"DON'T GO DOWN THE HALL!"

Paul Chapman unlocked the apartment door. There was no response when his wife Cheryl called out her sister's name. He told her to wait and cautiously entered the dark hallway. Slowly, one by one, he pushed open the three bedroom doors.

His eight-year old niece Melissa was behind the first door, lying on the floor, her legs spread open, nightgown pulled up to her breast area and a blue pillowcase tied tightly around her neck. Her mother Nancy was in the second bedroom, also half-naked and strangled with a pillowcase. In the last bedroom, two-year-old Angie was covered in blood, her throat slashed from ear to ear, and her nightgown bunched up above her waist.

Waves of nausea and shock crashing over him, Chapman headed back to his wife.

"Don't go down the hall," he said. "They're all dead."

Cheryl screamed and tried to force herself past him. He grabbed her tightly and pushed her out of the apartment, away from the nightmare.

BOOK YOUR PLACE ON OUR WEBSITE AND MAKE THE READING CONNECTION!

We've created a customized website just for our very special readers, where you can get the inside scoop on everything that's going on with Zebra, Pinnacle and Kensington books.

When you come online, you'll have the exciting opportunity to:

- View covers of upcoming books

- Read sample chapters

- Learn about our future publishing schedule (listed by publication month *and author*)

- Find out when your favorite authors will be visiting a city near you

- Search for and order backlist books from our online catalog

- Check out author bios and background information

- Send e-mail to your favorite authors

- Meet the Kensington staff online

- Join us in weekly chats with authors, readers and other guests

- Get writing guidelines

- AND MUCH MORE!

**Visit our website at
http://www.kensingtonbooks.com**

MURDER IN THE FAMILY

BURL BARER

PINNACLE BOOKS
KENSINGTON PUBLISHING CORP.

http://www.pinnaclebooks.com

Some names have been changed to protect the privacy of individuals connected to this story.

PINNACLE BOOKS are published by

Kensington Publishing Corp.
850 Third Avenue
New York, NY 10022

Pinnacle and the P logo Reg. U.S. Pat. & TM Off.

First Pinnacle Printing: August, 2000
10 9 8

Printed in the United States of America

For Stan—my brother, the lawyer

"There existeth in man a faculty which deterreth him from, and guardeth him against, whatever is unworthy and unseemly, and which is known as his sense of shame. This, however, is confined to but a few; all have not possessed and do not possess it."

—Bahá'u'lláh, *Epistle to the Son of the Wolf*

CHAPTER 1

For Paul and Cheryl Chapman, the nightmare began 8 A.M. Sunday, March 15, 1987. Their bedside telephone's incessant ringing roused them from slumber; Paul fumbled for the receiver. On the other end of the line was "Mama" Summerville of Gwennie's Restaurant, a popular Anchorage diner where Cheryl Chapman and her sister, Nancy Newman, worked as waitresses. Paul handed his wife the phone.

Summerville apologized for waking them, but she was seriously concerned. Nancy was two hours late for work, and her car was still parked in the same spot as it was the previous Friday evening. Panic immediately seized Cheryl Chapman—her sister, the married mother of two young girls, would never go without her car for two days, and she was never, ever, late for work.

The couple leapt from bed, quickly dressed, grabbed a Pepsi from the refrigerator, and took off for Nancy Newman's apartment. Cheryl remembered to take her cigarettes, Benson & Hedges Ultra Light Menthols; Paul left his Viceroys on the nightstand. As her husband piloted their little red Datsun pickup over Anchorage's frosty boulevards to Newman's Eide Street apartment, Cheryl's apprehension increased at every intersection. Her sister's husband, John, was in California; Nancy and the kids were alone. By the time the Datsun pulled into the apartment complex's parking lot, Cheryl Chapman was a nervous wreck.

Paul parked directly outside the doorway leading to a common hallway. The two raced inside and didn't bother knocking on Newman's door. Cheryl had keys to her sister's apartment, but was shaking so hard that Paul had to take them from her trembling fingers to unlock the door. Cheryl called out her sister's name, but all was silent. She went into the kitchen, sat down at the table, and looked around the room. Everything appeared perfectly normal, except for a large, empty cookie canister in the middle of the table—the canister in which Nancy kept her tip change. While Cheryl waited anxiously in the kitchen, her husband cautiously entered the apartment's dark hallway. Slowly, one by one, he pushed open the bedroom doors.

Behind the first door was eight-year-old Melissa Newman, victim of unspeakable cruelty. In the second room was her mother, Nancy Newman, half naked and lifeless on the bed. The third room contained the bloody remains of three-year-old Angie, her throat slit from ear to ear.

Paul was momentarily paralyzed and disoriented; waves of nausea and shock crashed over him. It was as if his entire world tilted precariously on its axis, then spun off into a black hole of horror. Fighting to maintain his composure, Paul turned away and headed back toward the kitchen. His wife saw him coming, and the look on his face told her something was terribly wrong.

"Don't go down the hall," he said, "they're all dead." Cheryl screamed, knocked over a chair, and tried forcing herself past him. He grabbed her, held her tight, and pushed his hysterical wife back through the living room and out the front door.

On the way, he grabbed the Newman's telephone. Stretching the long phone cord out the door, Paul Chapman dialed 911.

Officer Wayne Vance of the Anchorage Police Department was immediately dispatched to the Eide Street address. Upon arrival, he saw the distraught and anguished Cheryl Chapman weeping uncontrollably and wandering aimlessly in the parking lot. Her husband, clutching the telephone, guarded the apartment's front door. Vance called for backup and got out of his patrol car.

"Drop the phone," yelled Vance. Chapman threw it down and walked toward the flashing police lights. Vance quickly moved past him, entered the apartment, and checked the living room and kitchen to make sure no one was hiding inside. Discovering the same scenes of death and devastation as Chapman, Vance quickly exited the apartment. Within moments, the sirens of fire trucks and ambulances added their shrill screams to those of Cheryl Chapman.

The arriving paramedics demanded immediate entry, but Officer Vance held firm. Anchorage police policy dictated that if the first respondent observes unmistakable evidence of death, he or she is empowered to keep out anyone to protect the purity of the crime scene.

Officer Paul Schwartz, called in as backup, focused his professional concentration on the emotionally distraught Chapmans. He put them both in his patrol car's backseat, but Paul Chapman was too shaken up, crying, and nauseous to handle confinement. He wanted fresh air, room to move, and a cigarette. His were at home on the nightstand; Cheryl had left hers on Nancy's kitchen table. Officer Schwartz gave Chapman his Kools. Between them, the Chapmans smoked half a pack.

Detective Gregg Baker of the robbery division, the only detective working Sunday morning, also heard Vance's call for backup. Being mobile, he responded quickly. The second detective on-scene was Ken Spadafora of Anchorage's elite Homicide Response Team. Once inside, he saw what he would later describe as a "nightmare at the end of the hallway." Each room was worse than the previous one. Shocked and repulsed, he sealed the apartment and returned outside to await the arrival of his superior, Sergeant Mike Grimes. Spadafora told Baker what he witnessed inside. "I'll get this guy," he insisted, "I swear, honest to God, I'll never give up."

The Chapmans tearfully explained to police how they happened to find the bodies, beginning with their quiet Sunday morning being cut short by the call from Mama Summerville. They would tell their story again and again, each time prompted for every possible detail.

When Detective Sergeant Mike Grimes, head of the Homicide Response Team, arrived at the scene, he, too, experienced the triple homicide's emotional impact. His own daughter, like Melissa Newman, had red hair and glasses. "She looked so much like my little girl," he later recalled, "that my heart just broke. I knew how devastating this could be to the other cops, too. Usually, when a homicide detective in Anchorage deals with murder, you're dealing with one scumbag who got to the gun before the other scumbag—we call it 'NHI.' *No Humans Involved.* But this was different. This was a close, loving family—good people."

When the balance of his team arrived, Grimes did his best to prepare them. "I understand the effect this scene is going to have on you, and if you feel you can't deal with it, let me know now."

Grimes immediately assigned two groups of detectives to the Newman homicides: one for the immediate crime scene and forensic evidence; the other concentrating on leads, suspects, and other noncrime-scene aspects. For the latter, easygoing Detective Bill Reeder, experienced in investigating sex crimes against children, was teamed with the more aggressive Ken Spadafora. Already friends, the two men's opposite styles complemented each other perfectly.

Sergeant Bill Gifford's group, assigned to the crime scene, realized that the most inconsequential piece of physical evidence could be crucial. His team worked extensively on the bodies, carefully removing each and every hair and fiber. Pathologist Dr. Michael Propst joined Gifford at the Newman apartment, and according to his observations, Angie Newman, age three, was lying on her back on the floor of her bedroom, her legs spread completely apart. There was a compound knife-like cut to her neck, made by at least four slashes of a sharp-bladed instrument, that appeared to have started from the right side slicing across to the left.

These knife injuries, which transected the trachea and esophagus, extended deeply into the neck. Both her left carotid artery and jugular vein were severed. In essence, the child's throat was cut from ear to ear. Her body was virtually covered with blood, as was her nightgown, which was pulled up and bunched around her tiny torso, exposing her naked pelvic region. Defensive knife wounds were observed on the palm and fingers of the child's right hand. Several injuries to her face, forehead, nose, and right eye were also noted.

Although Angie Newman was covered extensively in blood across her naked stomach, there was a clean wiping of blood starting in the vicinity of her vagina and proceeding up the chest. The right side of this pattern was fairly straight without any rough edges, while the left side had a rough edge. This swipe was an inch wide and several inches long. It appeared to investigating officers that someone had made an effort to wipe, clean, or perhaps lick a portion of her vaginal and lower abdominal area.

The child's anal opening was somewhat enlarged, and an argon laser-light examination suggested the presence of seminal fluid, and another possible seminal stain was observed in the vicinity of the neck area injuries. Angie Newman had died from extreme blood loss.

The mother, Nancy Newman, was found with a pillowcase tied tightly around her neck. She had died of strangulation and had been struck several times in the face with a blunt instrument. Her dark-colored nightshirt was pulled up, exposing her naked breasts and pelvic area. Blood was on the sheets, as well as a small amount of fecal matter.

A pair of wool GI-type green gloves was found near Nancy Newman's body. Taken as evidence, the gloves would be sent to the FBI for microscopic examination.

Melissa Newman, age eight, was lying on the floor of her bedroom. She was on her back with her right arm under her back, and her left arm out to her left side. Both legs were bent back at the knees, and her legs were spread wide open. The right leg was bent back near her buttocks; her left leg was bent back pressing against the inside portion of her back. As with her mother, the child's nightgown was pulled up to her breast area, exposing her naked lower abdomen and pelvic region; a blue pillowcase, identical to the one used to strangle Nancy Newman, was tightly tied around her neck. Her panties were found on the floor a short distance away. Police also observed another pillowcase of a different color tied around her right wrist.

Dr. Propst found massive injuries to the girl's vagina, accompanied by large amounts of blood, apparently caused by a blunt object—not an erect penis or other body part—forcibly inserted into the vagina. An unusual blood smear was observed on Melissa's lower abdomen leading from the upper lips of the vagina upward toward her left breast. This peculiar swath of blood was eighteen inches long and approximately one to 1½ inches wide, an indication that someone had dragged a bloody object across the child's torso.

Investigators carefully vacuumed each bedroom, including the beds themselves, in search of hairs and/or fibers that the killer may have left behind. Gifford and his crew were on their hands and knees, sectioning off the floor into two-foot square grids. They laid down tape and lifted everything off the various carpet sections, then wrote down exactly where each hair or foreign fiber was found before they lifted and photographed it. The process, extremely tedious and boring, was an investigative imperative.

Officers also vacuumed the bathroom floor. While there, they found bloodstains on the underside of the light switch and on the inside of the door. There was more: a single damp washcloth wadded up in the sink. Careful processing of the bathroom's interior disclosed that someone had made a deliberate effort to wipe down the sink basin, the splash areas around the sink, below the medicine cabinet, and the vicinity of the toilet. This effort to destroy evidence was, police surmised, done with the washcloth given the fact that it was wet, wadded up, and left in the sink. There were also cloth wipe marks on the wall.

The washcloth, numerous hairs and fibers found on the bodies of the victims, fibers, samples of blood, and other physical and trace evidence seized by police in the apartment were carefully handled, labeled, and prepared for transport to the state crime lab. Officer James Ellis videotaped the entire crime scene in extensive detail, and all detectives assigned to the case viewed it in its entirety. One of them toured the crime scene outfitted in a disposable "moon suit"—a sanitary garb complete with hair net, gloves, and other protectorates to keep hairs or fibers from contaminating the evidence or area.

Even without scientific analysis, certain behavioral clues were blatantly obvious to Sergeant Grimes, a veteran of numerous sexual homicide investigations. For example, the killer had felt safe enough to stay in the apartment for a significant period of time.

"Killing and raping three people is not something you do in five minutes," Grimes explained. "Whoever did this not only knew the victims, he enjoyed himself while doing it. After most domestic homicides, there is tremendous remorse. The killer will most often cover the victims' faces. Not here. The person who raped and killed the Newmans not only had fun doing it, he splayed their bodies like that just to offend. This means the type of person we're looking for is the kind that is very adversarial, an 'in your face' kind of person. In short, we knew we were up against a sexual psychopath asshole."

A dozen Anchorage police detectives and patrol officers were pulled from their usual assignments to augment the investigation, Captain George Novaky told the press. "We've put a task force together to work on the thing. That's all they're going to do. We have a case that for all intents and purposes is the murder of an entire family. The case has high priority."

Novaky released only minimal details to the public, and only confirmed that two of the victims had been strangled, one stabbed, and that each was found in a separate bedroom. Police had no specific suspect, no motive, no weapon, and few leads.

John Newman, the husband and father, was notified Sunday night in California. Shocked and grieved, he told police that he was originally due to return from California on March 22, the week following the crimes. His wife and he were looking forward to his return after being away for almost 2½ months. Overwhelmed and distraught by the loss of his wife and children, John Newman kept the horror at bay by returning to his hometown of Twin Falls, Idaho. Heartbroken, he never viewed the bodies.

Nancy Newman and her daughters were unlikely murder victims. Born February 27, 1955, in Fresno, California, as Nancy Vantassel, she was one of five children born to Everett and Mearle Vantassel.

Moving to Idaho in 1970, she married John Newman in Twin Falls, on January 5, 1975. Their first daughter, Melissa, was born September 22, 1978; Angela was born August 17, 1983. Mrs. Newman worked as a certified public accountant for the J.B. Corporation before moving to Anchorage in 1985.

John Newman arrived in Alaska on May 1, 1985; Nancy and the girls came up on July 12. Mr. Newman secured work on Alaska's North Slope as a heavy-equipment operator for MarkAir in Prudhoe Bay, and Nancy Newman took the waitress position at Gwennie's. An outgoing and convivial lady with light-brown hair who worked part-time at H&R Block, and the morning shift at Anchorage's popular Gwennie's Old Alaska Restaurant, Nancy Newman made friends easily and earned a reputation for reliability.

"She worked here for a year and a half, and in that time, she was late once and took one week off about a year ago when her husband was injured at work," said Gwennie's owner, Ron Eagley. "She had a second job, as well, doing people's taxes. That's why, when she didn't show up Sunday, we were worried."

Regular Gwennie's customer Jack Keane remembered Newman as "kind of a fresh country girl—outgoing, friendly, but never flirtatious. You could tell she was working, that she wasn't there to play around. I'm sure she made pretty good tips. The tone at Gwennie's was good-looking waitresses that joked with you. They never came on to you, especially Nancy. She was a dedicated wife and mother, that was no secret."

John Newman sustained serious injuries on the job with MarkAir when a forklift he was driving flipped over. Workers' Compensation paid to have him retrained in California as a locksmith. John Newman departed Anchorage on January 3, 1987, leaving Nancy and the girls in their Eide Street apartment. With her husband out of town, Nancy drew continued emotional support from her sister and brother-in-law, Cheryl and Paul Chapman.

The sisterly bond between Nancy and Cheryl was deep, caring, and exemplary. Cheryl considered Nancy her dearest and best friend, and regarded Nancy's girls, Missy and Angie, as her own. Melissa was Cheryl Chapman's first niece, and her personality was similar to her mother's. Angie was a little spitfire, much like her aunt Cheryl—bold, spontaneous, and hot-tempered. The Chapmans and the Newmans were a close, loving extended family.

Originally from Rigby, Idaho, Paul Chapman came to Alaska in 1978 and secured employment from the Continental Motor Company. Smart and hardworking, Chapman advanced to sales manager by 1981. He also advanced from his first wife to Continental's bookkeeper, Cheryl Prather. Mr. Chapman subsequently became finance manager for Pioneer Honda in 1984, and in spring 1985 was hired as sales manager at Northern

Mazda. His new wife, Cheryl, went to work doing the books for S&S Engineers. In summer 1986, Cheryl Chapman joined her sister as a Gwennie's hostess.

In spring 1987, economic conditions prompted the merger of Northern Mazda and Continental Motors. As a result, many Mazda employees were suddenly unemployed, including Paul Chapman.

On Friday, March 13, 1987, Chapman anticipated an important two o'clock interview at Universal Motors. Between 8 and 8:30 that morning, Nancy Newman dropped by. She wanted to borrow the vacuum cleaner. Before he lent it to her, Chapman needed to use one of the vacuum's attachments to trim his beard. Adjourning to the bathroom, he clipped his beard, replaced the trimming attachment with the regular brush sweeper, and carried the vacuum cleaner down to her car.

Nancy Newman was a tidy and conscientious housekeeper, and it was no secret that her husband would soon be returning home. Despite her apartment having a central vacuum system, she preferred using her sister's more powerful upright.

"Her apartment was as clean as any place with two little kids could be," observed Sergeant Grimes. "Two cereal bowls were in the sink the day their bodies were discovered, there was a coffee cup on the kitchen table, and an ashtray with only a few cigarette butts in it. We had a basic time frame for the murders between midnight Friday night and about ten o'clock on Saturday morning. Although until the autopsy results came in, we considered it possible that it happened late Friday night. Anyone we talked to, we wanted to know where they were during that time. We knew for a fact that the last time the Chapmans saw Nancy and her kids alive was Friday night when they had a family get-together."

At 6 P.M. on Friday, March 13, 1987, Nancy Newman joined the Chapmans at Gwennie's. Cheryl's daughter from a previous marriage, Kelly Prather, had taken Nancy's two girls swimming at Service High School. She then treated the kids to dinner at Tastee-Freeze. This gave the adults a free evening, and the informal party soon moved to the Chapmans'. Rather than take two cars, Newman left hers in Gwennie's parking lot. At 9 P.M., the Chapmans drove Nancy home where the conviviality continued around Newman's kitchen table. An hour's worth of conversation, caffeine, and nicotine passed before Angie and Melissa Newman returned home ready for bed.

Although Newman's car remained at Gwennie's, Nancy said she would either get a ride on Saturday, or call the Chapmans if necessary. Her next scheduled work shift wasn't until early Sunday morning.

"Considering the hour the Newman kids came home from swimming on Friday night, and that they reportedly stopped at the Tastee-Freeze on the way home," reasoned Grimes, "the children did not eat again before going to bed Friday night. This would mean they were still alive first thing Saturday morning."

Based on information from the Chapmans, and the crime scene itself, police determined that the Newmans' Saturday routine included getting up fairly early because the kids watched television. While the two girls ate cereal and enjoyed cartoons, their mother sipped coffee and smoked her morning cigarettes. Newman's brand was Marlboro Lights.

"The cigarette brands, and the number of butts found in the ashtray are significant," asserted Grimes. "Nancy Newman must have emptied the ashtray before she went to bed Friday night. Otherwise, it would have been full from Friday night's socializing. Regardless of what brand they smoke, or if they're nonsmokers," he told the homicide team, "I want the name of every human being who has ever rightfully been inside that apartment within the last two months. I want prints, hairs, everything. And that includes Paul Chapman, Newman's friends, her coworkers, and anyone we can eliminate from being a viable suspect."

One such coworker was Shanaz Dalton, a former West Seattle native who moved to Alaska to get a better view of the Northern Lights. It was Dalton who served Nancy and the Chapmans on

March 13. Scheduled for her regular night shift, she was also awakened Sunday morning by Mama Summerville. Summoned to substitute for the missing Nancy Newman, Dalton discovered that the other night-shift workers had been called in, as well. It was then that she heard of Nancy's death and found herself accounting for her whereabouts since Friday night. Some employees were asked to provide rather personal samples to the Anchorage police. "With all the head and pubic hair we collected," stated Grimes flatly, "we could have knitted a sweater."

Jack Keane, a former California computer programmer, arrived shortly after Dalton. "I anticipated a pleasant morning breakfast, but when I walked in, there was a black pall around the place," he later recalled. "You can imagine all the women thinking there's some serial killer out there bumping off Gwennie's waitresses, and they might be next. Gwennie's had a real club feel to it in those days—we all felt close, customers and staff. When you see someone next to you count out their tips and go home, and then you never see them alive again, it's got to be hard."

Press reports and public speculation immediately put Grimes and his Homicide Response Team under intense pressure. Anytime a home is invaded, victims include a mother and two children, the suspect is unknown, and it all happens on a quiet, sleepy Sunday morning, no one feels safe.

"It immediately injected an undercurrent of fear and unease into the community," Grimes later said. "We had to work fast, work smart. We needed to find out everything we could about the victims—their lifestyle, their personal habits, their relatives."

Police asked the Chapmans if any other relatives lived in town. There was only one, also from Twin Falls, Idaho—a young nephew named Kirby D. Anthoney. Named for his paternal grandfather, he was the son of John Newman's sister. Cheryl Chapman had known Anthoney and his parents, Peggy and

Noah "Tony" Anthoney, ever since Nancy and John were married.

She became better acquainted with the nephew when he and his girlfriend, Debbie Heck, moved to Anchorage in October 1986. Chapman told police that the two stayed in Melissa's room during their visit, and moved out within a week after John Newman left for California on January 3. Anthoney and Heck traveled to Dutch Harbor where they secured work on a fishing boat, the *Arctic Enterprise.*

"Probably about a little over a month after they left, he came back," Cheryl Chapman told authorities. "Nancy and I drove up to her apartment one day—we'd been out shopping; Melissa and Angie were at the baby-sitter's—and he was sitting in a cab outside the apartment, waiting. As we came in, the taxi was sitting in front."

The three entered Newman's apartment, and Anthoney explained that he and Debbie Heck couldn't get along out on the boat, quarreled frequently, and were no longer an item. According to Chapman, Anthoney then moved back in with Nancy Newman and her children, moved out within a week, and now lived about a mile away with an auto-parts clerk and mechanic named Dan Grant.

Grimes discerned that Cheryl Chapman didn't care much for Kirby Anthoney, "but that doesn't mean she thought he committed these horrid acts," stated Grimes, "nor did we have an unusual interest in Anthoney based simply on her personal dislike for him. Even in a seasoned cop's mind it's hard to imagine that anyone in the family could do these things. Of course, we never eliminated anybody and we wanted immediate contact with Kirby Anthoney."

CHAPTER 2

Two and a half hours after the bodies were discovered, Sergeant Grimes, accompanied by Investigators Bill Reeder and Ken Spadafora, knocked on Kirby Anthoney's front door. When Dan Grant answered, they asked if they could speak to Mr. Anthoney. Soon, a tall, blond, disheveled, and shirtless young man shuffled out of the bedroom and through the living room. Bleary eyed and obviously hungover, Kirby D. Anthoney leaned against the doorway and asked what was going on.

"We understand that Nancy Newman is your aunt," said Sergeant Grimes sympathetically. "I'm afraid we have some tragic news. She was found dead this morning, along with your two cousins, Melissa and Angie."

Anthony cried out in despair, grabbed his head, and began wailing and ranting. Then, suddenly, he stopped cold. "Who found them?" he asked. "Her sister, Cheryl," answered Grimes. "Oh," responded Anthoney, "that makes sense—she's the only one who has a key."

Grimes and Spadafora cast quick glances back and forth in confirmation that they were having the same response to

Anthoney's behavior. The detectives told Anthoney that they needed to know everything about his aunt and nieces. He offered complete cooperation, and returned to his room to get dressed. As the investigators stepped outside, Grimes and Spadafora agreed that Anthoney's response struck them as "real weird."

Despite Anthoney's unusual remark and unbelievable reaction to news of the murders, he was not singled out as the prime suspect. "It is very important in police work," explained Grimes, "that you not focus on one suspect to the exclusion of other possibilities. The focus has to evolve from a preponderance of evidence. Our response Sunday was to do a contained crime scene investigation, utilize whatever information we could get from the Chapmans and our initial interviews with Anthoney."

Anthoney was told that the purpose of going to the police station was to provide information about the Newman family, but his perception changed once interrogation began. Detectives primarily questioned Anthoney concerning his activities between Friday night and Saturday afternoon. When pressed for details, he was unable to recollect anything with much coherence.

Anthoney initially acknowledged attending an all-night party at the home of a friend, Jeff Mullins. When questioned about drug use at the party, Anthoney initially denied the presence of cocaine. In truth, Anthoney had purchased a half gram of cocaine for $50 prior to the party.

The friends—Anthoney, Jeff Mullins, Sissy Altman, and a fellow named Mark—rolled dice, drank beer, and snorted coke until 3 or 4 A.M., but continued rolling dice until 7 A.M. As other guests contributed cocaine to the gathering, as well, Anthoney recalled consuming about a half gram on his own. He also drank twelve beers. As for leaving the party, he only did that long enough to get more beer from Major Liquor on Benson and Spenard. At no time did he leave alone on the beer runs, as one or more of Mullins's houseguests always accompanied him.

Anthoney told detectives that he left Jeff Mullins's house at 7:05 A.M. "The reason why it is so distinct to me," he said, "is because I remember that Dan Grant had to go to work in the morning and it was my impression that it was going to be at eight o'clock and I wanted to give him some time to get up and get around, because I know he normally doesn't get up until just before he has to go to work—he's up, puts his clothes on, and out the door he goes."

The home Anthoney shared with Dan Grant was just across the street. Anthoney said he turned on the TV, woke up Dan, went inside his own room, took off his shirt, went to the bathroom, washed his upper torso, and watched some cartoons.

"[Grant] laid in bed for a little while," recalled Anthoney, "but then he got up and had his coffee, which he normally does, and I believe he smoked some marijuana, and he was in the bathroom." While Grant was in the bathroom, Anthoney placed a phone call to "Aunt Nancy," basically "just to visit. I wanted to give her some money that I owed her," explained Anthoney, "and just to visit and talk with her. I don't know if I would have considered taking my laundry with me at that time, but that's where I always did my laundry, and I knew I had to do it, so I might have taken it then."

Anthoney had laundry on his mind because he'd borrowed a clean shirt from Jeff Mullins's brother, Kirk, the night before. Somehow, the shirt became stained. Anthoney wasn't sure of the stain's origin, he asserted, but he assumed it was feces from a dog or cat. Perhaps the cat stepped in dog dung and then stepped on the shirt.

When Grant left for work, Anthoney said he went right to the home of a friend, Kirk Mullins, arriving between 9 and 9:30 A.M. The balance of the day was consumed by loads of laundry at the Mullinses', smoking pot, and buying beer. All three went to Burger King between 11:45 and noon for a Whopper, two chicken sandwiches, and French fries.

Detective Spadafora assured Anthoney that they knew he'd lived with the Newmans and that his prints would certainly be present throughout the apartment. "We need to eliminate you from the suspect list by getting some samples from you—fingerprints, palm prints, hair samples—that way we can eliminate those people who would rightfully be there," he told Anthoney, "and we'll need to get a blood sample, as well."

Informed of the murders at 10 A.M., Anthoney didn't have an opportunity to call family members until the police were done interviewing him and he had returned home. He first called Cheryl Chapman, but she was too distressed to take the call. He then called his mother, Peggy Anthoney, in Idaho. Dan Grant overheard Anthoney's side of the conversation and later recalled hearing Anthoney say, "Sit down, Mom . . . Nancy and the girls are dead. Settle down, Mom . . . they won't tell me what happened to them, if they were raped or not . . . but, Mom, they think I did it. That's the fucked thing about it, Mom. They think I did it."

Anthoney didn't realize *every* friend, relative, and neighbor of the Newmans received the same intense scrutiny. The homicide victimology team's assignment was to find out the name of everybody who had been inside the Newman apartment in the previous two months. They wanted fingerprints, palm prints, everything from anyone who had legitimately been in the Newman apartment.

Identification technician Kathy Monfreda was called to the crime scene, and she worked closely with Bill Gifford. "There is a normal routine that we use for examining scenes of crimes," explained Monfreda. "David Weaver of the Department of Public Safety Crime Lab assisted me in developing any visible latent prints. Also Sergeant Gifford examined the front door and the door to the building itself. The three of us did processing of the building and the apartment. As latent prints were developed, we marked them and either removed them for photographing and lifting, or we photographed them at the scene as if it was an unmovable object."

Monfeda also utilized a technique known as Super Glue fuming to reveal any latent prints. "The way the process works,'' she elaborated, ''is that Super Glue will naturally emit fumes that are attracted to the moisture that's on fingerprint residue that's left when something is touched.''

Monfreda put Super Glue on specially treated cotton pads and placed them throughout the entire apartment, then sealed the area overnight. The next morning, the apartment was ventilated and brushed for prints. ''In the case of an apartment this size, there is no visible reaction, but what's actually happening is the fumes are attracted to the moisture in the residue and it will fix the prints so that they can be made visible using fingerprint powder.''

Grimes also wanted complete information on the victims' lifestyle and habits. ''I want to know everything, from what the kids ate for breakfast,'' he told the victimology team, ''to if Nancy took cream in her coffee. Find out their likes, dislikes, interests, everything and anything.''

While the fingerprint experts and victimology team were doing their jobs, Investigators Reeder and Spadafora checked out Kirby Anthoney's alibi for Saturday morning with Kirk Mullins and Deborah Dean. Yes, he had arrived Saturday morning. Together they did multiple loads of laundry. Everything was exactly as Anthoney told police, with one exception— Mullins said that Anthoney did not arrive at 9:30 A.M. He arrived sometime between 10 and 11 A.M. The detectives noted the discrepancy and made plans to ask Anthoney for clarification. However, at this early stage of the investigation—the first days after the bodies were discovered—everyone was a suspect until they were eliminated from suspicion, including Paul Chapman.

''He has no real alibi for where he was or what he was doing on Saturday morning,'' commented Grimes. ''His wife was at work and he was alone. Based upon the Chapmans' recollections of their Friday night get-together with Nancy Newman, we know they sat around the table smoking cigarettes and drinking coffee. We found five butts in the ashtray: four Marlboro Lights, and one Camel Filter. Friday the Thirteenth, the night before the murders, Paul Chapman bought a fresh pack of Camel Filters.''

''I normally smoke Viceroys,'' he told police, ''but I'd run out of cigarettes while at Gwennie's and bought a package out of the machine. They didn't stock Viceroys, so I got Camel Filters.''

A pack-and-a-half-a-day smoker, Chapman claimed he smoked more than one solitary cigarette while having coffee and conversation at the Newmans.' A thorough examination of Newman's garbage turned up several Benson & Hedges, Marlboro Light, and Camel Filter cigarette butts. Police submitted the single Camel Filter to the lab for analysis and took a saliva swab from the inside of Paul Chapman's mouth.

In addition to intensive questioning of Anthoney and the Chapmans, the Homicide Response Team's top priority was conducting a neighborhood canvass, but the location proved a logistical nightmare. The Eide Street complex in which the Newmans lived consisted of fifteen or twenty apartments. Multiunit apartments and trailers surrounded the immediate neighborhood. This largest concentration of high-transit residents included convicted felons and known sex offenders. Two suspected or formerly convicted rapists lived in the general area, and police were all over both of them, taking samples and asking extensive questions. One young man who recently moved in near the Newmans' was highly suspect—a nineteen-year-old named Frank Cornelius. Similar to Kirby Anthoney, Frank Cornelius came to Achorage to stay with family following an automobile accident.

''He hit a moose,'' explained his cousin Jody, ''and my father went to get him.'' Severely bruised by his unpleasant interaction with Alaskan wildlife, he stayed with relatives only a few weeks. ''He slept on the couch,'' said Jody Cornelius. ''He was going to have to move out because Gretchen didn't want him living there.'' Following the homicides, Frank Cornelius had Jody toss his suitcase out the window, and he promptly took off for Seattle.

The people in the apartment directly above the Newmans claimed they heard absolutely nothing unusual—not a sound, not a scream—making it difficult for police to ascertain time of death. The best way to know when somebody died is to find out the last time somebody saw him or her alive. A pathologist provides time parameters based upon physical characteristics.

"It was critical to find out where people were during certain periods of time," stated Grimes. "Our initial time frame was broad—we could tell that they were dead at least twenty-four hours, so our focus was from midnight Friday until late Saturday morning. We had to ask ourselves when would they have been killed, and what were they doing when it happened. We wanted to reconcile what we knew happened Friday night with the crime scene as found. We also had to confirm that John Newman, husband and father of the victims, was in California at the time of the crime—which he was. That immediately removed him from any list of possible suspects."

Within twenty-four hours, the murders were a high-publicity, high-profile case dominating the headlines and the television news. The police were under pressure, and several days transpired without a break in the case. Detectives laboriously ran down more than 500 leads. One of the most bizarre calls claiming insight into the crime actually came into police *before* the murders.

Friday the Thirteenth, the day prior to the Newman murders, was apparently significant for someone identified only by the initials J.S., an unnamed mental patient who experienced visions of human sacrifice and satanic cult murders, foretold under a full moon.

Officer Mark O'Brian conducted two interviews with J.S., then a patient at a local psychiatric hospital. According to O'Brian, J.S. had her doctor call the police on Friday, March 13, because she had a vision that some cult killings for the purposes of human sacrifice were going to take place over the weekend. Nancy Newman and her two children were killed the next day.

"She said that due to the time of the year it was, and the aligning of the moons, there would be multiple killings," said O'Brien. "She didn't know who was going to be killed, but it was going to be a human sacrifice."

O'Brien reported the conversation to colleagues following the murders and interviewed J.S. again on March 24. In the second interview, she described an apartment like the Newmans' and correctly detailed how the victims died: two by strangling and one from knife cuts. According to O'Brian, J.S. said the youngest child was cut because her blood had to be taken to another place for a ritual.

"It didn't have to be done then, but it had to be done," J.S. was quoted, explaining why no signs of ritual murder were found in the Newman apartment. She said her vision included three men, one about age thirty, pushing into the apartment after the youngest child opened the door for them.

"You're going to get things like that," said Sergeant Grimes, rolling his eyes, "they crawl out of the woodwork, especially if you get a case of this significance. We get calls like this all the time—nutcases or self-proclaimed psychics, especially on Friday the Thirteenth. These murders took place on Saturday the fourteenth, and had they not taken place, no one would have remembered J.S. or her so-called visions. I worked a lot of sexual homicide cases back when people were talking about Devil worship and Satanism, and all that stuff is absolute horseshit. Ninety-nine point nine pecent of the time, these 'leads' lead nowhere. What we really needed was effective neighborhood canvassing and some solid evidence."

Grimes and Gifford also wanted a working behavioral or personality profile of the type of person who might have done this horrid crime. They immediately contacted Special Agent Don McMullen, a profiler coordinator with the FBI's Anchorage Field Office.

"We contacted the FBI," explained Grimes, "because of their obvious experience and expertise. Just as medical specialists may be experts in a particular disease, and know far more than our best local general practitioner, the FBI has the advantage of a national or even international perspective on certain types of crimes. The reference points of the FBI are broader and more inclusive. Besides, having worked with Don McMullen before, I knew how good he was.''

McMullen, praised by coworkers as a first-rate agent, had previously worked as case coordinator in the murders committed by Robert Hansen, an Anchorage baker who kidnapped prostitutes, flew them to the wilderness in his private plane, then hunted them down like animals. Based on information shared by Grimes, McMullen prepared his initial evaluation of the Newman murders.

Working on the principle that behavior reflects personality, FBI agents divide the profiling process into specific, clearly defined steps:

1. Evaluation of the criminal act itself.
2. Evaluation of the crime scene's specifics.
3. Analysis of the victim or victims (victimology).
4. Evaluation of preliminary police reports.
5. Evaluation of the medical examiner's autopsy protocol.
6. Suggestions for investigation predicated on the profile.

''Offering a profile is usually just the beginning of the help offered by the FBI,'' said Grimes. ''McMullen distinguished himself here in previous cases by his consultation with our local investigators, and suggesting strategies we could use to bring the criminal to justice.''

Using McMullen's guidance, police initially thought they had viable suspects in Frank Cornelius, the young man who had recently moved near the Newmans, and another fellow who lived down the street.

''There was one guy that lived a few blocks away in a trailer court that sounded pretty good,'' acknowledged Reeder, ''but we were able to confirm he was on a winter camping trip with a college class. Frank Cornelius had no alibi at all, and his behavior was sort of erratic, but we were not about to rush into anything. He met many of the characteristics McMullen outlined for us, but McMullen himself strongly urged us to get further in-depth profiling.''

Reeder and Spadafora further questioned Kirby Anthoney about the missing one to two hours between when he left Dan Grant's and arrived at the Mullins residence. Anthoney clarified that he left home at about 8:45 A.M., but did not go straight to Mullins's. Instead, he stopped at the Burger King on Boniface and Northern Lights, purchased a croissant sandwich from the drive-through window, and ate it while sitting in his truck in the parking lot. Stated with affable confidence, Anthoney's expanded alibi was credible, reasonable, and easily verified or impeached by a simple visit to the Burger King.

On the Friday following the homicides, a department gag order remained in effect surrounding details of the killings, and authorities would only confirm that the victims were strangled and one stabbed. They also said one was raped, but would not identify her. The press wanted as much information as possible, and Captain George Novaky gave them sufficient quotable statements.

"We sit here each day and say hopefully one of the leads is going to provide positive results," Novaky told the press, "but in the meantime, we cannot ignore and will not ignore any lead. The leads have come from Crime Stoppers, from citizens who have just called in to the police department, and from people we've contacted. The mayor got a postcard from some guy saying there was a case three years ago that should be looked into in connection with this case. We're probably going to pull up records on that. Because each and every lead must be logged before being tracked, paperwork is piling up. It's a tedious and thankless job.''

The same day Novaky lamented lack of progress, Grimes and McMullen called the Behavioral Science Unit of the FBI in Quantico, Virginia. The agent to whom they spoke was Judson Ray. Before joining the FBI, a former Vietnam veteran, police officer, and homicide detective, Special Agent Ray's job was to help investigators track down America's worst killers. Ray's professional training and credentials were further reinforced by his own personal experience as an intended homicide victim.

On February 21, 1981, two thugs hired for a contract killing entered his apartment, shot him in the back, and left him for dead. Suffering from shock and a collapsed lung, Ray made his way to the bathroom where he tried to take a drink by cupping water in his hand. It was then he noticed the bullet embedded in his palm—it had passed through his back, his right lung, ripped out the front of his chest, and penetrated his hand.

An operator-assisted phone call to the DeKalb County Police Department, a quick response by emergency medical technicians, and thoracic surgery at DeKalb General Hospital, saved Ray's life. He did, however, spend twenty-one days with an armed guard at his hospital room's door.

Adding emotional insult to intense physical injury, the would-be killers were hired by Ray's wife. Their marriage on the rocks, she preferred being a life insurance beneficiary to being a divorcée. Ray survived; the wife and the two thugs each got ten years in prison.

"If I had died," said Ray, "I'm absolutely convinced she would have gotten away with it. It was well planned and her actions had prepared everyone in the neighborhood. She would have been completely believable as the grieving spouse. Having been near death, I think it gives me a deeper insight into the victimology of a particular crime scene. I bring that kind of awareness because I lived through mine."

"We had a conference call," related Grimes, " and we said, 'Look we have some urgency here . . .' "

"We hate to do these things off the cuff." replied Ray. "I'm going to get as much information from you as I can, then I'll get back to you. You're obviously dealing with someone out of control. I assure you that if he isn't stopped, this will happen again.''

When Gifford heard Ray say it will happen again, he became personally obsessed. ''I couldn't stop thinking about it, and I couldn't really sleep,'' he said. ''There were nights when I would go to bed at midnight and get up again at two A.M. I couldn't sleep—all I could do was think about the crime scene, gathering evidence, and finding new ways of getting better evidence. The thought that this killer would strike again was simply not acceptable to me at all. If there was any contribution I could make to capture this person, I couldn't let it slip away. We all eagerly awaited Ray's profile.''

Selected crime-scene photos were faxed immediately to Ray, and a full set arrived in Quantico on Tuesday morning. ''In a weird kind of way I can almost place myself in that crime scene,'' Ray said, ''and kind of project what this woman went through. As I look at the photo, I'm almost reflecting back on those seconds and minutes that I struggled through . . . that she didn't struggle through. And I use that to go about thinking what did happen and what didn't happen, what could have happened, what are the possibilities here? And it all kind of relates to having, in some sense, walked in her shoes, but managed to walk out of the dark that night.''

The FBI conducts an in-depth training for profilers, and many of their best men were on hand when Special Agent Ray agreed to help. He had them drop everything to work on the Newman homicides. ''What we were looking at were the deeds—the actions of the individual who did this,'' said Ray. ''All the details were evaluated. It was a disorganized crime scene, indicating low self-esteem. This is the type of person who sees society as rejecting him, and now it's his turn to reject society. Unfortunately, once an offender like this commits to an aggravated act like rape, there is no amount of reasoning at that point that would keep him from having to get rid of all the potential witnesses. A stranger would not necessarily have had to do this because he wouldn't have been recognized and identified. He wouldn't have assumed he was going to find materials in the house he could use for control devices. And I think he really wanted to humiliate this woman. That's why he tied her up, and I believe some of this activity may have been done with [Melissa] watching."

Grimes and the Homicide Response Team wanted Ray's opinion of Frank Cornelius as a prime suspect, but at that stage of the game, Ray didn't want to hear about any potential suspects. What he wanted was what he termed "freedom of neutrality." There was another problem with Cornelius being a suspect—he didn't know the victims.

"He fit all our basic criteria," said Grimes, "except the most important one. Agent Ray was absolutely convinced that the killer knew Nancy and her children. Nothing else mattered as much—not age, not occupation. As far as Ray was concerned, knowing the family was the key point in the profile. If Cornelius didn't know them, we had the wrong guy."

"If there's a lot of facial battery, that tends to indicate some familiarity, a lot of anger," explained Ray. "Tremendous infliction of trauma with the hand indicates a kind of closeness instead of the guy with a thirty-eight who stands back and shoots you in the head. All these things mean something when you look at them collectively."

How could Ray be so sure? Certitude in profiling is developmental, and Ray admitted initial doubts. "I'd had some reservations about the ability to sit down with a bunch of photographs and things like that and come up with concepts about what was going on at the scene," said Ray. "But later on I would realize it was not one particular discipline—profiling—that enabled people in the unit to do these kinds of things. Truly, it is a collection of all the disciplines and an understanding and a good depth of knowledge about forensic psychology, forensic pathology, cultural anthropology, social psychology, motivational psychology—all of the things that when they are properly aligned and understood with a sense of investigative technique behind you, you have all these things kind of synchronized . . .

I don't see how you can effectively work these kinds of cases without those kinds of understanding, all brought to bear upon an analytical process where you walk away saying, 'Hey, I'm reasonably sure that you got the wrong guy' . . . as I did in this case. The tremendous rage inflicted on these young children suggested that there is nothing that could justify this type of rage by a stranger," he confirmed, "he'd probably killed these people a hundred times in his mind."

McMullen and Ray also placed significance on the cloth washrag found in the bathroom sink "The killer obviously needed to get the blood off himself before he left the apartment," recalled McMullen. "This means that either the killer was a drifter—that he didn't have his own place—or he didn't live alone. It was important that whoever did this took the time to clean up because he had to look normal when he went outside, or went home. It also could mean that it was already light outside when he left the apartment."

Awaiting Ray's extended in-depth profile, detectives explored all angles, intensifying the crime scene analysis. There were no signs of forced entry to the Newman residence, but several items were missing, including a large serrated knife from the kitchen's wooden knife rack. Sergeant Gifford investigated this absence with the aid of advanced technology.

"You can actually see invisible blood traces using Luminol," explained Gifford. "It is used to enhance existing bloodstain patterns and find invisible traces of blood. This was the first time this technique was used by the Anchorage Police Department. I did locate an otherwise invisible blood pattern that was the impression of a knife. This was found in the bedroom of Angie Newman. This blood pattern matched the shape of a set of knives that were in the kitchen, one of which was missing. It appeared as if the intruder used the Newmans' kitchen knife to cut Angie's throat, and took the weapon with him."

Significant to investigators was the theft of approximately $200 in miscellaneous coins. The coins were kept in a large metal cookie tin in a cabinet above the kitchen microwave.

John Newman told police that some of the coins kept in the cookie tin had already been rolled in paper wrappers, and that coin wrappers were kept inside the large container. Accumulated from tips Nancy Newman earned at Gwennie's, this money was being saved up to help pay for a trip to Disneyland. The Chapmans knew about the tin, as did Kirby Anthoney and his former girlfriend, Debbie Heck. Significantly, another similar cookie tin that was never used to store money was left undisturbed, giving further weight to the perpetrator being someone intimately familiar with the Newmans' lives and possessions.

Also absent were Nancy Newman's purse and its contents, John Newman's keys, checkbook, jewelry, a wallet, and an expensive, high-quality 35mm camera, lens, case, flash unit, and related equipment. All the photographic equipment was kept in a camera bag that had also vanished.

With as much time as the killer spent in the apartment, he could have ransacked the entire place, but didn't. A professional burglar would have meticulously searched the apartment for valuables, replacing anything he didn't want; an amateur would have ripped the place apart. In the Newman household, aside from the human slaughter and selective theft, everything appeared fairly normal.

Grimes and the Homicide Response Team knew that the awaited personality profile from Agent Ray would indicate someone who was most assuredly not normal. Their expectations were more than confirmed when Jud Ray called them from Quantico, Virginia. According to Ray's expanded FBI profile, the person responsible was a lone white male between nineteen and twenty-four years of age; was well acquainted with the victims, and/or lived in the immediate area, was unmarried and heterosexual; had a history of previous crimes against the weak, young, or old; and had committed cruelty to animals and nuisance-type arson.

The suspect would also have a slight physical defect or abnormality that was magnified in his own mind. The offender also possibly suffered a recent emotionally traumatic event, such as loss of job or other type of severe rejection. The FBI profile also suggested that he was low in birth order, perhaps the youngest of several children, had an inability to maintain male-female relationships, and would work at menial jobs with no employment stability. He would also have animosity toward Nancy Newman and the children, an animosity that could erupt in carnal rage.

It was time to take a closer look at the personal history of Kirby D. Anthoney: the youngest of five children; a single heterosexual white male; twenty-three years of age; had formerly resided with the victims. He had also worked at menial jobs—fish processor and car wash attendant—and was very self-conscious of his broken and rotten front teeth. As for traumatic events, his three-year relationship with Debbie Heck had recently suffered an acrimonious breakup.

CHAPTER 3

Kirby Dale Anthoney, born in Twin Falls, Idaho, two days before Christmas, 1963, was the youngest of five children produced by the stormy union of Noah "Tony" Anthoney, truck driver, and Peggy Anthoney, bartender and waitress. His parents' marriage, less than exemplary, featured violence, injury, and gunplay.

The young Kirby Anthoney inaugurated his criminal career in March 1978, with first degree burglary. He received a suspended sentence and one year's probation. One year and three months after his probation expired—June 20, 1979—Kirby Anthoney, his brother Mike, and a friend were driving around in Mike's car when they ran out of gas. According to Anthoney's sworn statement, Mike suggested they siphon gas from a vehicle parked at the Friedman Bag Company, on Shoshone Street West, in Twin Falls. In Kirby Anthoney's version, he tried to convince Mike to simply go home and get some money to buy gas, but Mike could not be dissuaded. Kirby Anthoney said that he waited in the car while his brother siphoned the gas, but when he saw the police coming, he got out of the car and ran. The police apprehended him and took him to the police station.

Anthoney, already a heavy drinker, told Roberta Dahlin, his caseworker for the Department of Health and Welfare, that he never got involved with alcohol because he didn't like the taste. He was more frank concerning his family life and upbringing.

"My father is a truck driver," Anthoney told Dahlin. "He wasn't home very often but when he was, he would take it out on the kids what had built up inside him—anger. He was generally in a bad mood, and it scared me to be around him too much. He would ground us for the smallest thing. Like being late five minutes from school. One day he started hitting me because he thought I was mad at him for telling me to get off the phone. It slipped out of my hand and fell on the receiver, making a bang. When he started hitting me, my mother told him to stop. He started hitting her. I threw a polish can and hit him in the head because I've seen him hit her so hard it put her in the hospital and I couldn't stand it. I ran to my brother's trailer who was fifteen at the time. He moved out because of my father. I stayed there until he moved out of town. My mother shot my father in the hip one day because he was hitting my brother and kicked her on the ribs after he knocked her down. She crawled into the bedroom and got a thirty-eight special out of the drawer. He came into the bedroom after her. I heard her say, 'Get out of here.' He said, 'Go ahead and shoot me, Peg.' I heard the shot. He got into the car and went to the hospital. It was all because [my brother] didn't feed the cats milk. I resented my father very much. I was never happy or comfortable with him around. I love my mother very much and respect her very much for going through what she did for us. My mother and father were divorced or separated five times that I know of."

In her evaluation submitted to the court, Dahlin noted that although Anthoney said he did not want to become involved in criminal activity, it was her opinion that "because of his peer associations, he had the potential of becoming involved once again.'' Peggy Anthoney was characterized as a loving and concerned mother who had difficulty supervising her son. The court gave Kirby Anthoney two years' probation.

In February 1979, he was charged with bombing a building— Anthoney allegedly attempted burning down the school with acetylene-filled balloons. He admitted to the bombing charge, was sentenced to thirty days in Twin Falls County Juvenile Detention Facility, and his probation period was extended. Through arrangements made with Judge Edwards, Anthoney received a continuance on the bombing charge. The judge wanted to see if Kirby D. Anthoney could stay out of trouble for six months. He barely made it.

On the Fourth of July, 1980, he and two other boys were arrested for breaking into the Thometz building. The others raided the cash register while Anthoney amused himself with two pints of whiskey. By this time, the court realized that it was almost impossible to keep Anthoney from criminal behavior. They cited two primary factors: his inability to comprehend or think of the probable results of committing criminal acts, and his inability to accomplish the goals he had set for himself on his own initiative.

The court committed Anthoney to the Department of Health and Welfare for an indefinite period of time. They also recommended that he be transferred to the Youth Service Center in St. Anthony, Idaho, where he could receive vocational training and acquire his GED. Anthoney arrived there on August 3, 1980.

Ironically, Anthoney's four-month stay at the Youth Service Center was the most productive and encouraging time of his young life. In a report to the court filed April 30, 1981, the target behaviors addressed were Anthoney's rationalization and manipulation, assertiveness skills, impulsive behavior, and facade of self-adequacy.

Anthoney, subjected to a variety of psychological, behavioral, and personality assessments, portrayed himself as rather naively defensive and presented an image of virtuousness and strong moral character. He was perceived as egocentric, suggestible, and impulsive. The tests indicated that he was in the ''bright normal'' intellectual range, but was a scholastic underachiever. Results of personality testing indicated a failure to accept responsibility for his behavior through rationalization and manipulation of those in authoritative positions. He also showed a lack of appropriate assertiveness skills; utilization of denial as a defense against personal inadequacies; impulsive behavior patterns; facade of self-adequacy covering an insecure person; feelings of alienation and estrangement from adult authority figures.

For the next four months, Anthoney received counseling from his caseworker, participated in group therapy, and attended AA meetings. He received his GED diploma and a mechanic's certificate for completion of a vocational-skills course.

''It should be pointed out that Kirby Anthoney's stay of just four months at the Youth Service Center is extremely rare,'' stated his discharge report. ''[He] was able to go through the program there in a minimum amount of time.'' Anthoney's Release Institutional Behavioral Record indicated that he had a relatively low chance of engaging in subsequent delinquent activities—approximately 40 percent. He secured employment via the CETA (Comprehensive Employment Training Act) program, doing landscaping for various community agencies before switching to a job at Kimberly Nurseries. He began working for Kimberly on March 9, 1981, and was still gainfully employed there as of April 8.

''Considering that [Anthoney] has not attained the age of seventeen and is working steadily, it would appear that he has matured sufficiently to be given the opportunity to take responsibility for his own behavior. For this reason,'' concluded the report to the court. ''It is recommended that this case be dismissed effective immediately.''

Anthoney acquired a glowing recommendation, a GED, a mechanic certification, and Dena Mendenhall, whom he consid-

ered his common-law wife. He also graduated within the year
to armed robbery.

On January 6, 1982, at 9 P.M., Thelma Stull heard her doorbell
ring. Confined to a wheelchair, and living alone, the elderly
woman wheeled to the door and opened it. Standing in front
of her was Kirby D. Anthoney, a stocking cap pulled down
low around his face. Brandishing a handgun, Anthoney robbed
her of her money, tied her up, and sprayed Mace in her face.
Before leaving, Anthoney tore the telephone out of the wall
and took the receiver with him. According to Detective Ritchie
of Twin Falls, Mrs. Stull was discovered and rescued by her
son. He had attempted calling his mother several times, but
there was no response. Concerned, he went to her home, where
he found her tied up in her wheelchair. Mrs. Stull suffered
severely from the Mace sprayed directly in her face, as well
as the traumas of insult, injury, and armed robbery. Had her
son not rescued her, Mrs. Stull might have died from shock.

Two days later, Mrs. Stull easily identified Kirby Anthoney
as the culprit, and he was charged with armed robbery. Perhaps
imbued with criminal pride, he confessed. "I and Dena Mendenhall, my common-law wife, went to Mike Pulsofer's house,
where Mike Anthoney and Mike Pulsofer were. Mike said, we
got a couple of schemes. I said, what do you mean, schemes?
He told me he knew where he could get some money by going
into a couple of houses. He told me about Mrs. Stull and that
she was in a wheelchair but could still walk. He told me about
a drawer she kept money in or that he saw it there before. At
first I said no to myself, but started thinking how desperate I
was for money because I lost my job at Scott's Refrigeration
because of being late too many times. I had two hundred twenty-
nine dollars for my wife's medical bills. I couldn't or didn't
want to ask my mother again for help. I couldn't find a job,
even a spot job. When I decided I couldn't find help, I told
them I would help. My brother kept saying no, but he went
with us. I parked a block away on Ash and Fifth, I told Mike
and Mike to go down the alley and I went down the street. I

knocked on the door and asked her to let me use the phone. She didn't and I was going to leave but something in me said, do it. I sprayed her with Mace and asked her to do as I say. She did and I went to the back door to let them in. But Mike Anthoney kept saying don't do it, come on. But I went back in and she gave me her money. I pulled the gun and hanged it by my side. I wouldn't even cock it or point it at her. I didn't really want to scare her. The reason I used Mace was because I didn't think she could scream. I wasn't trying to hit her in the face. But I had it by my side and when I sprayed it, it hit her in the face. If she would have refused to give me her money, I would have left. There's no way I could use physical force on her. When she gave me [the money], I took the phone so she couldn't call anyone. When I left, she told me, 'I thought you needed help,' and I told her I did in money-wise and that I was very sorry. I went back to the car where they were waiting. My car was out of gas, so we went to a guy's house to use the phone. I called a friend to meet us at the Seven-Eleven. He did and we got gas for my car. We went to my car and put it in. We went back to the store to pick up Mike and Mike. Then we took Mike Pulsofer home and gave him ten dollars for gas. Mike spent the night at my apartment. The next day, the detectives came over to talk to me. I told them everything.''

In his tape-recorded confession to Investigator Walden of the Twin Falls police, Anthoney expressed interest in how he was tracked down. ''Just personally, between me and you,'' asked Anthoney conversationally, '' I wouldn't do anything about it, can you just inform me what took place, how you guys got on the track? I mean it really bugs me. I thought that I had it really covered a little bit.''

The answer, according to Walden, was simple: Twin Falls is a small town, and there is a limited number of young criminals. There was no ''track'' for Walden to ''get on''—the crime itself had ''Kirby D. Anthoney & Co.'' written all over it.

''I know there's nothing I can say to change what has happened,'' Anthoney told the court. ''All I can say is that I really wasn't myself. I didn't realize I had help when I did—my family. I'm very sorry for putting Mrs. Stull through this, and I have everything I get coming. But there's nothing on this earth I would do to jeopardize my freedom and love for my wife. If I did anything else to cause trouble, I would lose her and I could never face anyone again. This is going to be hard coping when I return to the community. I plan on getting a job of any source until I am financially stable. Or begin school for architecture or drafting. Raise a family with my wife the way a family should be raised. Stop the use of pot and beer completely. I realize I have responsibilities to hold, and I'm going to do everything possible to live a comfortable life honestly.''

The court-appointed investigator's advice to the presiding judge, however, was less optimistic. ''This appears to be the act of a self-centered, selfish, and uncaring person, a person who thinks only of himself. In committing this crime, it appears the subject is continuing his pattern of criminal behavior, a pattern that began during his recent juvenile years, and a pattern that he has brought with him into his adult life. He has a serious drug and alcohol problem, his debts are unmanageable, and he has no known source of income.''

Anthoney's previous employers were not standing in line to offer him prestigious positions. Contrary to Anthoney's statements to the court, David C. VanEngston of Scott's Refrigeration told authorities that Anthoney wasn't fired, he quit. VanEngston made it clear that because of the manner in which Anthoney quit, he would not be rehired. His previous employment history was equally lackluster—Mrs. Lloyd K. Wright of Kimberly Nurseries advised the court that Kirby Anthoney did not extend himself to help his employer when he worked for them, and she also would not rehire him.

''When you look at the profile Ray provided us with, then look at Anthoney's history, the matchup is astonishing,'' commented Grimes. ''Right down the line: arson, crimes against the weak . . . it's all there. Dena Mendenhall's relationship as

Anthoney's common-law wife was short-lived—she left him because he was violent and abusive.''

Even more upsetting was the story of little Michelle Bethel. On July 26, 1985, the innocent twelve-year-old was raped, beaten, strangled, and left for dead near a river in Rock Creek Canyon, a popular picnic area outside Twin Falls, Idaho. The prime suspect: Kirby D. Anthoney.

On Saturday morning, July 27, 1985, officers of the Twin Falls Police Department arrived at the Magic Valley Regional Hospital to investigate the previous night's rape and life-threatening assault on Michelle Bethel. They learned that during early Friday evening, several young men gathered for a party in the picnic area adjoining the riverbank where Bethel was assaulted. Found near the scene was a pair of men's thongs.

Police interviewed several of the party's participants, asking if any of their acquaintances arrived in thongs, but left the picnic grounds barefoot. They also wanted to know if anyone could identify the thongs discovered at the scene. The answer to both questions was yes. The thongs belonged to a young man named Sam Berry. The fellow who left barefoot, however, was not Berry. It was Berry's buddy Kirby D. Anthoney.

Sam Berry confirmed that the thongs were his, and that he lent them to Anthony to wear at the picnic. ''Right before I left,'' Berry told police, ''Kirby came to me and asked if I was ready to go. I said yes, then I noticed he had fallen down and got into some mud or something. I asked him what happened. He said he needed to wash his hands and feet. So he had been down by the river. Then he said, 'Sorry, Sam, I lost your thongs.' I asked where at, and he said down by the riverbank. Then I said, 'Let's go find them,' and I started walking toward where he told me he was, and then he grabbed me and said, 'No, let's get them tomorrow.' I said okay, then we left.''

Idaho police immediately contacted Anthoney, asking him how the thongs got near the victim. He explained that he was throwing things into the fire with his feet, got mud and ashes on the thongs, then went down to the creek to wash his feet.

He claimed that he left his thongs down by the creek because it would have been slippery to walk with his thongs. He didn't explain why he would not worry about getting his feet dirty again while walking back up.

Twin Falls police, highly suspicious, asked Anthoney for the clothing he wore Friday night so they could test for bloodstains. Anthoney then allegedly told his girlfriend, Debbie Heck, that he tore the pants at the party, that he was going to throw them away, and that Heck shouldn't say anything about it. The pants, stained with what looked like mud or blood, were not given to police. Instead, Anthoney provided investigators with a different pair of trousers. Heck, despite witnessing Anthoney deceive police, was unconcerned. She knew he was a suspect, but did not believe he did it.

The assault victim, Michelle Bethel, blind in one eye and deaf in one ear from severe head blows, had no memory of the attack and could not identify her assailant under any circumstances. Anthoney, after assuring police of his full cooperation, abruptly left for Alaska with Debbie Heck. Peggy Anthoney knew her son was the prime suspect in the rape and beating, but never told John and Nancy Newman.

"If I would have known that, he would have never walked around my family," John Newman said. "I have a resentment of her. She knew what he was up to, she knew. Why she couldn't let the family in on it, I'll never know."

Most parents of children with behavior histories similar to Kirby Anthoney's are well aware that something is wrong even before the child starts school, according to Dr. Robert Hare. "They are different from normal children—more difficult, willful, aggressive, and deceitful; harder to relate to or get close to. The parents are always asking themselves, 'What next?'"

Dr. Hare, who conducts training seminars for the FBI, pinpointed certain school-age traits as prime indicators of young psychopaths. "As I mentioned in my book *Without Conscience*, these hallmarks include repetitive, casual, and seemingly thoughtless lying; apparent indifference to, or inability to understand, the feelings, expectations, or pain of others; defiance of parents, teachers, and rules; continually in trouble and unresponsive to reprimands and threats of punishment; persistent aggression, bullying, and fighting; a record of unremitting truancy, staying out late, and absences from home; a pattern of hurting or killing animals; early experimentation with sex, vandalism, and fire setting.''

"More and more, all information, both physical and behavioral, pointed toward Anthoney," said Grimes. "Each day added more suspicion, and confirmed our previous ones."

Investigators Reeder, Spadafora, and Grimes interviewed Anthoney three times in person, twice via telephone. The second time officers visited Anthoney, they requested his leather jacket and a pair of shoes he'd worn the previous weekend. Anthoney let them in, even though they didn't have a search warrant.

"He said we could look around," confirmed Spadafora, "and started getting angry that we were 'harassing' him and not trying to find the killer. He flung a couple of cabinets open. I found what appeared to be a camera case in his closet. There it was—John Newman's stolen camera. Anthoney stated that yes, it was John's. He only did this after we caught him with it. He had no intention of volunteering the location of the camera. I removed it from his closet. His explanation for having it was that his aunt Nancy, knowing his love of photography, generously loaned it to him on the Thursday prior to the homicides. He also told us that Nancy said, 'Don't tell John, he'll have a shit fit,' and that he was going to use it and give it right back.''

John Newman, however, told detectives that Nancy would not lend his camera to anyone in his absence. Police also discovered that Anthoney already owned a least two other cameras, and possibly a third, at the time he allegedly borrowed the camera and equipment from Nancy Newman. Anthoney offered additional explanations—his other cameras were in storage, and he wanted to use Newman's high-power telephoto lens.

"After we recovered Newman's camera from Anthoney, we

learned that it still had film in it,'' explained Sergeant Grimes. ''We developed the pictures, and they were family photos taken at Christmastime, 1986. You'd think that the roll would have been completed and removed before loaning it out, or that at least there would be new frames shot by Anthoney. In fact, the camera was never used after he supposedly borrowed it.''

The more police talked to Kirby D. Anthoney, the more they doubted every aspect of his alibi. Most suspicious were his alleged activities on Saturday morning, March 14. The employees at Burger King had no recollection of him at all, and although he said he sat in the parking lot to eat his breakfast, they said no one sat in the parking lot all morning. When police mentioned this to Anthoney on April 25, he immediately said he meant the parking lot across the street. No matter what, he had an immediate answer or explanation for everything, including answers for questions not yet asked, and knowledge of facts not yet revealed. On the Wednesday following the murders, Anthoney called Carol Hawkins, mother of a former Idaho girlfriend. In the conversation, he revealed details of the Newman homicides only the killer could know.

''He called here after the murders wanting to talk to my daughter, Kimra,'' recalled Hawkins, ''and he told me Nancy was raped and one of the little girls was stabbed. He knew that, but it hadn't come out in the Twin Falls paper yet, so it was news to me.''

It should have been news to Anthoney. Neither the police nor press said who was raped or stabbed. News of the murders hit the Twin Falls newspaper on Thursday, March 19, one day after Sergeant Walt Monegan of the crime prevention division of the Anchorage Police Department contacted Twin Falls police. Monegan withheld details concerning sexual assault or stabbing, never mentioned Angie Newman's name, and reported that the murders took place Saturday night or Sunday morning.

''Right now, we have no motives for the killings, and there are no suspects we can point to and no arrests have been made,''

Monegan said. "Our homicide division is extremely busy, but the investigation team is concentrating on the Newman homicides."

"I was shocked by what Kirby told me in his phone call," stated Hawkins. "I recall saying, 'What kind of animal could do something like that,' and how whoever did it was less than human, and all that sort of thing. I told him that even if the cops didn't catch the monster that did this, sooner or later whoever it was would have to face judgment—if not from the courts, from God. He was dead quiet after I said that, and for a second I wondered if he was still there. In fact, I asked him if he was still on the line. He finally spoke, telling me that he was just choked up. He asked me for Kimra's phone number and address in Pennsylvania. Although I balked at first, under the circumstances I gave it to him. I was surprised to hear from him, although he had called my daughter before. She wouldn't tell me much about their conversations—she would just say he called to chat. This always struck me as a bit unusual considering their breakup had not been a smooth one."

Kim Hawkins first met Kirby Anthoney in 1982 at Harmon Park in Twin Falls. She was in *that* rebellious phase, where if her mother liked a boy, she didn't; if the mother didn't like him, she did.

"My first impression of Kirby Anthoney," said Kim's mother, "was that he looked clean-cut enough, but there was always something I didn't like that I couldn't put my finger on. I thought he was more than a little strange, but I figured I'd keep my opinion to myself and hope that the relationship would blow over. She now says the reason she went out with him in the first place is because he had such a tough-guy image. No one messed with Kirby Anthoney, and that meant no one would mess with her. He made her feel safe until she realized what she had gotten into."

What "she had gotten into" became apparent during an incident involving Anthoney, some other local toughs, and a box of bunny rabbits. The boys were up on Pine Bridge getting

ready to set the bunnies on fire and parachute them off the
bridge. Kim, protective of innocent animals, became upset and
started crying in the car. Anthoney made a big show of rescuing
the rabbits, taking the box away, and scolding the other boys.
He took Kim home and told her he'd take care of the rabbits.
She was very impressed by his heroic act until she later learned
that Anthoney returned the rabbits to Pine Bridge for their fatal
pyrotechnic aeronautics.

Anthoney's reputation for strength, violence, and stamina
was well-known in Twin Falls, and the other teens feared him.
He got into an argument one night with a fellow who promptly
pulled a gun and shot Anthoney in the neck. Thinking he'd
been clubbed, Anthoney tackled him and beat him to a pulp.
Drunk and bleeding, the two happily accompanied each other
to the hospital.

"Although she soon realized that he was violent and dangerous, it was exceptionally difficult for Kim to get away from
him," said Mrs. Hawkins. "He was a guy who didn't like the
word, 'no.' It turns out Kim tried to break up with him on more
than one occasion. Finally, he called one night and wanted to
come over. She told him, no, that she didn't want to see him.
He came over anyway. There was no one home at the time
except the two of them. Well, they got into an argument, he
went into a rage and started choking her. My son, Terry, and
his friends came home and saw what was happening. Anthoney
immediately took his hands off Kim when they came in. They
didn't want to mess with him because of his violent reputation,
but they got him to leave. After that, Kimra was scared to death
of him. A mother would hope that her own daughter would
confide in her about something like that, but she kept that from
me for quite a while. He even told her that if she took up with
someone else, he'd kill her."

According to Kim, Anthoney stalked her by telephone for
years, calling every Thanksgiving Day no matter where she
lived. On one occasion, some friends and she were socializing
at a bar when a long-distance call came in from a man who

identified himself as her secret admirer. Thinking it was her husband calling from New Jersey, she happily took the call. It wasn't her husband; it was Kirby Anthoney warning her that he knew everything about her—where she lived, her phone number, and even her car's license plate number. He promised her that someday, sometime, when she least expected it, she would turn around and see his face.

"He had more girlfriends after Kim," said Hawkins. "There was Dena Mendenhall, Jaree Conway, and another friend of Kim's who got pregnant by Kirby while he was going steady with Kim."

Following a typical rural Idaho teenage beer party, Anthoney gave Kim and her friend a ride home. He first dropped off Kim, then had sex with her friend, which resulted in a pregnancy and the young woman giving up the baby for adoption.

"Ashamed and humiliated, she never spoke to Kim again. She still hasn't, as a matter of fact, after all these years. And that's sad. After Kim and the others, of course, there was little Debbie Heck, another one of Twin Falls' troubled teens," said Hawkins.

Everyone who met Debbie Heck had the same question: What was this attractive, pleasant young woman doing with a rude and abusive psychopath like Kirby Anthoney? Perhaps there is no explanation that makes sense outside the world of family pain inhabited by both Heck and Anthoney. Although the two attended the same school, she didn't know him beyond his reputation as "a badass, a ladies' man, and a partyer." They met in August 1984 through mutual friends when they were both twenty years old. They dated for a little over a week before he asked her to go with him to California.

"I wanted to get out of Twin Falls," Heck later admitted. "I was drinking a lot. I'd broken up with a boyfriend, which hurt pretty bad, about five months before that and so I'd started drinking a lot, and I was ready to lose my job, and I wanted to get away from there. Kirby had, or so I understand, just broken up with his girlfriend, Jaree Conway—she was about twenty-three—they had been living together for about nine months, I guess, off and on, before that. She had the brains to get rid of him—like an idiot, I didn't.''

Debbie Heck was not an idiot. She was, however, a very troubled young woman having a bad life. Her 1984 decision to link herself with Kirby Anthoney may simply have been, ''any port in a storm.'' Sadly, she made it to Lost Harbor in more ways than one.

CHAPTER 4

The Friday following the murders, Detective Gregg Baker located Debbie Heck aboard the *Arctic Enterprise,* not far from Lost Harbor. Heck had absolutely no knowledge of the Newman homicides, and thought Baker was investigating another matter entirely.

Heck, stunned and tearful, kept repeating, ''I can't believe it, I can't believe it,'' when Baker broke the tragic news. ''I know how you must feel, okay,'' he said sympathetically, ''and I know how sudden it is. So, you gotta understand what we've got to do right now. And we've got to think as hard as we can.'' Baker sat Heck down for an extensive interview, first assuring her that her employment was not in jeopardy.

''There's no problem here on the boat with your job. Everybody's real cooperative with me,'' Baker told her. ''We've talked to a lot of people, got a lot of statements. We've got a lot of evidence. But obviously we don't have enough and that's why I'm talking to you.'' Baker knew some of his questions would be both personal and embarrassing, and he advised her accordingly.

"I'm gonna have to ask you some things that you may think are really weird, or they might be difficult. Believe me, the only reason I'm asking these questions is because I want to get the person that did it. I know you have information that can help me. Somewhere, somehow, you have some little bit of information that can help me."

"Nancy was like a big sister to me, you know, an older sister," said Heck, wiping away tears. "There was lots of stuff that I could talk to her about—stuff that I would talk to my own sister about. John was very lenient on the girls. Nancy tried to be stern, which didn't work too well with John's easygoing attitude, so the girls were spoiled," she said, laughing through tears. "Melissa, she was ornery and she'd get on your nerves. She was a little sweetie, though. She was spoiled but apparently she had come a long way from when she was younger. She was a good girl. Angie was a real spitfire. She was a good kid, though. I liked 'em both. Kirby didn't like kids. Melissa didn't much like Kirby. He doesn't have enough patience."

Baker asked Heck about Kirby Anthoney's parents, and she told him that she sincerely liked and respected Peggy Anthoney. "She's an ornery old lady. She reminds me of my grandmother. She's a very nice lady, very nice." As for Kirby's father, Heck described him as "overbearing and he has a temper," but had learned to control it. "From what I understand, he never used to be able to control it."

"What about Kirby," asked Baker, "did he have a temper? Could he control it?" Debbie Heck allowed herself a long, thoughtful pause before responding. When she spoke, it was as if years of tears and pain, having reached the point of saturation, released themselves in a torrent of words.

"Very violent temper and, no, he can't control it. He used to tell me that I was the one who could control his temper, and I said, ya gotta do it yourself. He—he—he couldn't control it," she stammered, "that's why I left him . . . he'd throw me up against walls, he'd smack me around . . . throw me on the floor. When he lost his temper, he would go completely out of control. He had no control over it. He couldn't stop. I was petrified because of his temper, you know, until I could be sure that he was cooled down where he wasn't gonna kill me. I was scared for my life when I was living with Kirby. I was scared for my life.''

Debbie Kay Heck, age twenty-three, daughter of Ralph and Dolly Heck of Twin Falls, Idaho, offered Baker more than ''some little bit of information.'' She detailed important facts and provided significant insights.

''When we first came to Anchorage, we stayed with friends of Kirby's—Jeff Mullins, Kirk Mullins, and also their father, Ron Mullins, lived there,'' recalled Heck, ''then we moved into our own place.'' Their own place was only half a house number away from the Mullinses.

The first year in Anchorage, she worked at Spenard Foodland and Family Market as a grocery checker; Anthoney secured employment installing Sheetrock. ''After a while he started working at Northern Lights Car Wash,'' added Heck, ''He also had a mobile cleaning business.'' In November 1986, the couple arranged jobs working on the *Arctic Enterprise* after the first of the year. ''We sold all our household goods. We had not planned on staying in Anchorage after we left the boat. So, we had sold everything, given stuff away.''

Reducing their possessions, Heck and Anthoney moved in with John and Nancy Newman on December 3, 1986. The Newmans graciously gave the couple Melissa's bedroom. They did not, however, give them keys to the apartment. If the Newmans weren't home, Heck and Anthoney came in through Melissa's bedroom window.

''Kirby would usually use a key or an ink pen and just slide that in through the screen. There was a little hole in the screen, and you could unlatch it pretty simply that way. It was a sliding window,'' explained Heck, ''and it was usually open, even if just a crack, and it was hardly ever latched while we stayed there. I believe Kirby also went through Nancy's window a few times.''

The couple spent one month and three days in Newman's apartment. Hospitality, according to Heck, was not all that Nancy Newman provided Anthoney. His aunt secretly loaned him $500, disclosing this clandestine financial arrangement to Anthoney's mother, Peggy, in a letter written February 27, 1987. Nancy confided that she didn't ask John before she did it, and that Kirby promised to repay the loan as soon as possible. She also informed Peggy that Kirby opened a new bank account with a paycheck of Debbie Heck's, and that he was going into business with Tony Marinelli, the young man from whom he was purchasing a flatbed truck.

Finally out of the Newmans' home and on the *Arctic Enterprise*, Heck and Anthoney slept separately for two weeks until they arranged a room trade. Although reunited nocturnally, they drifted apart romantically. She found herself attracted to boat mate, Doug Anderson.

"What happened was," explained Heck to Baker, "Kirby had made friends with this guy, right, and then this is the guy that I, of course, go for." She also admitted that there was more behind the breakup than libidinous interest in Anderson. "We split up because I can't take it any more, because he scares me. I just didn't know how to get out of the relationship. I was afraid of him."

A new love interest provided a way out; Anthoney's volatile reaction in a work-related environment insured her protection. "He was unstable and very irrational. It was scary. I asked the production manager, and I said I want him off the boat because he could hurt somebody and I don't want to see anybody hurt. Anyway, he let it ride. He changed Kirby's shift and then a few days later he said, Kirby is getting off the boat now, and I don't know what happened that morning or that day. I don't know anything about that. All I know is that they decided he had to go. You have to understand that on that day I was locked in a room until Kirby left."

"You were that scared?" asked Baker.

"Goddamned right I was," Heck declared.

Heck's employer confirmed that on February 13, 1987, Anthoney was terminated from employment and was pointedly asked to leave. When Anthoney initially refused to go peacefully, Heck and Anderson were both locked in a room for their own protection.

"After he left the boat," said Heck, "I wrote my sister and I said, be alert because I don't know what he's gonna do." Heck said she told her sister, "If you hear anything about him, stay away from him. He threatened Doug when he was on the boat, threatened Doug's life." Heck's new lover, Doug Anderson, soon lost his job on the *Arctic Enterprise,* as well. He returned to Anchorage shortly after Anthoney. "One of the persons Doug went back with had contact with Kirby," said Heck, "and Kirby told the guy that he wanted to kill Doug."

Detective Baker had to ask Ms. Heck very personal questions about her sex life with Anthoney because they were dealing with a sexually motivated triple homicide. "She wasn't comfortable talking about such intimate matters," Baker later recalled, "so I had to sort of bring up the topic bit by bit, approach it from different angles, so to speak."

Sporadically, over an extensive length of time, Baker returned to the topic of Anthoney's sexual proclivities. Gradually, she revealed disturbing details, reluctantly admitting that Kirby Anthoney enjoyed hurting her—grabbing her nipple, pinching it hard enough to leave marks. When she begged him to quit, he did it all the more.

"Yeah," confirmed Heck, "he would do it because I kept telling him to stop. I thought that if I would quit telling him to stop, then he wouldn't do it anymore, which wasn't the case. That wasn't true at all." Her pain and pleading only aroused Anthoney, and he would almost always want sex after inflicting pain. "He had to have sex constantly," she said, "or else he would go nuts. I mean two days and he would go nuts. He would drive me nuts. His sex drive was scary, very scary, it just wasn't normal to what I think is normal. Very overactive. If he didn't get it, he just thought he had to have it."

After two days without sex, Anthoney would become obsessive and demanding. When he finally got it, Heck said he would be in "a state of frenzy"—more rough and violent than usual, especially if he had been doing cocaine. "He would want more and more and more, and that's all there was to it. He had to have more. He had no self-control when it came to coke or sex. He used to scare me when he was doing coke. He would start talking about our relationship and things that needed to be different and blah, blah, blah. I used to try to just block it out and say, leave me alone. I would freak out. I would literally freak out because of him talking to me and he wouldn't stop. It's just really weird." If they both did coke, she would quit early and go to bed. He would stay up for hours doing more, then come to bed and have rougher, more aggressive sex.

"Did he hurt you," asked Baker, referring to Anthoney's sexual technique.

"He always hurt me," stated Heck.

Questioned if Anthoney wanted to experience pain in addition to inflicting it, Heck was again chagrined. "I asked her if Anthoney ever requested that she hurt him, and she said no. But the way she said it, I knew she wasn't being forthcoming. So, I said, 'I don't mean hurt him, *hurt him,* but a little pain?' She again gave me a weak little no, but her face was turning red."

"I'm not getting these questions out of random, believe me," Baker told her. "I mean I didn't really make 'em up."

"Well, you're just embarrassing me," admitted Heck, obviously uncomfortable with the line of questioning.

"I know, and I'm sorry, really I am," Baker said, "and I know how you feel, but this is real important."

"I understand," she said, then awkwardly explained by words and hand gestures that Anthoney wanted her to take hold of his testicles and squeeze them so hard he would almost pass out from the pain. As she scrunched them in the palm of her hand, he would tell her to do it harder and harder. She made it clear to Baker that this was not fondling, caressing, or anything of a gentle nature. He wanted her to inflict excruciating pain.

"I made sure I understood what she was saying by specifically asking her if she did this to the point where she thought it would hurt him," Baker recalled, " and she very emphatically said, 'Yeah, yeah, past the point. Way past the point.'

"How many times do you think he injured you, bruised you, or more? More than ten times? More than fifty?"

"Yeah, more than fifty," conjectured Heck. "It always seemed to me that we were fighting, and when he would slap me, I would slap him back. And one night we fought almost all night long, around and around. He would slap me and then I just hauled off and I hit him as hard as I could, and he would slap me again and so I would slap him, and he would just stand there—just stand there and laugh in my face."

Baker, looking for matches to the FBI profile, asked if Anthoney ever demonstrated cruelty to cats and dogs. "Oh, we had a female [dog]," she answered, "and he used to kick her and beat her. He used to take the cats and he would hold them down in his lap with their backs down, you know. A cat hates that to begin with. He would stretch out their paws and hold them to where they were screaming and crying. He did this for fun, to play with them, just be ornerier than hell, and when he was mad, it was ten times worse. When the cats would scream in pain, he'd tell them to knock it off, to straighten out their shit, then he would slap 'em around some more. I told him so many times that I wanted to get rid of the cats—I loved the cats, but I wanted to get rid of them."

Heck and Anthoney once owned a puppy. "He beat the dog bad, and he didn't take any time with him except to beat him. I had a hard time controlling the dog because of Kirby's attitude and he used to just kick the dog. I mean, he's bad with animals."

Heck, in a moment of reflection, shared a memory from before her days with Kirby Anthoney. "I was engaged to a guy at one time and I got a little kitten. Well, I kept the kitten at this guy's house, and one night the guy got mad at that cat because the cat was watching him eat. He picked the cat up and he threw him across the room. And that got me thinking—that incident right there got me to thinking if he can do that to a little kitten, what's he gonna do to me after I marry him, and the kids after we have kids? So, I broke up with the guy and had nothin' more to do with him after that. I don't know why I put up with it from Kirby. This guy just threw the cat across the room; Kirby used to literally scare the shit out of them.''

Another trait on the FBI's list was arson, and Baker inquired if there were any fires related to their lives together. It came as no surprise that, yes, when they were in Riverside, California, there was an unexplained fire at Kirby Anthoney's former place of employment.

Detective Baker then began broaching the most serious and disturbing questions. ''Has Kirby ever done anything you know of, or you suspect of, in the past? I mean, this is a pretty big step, you know what I mean? You don't usually start out doing this. Has he ever killed anybody that you know of, or that you suspect?''

''There's a possibility,'' she acknowledged. ''A native in Alaska that was killed—he was found next to the car wash that Kirby was working at. Well, Kirby kept teasing me, saying, 'I know who did it.' And he let this go on for quite some time . . . he kept saying, 'I know who did it.' And then finally it got to, 'Yeah, I'm the one who did it, I'm the one who killed him.' I was just blowin' it off, right? And then, one day, we walked past the place—the car wash—and Kirby talked about the guy again. Then we didn't say anything for about a block, and then Kirby said, 'Debbie, I've got something that I need to tell you.' Kirby never did this, he was always right up front and would tell you what was on his mind. So, I said, ''Well, tell me.' And he goes, 'I can't tell you right now.' Anyway, I think that maybe, you know, I suspect.'' It was then that Heck told Baker that she thought the car wash murder was the reason Baker had come to see her. ''Yeah, for sure,'' confirmed Heck.

"That's what I thought this was about. I've been thinking about that for the last year."

Heck also acknowledged that Anthoney made sexually charged comments about his aunt, Nancy Newman. "At one time I confided in him about a problem I had," she revealed to Baker, "a sexual problem with someone I was related to. He assured me that he knew how I felt because he'd been sexually involved with his aunt Nancy—that he had an affair with her. Later, he said he was just kidding, but I would expect that he would hit on her if he felt like it."

"You know, Debbie," Baker said, "we've got the FBI down there, we've got the state troopers. We've called in specialists from all over the country. Serious—I mean flown 'em up, flown 'em down, anything necessary. We have a two-year-old and a seven-year-old . . . and we're pretty sure that if we don't make some headway in this case, a similar thing's gonna happen again, somewhere. And the reason I'm telling you this is because it's important for you to realize how serious this is. And this is not a pretty thing. That's all I can tell you. Is there anybody you can think of, in the family, that could do this?"

"In the family? Kirby." Heck's answer was immediate and emphatic.

"Kirby? Do you think he could kill a two-year-old?"

Without a moment's hesitation, Debbie Heck said, "Yes, I do. Because I saw him when he left this boat, and I've seen him for the last three years, and that man scares me. He scares me terribly. I was afraid for my life."

Prior to the homicides, Heck wrote Anthoney a letter apologizing for the manner in which their relationship ended. In doing so, she hoped to lessen his anger and reduce the odds of violent reprisal. He wrote back, insisting that although he couldn't believe she would have sex with Doug Anderson, he didn't want to make her feel ashamed or guilty. He described himself as a hotheaded, selfish, no-good bum of a jerk; that he was a sorry excuse for a human; and that if he couldn't show her his love, it was going to crush him. In conclusion, he offered to send Doug and her at least four ounces, maybe a pound, of marijuana, and signed the letter, "Your husband." Heck, who was never much of a pot smoker, wanted nothing further to do with Kirby D. Anthoney under any circumstances.

CHAPTER 5

Kirby Anthoney left the *Arctic Enterprise,* in Debbie Heck's words, "on the verge of losing it." He detailed his mental state in a long letter to her and Doug Anderson, written upon his return to Anchorage. Anthoney complained of being mad, hurt, and confused. He also accused Anderson and Heck of enjoying his pain and being two-faced. Anthoney insisted that Heck was the only person with whom he felt comfortable, and that he needed her. The contradictions between expressions of love and outbursts of anger were consistent with Anthoney's previous behavior. Yet, within the ranting prose and disjointed syntax, she clearly perceived the warning signs of a man teetering on the brink of madness.

Anthoney admitted he felt hated and confessed that he didn't know if he were okay or not; that there were too many things going through his head; he didn't need anyone asking questions and was trying to get a hold on himself because "it's that bad." He concluded the three-page handwritten letter with an awkward poem originally entitled, "My Final Vision." He scratched out the title and renamed it, "My Last Cry," then added a postscript: "Sorry, but time is my enemy."

When Anthoney returned to Anchorage by plane, he took a taxi directly to Nancy Newman's apartment. Finding no one home, he waited outside until Cheryl Chapman and her sister returned from shopping. Once again, Anthoney became Newman's houseguest—a situation displeasing to the absent John Newman, and of serious concern to Cheryl Chapman. He also flashed $1,500 that he promptly spent on heavy-duty partying. Writing to Heck after the murders, Anthoney explained his partying as the only way he could keep from "losing it."

Something happened that made Nancy and Cheryl exceptionally uncomfortable about having Anthoney stay around. Perhaps it was failing to repay the loan, or maybe he'd come on to Mrs. Newman sexually, or possibly Melissa had previously complained about him. Whatever it was, it increased Cheryl Chapman's obvious distaste for Kirby Anthoney. Nancy told Cheryl that Kirby was giving her the creeps, and that she certainly did not feel safe or comfortable around him.

When detectives asked Kirby Anthoney if he had ever done anything to the kids to make Nancy mad at him, he replied, "You mean like molesting them?"

"Who is going to answer something like that?" asked Grimes rhetorically. "Most people would say, 'You mean yell at them, or spank them, or tease them or something?' But molesting them?" Detective Grimes developed his own theory, one decidedly unfavorable toward Newman's nephew.

"Even though Nancy Newman was sexually assaulted, Melissa seemed to be the focus. As bad as Angie looked, her death was quick. But Melissa was the focus of extended cruelty and painful degradation. I think Melissa went to her mother and said Kirby did something. You must understand that this is part of the family, so she tells Anthoney he has to leave. She doesn't make an issue out of what he did because it's family. She doesn't tell her husband, but perhaps confides eventually in her sister."

"If Anthoney touched those kids in a sexual way, and Nancy Newman knew about it, we would have heard about [it]—the police, I mean," said Spadafora. "She was the type of woman who would not have covered up something like that. And Cheryl Chapman most certainly would have called the authorities if she had the slightest hint that Kirby Anthoney had been inappropriate with Melissa. No, I think maybe Anthoney came on to Nancy, hit on her, or she was picking up on his sexual-predator vibes."

With family discord erupting, Cheryl Chapman had no intention of keeping quiet about Nancy's discomfort if Anthoney stayed. "I said that I would tell him to leave," confirmed Chapman, "or I said I will confront him with this. And I said that if Nancy didn't, I was going to call Johnny and tell him because she knew that if I told her husband, that Johnny would insist on him leaving because Johnny didn't want him to stay there, either."

John Newman found out his nephew was back in Anchorage when he called home in February. Anthoney answered the phone. "I asked him what he was doing there," Newman recalled. "When Nancy came to the phone, I asked her what was he doing there and I wanted him out. I knew he had a very hot temper and just didn't want him around my family when I wasn't there. He was the kind of person, you don't know what to expect of him. He made me uncomfortable to be around him."

Newman remembered that a visit to Anchorage the previous fall by Anthoney's parents was marred when a fistfight broke out between Kirby and "Tony" Anthoney after the father made a belittling remark that reduced the son to tears. According to Cheryl Chapman, Kirby shouted, "All I ever wanted was for you to love and respect me, and you never would."

"That's the first time I ever saw him explode like that," Newman said. Debbie Heck, also present for the altercation, recalled that, "it got kind of violent. They went outside and they smacked each other a few times, and they were screaming at each other. Kirby kept saying, 'I love you Dad and you've never loved me. You've always treated me like shit.' His dad kept trying to calm him down, but Kirby wouldn't listen.''

In addition to Anthoney's notorious and off-putting outbursts, his alleged depression over the breakup with Heck prompted additional concerns. In a phone call to his mother, Anthoney made veiled references to suicide. Peggy Anthoney quickly contacted Nancy Newman, asking her to watch over her troubled offspring. Because she and Peggy were close, Newman agreed.

''She didn't want Peggy worrying about him,'' confirmed Cheryl Chapman, who also noted that both Mr. and Mrs. Newman were seriously concerned that Anthoney might harm himself. Were he to attempt suicide, the effect on the children would be traumatic.

''I never put much credence in that,'' said Grimes. ''Psychopaths don't kill themselves; they kill somebody else. Kirby Anthoney was an attention grabber. He would talk suicide, but only as an attention-getting device. Debbie Heck had seen him use that ploy before, and she didn't take those threats seriously, either, I don't believe.''

While detectives interviewed Debbie Heck and Anthoney's other acquaintances, the state crime lab became overburdened with the plethora of physical evidence submitted for analysis. Again, Anchorage Police turned to the FBI, sending every hair and fiber sample to Washington, DC, on April 3, 1987. Included were the wool GI gloves, the washcloth, various nightclothes, toys, and sheets from the victims' rooms.

Analysis of fingerprints retrieved from the Newman apartment was done locally by Kathy Monfreda, an identification technician with 11½ years' experience, 4½ of that with the Anchorage Police Department and of that, 2 years with the Alaska State Troopers Crime Laboratory. Previous to her Alaska experience, Monfreda was in the Menomonee Falls, Wisconsin, Police Department.

Monfreda's comparisons revealed that John and Nancy Newman's fingerprints were everywhere in the apartment. More than half of John Newman's prints were found on the living room fireplace, where soot and other fire residue cause prints to last longer. Print dusting and comparisons revealed several from Cheryl Chapman in the kitchen area. Two of Anthoney's prints were found near the inside knob and the outside dead bolt on the front door to the Newmans' apartment, although Anthoney had moved out several weeks earlier and said he never had a key.

There was, however, a reasonable explanation for Anthoney's fresh prints. About twelve hours after the murders, Anthoney gave Jody Cornelius a ride in his truck. She said that as they passed the Newmans' apartment, Anthoney tried the knob to see if the door was open.

More troubling were fingerprints matching those of Kirby D. Anthoney in virtually every room, including the inner rim of Nancy Newman's tip tin. Nineteen prints found in sixteen locations belonged to him, and there was also one very disturbing left-palm print on the wall above Melissa Newman's bed.

"Were he leaning against the wall while sexually assaulting the child from behind, the palm print would be exactly in that spot," noted Grimes. "There is no other explanation how or why a fresh palm print of Kirby Anthoney would be right there, in that position. It wasn't smeared, it wasn't brushed over. And—this is very important—our fingerprint expert told us that when he lifted prints, that one just came right up. It is a perfect match to the left-palm print of Anthoney."

The only shoe prints found in the apartment also matched Anthoney's. Most significant were Anthoney's footprints on the fireplace—the place to stand if one wanted to look out the window—and on Angie Newman's bedroom dresser. Although police had mounting circumstantial and physical evidence, they were not about to make an arrest.

"Most of the prints were found in the room Anthoney used when he lived with the Newmans in February—Melissa Newman's room—and no one can say for sure how long they'd been there," said Grimes. "Once you make an arrest, an entire phase of the investigation ends. We didn't want the investigation to end, and we knew the longer he stayed out there, the more chances we had that he would screw up, say the wrong thing, do the wrong thing, or we would find more hard evidence. Also, Ray told us that the person who did it would be cooperative with the police, primarily to find out how much we knew. Anthoney would always call us and ask how the investigation was going."

Detective Bill Reeder, partnered with Ken Spadafora, interviewed Anthoney on five different occasions for a total of fifteen hours, all of it tape-recorded. They questioned him repeatedly about the same topics, including the "poop stain" on his borrowed shirt. Anthoney told Reeder that the shirt became stained when he took it off and put it on the floor.

"I asked Anthoney why he would take his shirt off," Reeder later recalled, "and if you listen to the tape you can almost hear the gears in his mind trying to mesh together, trying to crank out some sort of explanation. First he said it was when he went to bed, then he realized that he didn't go to bed that night, so he stops, and actually says something like 'when the fuck did I do it, let me see here' and he had to think for a while. Then he said it was when he was sorting his clothes to do laundry—that he took it off and put on another dirty shirt."

Reeder also asked Anthoney if he had any gloves—green wool GI gloves, to be exact. Anthoney told him that he previously used a pair of Nancy Newman's green gloves to graciously wipe snow off her car.

"I asked him about the snow," Reeder later confirmed, "and he said it was snowing real heavy. He didn't say there was some frost on her window. He said it was snowing real heavy. In fact, he may have even brushed that snow off with his hand. He told me he couldn't remember if he did that or pushed it off with a broom. Well, we checked the weather records. From February fourteenth to March fourteenth, the most it snowed on any one day was about half an inch, and that was once. I think we underestimated him a couple of times,'' he added thoughtfully. ''He could actually anticipate where we were going with a particular line of questioning. He would make an incorrect or misleading statement, and I would let it pass, simply making a mental note of it. Then, a few questions down the line, he would go back and correct his statement. This showed me that he wasn't stupid, far from it. His ego, however, was enormous.''

In the interview held March 15, Anthoney said he partied all Friday night to 7:05 A.M., left Dan Grant's at about 8:45, went directly to the home of a friend, Kirk Mullins, and arrived between 9 and 9:30 A.M. Mullins, however, told police that Anthoney arrived between 10 and 11 A.M. Reeder confronted Anthoney on April 20 about the missing one to two hours. Anthoney then said he left his home at about 8:45 A.M. but did not go straight to Mullins's home. Instead, he stopped at the Burger King on Boniface and Northern Lights, where he bought a croissant sandwich and ate it while sitting in his truck in the restaurant parking lot. In an interview on April 25, Reeder told Anthoney police had checked with Burger King employees and no one remembered him. ''The restaurant does very little business that early on Saturday mornings,'' Reeder said, ''and someone would have remembered.'' Anthoney's response was that Burger King employees can't be expected to remember everyone.

Anthoney offered additional explanations or excuses for everything, including small traces of blood found on his leather jacket and on the side of the shoes he wore the weekend of the murders. He told Reeder that cats may have scratched the kids, and that Angie especially liked to clomp around the apartment in his shoes. He also said that he was in a knife fight on the boat and the blood drops may have resulted from that incident. Debbie Heck confirmed that Anthoney was involved in a knife-wielding altercation aboard the *Arctic Enterprise*. One of the men drank pruno—an alcoholic beverage derived from prunes—for two days straight. "He stabbed a guy, and Kirby took the knife away," explained Heck, "and the guy told him that he 'wasn't nothing,' and flicked him on the nose. Kirby dove on the guy and kicked him."

"We couldn't determine anything about the tiny blood specks on the jacket and shoes," admitted Reeder, "except that they were human, but Anthoney didn't know that." Police also requested any rings that Anthoney wore the weekend of the murders. They told him that they wanted to see if the rings matched marks or scratches on the victims. By "coincidence," Anthoney had just given his ring as a gift to a young lady named Collette Cooper. Reeder and Spadafora, driving Anthoney home from a police interview, wanted to stop and retrieve the ring. Anthoney jumped out of the car.

"He didn't want to go pick up that ring," recalled Spadafora. "He insisted that he didn't have to go with us, and got out of the car at the corner before I even came to a stop. He actually called up Ms. Cooper before we made it over there because he didn't know if we found marks that could be traced directly to that ring. That whole approach didn't pan out, but his reaction to the request was certainly inconsistent with someone who was innocent."

Were Kirby Anthoney the rapist-killer, he would never admit it, asserted Reeder. "Not that he would be embarrassed about doing it, but confessing would mean he was inferior. It was obvious to me that Anthoney thought he was smarter than all of us put together."

Police were not worried about him killing anyone immediately because they were watching Anthoney virtually twenty-four hours a day, and he knew it. Despite police surveillance, he continued his normal social interactions—drinking, dancing, and attempting to charm females.

"Kirby can be very charming when he wants to be," said Debbie Heck. "He can charm just about anybody when he wants to. He starts off treating you good as gold, then he treats you like shit."

Victoria Kay Irvine encountered Anthoney at Chilkoot Charlie's, an Anchorage nightspot, on March 20, 1987, the Friday after the bodies were discovered. "He was writing poems and stuff, weird poems on napkins," she recalled. "He was passing them around."

Anthoney asked her if she had heard about the murders. "There was a mom and two girls," he told Irvine, "that was my aunt and my nieces. The worst thing was that the mom had to watch." He also told her the oldest child had been sexually assaulted, and admitted to Irvine that he was a suspect in the slayings. "He wasn't worried," Irvine recalled, "because he had alibis."

"While we waited for those reports from the Washington, DC, crime lab," Grimes said, "we took a look through our records to see if the APD had any previous encounters of any kind with Kirby Anthoney." There was one previous contact documented in Alaska Police Department report No. 86-88747. Officers arrested Kirby Anthoney when they could not calm him. The woman with him insisted she was frightened of what Anthoney would do to her after police left. She had red marks on her throat, neck, and forearms. Anthoney was arrested and charged with assault. The victim's name: Debbie K. Heck.

"I was busy in the house doing cleaning," recalled Debbie Heck of the incident, "and Kirby was yelling at me to come out and move the car. I kept telling him that I was busy and that he could do it himself. He told me that I better get out there right now, blah, blah, blah, and it turned into a big argument. I walked out on the porch to just get away and cool off. He reached out and pushed me." Heck smacked into the wall, turned, and tried to walk past him. "He went to reach to stop me, but snagged onto my necklace and he broke it. After he had broken my necklace, I went out the back door, and I was crying. I was scared, and I ran around the side of the house and Kirby came after me, following me. Like a dummy, I stopped right there. I don't know why, but I stopped because I was scared that if he caught me, he would hurt me. I was screaming at him to leave me alone, and then the neighbors heard. We went back into the house, and we were screaming at each other in the house, and then the cops came. Kirby was begging and pleading [with the cops] and that scared me. He was losing it—he was on the verge of losing it then. Then the cops took him away." At the time of the incident, police noticed visible signs of abuse on Heck's face, arms, and throat. Heck, fearful, later dropped the charges.

More significant than the assault on Heck was a brief, easily overlooked contact with Anthoney following the unsolved homicide of Walter Napageak, a native male transvestite.

Napageak, who dressed as a woman and represented himself as one, frequented Anchorage's Fourth Avenue district. He was known for soliciting sex with men. Naturally, this could cause problems if he had intimate relations with a man, and his partner then discovered that Walter wasn't really a woman. Police reasoned Napageak's murder was a violent and deadly result of buyer's regret. His body, stripped to the waist, was found behind Anchorage's Northern Lights Car Wash. Repeated vicious blows had cracked Napageak's skull, and his jeans had been tied around his neck.

While there was perhaps motive in the Napageak homicide, at the time the body was discovered, there were no suspects, no weapon, and no arrests. Investigators were mystified by certain aspects of the case—Napageak's body was soaking wet, there was very little blood, and police could only find one tire track leading to the body, and that track was impossible to match. Detectives guessed that the body was driven to the site in the back of a pickup, and the ice had kept the other tire tracks from showing up.

A new review of the Napageak crime scene photos revealed striking similarities to the posed bodies found in the Newman apartment. Just as they had pillowcases tied around their necks, Napageak had his pants tied around his head. He was also splayed out in much the same manner—stripped to the waist—with massive blunt-force trauma to the face and head.

"Now we were into a real cat-and-mouse game with Anthoney. We followed him everywhere," Grimes said, "and when he went to visit his friends, we would go there immediately after. Basically, we wanted to isolate him. When you figure the lifestyle of his friends, they didn't like cops coming by, and anyone would find the idea of having a child rapist and killer in their home upsetting. Our obvious concentration of attention on Anthoney didn't make his pals comfortable. If he did it, they wanted nothing to do with him."

Police also took hair samples from Anthoney's roommate, Dan Grant, and even hair and fur samples from Grant's dog and cat. "We also relocated our original suspect who had thrown his suitcase out the window and took off—Frank Cornelius. The suitcase had old bloodstains on the inside, strangely enough, so we took hair samples from this guy and a swab from inside his mouth. There was always the off-chance that Anthoney wasn't the killer, and we had to explore all clues, all suspects."

Police also alternately increased and decreased surveillance of Anthoney to the point where he became outraged and confused. "He called me up just screaming," said Grimes, "demanding that we stop watching him. The funny thing was that we had pulled back significantly at that time—he was seeing cops everywhere, all the time, if we were there or not."

This served two purposes: First, it kept Anthoney from acting out in any way that would prompt immediate arrest, and second, increased the odds that Anthoney would make an important error. "I was increasingly convinced that he was responsible for the Newman homicides," admitted Grimes. "We just didn't want to make an arrest until we had absolutely everything we could get—and that meant lab results from the FBI."

"My biggest fear," acknowledged Reeder, "was that Anthoney would clam up and say 'Screw you guys.' I thought that if I could keep an avenue open to him, let him vent to me how much he disliked Ken Spadafora, it would help."

"Anthoney hated me," explained Spadafora, "because I was

his accuser. I was the bad cop to Bill's good cop. I called him on his lies. I was the one that labeled him a baby killer and a rapist. I would never believe him and he got angry when he could not manipulate me. He could not manipulate Bill, either, but Bill let him think he could. I held him accountable during the interviews.''

Jud Ray of the FBI told Reeder that the killer was the type to interject himself into the investigation, and that gave police hope that if Anthoney was the killer, he would keep right on talking.

CHAPTER 6

"Had this homicide happened in the 1970s or the early 1980s," stated longtime police officer Sergeant Richard Coffee, "things would have been different—much different. At the end of the 1970s, the success rate of our homicide investigations was less than forty percent."

"And in those days," recalled Grimes, who joined the Anchorage Police Department in 1972, "Anchorage was pretty much a small town. The oil boom and all that came with it caught us off guard. It became a regular circus." Rugged in nature, liberal by lifestyle, Alaskans during the the Alaskan Pipeline boom treasured their extensive personal freedom and the easy availability of vices. Anchorage built a new reputation erected on its thriving sex industry, gambling dens, and legalized marijuana.

"The money was the magnet," recalled former Californian Jack Keane. He came to Alaska on a whim and discovered a natural affinity for endless elbowroom and the lucrative fishing industry. In Anchorage, he saw it all, from entrepreneurial daytime home builders to opportunistic all-night ingenues. "All those cheap bed and breakfasts you see nowadays were houses of prostitution back then. The attitude was that all these guys needed to do something, and that was one thing they were certainly going to need. Another thing needed was Gwennie's good food and a convivial atmosphere." It was at this popular meeting place for fishermen, friends, and family that Keane also encountered Nancy Newman—part of the new influx of willing workers from the lower forty-eight who increased the forty-ninth state's population in the '70s and '80s.

As with all migrants and immigrants, some were drawn by an intangible longing, or summoned by the lure of increased income. And then there are those who didn't come running *to* Alaska, they came running *away* from somewhere else: escaping their past, avoiding indictment, or a combination of both.

"And they drank, drugged, gambled, and had plenty of sex," Grimes recalled. "Alaska's taverns only had to close three hours a day—any three hours. Most selected the hours between five and eight in the morning. Anchorage's downtown became endless, interconnected taverns; the streets swarmed with eager prostitutes, and massage parlors were opening one right after the other." It was then that Mike Grimes found himself on the vice squad.

"Squad? There were only three of us for the entire city, if you can imagine that. Three vice cops and hundreds and hundreds of hookers. All our obscenity laws had been struck down for being unconstitutional. We were overwhelmed. We would have over two hundred prostitutes working the streets in a two-block area, and that's not counting those working indoors, in the bars, hotels, or massage parlors. The Mob, or people who wished they were the Mob, also had about fifty illegal gambling dens operating, and all we had were three guys working vice."

The three officers may have been overwhelmed and over-worked, but they loved the job. "I couldn't believe I was actually getting paid to do the things I was doing. It was a dream job," confirmed Grimes. "I was getting paid to go out at night and get drunk—you couldn't sip Seven-Up in those taverns and be believable—then get naked, get massaged, and ultimately propositioned by prostitutes. We'd make an arrest and go out and do it again. It was crazy. No doubt coming home drunk every night at five A.M. contributed to the end of my first marriage. It went on like that for about three years.''

In 1980, the Anchorage Police received an Alaskan state grant for felony suppression. Grimes, then a corporal, was assigned to this special task force targeting violent career criminals. Soon advancing to sergeant, Grimes left his vice days behind, concentrating his energies on preventing and solving violent crimes.

"We had a small-town outlook, and major big-city problems,'' he recalled, "and it happened so fast, it was so abrupt, and we were operating with a local hometown way of doing things. Basically, the situation was out of control. That's why the state gave us that grant. We formed a target group to get the most violent criminals off the street.''

As Anchorage developed a more modern approach, overhauling the homicide division took top priority. "There was no crime scene investigation of any quality or consistency in those days, and we were getting up to twenty homicides a year. Our first improvement was to use the new Felony Suppression Team for homicide response. The homicide unit is supposed to be the elite—the best. Well, we had a lot of work to do, and a lot of changes to make. The department gave me an incredible amount of autonomy, and I brought in really good people. The chief, the captain, both were great and incredibly supportive.''

Grimes met with his superiors, proffering a rather expensive, expansive, and grandiose plan: a highly specialized and well-trained Homicide Response Team. "It was expensive to begin with, but a cost saver in the long run. Before we had the full Homicide Response Team, I was losing all my detectives to the crime scene. We had no separate crime scene team, so I had to utilize my homicide detectives at the scene rather than out on the street. I wanted to have my detectives work people—

I wanted two coordinated groups: one that worked the crime scene, and another that worked the people.''

With the concept formalized, Grimes was allocated three teams of homicide investigators. The immediate response to the department-wide applicant search surprised everyone. ''We found people who had astonishing talents and expertise that wasn't being tapped. We had patrol officers with education and practical knowledge we were completely unaware of. There was so much talent out there that we were not taking advantage of previously. This police force was alive with talent, knowledge, and resolute willingness. You couldn't ask for a better bunch of people, or a more dynamic commitment to professionalism, people such as Bill Gifford, for example.'' Gifford aided in the planning of the Homicide Response Team and was one of the original members.

''I was one of twelve officers whose job it was to process all felony cases,'' recalled Gifford. ''I had done a lot of learning on my own and had developed some skills that were used a lot at that time. I also had redeveloped the crime scene processing program at the PD, and developed a state-certified forty-hour training class. This class was certified through the Police Standards Council and is still used today. I had taught many classes for the Anchorage Police Department and for other agencies around the state. At the time of the Newman murders, I was assigned to assist the homicide unit in scene investigations.''

Had the Newman homicides taken place a few years earlier, insisted Grimes, the crime scene's integrity may have been compromised. ''You can't fault the patrol cops themselves, it was simply that responding officers were not trained in that type of thing back then,'' he explained. ''I showed up at a homicide scene one time years ago where a lady had shot her husband in a domestic dispute. He's lying in the kitchen, blood everywhere. She's still sitting there, drinking at the dining room table. The cops keep moving the gun on the table farther away from her. When I got there, there must have been six or seven guys walking all over the crime scene, tracking blood all over the place. It was crazy. Had we faced that with the Newman case, we would have been sunk.''

As for dealing with physical crime-scene evidence, Grimes developed another productive concept. ''A police officer, in the normal course of his duties, goes to call after call after call. In the process, he develops a sixth sense about what's important,'' he explained. ''You give someone like this training and equipment, and they're going to be a better crime scene investigator than a lab technician. The lab guys work in a sterile environment and they don't know what to look for. But if you put a detective with them, the detective tells them what to photograph, what samples to take, and so forth. I didn't want to give up a detective to stand around and do that. I wanted detectives who were trained to be crime scene investigators.''

In the old days, according to Sergeant Coffee, ''a homicide crime scene investigation consisted of one cop and a guy with a camera. The new concepts, put into action, proved successful beyond anyone's expectations. In the following twelve to fourteen years, the Anchorage Police Department's clearance rate on homicides went up to over ninety percent; conviction rate almost one hundred percent.''

Anchorage Police also got on the fast track with the District Attorney's Office for instantly issued crime scene search warrants. In addition to actual on-scene response from the Prosecutor's Office, forensic psychologists and pathologists also signed on for immediate on-site participation. The new Homicide Response Team had been in existence for about 1½ years when the 911 call came in from Paul Chapman.

''We depend so much on the initial response of the patrol officer,'' explained Grimes. ''If we show up at a botched crime scene, it's almost impossible to rehabilitate it. Vance did exactly what he knew was correct—he went directly into Newman's apartment, touched nothing, and saw just enough to recognize that the occupants were dead, that this was a forensic crime scene, and that solving this case would depend upon exceptionally fragile trace evidence. Cheryl understandably went berserk when Paul told her everyone was dead. She knocked over a chair and left her purse and cigarettes in the kitchen when he pulled her out. But thankfully, not much aside from that was disturbed. Crime scenes and evidence don't go anywhere, unless you're outside and the elements get to it. But inside, as with this case, as long as the purity is maintained, you have all the time in the world. We were on the Newman crime scene for eight straight days," said Grimes. "Gifford really must be complimented on his extensive and thorough investigation. He used equipment and methods that were, for the time, quite advanced."

One new method utilized, Gifford explained, was argon laser light. "Using the state crime lab's argon laser, green fibers were found on the bodies at time of autopsy. What we needed was a portable unit for examination of the crime scene. There were no portable lasers in the state at the time, so George Taft at the crime lab made arrangements for the Omni Chrome Corp. to bring up a demo unit. I spoke with the representative from Omni, and he agreed to let me keep the portable unit and use it in this case. The use of this machine is very time-consuming. I went over the scene three times looking for the source of the green fibers. I then checked out all the evidence at the station and went over it. The source of the fibers was the pair of green gloves found in Nancy Newman's bedroom."

Agent Doug Deedrick of the FBI verified this important bit of physical evidence, among others, in Washington, DC. "The FBI laboratory has been chartered for many years by congress to examine physical evidence from duly authorized law enforcement agencies throughout the country," Deedrick explained. "It doesn't have to be a federal investigation for the FBI laboratory to become involved and examine physical evidence. We only have one laboratory, which is in Washington, DC, and we also do all FBI investigation–type examinations, as well."

"The successful investigation and prosecution of the Newman murders," Gifford said, "would depend upon scientific analysis of crime scene evidence. The FBI laboratory is one of the largest and most comprehensive forensic laboratories in the world. It's the only full-service federal forensic laboratory, and it examines evidence free of charge for federal, state, and local law enforcement agencies. Examiners also provide expert witness testimony in court regarding the results of the forensic examinations."

"Most of the testimonies are at the request of the prosecution," said Deedrick, "but I've had a number of cases where I have testified at the request of the defense because sometimes the findings indicate that perhaps the individual had not committed this crime."

Deedrick, who came to the FBI in 1972 with a bachelor's degree in biology from Indiana University, is one of the few hair, fiber, and feather experts in the world. "I was involved in writing an article of feather identification for the law enforcement bulletin," stated Deedrick. "That's another area of specialty that I have. I was also coauthor on an article in the proceedings of the International Hair Symposium."

"Deedrick is really amazing," said Grimes. "That man knows more about hairs than there are hairs on your head. It's fascinating that one man can know so much about something most people seldom think about, except whether or not they're losing their hair or having a bad hair day."

"Well, you can't learn by just reading magazines and books," explained Deedrick. "There's a one-year training period in the laboratory that consists of looking at reference material of known hairs, and known fibers, and known fabric samples. There are courses taught at the FBI Academy that deal with hair and fiber identification, the use of various microscopes in helping to identify types of evidence. For instance, a polarizing microscope course that uses a polarizing microscope to identify textile fibers. I took a course in the identification of forcibly removed human hairs."

Deedrick's most valuable area of expertise, however, was microscopy—the use of microscopes to discern the transfer of hairs and fibers from one individual to another, or from one place to another. If someone wanted to know how a hair from the bathroom ended up in the kids' playroom, Agent Deedrick could probably explain it.

He also worked numerous high-profile investigations, including the tragic space shuttle explosion, bombings in Lebanon, the killing of nuns in El Salvador, and the hijacking of a ship in Cypress.

"All of my time is devoted to the science of identifying and comparing human hairs," commented Deedrick. "That's my workday, except for times when I'm testifying or times when I'm trying to teach someone else about it. I deal strictly with hair and fiber evidence. I've probably testified somewhere between two hundred fifty and three hundred times in perhaps thirty to thirty-five different states and territories. This includes federal courts as well as state courts." Because of his success in clearing innocent suspects, Deedrick earned the nickname "Mr. Defense."

As training coordinator of the FBI's hair and fibers unit, he conducted examinations of evidence, "primarily from crimes of violence, sexual assaults, homicides, and other assaults where an exchange of hair evidence and fiber evidence may occur. I examine the evidence that's submitted in these cases," he explained. "I've probably worked close to four thousand cases. Hundreds of thousands of hairs have crossed my microscope at one point or another during the last ten years."

Investigating the Newman case, Deedrick examined almost four hundred individual hairs and fibers. A daunting task, he utilized two interconnected electronic microscopes to compare samples. When Grimes, Gifford, and the other detectives heard back from the FBI crime lab, the results were not surprising. They were, however, disconcerting. "Hairs cannot be matched exactly to people the way fingerprints can," Deedrick said, reminding them that hair comparisons do not constitute a basis for absolute personal identification. He did report that " brown Caucasian pubic hairs that exhibit the same microscopic characteristics" as those of Kirby D. Anthoney were found on the body of Melissa Newman. Nine more such hairs were found in the sweepings from the bedroom floor. Finally, two additional pubic hairs like those of Anthoney were found on Melissa's bed.

Sergeant Gifford had handpicked the three hairs on Melissa Newman's bed from exposed areas. "I picked some hairs from the comforter and from her blanket," he said. "We didn't find these hairs buried in the sheets somewhere."

"A total of thirteen pubic hairs like those of Kirby D. Anthoney were found on or near the remains of Melissa Newman," reported Deedrick. "Anthoney's hair has distinctive characteristics that make it possible to match samples with more certainty than in the average. I felt I could come to a very strong conclusion as to the origins of those hairs."

Pubic hairs matching Anthoney's were not found on Nancy Newman, nor were any such hairs found about her body or in the room. There was one pubic hair matching Anthoney's found on Angie Newman, and two more were taken from floor sweepings. Also, one head hair like Anthoney's was found on the floor near the body. No head or pubic hairs like Anthoney's were found on Angie's bed.

FBI personnel also closely examined the damp washcloth recovered from the bathroom sink. There was only one identifiable hair on the washrag—one from a Caucasian adult having attached to it a small amount of tissue suggesting it was forcibly removed. This single hair was like the sample of pubic hair provided by Kirby D. Anthoney.

Under microscopic examination, the washcloth showed the presence of green wool fibers matching the GI gloves found near Nancy Newman's body, and fibers found on the bodies themselves. The gloves also contained a large number of Newman's forcibly removed head hairs.

Some of the pubic hairs matched to Anthoney also had lice egg casings at the roots. If Anthoney had pubic lice, evidence was mounting. "This was a significant turning point in the investigation," stated Reeder. "Kirby D. Anthoney had always been a suspect, now he was *the* suspect. However, as Deedrick said, you can't match hair with the certainty that you can fingerprints, and establishing how old the hairs are is extra difficult. Anthoney would have, as usual, a reasonable explanation. After all, he had lived there for over a month, and was a frequent visitor up to the time of the murder. But the presence of pubic lice is such a definitive marker. I think this was the first time in my life that the sight of pubic lice gave me anything akin to hope.''

''We had briefings once a day about the status of the case,'' recalled Gifford, ''and we were talking about the problems with the evidence—how could we establish that Anthoney's hair samples were recent and not left over from when he lived there? I recall we discussed Nancy Newman had borrowed the Chapmans' vacuum cleaner on Friday the thirteenth, immediately after Paul Chapman used it to trim his beard. Only hours before the murders, Newman told her niece, Kelly, that she just had the entire apartment vacuumed. The upstairs neighbor girl who baby-sat for the Newmans every Monday and Wednesday, Jody Cornelius, said that she did the vacuuming for Mrs. Newman, and helped her tidy up the place.''

The District Attorney's Office made it clear to Gifford that young Cornelius's unverified statement was ineffective, and perhaps not admissible in court. ''We have a real problem,'' Gifford told Sergeant Grimes, ''because the FBI can't say how old the hairs are, or how long ago they came from Anthoney's body. Especially when you consider that one of Debbie Heck's old hairs was found in Melissa's room from when she'd stayed there previously.''

''Is there a way,'' asked Grimes, ''any way at all, to prove the Newman apartment had been vacuumed immediately prior to the murders, and can we show that the hairs matching those from Anthoney were more recent?'' Sergeant Bill Gifford gave the conundrum serious consideration. If he could find the answer, it would make all the difference in the world.

CHAPTER 7

Paul Chapman trimmed his beard the morning of Friday, March 13, then lent the upright vacuum to Nancy Newman. Inside the vacuum cleaner was the bag, and inside the bag were the beard trimmings. "If we could examine the contents of the vacuum bag the same way an archeologist examines a dig," Gifford told Grimes, "we could tell if the vacuum had been used after leaving the Chapmans." Gifford immediately contacted Agent Deedrick, asking if he could send the bag to the FBI's lab. The answer was quick and emphatic.

"Deedrick said no way, and his boss said, 'Do not send the bag back here, we will not do it. There are hundreds of thousands of hairs and all manner of debris in there. It would be so time-consuming that it would shut down the entire lab.' " Gifford, not easily dissuaded, personally removed the vacuum bag, brought it to an illumined work area, and slowly sliced it open with a razor blade. "I dissected it as if it were a biological sample or unique life-form, and spent six hours going through four inches of debris," said Gifford. "There were two separate compacted layers above Chapman's beard trimmings. I could prove that the vacuum cleaner was used twice after the morning of the thirteenth. I would pull debris over an area of the desk, and using a magnifying glass and a pair of tweezers, I'd search through it and pluck out things that looked like pubic hairs and head hairs. If the contents of the vacuum cleaner could establish that the apartment was cleaned before the murders, then the hairs and fiber evidence from Anthoney would be recent and damning. It [was] with a certain degree of irony that I noted the vacuum's brand name: Kirby.''

The Anchorage Police Department drew the hard evidence and circumstantial evidence together, hoping to build a strong case worthy of the grand jury. The physical evidence from the lab linking Anthoney to the crime scene—fingerprints, washrag, gloves, hair and fibers, the soiled shirt—and then such things as Anthoney's possession of John Newman's camera and the wrapped coins possibly from Nancy Newman's tip tin. Detectives learned that four days after the murders, Anthoney bought Dan Grant lunch at Burger Jim's, paying part of the $12 tab with a role of dimes. John Newman had previously told police that some of the coins in the cookie tin were already rolled in wrappers and additional wrappers were kept in the tin.

''We spent a considerable amount of time attempting to reconstruct Anthoney's precise whereabouts at all times before, during, and after the homicides,'' explained Reeder. ''He spoke to us extensively about that, and even told us he had 'an airtight alibi.' In truth, Anthoney could not account for his whereabouts between eight-thirty A.M. and ten-thirty A.M., Saturday, March fourteenth. Everything he told us about where he was, and what he did during that time, seemed more and more a complete fabrication.''

On April 13, 1987, Kirby D. Anthoney called Reeder, asking about the status of the investigation. ''I told him that we had just received some results from the FBI lab in connection with the hairs and fibers we sent to them for analysis. I told him that I wanted to get together and talk about those results. In

fact, I set up an appointment to interview him at the Anchorage
Police Department the next day, April fourteenth.''

Anthoney, however, did not keep the appointment. Calling
the Anchorage Police Department, he left a message for Reeder
explaining that he was helping a friend with a truck and would
be unable to make the appointment. In reality, Kirby D. Anthoney was on his way to the Canadian border. Anthoney didn't
bother fixing the defective steering or repairing the damaged
brakes on his truck. He also didn't call his friends to say good-
bye—he called the Pennsylvania home of ex-girlfriend Kim
Hawkins, the married mother of two young children.

''Anthoney asked me for her number when he called after
the murders,'' said Carol Hawkins. ''He called her then, and
he called her the day he left Anchorage.'' Anthoney, intoxicated
and wound up tighter than a $2 watch, told her everything
''was going wonderful for him, that he owned a car wash where
he was making hundreds of thousands of dollars a year,'' and
that he was coming to see her and her kids.

''He wanted Kimra to tell me that he was going to come see
me, too,'' recalled Hawkins. ''At that point she was the only
one who knew Kirby Anthoney was leaving Alaska. By the
time her husband got home from working the graveyard shift,
Kim had already packed her bags. When he walked in the door,
she told him, 'We're moving, and we're moving right now.' ''

''Anthoney was under intense surveillance during most of the
investigation,'' said Captain Novaky of the Anchorage Police
Department, '' but it was reduced because more officers were
needed to help with the investigation, and we weren't getting
anything out of it.''

''He told Dan Grant he was leaving,'' Grimes recalled, ''but
insisted that Grant not notify the police. Thankfully, Grant
eventually got up the nerve to call Spadafora.'' Grant told
police Anthoney had taken off for Canada. When asked how
long ago he'd left, Grant broke the bad news: seven hours. ''I
yelled 'holy shit' when I heard that,'' said Grimes. ''It's about
eight hours to the border. There was a slim chance he hadn't

already made it out of the country.'' Grimes called the American side of the border, telling them to be on the lookout for a flatbed dual-wheeled truck, and that the driver was a homicide suspect. "They told me I was too late, that he had already crossed the border, but between American customs and Canadian customs there is twenty-six miles of no-man's-land. They gave me the number of Canadian customs and said there's a chance he hasn't made it through yet."

Grimes quickly dialed, praying Anthoney hadn't already entered Canada. "I called Canadian customs and said, 'We got a guy who's a suspect in a triple homicide, has a prior felony conviction, and is also the suspect in a rape and attempted murder in Idaho. I don't think you really want this guy in Canada.' " The Canadian customs agent looked out his glass-enclosed booth. Kirby D. Anthoney's flatbed truck was approaching at that very moment.

"Here he comes now, hold the phone. I'll be right back." Grimes waited, straining to hear what was happening on the other end of the line. "I told him to bugger-off," the agent reported, "and he's heading back your way. He's not coming into our country."

Grimes then called the American side, alerting Supervisory Customs Inspector Patrick O. McGownd. As luck would have it, the state troopers assigned to the border area had just pulled up. Grimes reported the situation and advised troopers that Anthoney was driving with a suspended license.

"At about 11:30 P.M. Alaskan State Troopers arrested him for driving with a suspended license—a misdemeanor offense. As he was passing through American customs, Inspector McGownd had his people search the truck. They found a marijuana pipe with resin in it, and seeds in the ashtray. This meant his truck was impounded under customs' law. Anthoney was really aggravated because not only was his truck gone, but he was jailed in a little border town. The judge held him on a five-thousand-dollar bail for driving with a suspended license."

Detective Baker flew up in a private plane to recover Anthoney's truck, then arranged to have it towed down to Anchorage. "With Anthoney in custody, the district attorney worked up the charging documents," said Baker, "and had warrants issued for three counts of murder in the first degree, two counts of sexual assault in the first degree, and threw in one count of kidnapping." The charges were filed at 4 P.M., April 24, 1987, in the trial court for the third judicial district for the state of Alaska.

"In Alaska," explained Grimes, "we have a statute that says if you restrain any person in any significant way to perform an act of sexual assault, it adds another count of kidnapping punishable by up to ninety-nine years. Melissa Newman had a pillowcase knotted around her wrist, indicating that she had been restrained. We were sure that she had been tied to the bed when he raped her. Since her wrists were tied, that added a count of kidnapping."

Anthony, transported to the Fairbanks Correctional Facility, lodged there for a week on the suspended-license charge. The new, far more serious charges were sent off to Fairbanks. The following day, Grimes notified authorities that he and Spadafora were coming up to get Anthoney.

"Spadafora and I flew up there to get him because he hated both of us. We go up there, get off the airplane, and there is Anthoney with belly chains on, and he's holding the paperwork in his hand. The guy was in an absolute rage, and he screams at us, 'What is this kidnapping shit?' Three counts of murder, three counts of sexual assault, and Anthoney is screaming about being charged with kidnapping. He didn't understand why we charged him with that. He wasn't complaining about being charged with murder and sexual assault, only about kidnapping."

On Saturday, April 25, 1987, Kirby D. Anthoney returned to Anchorage held on a cash-only bail of $3 million. Police informed the press that the case would go to the grand jury on May 4, and that charges were officially filed on Friday, April 24, 1987.

Monday, April 27, 1987, behind a tight wall of security, Kirby D. Anthoney appeared in district court. After a fifteen-minute videotape of a magistrate explaining Anthoney's rights under state and federal law, Magistrate Janna Stewart began asking questions. Anthoney, quiet and self-contained, answered Stewart's questions with stilted courtesy, correcting the misspelling of his name on court documents and conferring briefly with his court-appointed attorney. Courthouse guards searching for weapons patted down reporters and photographers who arrived to record Anthoney's first appearance since his arrest at the Canadian border.

"Reporters aren't notorious for shooting defendants," noted Grimes, "but increased security was imperative. So many people were outraged by this crime, that it was not unreasonable to fear that someone might try to short-circuit justice by shooting Anthoney right there in the courtroom."

Five days after charges were filed against Kirby D. Anthoney, police received an unexpected phone call from Mr. Jess O'Dell, Anthoney's next-door neighbor. He offered information regarding a certain 35mm camera, complete with telephoto attachments. According to O'Dell, Anthoney tried to sell him the camera on the Tuesday following the homicides.

"It was Tuesday after the officers had taken samples of hair from him and stuff," said O'Dell. "I went over there and he owed me some money, fifty dollars, and he paid me with some coins, two days after, I guess, the bodies were discovered. And there was a roll of dimes and a roll of quarters. He paid me about thirty dollars. I said to him, 'Where'd you get these, the car wash?' He said, no, and sort of put his head down. He told me that the police were coming back to search his house again. He was cleaning everything and he was acting real nervous. I figured he was just sad because it was someone he knew and stuff and he told me about it. And I didn't even think that he would do anything like that. He just told me, 'I can't believe it, I'm a suspect,' and they took samples of pubic hair from him and that's about all he said. He was acting real weird. He said that they were coming back for something and he was just like cleaning really fast and going through his closet and acting real hyped out, like he was looking around for stuff. He just pulled [the camera] out and said, 'Hey, you know of anybody wants to buy this?' I asked him if it was hot, and he says, no, somebody he knew was hurting and he got it from him cheap or something. I had too many bills piled up, I didn't even want it, you know even if I would have got a good deal on it.''

O'Dell easily identified John Newman's recovered camera, bag, and attachments. ''I told the police that I didn't know exactly the brand,'' recalled O'Dell, ''but I told them it was a nylon blue case and it had red writing on it. It had a couple extra lenses, and flash, and a couple filters or something.''

Six days after O'Dell contacted the police, May 4, 1987, seventeen witnesses, including O'Dell, the Chapmans, Debbie Heck, both Mullins brothers, Dan Grant, and various investigative officers and forensic experts testified before the grand jury. Representing the state was Assistant District Attorney Stephen E. Branchflower; court appointed to defend Anthoney were John Salemi and Craig Howard.

The grand jury indicted Anthoney, but his attorneys wanted the indictment dismissed on the grounds of improper testimony. They alleged that various witnesses made remarks suggesting that Anthoney was a person of bad character. Some of the statements considered unfairly prejudicial by the defense included Cheryl Chapman telling jurors that Nancy Newman was unwilling to leave her children alone with Anthoney and unwilling to let him have a key to the apartment.

''The grand jury was left with the impression that Mr. Anthoney was not trustworthy enough to be left in the house without supervision,'' defense attorney John Salemi argued. ''The inference is that Ms. Newman did not trust Mr. Anthoney with her two daughters. This blatant elicitation of character evidence is clearly contrary to the rules governing these proceedings.''

Salemi also objected to a ''now or never'' explanation to the jury made by Assistant District Attorney Steve Branchflower.

When one juror asked if Kirby could be indicted later if the jury failed to indict him the first time around, Branchflower said it was possible but unlikely.

The defense also asked Superior Court Judge Seaborn Buckalew to let Anthoney act as cocounsel at his trial. The judge rejected Salemi's dismissal request, but affirmed Anthoney's right to question witnesses or argue to the jury. The trial, tentatively scheduled to begin February 8 of the following calendar year, would mark the one-year anniversary of the day on the *Arctic Enterprise* when Debbie Heck, sick and tired of being scared for her life, told Kirby D. Anthoney that he had abused her for the last time.

From his arrival in Anchorage to the conclusion of his trial, Anthoney was housed at the Cook Inlet Pre-Trial Facility. In the same module were Dwaine Chambers, convicted of stabbing a stranger to death; Tom Warren, who pleaded no contest to more than a dozen rapes; Gary Newcomb, convicted of attempted murder and assault after shooting two police officers; and Kevin Collins, a former drug dealer convicted of killing four people on purpose and one by accident in a drug-related shoot-out.

Collins despised Kirby D. Anthoney from the moment he read of the Newman murders. "There's never no need to kill a woman and two little girls," he said. "I have a young daughter myself. I've hated him since I read about his arrest."

Collins's displeasure increased through personal interaction. Anthoney infuriated Collins by accusing him of stealing a newspaper from Anthoney's room.

"I don't go into other people's rooms," insisted Collins. "He then got all up in my face; called me nigger. When he went into my room and took my newspaper, I decided to kill him. I waited until he came out of my room, then I punched him in the face. Then the goon squad came, and the guards broke it up."

Collins was in lockdown for three weeks but not charged with a crime. "If I'd known I would have been locked down for three weeks,'' Collins said, ''I would have tried to do more damage. If I ever get another chance, he won't need no trial.'' Anthoney required six stitches to close the cut caused by Collins's fist, and a series of violent encounters prior to, and during, the trial with several different inmates.

In those same months, the owners of the apartment building where the Newmans died wondered who would pay for the estimated $10,000 in damages. During their investigation leading to Anthoney's arrest, police inspected nearly every square foot of the three-bedroom apartment, dusting black fingerprint powder in three-foot-wide strips running along walls and hallways. Pieces of wall were removed, several doors were relocated, and large holes had been cut in the rug pads and in the carpets. Police also used ink markers to write on wood surfaces, and the refrigerator was covered with indelible fingerprint powder.

Two of the building's three owners, Karen Baker and Neil Stock, stated that the Anchorage Police Department acknowledged responsibility for the damage, and the claim was referred to the municipality. Harry Sjoberj, representing the city's Risk Management Department, anticipated a decision regarding liability. Baker said she understood the reluctance of the city and her own insurance company to pay for the damages, but she was worried about making the mortgage payment on an empty apartment. The situation was soon resolved to the owners' satisfaction. It was not easy, however, to find eager renters. The aura of death is powerfully dissuasive.

Bill Reeder and Ken Spadafora, the official case officers, worked for almost another full year with prosecutor Branchflower and Assistant Prosecuting Attorney Bill Ingaldson, closing off Kirby's defenses, and FBI Agents Ray and Deedrick were diligent, as well.

Preparing for trial, Branchflower wanted to know if anyone from the FBI's Investigate Support Unit had ever testified as an expert witness. Profiling and behavioral analysis were new to law enforcement, and he wanted the jury to know what type of person commits such horrid acts.

Agent Ray followed up by contacting the FBI's legal counsel, who was unable despite extensive research to find any precedent for such testimony. The FBI itself had no objection, Ray informed Branchflower, but it had never been done before.

"Well, I think I can get you qualified with your background in police work," Branchflower told Ray, "and having worked homicide for a number of years. At least we want to try it." Hoping to secure Ray "expert witness" status, he flew him to Anchorage for the trial.

According to Ray's superior in the Behavioral Science Unit of the FBI, John Douglas, jurors have difficulty believing that ordinary-appearing people, who, for the most part, seem normal, can commit such shocking crimes. The FBI terms acts such as those perpetrated against the Newmans as "sex-power killings"—premeditated acts willfully committed by a sane individual with a character disorder such that, while knowing the difference between right and wrong, the individual is not deterred from committing the acts. When the light of a moral and ethical upbringing is denied a child, or if the child is incapable of internalizing those ethics, the individual is, as Dr. Hare noted earlier, without conscience.

Conscience, however, is not an unchangeable absolute. One dictionary definition presents the common understanding of the word "conscience" as "the sense of right and wrong as regards things for which one is responsible; the faculty or principle which pronounces upon the moral quality of one's actions or motives, approving the right and condemning the wrong." The functioning of one's conscience, then, depends upon one's understanding of right and wrong. The conscience of one person may be established upon a disinterested striving after truth and justice, while that of another may rest on an unthinking predisposition, or to act in accordance with that pattern of standards, principles, and prohibitions that is a product of his social environment. Conscience, therefore, can serve either as a bulwark of an upright character or can represent an accumulation of prejudices learned from one's forebears or absorbed from a limited social code. Some people have little or no conscience beyond unthinking predisposition.

Traditionally positive ethical/moral teachings come to us from the world's religious systems such as Judaism, Christianity, Buddhism, Islam, Bahá'í, and others. These systems, employing a spiritual perspective, inculcate behavioral and social standards that deter individuals from transgressing the bounds of civilized and enlightened society, perhaps it is because such spiritual approaches instill an inner moral component and a healthy sense of shame. Murderous rule-breakers lack the sense of shame or remorse because this sense derives from a philosophical or theological idea of good and evil. Obviously, fear of punishment is not the primary reason "normal" people don't commit horrid acts of human slaughter.

"There are other reasons why we follow the rules," explained Dr. Hare. "Most important perhaps is the capacity for thinking about, and being moved by, the feelings, rights, and well-being of others. There is also an appreciation of the need for harmony and social cooperation, and the ideas of right and wrong instilled in us since childhood."

The FBI's Behavioral Science Unit believes that this sense of right and wrong, conscience or a sense of shame, is missing among lust murderers. They actually enjoy killing, don't feel remorse, and show no signs of guilt afterward. Psychopaths do their deeds without any anxieties, doubts, or concerns about being humiliated, causing pain, sabotaging future plans, or having others be critical of their behavior. It is almost impossible for people who have been successfully socialized to imagine the world as psychopaths experience it.

The extreme savagery of the assaults in the Newman case, especially upon tiny Angie Newman, was beyond the comprehension of even the FBI's most seasoned veterans, who would search naturally for some "cause" or "reason" for the acts.

"I don't think you can isolate one thing that would throw a

man into a homicidal rage like Kirby Anthoney did," said Ray, "and for the most part, I don't think even Kirby Anthoney himself could tell you why he did something like that."

"The Kirby Anthoney killings were beyond anything we'd ever seen," said Grimes. "In preparation for the trial, we were driven; we were determined. All of us—the detectives, the FBI agents—we were relentless. What he did to those two little girls is so repellent, so horrid, I doubt even God can forgive him. You must realize that DNA testing and evidence was not as advanced then as it is now, and the percentage of certainty you could claim in hair, semen, and blood comparisons was simply not enough on its own to convince a jury beyond a reasonable doubt. In fact, when Nancy Newman and her two daughters were found murdered in their Eide Street apartment in March of 1987, the FBI had not yet approved the methodology of any of the labs doing DNA analysis. That approval didn't happen until the following December. The FBI did, however, send blood and semen samples to Dr. Moses Schanfield, one of the leading experts when it comes to analyzing that type of evidence."

The trial, expected to last four to six weeks, was anticipated as an ordeal of extremes, involving emotional testimony from family members, on the one hand, and on the other, technical testimony from experts who analyze hair, fiber, and body fluids. Among these experts was the aforementioned Dr. Schanfield, president of the Council on Forensic Science Education, a member of the American Society of Crime Laboratory Directors, the International Society of Haemogenetics, and a fellow of the American Academy of Forensic Sciences.

Dr. Schanfield's analytical report of samples provided to him by the FBI informed the prosecution that he had absolutely identified an unusual genetic marker in the semen found by police at the Newman apartment. Now, if he had a semen sample from Kirby Anthoney, he could make comparisons and determine if Anthoney's semen contained this same distinctive genetic marker.

There were only two ways to secure a semen sample from Anthoney: voluntarily or involuntarily. In the first instance, Anthoney would sexually arouse himself, masturbate, ejaculate, and hand the outcome to the prosecution. The alternate method was for a nurse or physician to insert his or her finger into Anthoney's rectum, manually manipulating the prostrate, and forcing seminal fluid out Anthoney's flaccid penis. Several nonmedical personnel made informal offers to extract the sample by any means necessary. Deferring to propriety, Ingaldson sought a court order compelling Anthoney to loosen his resolve and bend to the prosecution's insistence. In his efforts, he arranged for Dr. Moses Schanfield to testify in support of his pretrial motion by telephone from Atlanta, Georgia.

Defense counsel John Salemi objected to Schanfield testifying about anything. "I'll be bringing up the Frye test and objecting on those grounds," he told the judge. The Frye test means that prosecutors have to be able to demonstrate that the scientific community accepts the new technique as reliable. Information obtained under hypnosis, for example, is not considered reliable by the majority of the scientific community—it doesn't pass the Frye test, so is usually not allowed in the courtroom.

"We're talking about allotyping," explained Salemi, "and I'm going to object to Schanfield testifying based on his area of expertise, his methodology not meeting the Frye standard. I don't know if the court had ever heard of it before this case."

Buckalew, Ingaldson, and Salemi interviewed Dr. Moses Schanfield via a long-distance call. "I believe he's on the phone now," said Ingaldson, "so, if we could give him an oath, and then I'll begin questioning, Mr. Salemi would have an opportunity to cross-examine him concerning the type of testing to be done and why there is a need for a semen sample as opposed to just gathering blood in this case."

The clerk asked Schanfield if he could hear the conversation, and Schanfield replied, "I can hear you, but you sound like you're in a big cave."

"Well, it's kind of a cave," commented Buckalew, "it's kind of in a cave. They call it a courtroom."

After Schanfield provided his credentials in abbreviated form, Ingaldson asked him to explain allotyping. "Allotypes, or allotyping, is a name applied to genetic markers that occur on antibody molecules," he explained, informing the court that the test procedure for them was very similar to the tests for determining the ABO blood groups in body fluids, such as semen or saliva. "The markers are in almost all human fluids. They were actually the second system used to identify human blood. They have been used widely in Europe and all over the world. These markers were originally discovered in 1956. [The year] 1961 was the first publication of forensic application."

Schanfield told the court that allotypes were more reliable for testing because the ABO blood groups share structures with bacteria. "It's fairly common to find ABO structures in denim jeans or the soil, [but] allotypes or the genetic markers are unique to humans and their closest primate relatives. As far as stability goes," he asserted, "of the markers used in forensics currently, they are probably the most stable."

Ingaldson, concerned that allotypes were not commonly used in Alaska, prompted Schanfield to mention where they had been used in the United States, Canada, and Europe. "They have been used worldwide because they are useful in discriminating people in all human populations, they've been used in anthropological studies on a worldwide basis for many years," said Schanfield, who then corrected Ingaldson's mistaken assumption. "We've probably studied several thousand of your native population. . . . [allotypes] have been used in paternity testing in the United States since the 1970s, and in Europe since the early 1960s. Literally every country in the world has used allotyping if it has a laboratory that's doing any kind of work."

Turning to the specific topic of Kirby D. Anthoney, Ingaldson asked, "Is it not true that it's your request to be able to draw more discriminatory conclusions, that you need a semen sample as opposed to just testing Mr. Anthoney's blood?''

"It was a suggestion and a recommendation on my part," he confirmed, "that we gain some insight by looking at Mr. Anthoney's semen versus his blood."

Dr. Schanfield then explained the difference between information gleaned from blood analysis versus semen testing. "The body can be thought of as compartments with different kinds of plumbing and fixtures in it. The blood is—I guess the best example. It's your water system, and things get pumped around in it. Saliva, semen, and vaginal secretions really are not part of that plumbing system. They're parts that connect to it in some way, but each of them has its own unique ability to produce things. For instance, saliva, which is what we use to determine whether or not somebody is a secreter, is really a different compartment biologically. The blood group substances produced in saliva are very different."

Schanfield then addressed the primary topic and said, "What we have found is that no two semen stains appear to be exactly the same. We are just starting to do detailed studies of what the exact differences are among individuals, but it appears that there are enough differences between individuals that the final product we look at, which is a stain, which is [often] a mixture of body fluids, vaginal secretions, semen, and perhaps saliva, tend to come up with very distinct patterns, and those patterns can be relatively characteristic."

"Would it be fair to say," asked Ingaldson, "on some of the samples you've gotten, you've observed characteristics that if you were able to compare them with Mr. Anthoney's semen, you would be able to tell with a great degree of certainty whether or not that came from Mr. Anthoney or whether it could not have come from him?"

"Well," he answered, "I think we would be looking at a pattern. I think potentially we could get some exculpatory information out of this."

Dr. Schanfield further explained to the court that certain

markers in the crime scene semen were abnormal, "and a determination as to whether the defendant could be excluded or included could be determined from examining his semen. Examining his blood, because of this possible 'abnormal secretor' status, would not reveal the necessary information."

John Salemi cross-examined Dr. Schanfield, taking a dim view of both allotyping and Schanfield's motives. If eight states accepted allotyping results in criminal cases, "that would mean forty-two states are not so sure about it," Salemi said.

"Dr. Schanfield, would it be fair to say that you have some financial interest in allotyping?" asked Salemi. "I noticed that you have an actual corporation that does this, correct? And in order to do this type of testing, isn't it true that you have to have a specific type of antiserum, and there are only two people in the United States who sell that serum? And you're one of them, and you also go around the country and train other people? I assume you get paid for that, and you testify in court—I assume you have a fee for that also, and then doing the testing in your lab, that I assume involves some expense?"

Dr. Schanfield answered affirmative to all of the above, then Salemi addressed the specific test in question as it pertained to Anthoney.

"Your report which is dated February tenth, 1988, and is based on analysis that you did of certain items sent to you from the FBI related to the Kirby Anthoney case. First of all, there seems to be a suggestion that you would be able to include or exclude Mr. Anthoney within one percent of the population if you were able to test his semen. Is that really an accurate figure?"

When Dr. Schanfield referred to the percentage as "a dirty number," Salemi started hammering him about what the percentage would mean using different population tables, and if other experts would differ with his conclusion that the crime scene semen had unusual markers.

"I'm going to object," interrupted Ingaldson, "if he's being asked to speculate what other experts might say."

During the commotion that followed, both Salemi and Schanfield lost their train of thought. "I think there was an objection," offered Schanfield helpfully.

"Yeah, there was," replied Salemi testily. "You've been in court before, you know when not to answer, I can tell that. I guess it doesn't take an expert in sereology to tell us that one percent of the United States population—assuming that males are roughly half the population—we're talking about a pool of one million people, correct?"

"Yes, certainly," agreed Schanfield, "on a national basis we're talking about potentially a very large number of individuals."

"Doctor, I was wondering, if you got this semen sample, what do you think the chances are that you wouldn't be able to tell why this atypical result occurred?"

"That's a very good question," said Schanfield, "and I'm afraid I don't have a very good answer for you."

Why the atypical result occurred was not important to establishing evidence of probable guilt or absolute innocence. The test would ascertain if Anthoney's semen contained that unique abnormality as found at the crime scene.

"If the judge orders a semen sample," asked Ingaldson, "and you get the sample, and on the basis of that sample it's your opinion that the defendant, Kirby Anthoney, did not leave this semen, would your charge for your services to the Anchorage District Attorney's Office be any less?"

"No," answered Dr. Schanfield, and the long-distance conversation concluded.

Judge Buckalew ruled that Schanfield could testify as an expert for the prosecution, but Ingaldson specifically wanted Buckalew to also rule that Anthoney could be forced to provide a semen sample. Salemi and Howard fought it diligently, and told Judge Buckalew that if he ruled in favor of the prosecution, Anthoney absolutely was not going to provide the sample in a participatory fashion.

"He's not going to be masturbating for the state," insisted

Salemi. "Can I justify subjecting him to this type of indignity, to this type of embarrassment, to this type of discomfort? We might as well delete the right of privacy that is in the Alaska constitution. I think the privacy issue is primary. Along with that, of course, is the unreasonableness of this request and the unreasonableness of this search. And then, thirdly, what does the state expect to obtain, what are they hoping for? Mr. Ingaldson states essentially, and rather unequivocally, that they're going to be able to exclude or include Mr. Anthoney within one percent of the population. That kind of percentage, when used in a courtroom, can be potentially misleading to a jury. They say, 'Oh, one percent, well, that means that he's ninety-nine percent sure. Well, that sounds like proof beyond a reasonable doubt to me.' And the next thing you know, we've got an expert from Atlanta, Georgia, deciding this case rather than a jury of twelve people. . . ."

"I don't think that would happen," commented the judge.

"Have you ever seen," Salemi asked Buckalew, "the look in the eyes of the people when Dr. Propst and other experts get up and start talking about their scientific and medical findings? I wish their eyes would glaze over, but they're on the edge of their seats."

"Well," stated the judge, "Dr. Propst is a good witness."

"He is a good witness," agreed Salemi, "I'm glad he's not doing allotyping. He probably will after he finds out how lucrative it is."

"The privacy issue," said Buckalew, ignoring Salemi's remark, "is really a substantial concern to the court."

The express right of privacy in the Alaskan constitution is broader than the U.S. Constitution or the federal case law. Alaska, of all the states in the union, is special in terms of granting its citizens, and those visiting Alaska, a right of privacy. They are also entitled to an expectation of privacy.

"In other words," said Salemi, "would he normally think that he is free from having state law-enforcement people getting a court order allowing somebody to essentially put a finger up his rear end against his will? And I think most of us think that we probably have the right to be free from that kind of intrusion from state authorities.

"Obviously the state has a reason for wanting to invade and to abrogate Mr. Anthoney's privacy rights. They must establish a compelling state interest to abrogate the right of privacy that Mr. Anthoney would otherwise enjoy. We're talking about a physical invasion of Mr. Anthoney's body, the most intimate of bodily functions. We're talking about Mr. Anthoney's potential sexual function. We're talking about his sexuality, genitalia, discomfort, embarrassment, and the resulting loss of dignity. What really is the state going to get out of this? And I would submit to the court," said Salemi, "that based on the testimony of Dr. Schanfield, that the chances—I mean, I don't know how to put the odds, but we're dealing with dirty numbers. A lot of Dr. Schanfield's answers to my questions started off with, 'that's a good question.' "

Salemi argued that the character of the evidence was questionable in terms of whether it should even be brought into a courtroom. "Courts are traditionally very conservative about what they let the jury hear. We don't want to bring in evidence which later, through other scientific theory, is found not to be valid."

Ingaldson countered Salemi's argument by drawing the court's attention to sexual assault cases where "someone's penis is stretched out and scraped" to get blood off it. "Or where persons are allowed to examine the penis in a rape case and conduct close-up visual exams of it, which certainly are extremely embarrassing types of situations. And then we have drug cases with anal searches."

"Don't you think," asked the judge, "that this procedure is quite a bit different than removing a balloon that's got, you know—in the narcotics cases they remove foreign objects that have been inserted into the rectum to conceal it—"

"Obviously, there is," answered Ingaldson. "You aren't massaging the prostate when you're taking out balloons, but you're also not digging out balloons probably—I don't know, I certainly haven't had that done. . . ."

"Probably would be less painful," offered Buckalew.

"Considering the number they found that might . . . ," Ingaldson agreed. "The main discomfort from massaging the prostate is going to be apparently a strong need to urinate. It's not particularly painful, but the embarrassment factor, I think, would be about the same of having someone in that orifice."

"We're not going to do *that* in the courtroom," stated the judge. "I can see a difference between removing an object that a person has put up their rectum as opposed to massaging the prostate to recover semen. That's a different kind of invasion."

"As far as pain," Ingaldson said, "I would imagine it's not comfortable having someone reaching up into the colon for balloons and drugs."

"It wouldn't be the colon," Buckalew interrupted, "it would be the distal portion of the rectum, the distal portion of the intestine. Isn't that the definition of rectum? The rectum is the distal portion of the large intestine."

"I'm certainly not a biology expert," noted Ingaldson, "so I'll take the court's word for it."

"I think Mr. Ingaldson needs one of these procedures performed on him," said Salemi pleasantly.

"Digging into the rectum," continued Ingaldson thoughtfully, " I mean some of these cases have twenty or thirty balloons up there."

The state allowed Buckalew and Salemi a moment of shared visualization before resuming. "Persons actually shove these things up themselves, and you're digging out something they've shoved up. I think it's analogous in the present situation because there's no proof that the person has it up there other than what's presented to the court beforehand. In this case, you have someone that has deposited semen, and specifically in this case, on an eight-year-old girl. And has in fact deposited to the extent that it has ripped the wall between the vagina and the anus, a very violent sexual assault, and that semen has been deposited.

If he hadn't deposited semen, if we hadn't found semen, of course we wouldn't be requesting it. And we know he's deposited semen—''

"Of course you understand," interrupted Buckalew, "that I'm required to presume at this stage he's innocent."

"If there was a search warrant hearing before Your Honor for drugs, you'd still presume that he's innocent, but that doesn't mean you'd close your eyes to the probable cause that you might find."

The state argued that the seriousness of the crime warranted compelling Anthoney to provide a semen sample. "If you take a look at this case, you have the most serious type of offense imaginable. You have three murders, three violent sexual assaults. The murders were violent murders. One of them particularly so. One of the victims had her head almost completely cut off. I mean, you can't imagine from the community's standpoint a worse crime than this."

Judge Buckalew took the motion under advisement, promising to issue his ruling on March 6, 1988. "The issuance of such an order requires a twofold determination," he explained. "First, the type of search requested must be reasonable. Second, the particular search must be reasonable." Buckalew then offered three observations: "One, the method proposed by the state, prostate manipulation, is a reasonable means for gathering semen samples for the purpose of medical diagnosis, but that fact alone does not make it a reasonable procedure for general application in criminal matters. Two, the test methodology, genetic allotyping, although persuasive in theory, has not been practiced or accepted to the extent that would render it commonplace as that term is understood in the blood-draw context. Three, despite this latter finding, the court issues no opinion on whether the results of a sample tested by that means would be admissible.

"Having balanced the need for this particular search against the invasion it entails," the judge continued, "the court finds in favor of the defendant. The search proposed by the state is a substantial intrusion into the defendant's right to privacy. The right to privacy is among those specifically enumerated in the Alaskan constitution. Alaskan courts have consistently interpreted this right to be broader in scope than its federal counterparts. They have also consistently held the Alaskan right to be free from unreasonable searches and seizures contains a more expansive guarantee than that embodied in the federal standard. The primary purpose of these constitutional provisions is the protection of personal privacy and dignity against unwarranted intrusions by the state.

"Due to the fundamental nature of the rights involved, and the degree of intrusiveness the proposed search entails, the state must put forth a compelling justification to support its need for the evidence requested. This is true even under Alaska's flexible constitutional analysis. The state has put forth no such justification," concluded Buckalew. "The state has substantial real evidence in the form of hair, fibers, and fingerprints; it has additional circumstantial evidence; and it has not shown that the evidence sought would necessarily be of value to the prosecution."

CHAPTER 8

Building a cohesive presentation of evidence to use against Kirby Anthoney was a stress-inducing undertaking for everyone working with the District Attorney's Office. "At times the tension was fairly high," recalled Gifford. "We had a lot of evidence—both physical and circumstantial—but we were short some absolute facts."

One fact was clear to police and prosecutors alike: Anthoney's defense attorney John Salemi was among Alaska's finest. "Salemi is an excellent attorney and a tough adversary in the courtroom," acknowledged Ingaldson. "I'd been up against him before, and in two previous murder trials the defense was victorious. I have great respect for John Salemi both as a lawyer and an individual."

Another unavoidable reality was that much of the evidence against Anthoney was circumstantial, inferential, and open to technical debate. The jury could not be told that Anthoney was the prime suspect in the rape and near murder of a twelve-year-old Idaho girl, or that Heck broke up with him because he beat her. The jury wouldn't know that he once pleaded guilty to Macing and robbing a wheelchair-bound old woman, that Nancy Newman did not want her children left alone with him, nor would they be informed of his extensive juvenile burglary record.

"They may be told something of his drug habit," explained Assistant District Attorney Bill Ingaldson to the press, "how he often came to his aunt to borrow money, and perhaps did so the morning of the murders. So much of Anthoney's history is barred from trial because it is not fair to convict a person of a crime on the grounds that he has a bad character, or because he has displayed a propensity for similar violence in the past. To convict any defendant, the state must present evidence from the case at hand, proving guilt beyond a reasonable doubt."

This did not mean that the prosecution wouldn't try to give the jury an accurate picture, within the law, of Anthoney's mind-set prior to the homicides. Such efforts were assiduously assailed by the defense in pretrial hearings. They strongly protested any mention of Anthoney's depression and threats of suicide.

"If they want to say he was depressed because of the breakup, that's fine," said Defense Counsel Craig Howard. "But there is nothing to show that he's out there trying to slit his wrists, that he's tried to run off the road, or anything like that . . . if [the prosecution] can show that he decided to kill these people somewhere along the line because he was suicidal and decided better them than him, then perhaps it comes in. But at this point, we're asking for a protective order on that."

Ingaldson agreed to make no mention of suicide in his opening remarks, giving Judge Buckalew more time to consider a decision. The defense requested assurances that the prosecution would never offer opinions about "the thoroughness of the investigation in this case, how this was the biggest manhunt in Anchorage, the number of officers, the number of man-hours, [or] this being the most gruesome crime scene in Anchorage history."

The defense wanted Ingaldson's planned presentation of

Anthoney's postcrime letters and postarrest poetry disallowed, as well. The state had three arguments as to why the letters and poetry should be allowed, and Ingaldson presented his justifications to Buckalew.

"I think his emotional state at that time is extremely important," said Ingaldson to the judge, "and you'll see it in letters he's written to people afterward. Here's someone that's a powder keg ready to explode, and I think I need to present that to the jury so they can see what state of mind he was [in] at that time." Ingaldson raised another reason why these letters and poems were important—the marked transformation in Anthoney's appearance and demeanor. "We have someone who is coming in here now, who is cleaned up, who doesn't look anything like he did a year ago. His beard's trimmed, his hair's cut. He's wearing glasses that he's never worn before so that the jury won't be able to see his eyes. We have someone here that looks right now like he wouldn't hurt a fly. I'm not going to emphasize his bad past," promised Ingaldson, "I'm not talking about the explosive things that he did beforehand, the fight that he got into with his father in the fall, the times the whole year before that when he beat his girlfriend many times, choked her many times. I can't get into those things—the rules of evidence don't allow it, but they do allow me to get into his state of mind at the time."

Ingaldson's third argument was the most controversial—he believed Anthoney's bizarre poetry contained direct admissions of guilt, and specific descriptions of the Newman homicide. The state wanted the poems admitted as evidence; Salemi and Howard insisted they were not admissible.

"He sent these poems to a lot of persons, and they are confessions," Ingaldson insisted. "They are a way of him confessing, probably trying to absolve himself. And I think it is quite clear when you look at these poems."

"The only thing the jury would learn from reading this poetry," said Salemi, "is that Mr. Anthoney is never going to earn a living as a poet. It's the kind of stuff that anybody who maybe has too much time on his hands sitting in jail awaiting trial might write. And it doesn't relate in any respect to the offense.''

Buckalew didn't quite understand. "I'm going to admit these things because it's an admission? I want to know what you're talking about."

What Ingaldson was talking about was that Anthoney's education and proclivities were not of a literary bent. His sudden burst of questionable creativity began after the homicides and continued unabated after his arrest and incarceration.

"That's the motivation for him to write these, and that's his way of expressing what happened. If you look at the poem entitled, 'Endless Serenity.' ''

"I've got 'Endless Serenity' in front of me," said Buckalew, and he followed along as Ingaldson dissected the most telling of Anthoney's poems:

> Horizons lined with charitable mountains
> Perfections of the world's admirable beauty
> Dispensing rivers flowing as fountains
> Holding powers of an endless serenity.

The above stanza framed the poem. Between these bookends of beauty, Anthoney vividly described a scene analogous to the rage-driven violation and murder of the innocent Newmans:

> In the distance sweeps a serpent of danger
> racing towards the amiable height
> creatures plead with the raging anger
> defenseless in this destructive fight
> suddenly invaded by a foreign alienation
> disrupted by insatiable desire
> forces begin to weaken nature's creation
> destroying the silence with vicious fire
> blinded from the deadly obscurant haze
> consuming all of precious life's faith

engulfed by the obtrusive tyrant's blaze
mercilessly devouring with ferocious wrath.

"That is exactly a summary," insisted Ingaldson. "It's an admission as to what he did, and he's doing it through these poems."

"Endless Serenity" also struck Sergeant Grimes as a confession the first time he read it. "Anthoney even talks about them pleading with the raging anger," commented Grimes outside the courtroom, "and how they're defenseless. If he's talking about himself, which I think he is, he's saying that he lost it, just as Debbie Heck feared—his insatiable desires blinded him, that his victims were treated mercilessly, his wrath was ferocious, and on and on."

Salemi, speaking on behalf of his client's best interests, said, "I thought the poem was about a forest fire, and it certainly doesn't necessarily refer to this offense. Again, you have to understand that these poems were written for the most part while Mr. Anthoney was in jail to Debbie Heck. She received all these after she had heard of the offense and Mr. Anthoney was arrested. I think it really cuts against the presumption of innocence. You know," he stated, "we don't let the jury see Mr. Anthoney in handcuffs because it cuts against the presumption of innocence. And then to allow in some marginal poetry. . . ."

"The other thing that's very significant," countered Ingaldson, "is that a week after [the crime] he was writing poems of a similar nature at Chilkoot Charlie's. And another witness, Ms. Irvine, will testify to that. He was writing them on napkins, and she read them, and they were of this nature, this type of poem."

The judge ruled that Ingaldson could not reference the poetry in his opening remarks to the jury, nor could Ms. Irvine offer critique or interpretations of the tone or contents of the poetry shared with her at the nightclub. The jury, however, would be allowed to read, discuss, and interpret Anthoney's poetic efforts at a later date.

The case, Anchorage's first brush with the sex murder of a child, raised serious concern about how jurors would react to the grisly physical evidence. Assistant District Attorney Bill Ingaldson indicated that he intended to only play an edited version of the police death-scene videotape.

"The original was about three hours long," said Grimes, "but we cut it down to about thirty-eight minutes. The tape, which we would play on a television monitor, had no sound. Officer James Ellis, the videographer, would narrate it live."

Aware that the prosecution wanted the jury to see the tape, and also hear the Chapmans' call to 911, Salemi asked the court, "Why does he need both? I think the court is supposed to control evidence which might appeal to the emotions, which might offend a jury, and which is duplicative."

"Murder is a foul, foul deed," answered Buckalew, "and it's tough to sanitize. I mean, I can tone it down, but we've got three homicides here, and the jury has to have an opportunity to understand what happened."

"You don't have to show in living color the bruised, crushed larynx of a seven-year-old child," insisted Howard, "unless you want to have an emotional impact upon the jury." He and Salemi also wanted only black-and-white photos or slides presented as evidence.

"We're dealing with flesh and blood," responded Judge Buckalew, "and blood's red and these pictures demonstrate, I'd say graphically, the circumstances. I don't like to look at them, but I think the state's got a right to use the pictures."

Ingaldson, to help expedite matters, compiled a synopsis of the specific pictures and the defense's objections to each one of them. "Starting with Nancy Newman, there were objections to pictures of her anal area, around her buttocks, and the picture of her stomach," said Ingaldson. "The stomach shows a dropped spot of blood and it also shows a fecal smear. These pictures are extremely important to this case to show, number one, where the fecal matter came from . . . Mr. Anthoney complained about having fecal matter on his shirt afterward, and it's our position that he was sexually assaulting Nancy Newman at the time and got fecal matter from her on his shirt, not dog crap, as he told the police.''

Ingaldson argued that it was imperative that the jury see Newman's anal area and the fecal matter. ''She obviously had a bowel movement,'' continued Ingaldson, insisting that the fecal smear on her stomach was from being moved, and that the blood drop showed ''that someone deposited blood on her stomach after she was killed.''

Over Howard's objections, the judge ruled the pictures admissible. Howard and Salemi also objected to numerous close-up photos of Melissa and Angie. They specifically wanted excluded the picture detailing the smear on Melissa Newman's stomach.

''That's of vital importance in this case,'' pleaded Ingaldson, ''because that's where semen was found and a swab taken . . . this is extremely important because later the jury will be seeing pictures of the comforter on her bed, and on the corner of the bed they will see there's a smear that's about the same size. It also had semen on it, which had crystallized on top of the blood that matched Mr. Anthoney. He has a relatively rare blood type, and that's important information.''

One by one they argued over each and every crime scene photograph, compromising on some, pleading their case to the court on others. Overall, the judge allowed the majority of Ingaldson's photos.

By April 1988, all elements converged for the most high-profile murder trial in Alaskan history. Immediately prior to jury selection, Defense Council Salemi suggested that each potential juror be interviewed individually. ''The reason for that,'' he explained, ''is because I think that we're going to have to go into some detail regarding individual prospective jurors' knowledge about the case. And specifically information they have received from the media.''

Salemi's reference to media was not unexpected—television, radio, and newspaper correspondents were already a significant presence in Judge Buckalew's courtroom. "It's obviously a high-profile case," said Salemi. "A significant amount of journalism was generated and other media attention, and not only was it significant in terms of quantity, but its quality—the reporting was such that it stirred controversy in the community. In fact some of the articles drew some criticism from individuals in the community. They took it upon themselves to write letters to the editor." The complaints, directed at the graphic details described in the *Anchorage Daily News,* prompted an apology from editor Howard Weaver.

"Because of the nature of this case," continued Salemi, "it's likely that the people who are called will have some knowledge as to the case. If you have twelve people in the jury box and you say to juror number one, 'Can you tell me what you've read about the case,' and he or she starts telling us, then the other eleven, if they hadn't read it, their experience is going to be somewhat polluted."

"I suspect you might find that sixty percent of the people you call won't remember anything about this at all," responded Buckalew. "People have a constitutional right not to read the papers. Some of them figure they're more enlightened by not picking it up off the porch, just leave it unwrapped. I don't know. All right. We've all agreed if anybody has any acquired knowledge of this case through the media, its going to be individual voir dire. And the mechanics of it we can work out."

The process of jury selection revealed an important piece of information for the defense—Anthoney's eyes unnerved most prospective jurors. "He has very strange eyes," confirmed Spadafora, "and lots of folks get uncomfortable just looking at him. Realizing this, the defense had Anthoney wear glasses with tinted lenses so you couldn't actually see that look in his eyes—kind of a creepy look that isn't that uncommon to guys like him."

"Guys like him," according to recent research, indeed have

peculiar eyes. "Their eyes are those of an emotionless preda-tor," Dr. Hare has stated, "and many people find it difficult to deal with. Sometimes the eyes are described as 'empty,' 'unsettling,' 'riveting,' 'reptilian,' 'amphibian,' or even as 'goat eyes.'"

Hare reminds people, however, that they cannot reliably spot a psychopath simply by his or her eyes. "It's all too easy to misread another's eyes and draw false conclusions about their character, intentions, or honesty. Although it is clear that intense eye contact is an important factor in the ability of some psycho-paths to control, manipulate, or dominate."

Superior Court Judge Seaborn Buckalew had more initial concerns than the unnerving effect of Anthoney's gaze. Special security precautions were in place once the trial opened because of death threats against the defendant. "We're not going to have any blood on the carpet around here," the judge said.

The defense strategy for Kirby D. Anthoney would not include assertions of insanity, mental illness, brain damage from childhood beatings, or multiple personality disorder. Quite simply, Kirby D. Anthoney would insist that he didn't do it.

"Anthoney is an inveterate and unrelenting liar," stated Ken Spadafora. "I walked by him in a holding cell and he was still trying to manipulate me, still lying. He started crying—something he could now do at will—and said, 'Detective Spada-fora, you got the wrong guy, you got the wrong guy.' I looked him in the eye and stated, 'Who *do you* think you're talking to, Kirby?' He shut the tears off instantly and became angry. He never quit lying, he never will. I believe [it was] Debbie Heck [who] said that Anthoney was almost incapable of *not* lying."

On April 21, 1988, after six days of questioning more than sixty prospective jurors, lawyers in the Anthoney murder case declared themselves satisfied with the panel. Six men and six women were sworn in as jurors: a pastor, a housewife, a civil engineer, a building mechanic, an electrical mechanic, a soldier, a custodial worker, a pacifist preschool teacher, a supply expediter, an accountant, a secretary, and an IRS agent. Three alternates also took the oath.

The defendant, Kirby D. Anthoney, had a noticeable paucity of familial support in Buckalew's courtroom. His mother, supportive from a distance, did not attend the trial. "She refused to come up here," explained Ingaldson. "She was subpoenaed, and Idaho has a law that prevents the interstate subpoena act from applying to people that have to travel over a thousand miles. So, she's got a judge down there saying, 'You don't have to come.' "

"With the exception of his legal defense team, Anthoney was absolutely on his own," recalled Grimes. "His so-called pals and best buddies were not all there in the courtroom rooting for him, no dedicated sweetheart on the bench behind the defense table giving a show of support. Debbie Heck was there, but as a witness for the prosecution, not as a supporter of Kirby Anthoney. The Anthoneys and the Newmans are part of one big family forced to choose between Anthoney and the Newmans. Kirby Anthoney lost."

"Most of Anthoney's associates distanced themselves from him," confirmed Spadafora. "After all, who wants a possible child rapist and murderer for a friend? There were two, however, who stayed close—Kirk Mullins and Deborah Dean. After he was arrested, he spent a good hour on the phone with Dean and Mullins. All through the trial they stayed pretty much in his camp. There was a connection there, I believed, that was not simply friendship, kindness, or loyalty. I thought then, and still do now, that there was some other tie binding them."

Before the state's and defense's opening statements, Ingaldson raised two remaining issues. "One of them is the present relationship between Paul and Cheryl Chapman. They are the two people who found the bodies, and they are presently still married, but they're presently separated. This is something that to me doesn't really have anything to do with the case, and I want to avoid going into their private lives in that area. I talked to Mr. Howard earlier and he didn't seem to have a problem—"

"You don't have to litigate their marital problems in this trial, do you?" asked the judge jokingly. "All right. At this time that's a nonissue. What else?"

"The final area," explained Ingaldson, involved "a series of obscene phone calls prior to the murder. From my gathering of facts and from various other people . . . all the phone calls [were] made [after] Mr. Anthoney got into Anchorage, and they ended sometime shortly after the murders. And none of the calls happened when he was present. There was an inference certainly that he may have made some or all of these calls."

Ingaldson had no intention of bringing up the obscene phone calls in statements to the jury, and he wanted assurances that Salemi would not make reference to them without making application to the court well in advance. "I don't want the defense to go into that area in their case or in their cross-examination or something to make it look like, you know, some other mystery person is making the calls. Then it will look like I purposely didn't bring it up because I don't think Mr. Anthoney made it."

The judge ruled that Salemi must make application should he desire to discuss obscene phone calls, or elicit testimony regarding such calls from any witness. The jury entered, and Buckalew said, "Good morning, ladies and gentlemen. I think I advised you not even to advise anybody what case you were on. Upon reflection, I don't think that's such a wise idea. I think you should—if anybody inquires about it, you should tell them you're on the Anthoney case and the judge says you can't talk to anybody about it."

"Yes, Your Honor," responded Ingaldson, and the trial was under way.

CHAPTER 9

The purpose of opening statements is to prepare the jury for what they will see and hear as evidence, and to explain how and why that evidence will establish proof of guilt. Ingaldson, considered by Ken Spadafora to be among the best prosecuting attorneys in Anchorage history, addressed the jurors from a strong foundation of intense preparation.

"If it please the court, counsel," he began. "Ladies and gentlemen, last April, shortly after Kirby Anthoney was arrested at the Canadian border, he was taken back to Anchorage. He arrived in Anchorage and he had a conversation with Anchorage Police Officer Bill Reeder. During that interview, Investigator Reeder at one point confronted Kirby Anthoney with some of the evidence against him—evidence of hairs, fingerprints, blood, items found at his house, and many other pieces of evidence. After being confronted with this, Kirby Anthoney replied, 'I didn't screw up, Bill. I didn't screw up.' Well, we're going to show you evidence during the next several weeks that contradicts that statement."

The question of "what type of person could do this?" was

not to be addressed in court, and it was also not the purpose of the trial. "Why would someone ever do something like this? Who knows? Something goes wrong," Ingaldson told the jury succinctly. "Something snaps when anyone does something like this. And that's what happened with Kirby Anthoney that day."

Saying it is one thing, proving it beyond a reasonable doubt is another. "The only one who knows for sure what happened that Saturday morning is Kirby D. Anthoney," stated Ingaldson, "but we can reconstruct, with some degree of accuracy, the sequence of events." The prosecution then painstakingly detailed their version of events

The jury heard that sometime between 8:30 A.M. and 10:30 A.M., after an all-night party of beer and cocaine, Kirby Anthoney went to the Newman apartment for reasons unknown. He perhaps entered through the bedroom window, as he had numerous times before. Nancy Newman, shocked at his arrival, may have ordered him out, berated him for his behavior, reminded him that he still owed her $500, or simply told him to leave and never come back. Drug-crazed, hostile, and rejected by a woman for whom he had always harbored sexual desire, Anthoney snapped.

"You know Nancy probably had to be killed first," asserted Ingaldson, noting that there were no screams for help, "any mother is not going to let her kids be sexually assaulted and killed in that manner without going completely crazy and yelling and screaming." She didn't scream for help, the prosecution theorized, because there was an element of forced cooperation on her part. Although the rape was coerced, and she was physically restrained during the act, she may have allowed it as a means of protecting her girls, hoping they would be spared if Anthoney got what he wanted from her.

The prosecution detailed how Anthoney restrained and raped Melissa on her own bed before turning his intense rage on little Angie, cutting her throat to the point of near decapitation.

"Angie couldn't have been killed other than last," Ingaldson said, "because her blood's nowhere except in her room."

In Ingaldson's scenario, Kirby D. Anthoney raped and killed his aunt and nieces in a wild rage of sexually charged violence, then robbed the apartment of John Newman's camera and Nancy Newman's collected tips. He portrayed Anthoney as an inveterate liar, whose excuses and explanations would be shown to be falsehoods, and told the jury that Anthoney made a run for the border when he knew the FBI results identified him as the killer. He assured the jury that he would present solid evidence confirming Anthoney's guilt—evidence of hairs, fibers, and bloodstains that could neither be refuted nor denied.

His opening remarks concluded, Ingaldson thanked the jury and sat down. Buckalew called a ten-minute recess, and Kirby Anthoney consulted with his lawyers. Next on the agenda was John Salemi for the defense.

"We have our trial jury, Mr. Salemi," said Buckalew, and he nodded toward the defense. John Salemi stood, walked casually toward the jury box, and placed one hand in his pocket.

"Thank you, Your Honor. Ladies and gentlemen of the jury, we have a lot to talk about—and this is something of a preview from the defense perspective." Salemi characterized Ingaldson's opening remarks as the first clue that the state did not really have a case against Mr. Anthoney.

"His opening statement isn't so much a road map of the evidence which he will be able to establish, but more a wish list," said Salemi. "He told you today what he wishes he could prove in an ideal world with an ideal prosecution of this case, and it's what he wishes that you believe at the conclusion of this case." What the circumstantial evidence would establish, Salemi said, "is that you will have spent four to six weeks sitting as a trial jury on a murder which is yet to be solved."

The skilled defense attorney was quick to point out that the prosecution mentioned only circumstantial evidence, not direct evidence. The reason, Salemi asserted, was simply that there wasn't any direct evidence. "There are no eyewitnesses to these tragic and terrible murders and other crimes. There is no weapon which would link Mr. Anthoney in any way. There is no one who even heard anything associated with the acts which make up these terrible crimes.

"It's going to be an emotional event for you at times," Salemi said, preparing the jury for the impact of the photographs and the testimony of Newman's close friends and family. "We don't expect you to sit here without emotion during the entire course of the trial. What we ask of you is that you don't get caught up in emotion, that you don't do anything which would cause you to focus on events or circumstances which are separate from the evidence."

He reminded them of the state's burden of proof, the importance of keeping an open mind, and their job as jurors to store information, not draw conclusions. "I can't stress how important it is for you, in taking your oath as jurors, to presume Mr. Anthoney innocent, because the prosecution is dealing with what is called circumstantial evidence, and that is circumstance—maybe a hair which they believe leads you to believe something about this case and the perpetrator of the crime, because we're dealing with that type of evidence—"

Ingaldson, irritated, could take no more. "Your Honor, I'm going to object. I'd ask the court to instruct the jury as to the definition of direct evidence. This argument is clearly misleading as to the weight to give that. And I'd ask that Mr. Salemi not discuss circumstantial evidence as being less important because the law clearly—"

"I think I'm entitled to comment on the evidence," interjected Salemi, "including its character, Your Honor, and I ask to be allowed to do that."

"Well, I disagree with you," said Judge Buckalew. "I don't think you're entitled to comment on the evidence at this stage of the game. I can read you Rule Twenty-seven: Defendant of his counsel may then state his defense, and he may briefly state the evidence he expects to offer in support of it."

Salemi took a deep breath, then spoke in a most conciliatory and deferential fashion. "Your Honor, I think that the one defense in all criminal cases is the lack of proof by reasonable doubt. Just what I'm explaining at this point."

"I have no objection if he points out lack of evidence," agreed Ingaldson, "but he's misleading the jury as to character of evidence, which is very important in this case. And misleading them as to the law. And it sounds like his final argument, what he's talking now."

Buckalew agreed that Salemi's opening remarks were sounding more like a closing argument, and said he would instruct the jury that circumstantial evidence is just as good as real evidence. John Salemi didn't mind the judge giving those instructions. "But I would just ask that it be done at the conclusion of my opening argument . . ."

"Your opening argument? Or your opening statement?" Buckalew couldn't resist chiding Salemi for his unintentional malaprop. Salemi, slightly chagrined, responded, "Either one, Your Honor. Whichever you wish to call it."

With one more minibattle out of the way, Salemi continued his opening statement. "During the course of this case you will learn the following: Mr. Anthoney, at the time these crimes were committed, was someplace else. It was physically impossible for him to have committed these crimes. There is absolutely no motive or no reason. There is no evidence on Mr. Anthoney, he's not bruised, he's not cut, he's not scarred. There's no fiber or hair transfers on him, or on any of the clothes which were confiscated.

"If anybody is going to do something like this," Salemi continued, "it might make sense to figure out if the person that is being accused would have had a reason—even if it is a bad reason for doing it. There is no direct credible evidence with Mr. Anthoney being involved anyway in this criminal activity, or even being at the apartment that day, or in the evening before . . . there are no eyewitnesses, nobody sees his truck there, and nobody hears his truck there. He's not seen near the place until like seven-thirty or eight that night. He's not seen on foot leaving the place. There is no sort of admission, confession, no confiding to his parents that he had done this. None of that exists.

"There's no noise, no gun, there's no struggle," noted Salemi. "There are two separate methods of killing—two of them were strangled and one of them was cut. If you look at how these people were killed, you see that there are two MOs. One person's MO for killing is strangulation. Another person's MO is by cutting—consistent with the theory that this was an assault on three people involving two or more assailants."

Salemi summarized the state's case as being a scenario in which Kirby D. Anthoney "snapped because he was drug crazed. The kernel of their theory is that there was some sort of argument, and this argument led to this terrible tragedy where Mrs. Newman was killed, and then Mr. Anthoney had to kill the other occupants because they were potential witnesses. Well, if he were doing that, the whole purpose would be so that he wouldn't be discovered—the state's theory seems to be that the other two were killed to cover up the initial argument and the terrible tragedy involving Mrs. Newman."

Seeing the state's theory as inconsistent and unreasonable, Salemi insisted someone killing to keep from being discovered or identified is not going to commit sexual assaults, and that if the killer "snapped," the killer was not Kirby D. Anthoney.

"[Mr. Anthoney] wasn't snapped at seven-oh-five. He wasn't snapped at midnight. He wasn't snapped at a quarter to nine, and he wasn't snapped at ten-thirty or eleven in the morning. So, this man just snaps for the period of time it takes to commit these crimes, and then basically goes back to normal? It doesn't make sense."

Salemi also discounted the idea that the murders could have erupted following an argument between Anthoney and Newman regarding the $500 loan. "Is Mr. Anthoney going to kill her because she's asking for the money on Saturday when he's got all day Saturday, all day Sunday, all day Monday, all day

Tuesday to get that money before Mr. Newman comes back on Wednesday?''

The defense also mocked the prosecution's theory that perhaps Anthoney wanted more drugs. ''If Mr. Anthoney was going to concoct some phony alibi about where he was, then he certainly wouldn't put himself in a place where he was partying all night and using cocaine and alcohol. He'd come up with something better than that, something a little more sanitized. Something that would go over a little bit better with the police.

''You will learn through evidence,'' asserted Salemi, ''that the police were under a great deal of pressure to solve the case. Perhaps, as a result of this pressure they not only talked to Mr. Anthoney, but they harassed him, they hounded him for close to a month, they contacted his friends, told them that Mr. Anthoney was a killer, that they shouldn't let their children around him. They tried to influence his friends' testimony to change the times, to change dates. They contacted his family and said that they knew that Mr. Anthoney was guilty. This was anything but an objective investigation.''

Salemi informed the jury that Anthoney's departure from Alaska to the Canadian border was not a clandestine midnight flight. His client, not charged with any crime, was free to leave Alaska at any time. ''They lied to Mr. Anthoney,'' he asserted. ''They knew they had no authority and no power to hold Mr. Anthoney in the area. And when he did leave, after he told them he was going to leave, the police had him arrested at the Canadian border. More than a month after these murders, after an extensive investigation, they had him arrested''—he paused for dramatic emphasis—''for driving with his license suspended.

''I could talk for hours, I suppose,'' stated Salemi affably, ''but I'll stop in just a few minutes because what's most important is what's going to be established in the next four weeks. Not that nice, neat package or these little diagrams that the prosecution used during his opening argument.''

After lamenting that his client, Mr. Anthoney, had to live through the ordeal of the trial, Salemi concluded his opening statement. "At the end of this case, we assert not only will you have a reasonable doubt, but you will have many reasonable doubts. Thank you."

CHAPTER 10

The state of Alaska, well represented by the youthful, rugged, and athletic William Ingaldson, began its presentation Monday, April 25, 1988, with testimony from Investigator Spadafora and Officer Wayne Vance. Each detailed his experience upon arrival at the Newman's Eide Street address. Vance told the jury about his first encounter with Paul Chapman.

"He was very upset and shaking," recalled Vance. "He was on the telephone. I told him to put the phone down. He threw the phone down and walked out toward the parking lot. I went inside, I checked the living room, around into the kitchen to make sure no one was there."

Spadafora, representing the Homicide Response Team, explained his actions, discoveries, and perceptions. "I went inside," Spadafora recalled, "and from the center hallway in the apartment I saw what I would describe as a 'nightmare' at the end of the hallway. As I turned and looked into each of the bedrooms, one at a time, each scene was worse than the previous. I still remember seeing Nancy on her bed, then turning and seeing little Melissa sprawled half naked on her floor, and turning back toward the front door and then seeing baby Angie spread out in the center of her room, butchered. I left and sealed the apartment. I still remember saying that whatever it took I would get this guy and I knew I would never give up.''

The jury then viewed the edited videotape of Nancy Newman and her two daughters just as police found them, stabbed and strangled to death. When the final image faded from the television monitor, Buckalew excused the jury from the courtroom, and Defense Attorney Howard addressed the court. ''I guess the state next wants to play the nine-one-one tape,'' he said. ''Is that correct, Mr. Ingaldson?''

The prosecution confirmed the accuracy of Howard's guess; playing the full audio recording of the 911 call was always his plan. Howard immediately objected. ''All you hear on the tape is bloodcurdling screams,'' complained Howard, ''and it's the most prejudicial type of evidence that I could conceive of on the audiological level and has no probative value at all except to assault the jury's senses, and so we're objecting to it.''

''I don't want to just assault the jurors' senses,'' countered Ingaldson, ''and originally I had not intended to play that until—until I had indications maybe the defense might be pointing their fingers at Paul Chapman. If they want to stipulate that he had nothing to do with the murders, then they're right. There would be no need for playing that. Obviously, the state of mind of Mr. Chapman is going to be extremely important in this case depending on what the defense is, but we have to also eliminate people.''

Because all the evidence would clearly show that someone who knew the family and had access to the apartment committed the crime, Ingaldson insisted that the jury hear how shocked and upset Chapman was after discovering the bodies.

''This is just a pipe dream that Mr. Ingaldson has that we're trying to blame Mr. Chapman for this offense,'' said Howard, ''but if somewhere along the line we do point the finger at Mr. Chapman—which I cannot conceive of it happening, then the state would be allowed on rebuttal to play the tape. If you're even considering playing the tape—''

"I am considering it," interrupted Judge Buckalew.

Howard pleaded with the judge, begging, "Let's don't play it for the first time in front of these jurors—it's bloodcurdling screaming, and most of the screaming is from Mrs. Chapman, not Mr. Chapman. And if what they're trying to do is eliminate Mr. Chapman as a suspect, when he's interviewed by Officer Schwartz, he's crying throughout the tape. So, why don't they just play the tape of Officer Schwartz to say, well, he's crying during the tape? So, we aren't going to stipulate to anything in a murder trial . . .''

"I wasn't even going to ask you whether you'd stipulate," said Buckalew, then added, "I'm going to have to listen to that tape."

"I do take offense at Mr. Howard suggesting what order I put on my witnesses," Ingaldson told the judge, and he prepared to call Debbie Heck to the witness stand. Intimately familiar with Kirby D. Anthoney, she was a valuable witness for the prosecution, and a potentially damning one for the defense. Salemi and Howard would not allow her to take the stand without first requesting more protective orders from the judge. They wanted affirmation concerning exactly what Debbie Heck could *not* say.

"Just to be sure that we know the parameters with Miss Heck," said Howard when the jury was out of the courtroom, "what I'd like to do, is go through areas which I have concerns with. The first area, Your Honor, is that there was some discussion with Investigator Baker as to a homicide at the Northern Lights Car Wash. Mr. Anthoney mentioned that in some context, at least jokingly. The second area is his temper, and his failure to be able to control his temper. Third, she told investigators that she had received numerous beatings. In fact, there was one incident where the police were actually called in and Mr. Anthoney was arrested about several months before this incident. We ask that there be a protective order on that. The next area is the defendant's attitude toward children, and the corollary to that is also the children's view of Mr. Anthoney.''

Next Howard asked that there be no reference to Anthoney's extensive drug usage, or history of drug usage other than at the time of the incident. Heck would not be allowed to testify about his client's ability to lie and deceive people, nor would she be allowed to describe how she used to squeeze Anthoney's testicles as if crushing walnuts.

"There's other areas here," added Howard, "abuse of animals or pets, or her statement that he lost something like eight thousand dollars in cocaine deals, or the possibility of him stealing from a car wash he worked at, and the last two areas, Your Honor, well . . . actually we're asking for a protective order on getting into too much detail on the breakup of this relationship on the boat and Mr. Anthoney's reactions to it on the boat.''

The most problematic area of disagreement concerned the prosecution's proposed use of letters written to Heck by Anthoney after his arrest. "What I intend to do there, Your Honor," explained Ingaldson, "to avoid any problems with objections is I'll have the letters marked and then after she's done testifying, before anything's published to the jury, [the defense] would have the opportunity to object to any of them that they find objectionable.''

Debbie Heck testified about what happened on the boat and characterized Anthoney as seeming "unstable" and "acting irrational" before he was asked to leave. Heck was not allowed to reveal that Anthoney refused to leave when first told to do so, nor that there were acts of violence toward her or others aboard the boat. Heck was also questioned about her sex life with Anthoney, although no one probed into aberrant or violent sexual proclivities on his part. She testified that she had sex with Anthoney fifteen times in what had been, and later was, Melissa's bedroom, and another fifteen times out on the boat. Asked if she had ever contracted pubic lice from Anthoney during their sexual unions, Heck responded most firmly in the negative.

Under the prosecution's direct examination, Heck was asked what type of cigarettes Anthoney smoked. "Camel Filters and Marlboros," she replied softly.

"Now, at any time, did Mr. Anthoney say anything to you about any type of interest in Nancy Newman?"

"After we were first together, he did, yes," said Heck, and Mr. Howard immediately requested permission to approach the bench. Judge Buckalew excused the jury for a few minutes, and Bill Ingaldson explained where he was going with that line of questioning.

"Your Honor, by way of proof, it's my understanding that at one time Mr. Anthoney had indicated that he'd had an affair with Nancy Newman. Then at a later time, he joked about it and denied it. To me, I think that that's something—I'm offering it to show Mr. Anthoney had an interest beyond just an aunt-nephew type of interest in Nancy Newman. Which I think is crucial in this case since there was a sexual assault, and under I guess our theory of the case of how things started to get out of hand in this incident. I think it goes toward proving motive and intent at the time. If you weigh that versus any prejudicial value, it will come across that he's later saying he didn't have an affair, so it's not—I don't think it's something that's going to have that much prejudicial value. But it shows interest in Nancy Newman beyond something that you'd expect—even to be joking about from just a nephew talking about his aunt."

Howard requested permission to question Ms. Heck and asked her, "Did Mr. Anthoney claim that he wanted to have an affair with his aunt, or that he had an affair?"

"That he had an affair," confirmed Heck, adding that Anthoney later told her that he was joking. Howard then steered his questioning on a slightly altered course. "Have you had problems—sexual problems with someone in the past?"

Heck answered in the affirmative. Howard then asked, "Have you had sexual problems with your brother?"

She said, "Yes."

"What kind of sexual problems are we talking about with your brother?"

Debbie Heck paused, took a deep breath, and said, "My brother—"

"Your Honor," interrupted Ingaldson, "I think this area is covered under the rape shield statute. I don't know anything about what he's going into, but I don't see the relevance of it, number one. And number two, I think it's covered clearly under the statute as an area that's precluded from inquiring into."

Howard withdrew the question, the intimate details remained confidential, and he approached the topic differently. "Would it be fair to say that after you had talked about having the sexual problems with a family member, that he had then in turn mentioned that this comment about having had an affair with his aunt? Isn't that the way it went?"

"Possibly," she answered.

"And so you don't know whether Mr. Anthoney was basically trying to make you feel, you know, better or more at ease about this issue by telling you something, don't you?"

"No, I don't," Heck admitted.

Howard had no further questions, and Ingaldson presented a brief response. "It doesn't matter if [the affair] happened or not, but there's an interest and that shows intent," he argued. "And if it had happened, of course, with the sexual nature of this, it's clearly admissible to go into prior sexual relationships between victims and the alleged perpetrator of the sexual offense."

A second justification set forth by Ingaldson was that the testimony showed "an interest that he may have had in his aunt, which I don't think is a normal type of interest, and which goes toward intent in this offense." Although Anthoney made the remark two years ago, Ingaldson portrayed it as a "strong early cue"—an early warning indicator of the lust harbored for Nancy Newman by her obsessive nephew.

"It's a pretty long time ago," noted the judge, "and then I

can't tell exactly how long ago it was. It could be as much as nearly three years. And those are all the circumstances, and then within a week the declaration that it didn't really happen. The prejudicial effect weighed against it—I don't think I should admit it.''

The jury returned; Heck completed her trimmed-down testimony. Ingaldson then attempted submitting two sections of a letter Anthoney wrote to Heck after his arrest when he was well aware of what Heck told Detective Baker aboard the *Arctic Enterprise*. In the letter, Anthoney specifically referenced his temper, attempts to control it, and how he relied on Heck to control it for him. Buckalew again sent the jury out of the room.

''The state has already agreed to every protective order we've requested with respect to Mr. Anthoney's purported temper or inability to control himself,'' said Salemi, reminding the court that all references to Anthoney's temper were disallowed by previous protective orders. ''I'm not sure how they carve an exception out of these protective orders by the mere fact that Anthoney has apparently drafted a letter and talked on the subject matter. Obviously, to whatever extent his temper, his character in that regard, would be relevant, it would certainly be outweighed by the unfair prejudice. And it's a very vague statement. It's a response to who knows what. And I see no relevance, as I said.''

Buckalew, aware that Salemi intended objecting to more than one excerpt, suggested that Ingaldson address Salemi's objections one at a time. ''Your Honor, the two portions of the letter are being offered for similar reasons. The first section about his temper is a closer call—I guess it would be easier for me to argue both of them at once. He's talking about having trouble controlling his temper and needing Debbie Heck to control it, and put that in context with breaking up with Debbie Heck and leaving the boat, I think it's very clear—it will help the jury understand his state of mind during this time period. Now, obviously, I don't have to prove motive,'' stated Ingaldson, "but one of the things Mr. Salemi stressed in his opening was that there was no motive for this, and I think for me to put together his state of mind is going to be something that is important."

In Ingaldson's view, the first statement regarding Anthoney's temper would aid the jurors to understand his state of mind; the second statement, however, was more volatile. The statement in question was, "You said you thought I could kill a two-year-old."

"This is Debbie Heck's opinion as to whether or not this man is capable of killing a two-year-old," complained Salemi. "That's improper opinion evidence under the evidence rules. He's just responding to it. But in order for him to respond to it, you have to allow the opinion in, and the opinion is clearly inadmissible. So is his response taken out of context."

The potential for unfair prejudice toward his client was overwhelming, he asserted. "I don't think the jury would be assisted by someone reflecting on whether or not under some vague or unknown circumstances they might be able to kill a particular person or persons from a particular age group."

Judge Buckalew, finding the defendant's prose confusing, asked, "What does this last paragraph mean where he talks about the killing of the child? It sounds like he'd previously told her he'd killed a child. Is that what it says?"

"I don't know," admitted Salemi. "It says: 'I know I hurt you, but my God, to kill a child or anyone for the matter. I know I've said it.' When he says, 'I know I've said it,' we don't know whether he's referring to killing a child or anyone else for that matter. Beyond that, we could assume that perhaps Mr. Anthoney was referring to this joke he apparently made when he talked to Miss Heck. A car wash where he worked—someone had been killed nearby. At one point, Mr. Anthoney was apparently joking with Debbie Heck about him being responsible for that."

"I think it is self-evident what it says here," countered Ingaldson. "And I'll tell you what—Mr. Salemi may say some people could joke about certain situations where they could kill a two-year-old. I can't think of anyone would talk in any seriousness about killing a two-year-old. And I think this statement here is very clear.''

"I don't think that it's character evidence," said Buckalew, ruling in the prosecution's favor. "I think it's more in the nature of an admission."

Judge Buckalew ruled the passage admissible after the defense further argued that the phrase "I know I hurt you" would inform the jury that Anthoney physically mistreated Heck. This interpretation never initially occurred to either Salemi or Ingaldson. It was John Salemi's wife, sitting in the courtroom, who told him that was her take on the statement. Sensitive to his wife's opinion, Salemi formed an additional objection.

"I took it as emotional hurt," said Ingaldson. "There's been no evidence in front of the jury about the domestic problems that they've had. My proposal is that we just continue with your [previous] ruling."

Buckalew agreed. "Counsel, I have a pretty firm conviction that that's admissible," he told Salemi. "I think if I got an adverse verdict, it will probably survive on appeal. That's how strongly I feel about it." With that, the first day in the Kirby D. Anthoney murder trial was over.

CHAPTER 11

The morning of Tuesday, April 26, 1988, began with Debbie Heck returning to the witness stand. Speaking softly, she told them about the letter she received from Kirby Anthoney that said, in part, "You said I could kill a 2 year old [*sic*]. I don't believe that, but whatever. I know I hurt you but, my God, to kill a child or anyone for that matter. I knew [*sic*] I've said it but doing it's another thing. I guess I scared you bad huh?" From that point on, jurors knew that Heck believed Anthoney was capable of killing a child.

Judge Buckalew also ruled that the prosecution could play the opening moments of Paul Chapman's call to 911. Ingaldson set up a tape recorder, pushed the play button, and the jurors heard a traumatized Paul Chapman's desperate pleas for assistance. His voice cracking with emotion and choked by tears, he described the carnage to a police dispatcher, answered questions about whether there was a gunman in the apartment, and, at the same time, kept his wife from going into the bedrooms where her sister's and nieces' bodies were found. Much of the conversation was hard to understand, but Cheryl Chapman's blood-chilling screams were perfectly clear.

As the tape played, tears streamed down Cheryl Chapman's cheeks. As agreed, Assistant District Attorney Bill Ingaldson cut the tape off early and told jurors they could listen to the rest later if they so desired. Paul Chapman took the stand and recounted the entire story of the 8 A.M. wake-up call from Mama Summerville, the drive to Nancy Newman's apartment, and discovering the bodies.

"Cheryl went into the kitchen area, and I went down the hall, calling out Nancy's name," he explained. "When I first looked into Nancy's bedroom, nothing caught my eye. Then I looked in Melissa's room, and that's when I realized that something was very, very wrong in the house. Melissa wasn't moving—she was on her back, uncovered, and her legs were bent back behind her. As soon as I realized what I was looking at, I went back to Nancy's room, moving in a little bit farther. She was laying on her bed in a kind of twisted position. She was naked. I realized that both Melissa and Nancy were dead. I wondered what happened to Angie. I remember thinking that maybe somebody tied her up or she was in the closet or something, or she'd hid."

When asked to describe what he saw in Angie's room, Chapman closed his eyes for a moment, steeling himself against rising emotions. "It was very, very dark in there. She was lying on the floor, and as soon as I realized it was her, I noticed there was blood, a lot of blood. And at that time, I just couldn't deal with it anymore." During Chapman's testimony, sobs were heard throughout the courtroom.

Ingaldson also made sure that the jury knew that Nancy Newman borrowed the Chapmans' vacuum cleaner on the morning of Friday, March 13, 1987. "I told her that I had a job interview that afternoon," recalled Chapman, "and I wanted to use the vacuum cleaner for a few minutes. It had a lot of attachments," he explained. "One of them was for hair clipping. I took the vacuum cleaner, went into the bathroom, trimmed my beard, finished using it, took the hair trimming attachment off of it, took the long hose off, put the original brush sweeper attachment on, carried it down, and put it in her car.''

The prosecution's strategy was simple and straightforward on this point—Chapman testified about the beard trimming; Jody Cornelius would testify that she vacuumed the residence; Kelly Prather Nicholson (Nancy Newman's niece) would testify that she intended to postvacuum steam-clean the apartment Saturday, March 14; and Bill Gifford would explain how he dissected the vacuum's bag to ascertain how recent were the hairs discovered at the crime scene.

Jody Cornelius, the Newmans' sometime baby-sitter, took the stand and insisted that she was the one who vacuumed the apartment on Friday, March 13. ''I might not have done that good a job, but I did vacuum,'' she testified. ''Nancy had gotten a root canal and she wasn't feeling very good, and I went downstairs to make sure she was okay and I helped her clean up around her house a little bit. When I went down there, she was doing some laundry. I stacked a few dishes and picked up some garbage off the floor and vacuumed.''

Cornelius told the jury that she used the upright Nancy borrowed from Cheryl Chapman rather than the central system built into the apartment complex. ''After vacuuming the living room and dining area, I took it down the hall in Melissa's room, around her bed, down into Angie's room, around and down by her bed, and then I went into Nancy's room.''

Ingaldson then asked her to detail the Saturday-night phone conversations and activities with Kirby Anthony. ''He called me up and asked me what I was doing,'' Cornelius, who was sixteen at the time of the homicides, replied, ''and I said I was going to a dance, but I didn't have a ride. He agreed to come and get me. He was acting kind of weird. I thought he was on drugs. I did not call him and ask for a ride home from my friend's [because] I got the ride from my friend.''

The defense would have preferred that she called Anthoney

rather than the other way around. "Isn't it true with respect to this whole evening," asked Salemi on cross-examination, "that Mr. Anthoney didn't call you, that you called him and started talking about a dance because you were trying to get out of the house to go visit your friend out on DeArmoun Road?"

"No," Cornelius stated emphatically.

On the topic of Kirby Anthoney possibly having a key to the Newman residence, Cornelius was equally precise that before the homicides she was baby-sitting Melissa in the late afternoon while Nancy Newman was working at either Gwennie's or H&R Block, when Anthoney let himself into the locked apartment. "I asked him how he got in the house, and he says, 'I unlocked the door and came in.'" She also said she saw Kirby Anthoney let himself into the Newman apartment on another occasion. Although his back was toward her, she insisted that she "heard the keys."

The defense did its best to undermine the young woman's credibility by reminding her that she didn't mention vacuuming the apartment when first interviewed. She quickly made it clear that she simply provided additional details about her activities when she understood the level of detail desired.

Kelly Prather Nicholson, Cheryl Chapman's daughter, testified on behalf of the prosecution. Exceptionally close to her aunt Nancy, Kelly Prather was seventeen, pregnant, and engaged to and living with John Nicholson of American Building Maintenance at the time of the murders.

Nancy Newman was more than an aunt to Kelly Prather, she was a second mom. Kelly was with Nancy when Melissa was born, helped out when Nancy brought the baby home from the hospital, and lived with the Newmans when she was about nine or ten years old. She actually helped raise Melissa Newman the first few years of her life and regarded her more as a little sister than as a niece.

Kelly Nicholson, per Ingaldson's plan, would testify that she and John Nicholson planned to deep-clean Nancy Newman's carpet at 9 Saturday morning, March 14, 1987. Sadly, they both overslept. Waking up at 9:30, Kelly called her aunt Nancy to apologize for being late, but there was no answer. Had she and her husband-to-be kept their appointment, they might have arrived with the crime in progress.

"Your Honor, if he's going to call Mrs. Nicholson," complained Howard, "we do have some evidentiary matters that were never addressed."

"All the evidentiary issues were addressed," Ingaldson disagreed.

"No," insisted Howard, "Nicholson is going to testify as to two statements allegedly made by Nancy Newman. One is that Nancy told her that she had been vacuuming the place—the residence on Friday, the thirteenth. That's hearsay. The implied assertion of fact is that she vacuumed the residence."

The defense wanted no mention of steam cleaning and further objected to Nicholson's anticipated testimony that Nancy Newman said she didn't want Anthoney in her house. This would come out if Nicholson discussed what became known as the "Price Saver card incident."

"Kelly Prather borrowed Nancy Newman's Price Saver card one day," Grimes later explained, "and used it for shopping at the Price Saver store. When she was done, she went by Nancy's to return the card. Nancy wasn't home, so Kelly simply slid the card under the door. Later Kelly called Nancy, but it was Kirby Anthoney who answered the phone. He told her that he put the Price Saver card on the kitchen table so Nancy would find it. When Nancy came home and found the card on the table, she called Kelly and asked her how she got in the apartment. Kelly explained that she didn't get into the apartment, and that it was Kirby Anthoney who put the card on the table. According to Nicholson, Nancy Newman wasn't happy about that at all, and told Kelly that she didn't want Anthoney in the house. The defense team, of course, did not want the jury to hear this and argued against it."

Exasperated by Howard's objections, Ingaldson complained to Buckalew, "If we're going to reargue these issues, I don't know why we ever have any hearings! We spent half a day talking about these issues. You *did* rule on this. You ruled that I couldn't get into the statement about her vacuuming. You ruled that I could go into the Price Saver. You ruled on that already. You ruled that wasn't hearsay. You ruled that talking about the vacuum cleaner was [hearsay].''

Ingaldson explained that he only intended to ask Nicholson if she and Nancy had had a general discussion about the carpet, and if Nancy asked her if John Nicholson would steam-clean it for her. ''That's not a hearsay statement,'' said Ingaldson, ''because it's not being offered for the truth of the matter asserted. It's not, 'I had my carpet steam cleaned'; it's, 'Do you think John will steam-clean my apartment,' so that's the only thing I'm going to do. You've already ruled on that,'' he reminded the judge. ''You've ruled that I can't get into the fact that she said, you know, 'I've been vacuuming all day and how does it look,' or something like that. You ruled I couldn't get into that. I disagree—respectfully disagree with your ruling, but I accept it. You ruled on the Price Saver card already that I can go into that. I don't know why we're taking time going over this again. It just seems to me,'' complained Ingaldson, ''that we're consuming time needlessly. We've been taking fifteen minutes before every witness.''

''That's fine,'' Howard said, ''we're in a triple-murder trial and I'm not concerned about time.''

''Well, I'm concerned about time,'' asserted Judge Buck-alew.

''I'm not, sir,'' replied Howard. ''The criminal-justice system doesn't care how much money you spend, and time is money, and I don't think we should be concerned about time.''

''You lawyers are ...'' Buckalew thought better of his intended statement, and concluded, ''I'm not going to say anything.''

Howard again argued that having Kelly Nicholson mention steam cleaning was a backdoor method of telling the jury that the carpet had been vacuumed, ''because you don't steam-clean unless you vacuum it. That's the implied fact which he's trying to establish. I think it is hearsay.''

These evidentiary battles, while important to the lawyers, raised honest concerns about the jury spending too much time waiting in the jury room. Buckalew remembered very well a case where the jury was out of the courtroom for a week, and only in the courtroom a matter of minutes. ''And they reached a verdict—not guilty,'' Buckalew told Salemi and Ingaldson. ''And if you listened to the jurors talk, they said, 'If they can't put a case together any quicker than that, they know what they can do with the system.' And so, they were just out of the courtroom to the point where they gave up on it. I don't want to get in that posture that I never get the case tried because we've got to bruise our way through these—and I know it's a triple-homicide case. I would hope that some mornings we wouldn't have any problems.''

At last, Kelly Prather Nicholson was allowed to take the stand. She testified, within boundaries, about her profession. ''Before we went on a job, before we extracted,'' she explained, ''we would vacuum because the dirt deposit is so great in it that you have to vacuum to get up the loose dirt at least. And what the chemical does is it eats away at the carpet, so you don't want to do it too often to your carpet, an extracting job, because eventually you will find that it will eat away at the carpet because of the chemicals. And all you'll end up with is a carpet pad.'' When cleaning private residences, such as the Newmans', it was their normal habit to have the owner vacuum. ''We'd tell them beforehand that it needed to be vacuumed,'' confirmed Nicholson, who also testified in a most limited manner about the Price Saver incident. She was not allowed, however, to mention Nancy's aversion to Anthoney, nor her displeasure with him being in her apartment.

The third day of Ingaldson's presentation began with short testimony from Jeff Mullins and Sissy Altman, both verifying the time Anthoney left Mullins's all-night party and identifying the white shirt worn by Anthoney. On cross-examination,

Salemi 's questioning confirmed that Anthoney did not appear crazy, dangerous, or severely disturbed in the early morning of Saturday, March 14.

The manager of Burger King testified that he had no recollection of Kirby D. Anthoney, Anthoney's hard-to-miss flatbed truck, or the alleged croissant sandwich consumed in the parking lot on that same Saturday morning. Ingaldson was slowly, methodically, building up to the expert testimonies of Gifford, Deedrick, Schanfield, Monfreda, and Propst.

"Ingaldson was very thorough," Grimes later commented. "First he established, as best he could, that Nancy Newman's apartment was vacuumed prior to the homicides, that Anthoney spent the night ingesting drugs and alcohol, and that the Burger King alibi was hogwash. Then he would have a series of expert witnesses present scientific evidence that Kirby D. Anthoney was the rapist and murderer responsible for the deaths of Nancy Newman and her two little girls."

Sergeant Gifford, head of the crime scene investigation, flawlessly presented a compelling slide show of the crime scene and the process by which physical evidence was gathered. It was illustration-intense and required coordinated technical expertise.

"We decided that with the complexity of the case that we would use slides and diagrams," Gifford recalled. "It became necessary to use two projectors showing two photos at one time. How it worked was one slide showed the view from a bedroom door, and the other showed specific items in that room. Then we would move to the next. There was a lot to remember."

When Gifford detailed how he recovered hairs from the dead bodies, the defense put forth an objection that Sergeant Gifford could not identify a pubic hair. The objection was overruled when Ingaldson convinced Buckalew, without much difficulty, that anyone past puberty could ID a pubic hair. Gifford also explained his use of the special police vacuum and the recovery of over 500 hairs from the crime scene—each and every one later checked by the FBI. He also told of dissecting the Chapmans' vacuum cleaner bag's contents.

On cross-examination, Howard elicited confirmation that not one single pubic hair from Anthoney was found either in Nancy Newman's bedroom or on her body. He also challenged Gifford regarding the accuracy of his evidence-collection methods. Although Gifford sectioned the room into grids while vacuuming, the resultant contents were all placed in one bag per room. The pluckings from the bodies were all put in one bag per victim, but no record was kept of exactly where on the body they came from. Gifford acknowledged that the Anchorage Police Department had recently altered its method of evidence collection.

"Gifford did very well on the stand," Grimes later commented, "but there was just enough room for the defense to make an issue out of a few things. Howard did everything he could to portray the vacuum evidence collection as sloppy and imprecise—but that was a complete exaggeration."

"None of that would have meant anything," agreed Gifford, "except that Anthoney lived in the apartment at one time. As with many defense issues, it still didn't mean a whole lot because of the totality of the number of hairs, as well as the absence of Nancy Newman's pubic hairs. Why would Nancy not leave pubic hairs while Kirby did?"

The topic of hairs, both pubic and nonpubic, continued during the testimony of FBI Special Agent Doug Deedrick, who first explained his area of expertise to an enraptured jury. After listing his impressive credentials, Ingaldson asked him, "Have you received a nickname in the laboratory?"

"Objection, Your Honor," said Salemi, "may we approach the bench? The objection is to relevancy."

Buckalew sent the jury to their waiting room. "What is his nickname? That kind of worries me. How is it relevant?"

"He's been called," said Ingaldson, "*Mr. Defense*. And the reason I want to get that out is to show—"

"Well," interrupted the judge, "I thought it was something

like 'Spider.' '' He sustained the objection; the jury was re-seated.

Under oath, Agent Deedrick explained hair's telltale characteristics. ''With regard to human hairs,'' he said, ''it's possible to determine racial origin. There's three main racial groups: the Caucasian race, the Negroid race, and the Mongoloid race. The Mongoloid race would include hairs from Orientals, Alaska natives, and American Indians. It's possible to determine the part of the body hair came from, how the hair was removed, if it's been artificially treated, if it's been damaged in any way. These are the first things that have to be determined from a microscopic examination of a hair.''

''Can you say that a hair came from a white French poodle versus a brown schnauzer or something like that?'' asked Ingaldson.

''Animal hairs don't possess enough unique characteristics to say with absolute certainty that it came from a particular breed,'' answered Deedrick, ''or from a particular animal to the exclusion of all other similar animals. Now, if the animals are grossly different, obviously, then you can make that determination a little bit easier.''

Agent Deedrick, with the court's permission, drew an enormous illustration for the jury's edification and enlightenment. He explained the matrix, basal, distal, and medial areas, and discussed the importance of the distal, or tip, end.

''It depends upon the time when the hair sample is collected and when the hair sample is deposited at the crime scene,'' said Deedrick. ''The longer the time between the deposition you would expect to see maybe more changes that occur between the known sample and the characteristics of the hairs found at the crime scene. If the hair's been cut with scissors, it would generally be rather straight across. And as time progresses on the head of that individual, the edges of the hair will tend to round off through combing and whatever processing, and so forth. If the hair has been razor cut, the edges are often very sharp. Sometimes an individual's hair may split and may break and be frayed at the ends, split tips, people are aware of that term. Again, that may be characteristic of the person's hair sample.''

"How about pubic hair," asked Ingaldson, gradually steering Deedrick toward the payoff. Flanked by charts and photographs of hairs enlarged a thousand times, he told jurors that he found Anthoney's pubic hair on bedclothes and in carpet sweepings. Fibers from the green wool gloves were found on the pillowcase tied around Nancy Newman's throat and on the washcloth, which also contained one of Anthoney's pubic hairs. Deedrick testified that he found numerous other hairs in the apartment, including some that he could not identify.

In cross-examination, Defense Attorney Craig Howard focused on the big weakness in Deedrick's findings—his inability to say how old the hairs were; how long ago they had fallen or been torn from Anthoney's body. Every expert the prosecution presented was assaulted either on credentials, believability, or admissibility of evidence. It was a monumental battle, for example, to get Jud Ray on the stand.

"The state intends to call Mr. Ray to the stand," wrote Assistant Public Defender Craig Howard to the court, "to testify on the issue of whether a person who engaged in a triple sexual homicide would be 'tired and spent' in the hours afterwards. The defendant objects to said testimony. The testimony of Mr. Ray is not within the purview of Alaska Rule of Evidence 702 and 703. These rules permit persons with specialized knowledge to render an opinion on a controverted issue at trial. Rule 703 requires that the data relied upon must be of a type reasonably relied upon by experts in the particular field in forming opinions. Anthoney submits that Ray's testimony does not even comport with the threshold requirements of the Alaska Rules of Evidence 702 and 703."

Howard argued that even under the "liberal" rules pertaining to expert testimony, not all "expert" testimony is admissible, and that Ray's testimony would not assist the jury in any mode or manner.

"Ray's testimony will conclude that behaviors that are manifested by innocent citizens may also be expected," Howard stated. He characterized Ray's proposed testimony as "highly speculative, and will not add anything to pre-existing common-sense principles of the jurors." On behalf of Anthoney, Howard submitted that it would be "an abuse of discretion to permit Mr. Ray to testify."

The defense also argued that Ray's testimony did not meet the Frye standards test for "novel, scientific evidence." Anthoney's attorneys said that Ray's expertise was so novel and untested that it was "inherently unreliable and suspect."

Howard reminded the court that in a recent case before the Alaska court of appeals, *Anderson v. State* (1988), the court ruled that "it was error to permit expert testimony regarding the existence of common behavioral traits of a certain group. Indeed," stressed Howard, "it stated that such expert testimony has never been authorized as competent evidence. Ray's testimony is exactly the type of evidence which the Anderson court condemned; to-wit: that Anthoney's conduct may have been consistent with a sexual murderer's."

Judge Buckalew, after serious consideration, ruled that Ray could testify. He did, however, make limiting stipulations the prosecution found restrictive. Still, for maximum potential impact, Ingaldson scheduled Ray to testify immediately prior to John Newman at the very end of the prosecution's presentation. For now, Ingaldson wanted to complete the testimony of Gifford, Deedrick, and Schanfield.

Dr. Moses Schanfield, approved as an expert by Judge Buckalew, took the stand. Had he gestured hypnotically like Mandrake the Magician, he could not have been more mystifying. Undisputedly knowledgeable, Schanfield explained allotyping and blood analysis to a jury fighting involuntary slumber.

"It was highly technical, very detailed, and far, far over the heads of almost everyone in the courtroom," Grimes commented later. "He did, however, make it perfectly clear that there were strong indications that the semen samples found at the crime scene were from someone who had the same unusual blood allotype classification—B secretor—as Kirby D. Anthoney.''

Ingaldson then returned to more personal testimony by calling both Kirk Mullins and Deborah Dean to the witness stand. The couple, individually, confirmed that Anthoney did not arrive at 9:30 A.M.—it was closer to 11 A.M. Cheryl Chapman added another needed dose of personalization when she took the stand and told how she, Nancy, and John fixed up Melissa's room for Anthoney and Heck with a double bed borrowed from another Gwennie's waitress. During the couple's stay, Melissa shared a room with Angie; when they left, she returned to her own room and her own single bed. The borrowed double bed, Chapman testified, was returned to its owner.

She also told the jury that Melissa and Angie were across the street at the home of Cynthia Crowson, a baby-sitter, who lived in the trailer park, on the day Kirby Anthoney showed up at the Newmans' apartment after leaving the *Arctic Enterprise*.

''Just prior to Mr. Anthoney leaving and moving out,'' Ingaldson asked, ''did you have a conversation with Nancy Newman concerning Mr. Anthoney?'' Cheryl replied in the affirmative. ''And did you give any advice to Nancy Newman?''

Salemi was on his feet in a heartbeat. ''Excuse me, Your Honor. Could we approach the bench?'' The attorneys entered a whispered conversation before Buckalew excused the jury from the room. ''Your Honor,'' continued Salemi, ''while I'm not sure what Mr. Ingaldson intends to do with this line of questioning, my suspicions are, he intends to elicit from Miss Chapman that Miss Chapman advised her sister, Nancy Newman, to kick Mr. Anthoney out of her residence. Is that about right?''

''No, it isn't,'' replied Ingaldson.

''Oh, okay, then I'm wrong already,'' Salemi said. ''Maybe we should find out what he intended to elicit from Miss Chapman.''

Ingaldson entreated the judge to allow further testimony from Cheryl Chapman regarding Anthoney's mental state following the breakup with Heck. He wanted to get in the part about Nancy telling Cheryl that she wanted Anthoney out of the house, not Cheryl telling Nancy to get him out.

Salemi would have none of it. Strongly objecting, he insisted, "Ingaldson wants to mislead this jury rather than give them facts. He wants to leave them with the impression . . . that Mr. Anthoney was asked to leave, when, in fact, we know that he wasn't. They want to paint a picture where Mr. Anthoney is angry or upset because he was asked to leave the house. He doesn't talk about the accuracy or the inaccuracy of what he intends to bring out."

Upon reflection, the judge told Ingaldson that Chapman's expanded testimony would not be allowed. Ingaldson asked for a reason. "If the defense gets an adverse verdict," explained the judge, "this ruling is going to come back to haunt me to a significant extent. I have some real questions about its relevance." Ingaldson, exasperated, tried another tactic. "Well, Judge, it's—I mean my hands are being cut right and left here about anything with motive . . . I don't know how I'm going to paint any type of motive here if I can't go into these things . . . it's important to show his state of mind at the time. I've asked you to consider this thing even about the suicide—"

"When did this suicide business come up?" asked Judge Buckalew, "How close is it to the killings?"

"Within a couple weeks," Ingaldson quickly asserted.

"No! That's not true, Your Honor," insisted Salemi. "It's not within a couple of weeks . . . I think it's further than that . . . there is the remoteness question with respect to suicide, but anyway," he reminded the court, "you've already ruled on that."

"I can always reverse myself," Buckalew reminded Salemi.

"Yeah, you can," responded the defense attorney, "but you see, Mr. Ingaldson gets up here and Mr. Ingaldson is a real nice man and everything like that, and so he's saying, 'Gosh,

Judge, every ruling that you've made about motive is going against me, can't you give me one finally?' And that's not the way—we go by rules of evidence. We don't just try to balance things out.''

Buckalew, not warming to Salemi's line of reasoning, expressed his understanding of Ingaldson's position. ''What he's saying is that this court's not giving the state a fair trial. He didn't put it in that language, but that's what he's saying, and when a prosecutor says something like that, I give it some more reflection. Maybe I—''

''But, but . . . ,'' interrupted Salemi, ''but the rulings are based on the evidence.'' Turning to Ingaldson, Salemi became more pointed. ''You just make this general argument about 'gee whiz, my hands are cut.' He's saying 'my hands are being cut.' I think he means tied, but that is not an evidentiary argument. I don't see anything in this that says, you know—''

Buckalew, passing beyond saturation on the topic, cut Salemi off short. ''All right—that argument's not going to help me. I'm going to take a five-minute recess.''

Recess concluded, Ingaldson and Salemi reached an agreement whereby Cheryl Chapman could be called again to the stand and asked if she and Nancy discussed Anthoney's mental state, but she would not be allowed to elaborate, nor would Ingaldson be allowed to ask any specifics.

''You mentioned that you had some conversation with Nancy Newman about Mr. Anthoney. Did you talk to her in that conversation at all about Mr. Anthoney's emotional state at that time?''

''Yes, I did,'' Chapman answered. Ingaldson then changed the subject. Salemi was not happy about the question or the answer. ''I think it would cause the jury to speculate,'' said Salemi, ''as to what the conversation was about Mr. Anthoney's mental state, and the court's already ruled that wouldn't be admissible.'' In short, Salemi accused Ingaldson of attempting to ''subtly bring out evidence which the court has already proscribed him from bringing out.''

When Cheryl Chapman stepped down, Kirby Anthoney made what could be interpreted as an intimidating remark. According to Ingaldson, he whispered to Chapman as she walked past the defense table, "I'm so sorry, Cheryl." Ingaldson then asked for permission to repeat the remark to the jury, insisting that the remark was made with a smirk and was meant to be intimidating.

Defense Attorney John Salemi said Anthoney actually whispered, "I love you, Cheryl." Judge Buckalew said the whole incident was "subject to diverse interpretation" and denied Ingaldson's request. He did, however, acknowledge that such remarks by Anthoney "very well could be a form of intimidation." When Salemi challenged him to explain on what he based his conclusion, Buckalew replied, "Just looking at him. He's just a scary person. He has an intimidating presence."

Cheryl Chapman was not intimidated, she was furious. She bluntly told reporters on Monday, May 2, 1988, that she intended to kill Anthoney if he were acquitted. "He will never walk a free man again," Chapman said. Asked point-blank if she planned to kill Anthoney if he were not convicted, Chapman replied, "Yes, definitely. If they would give me the opportunity now, we wouldn't even be having a trial."

Aware of Chapman's intense hatred of Anthoney, security personnel watched her closely, occasionally frisked her, and did not allow her to take her purse with her into the courtroom when she testified. Frank Garfield, courthouse security chief, heard Chapman's direct threats and ruled she would have to watch the rest of the trial from the media booth—a soundproof room separated from the rear of the courtroom by double-paned one-way glass. Sound from the court could be heard through a loudspeaker.

"Anybody that sees a grisly scene that she had to see has a right to feelings like that," Garfield said at the time, referring to the triple murder and rape discovery. "But that doesn't give her the right to subvert the judicial system."

CHAPTER 12

The Northern Lights Car Wash was long defunct by the time Ken Larson and Curtis Cumiford were called to testify at the trial of former employee and coworker, Kirby D. Anthoney. The purpose of their testimony was to establish that Anthoney was an accomplished liar who could cry on cue. Before Larson could testify, Ingaldson had to win another battle with John Salemi. Buckalew excused the jury; Ingaldson made his argument.

"I would ask to be allowed to ask Curtis Cumiford concerning an incident that happened just the week before these murders wherein Kirby Anthoney called into work, asked to have time off, saying his mother had died; he was crying, very upset, and he was very believable at that point. The reason for that is twofold. The initial reason is to show his state of mind at the time. I think it's become important now."

Ingaldson reminded the court that the defense asked several witnesses how Anthoney acted before and after the murders. "They've opened the door, and I think I have a right to correct misimpression of the jury and to basically give them the real picture, a true picture. Also I think this is important just to show his state of mind up to the murders. The evidence is, I think, probative to show his state of mind prior to the offense, and also show his ability to turn on and off his emotions, what has been put squarely in issue by the defense through their witnesses. I think it is only fair for the jury to get an honest impression of Mr. Anthoney concerning that, that I be allowed to present this evidence.''

Defense Counsel Howard firmly disagreed. ''My understanding,'' he said, ''is that the state wants to bring in these two people, Ken Larson, who operates this car wash, and approximately around the first of March had hired Mr. Anthoney. Five or six days before the homicide, Mr. Anthoney called up and said that his mother had died, that he seemed emotionally upset and he needed some time off, and Mr. Larson said, take all the time off you need. The same thing with Mr. Cumiford, who allegedly saw Mr. Anthoney sometime, and Mr. Anthoney seemed to have been crying or been emotionally upset about this episode. Obviously, they're trying to show Mr. Anthoney is a liar.''

''Is his mother alive? Is that it?'' asked the judge.

''His mother is alive and well,'' Howard answered, then asserted that the proposed testimony violated the defendant's rights to due process. The exclusion rule, as previously noted, prohibits the jury from hearing about a defendant's prior crimes, wrongs, or bad acts. ''I would say, Your Honor, that the act of lying to your employer—the act of deception—that's what [the exclusion rule] goes to. That is, evidence of other crimes is not admissible to prove the character in order to show that he acted in conformity therewith. Well, obviously, the point is going to be made by the prosecution that Mr. Anthoney is very adept at deceiving people. Which, obviously, goes to character. It doesn't go to things like motive, opportunity, intent, preparation, plan, knowledge, identity, or absence of mistake. He's arguing,'' Howard said of Ingaldson, ''that somehow [what] it shows is state of mind. Apparently, the nexus is that [Anthoney] can lie and deceive people and he's real good at it. And that strikes at the heart of character, and we do not let that kind of evidence in. I think everyone would agree that it's wrong, it's a very bad act, to lie to your employer so you can get the day off.''

"That's pretty contemptible," agreed Buckalew, "to tell your employer, 'My mom's died,' and crying over the phone.''

"And that's exactly why the jury should be kept from hearing it—because it's a bad act. It has nothing to do but prejudice Mr. Anthoney in front of the jury. It has absolutely nothing to do with this case. Especially if Mr. Ingaldson later on is going to try to link it up to say that, well, Mr. Anthoney is a very good liar—he lied to the police—or the remorse he showed— he's very good at it. And that's what it's going to," insisted Howard. "It's going to a propensity that he is able to act in character and conformity with that character. He is very good at deceiving and very good at lying to people, will basically do anything to get his way. That is what you're looking at in this case, and that's what the evidence is going to be. Character evidence, Judge, rears its head in different ways. Sometimes it just doesn't say character—written, stamped, on it.''

The two lawyers tossed previous rulings and legal precedents back and forth while Buckalew kept score. They reached a compromise in the final round. "Your Honor," said Ingaldson, "I have no objection to any type of limiting instruction if the defense has one. A suggestion might be to inform the jury that they're to consider only Mr. Anthoney's state of mind, not as to whether or not he's a truthful person. That's not at issue here.''

"So, my understanding is," commented Howard, "that he's going to call Mr. Cumiford and Mr. Larson and he's going to elicit testimony that sometime that week Mr. Anthoney had called in, told them that his mother had died, and was upset.''

"That's about it," agreed Ingaldson, "and it's going to be very short. I'm not going to get into Mr. Anthoney's reputation at work, and I'm not going into that area. It's true that at one time in his statements he said that [Anthoney] was an excellent worker, but I know he also has accused him of stealing things and stuff, and I realize that I can't get into those types of things."

"All right," Buckalew said, "let's get your witness."

Kenneth W. Larson, manager of Northern Lights Car Wash, took the stand, and Ingaldson asked him, "Do you recall whether Mr. Anthoney ever called in concerning a problem as to whether he'd be able to work?"

"Yes," replied Larson, "he called me March eighth. He told me that his mother had passed away and that he just couldn't come into work. I just talked to him for twenty seconds on the phone. And then, later in the day, he stopped by to see me." Anthoney cried while visiting Larson, and the car wash manager had no doubt whatsoever, based on Anthoney's emotional reaction, that Peggy Anthoney was dead. Ingaldson then called Curtis Cumiford, the car washer who filled in for Anthoney that day. Cumiford saw Anthoney at the car wash in the afternoon. "He pulled up and he couldn't really talk. He had tears in his eyes and before he pulled up, I heard that his mother had died."

"What was his emotional state like when he was talking to you?" asked Ingaldson.

"He had tears in his eyes."

Ingaldson switched the topic, asking Cumiford if he gets tips from people at the car wash.

"I make anywhere from five to fifteen dollars a day. It's usually in dollar bills."

"How rare would it be to get change?"

"Real rare," Cumiford answered. "I've only had one lady give me change, and that was only two quarters."

Tony Marinelli, next on Ingaldson's witness list, testified that he did not speak with Anthoney on the day of the murders. While it was true that they had a telephone conversation, it actually took place a week earlier. He was able to produce his time cards as proof that he was not working that day, and telephone records showed that he did not speak to Anthoney on Saturday, March 14, 1987.

When Ingaldson wanted testimony from Jess O'Dell, the neighbor who claimed that Anthoney tried to sell him John Newman's camera following the murders, Salemi said O'Dell was a liar, burglar, and big-time drug dealer. He and Ingaldson got into another verbal altercation in court before the jury was allowed back in the courtroom, or O'Dell took the stand.

"Mr. O'Dell was involved in an incident," explained Ingaldson to the judge, "wherein he and some other people ripped off another drug dealer in Palmer, Alaska. O'Dell's role in it was he went in and took some marijuana plants. In the meantime, two other persons went in and held up people in the house and might have taken some money or something. Some of the other people involved were involved in some other cases also. Mr. O'Dell was not involved in the other cases, but he testified on behalf of the state in Palmer and was given an agreement prior to [the Newman homicides]. His agreement was that he would plead to burglary and the state would recommend that he not receive extra jail time. There was no deal made with this case," Ingaldson emphasized, "and I would ask the court to refrain from Mr. Salami characterizing Mr. O'Dell in terms such as 'armed robber.'. . ."

"How would he feel about an accomplice to an armed robbery?" asked Salemi pointedly.

"Why is all of this business relevant?" asked Buckalew. "Why should I try that kind of business in this trial? I mean, it's a collateral issue."

"It's not exactly that simple, Your Honor," said Salemi. "When the police started getting close to him, putting the heat on Mr. O'Dell, the prosecution witness that they're going to be calling, he called an attorney and worked out a deal."

"That's done every day," stated Buckalew, unimpressed.

"Yes, I understand that," Salemi assured the court, "and also when those people are called as prosecution witnesses, and they've been given concessions by the state in exchange for their testimony, those things come out on cross-examination. This is a little bit different because that was a separate case.''

Encouraged to continue, Salemi began his assault on Jess O'Dell. ''He busted his deal with the state, he fled jurisdiction. He wasn't supposed to do that, and then he came back. And all of a sudden he comes up with this other information, not only on that case where he was involved, but all of a sudden he knows Mr. Anthoney, he's lived next door, and he's got information about Mr. Anthoney which the police are very interested in. So, he calls up his new attorney and he says, 'I've got this good information about this murder case,' and his expectation was that he was going to get a benefit from that. So, we need to show that here's a man . . .''

''He's never been given any benefits, any deals,'' said Ingaldson forcefully. ''He's been given it in the other case . . . before this even happened. Mr Salemi is right—he did flee in October because he was afraid that these persons were going to come after him. It had nothing to do with this case.''

Ingaldson was highly critical of Salemi even mentioning O'Dell's previous brush with the law. ''The only purpose is to paint him as a bad person; the only reason is to have the jury emotionally dislike him. If Mr. Salemi starts branding him as an armed robber—I mean, I certainly can't do that about Mr. Anthoney, with his armed robbery convictions.''

''[O'Dell] had an expectation that he was going to get favorable treatment,'' Salemi insisted. ''He called his attorney for the purpose of selling information to the police in the hopes that he would receive more favorable treatment. And there are other things going on here. Mr. O'Dell was a drug dealer, and he lied to us about that when we interviewed him. I said, 'Okay, were you dealing any cocaine or anything like that?' He says no. He lied right to our face. Five minutes later he comes back in the office with his attorney and says, 'Oh, we've got to clear up something—Jess lied to you—he was dealing cocaine.' I'm going to bring that up because he lied right to my face. And he's a liar, and I think the jury should know that!''

"He can't ask him about things like that," Ingaldson protested. "If he wants to do that, and he wants to get into prior bad acts, and open the door to all the witnesses, fine! Let's do it with Mr. Anthoney, too!"

"It's allowed with Mr. O'Dell," Salemi argued, "because he's trying to curry favor with the prosecution, he doesn't want to be convicted. Your Honor, we've got a prosecution witness here who is not as clean as the driven snow, and I should be permitted to point that out to the jury."

"I'm not going to let any of that drug business in," decided Buckalew.

Ingaldson said Salemi could mention the fact that Mr. O'Dell sold Anthoney marijuana and was owed money. "But the fact that he's a drug dealer, this big picture of selling cocaine and things, is clearly much more prejudicial than any probative value. What I'm concerned about is characterizations—inflaming the jury, saying he's an armed robber. If I started saying, you know, Mr. Anthoney is a baby killer, that's the same type of thing because it's the type of words that just evoke an emotional response."

"All right," said the judge, "this O'Dell didn't have a handgun in his hand. I'm not going to permit [Salemi] to refer to him as an armed robber unless he can put the handgun in his hand."

"I'll shift from the drug involvement," agreed Salemi. "I'll ask, 'Are you generally an honest person,' and he'll probably say yes. And he just took an oath and stuff like that. And then I'll say, 'Well, isn't it true that when I asked you about your drug involvement, you lied right to my face? In front of your attorney, the district attorney, my investigator,' and he's going to have to say yes."

"I'm not going to let him ask that question," ruled Buckalew, "and if I'm wrong, the appellate court will tell me about it. But that seems pretty clear that's not admissible."

Salemi, refusing to give up, said, "We're going to have a problem with this one, Judge. I'd like a stay of proceedings so

I can take this issue to the Court of Appeals. I mean, it's critical
to the case. I'd really like it if the jury knew he was a liar,
which he is.''

"I'm not going to stay the case," said Buckalew flatly. He
reseated the jury and called the court to order.

"Right now I'm a doorman at the Gaslight," answered Jess
O'Dell when Ingaldson asked him what he did for a living.
Guided by Ingaldson's questions, O'Dell explained his coopera-
tion with police and prosecutors on the Palmer burglary case.
Ingaldson made sure the jury knew any benefits received by
O'Dell were prior to the Newman homicides, and that O'Dell
would receive no direct benefits for testifying against Kirby
Anthoney.

"I first went over to Kirby's house because I saw an
unmarked cop car down the road," testified O'Dell on direct
examination, "and I went over there and he seemed pretty
upset, and I asked him what was wrong. He told me that they
had come over, and his aunt and two nieces had been murdered.
He said that [police] had been there and they were probably
going to be coming back."

"Tell me a little bit about the camera," said Ingaldson.
"Where did you see the camera?"

"In his room. He had placed it on his bed and asked me
what I thought it was worth, if I wanted to buy it. He asked
me to come in [his room] and he showed it to me."

O'Dell said Anthoney set the Pentax camera on the bed, and
inside the case were lens filters and a telephoto lens extender.
"I'm not sure, but there was a smaller lens in there. There was
a larger lens also. And just a bunch of film containers on the
side where you put them inside."

Ingaldson produced state's exhibit #51—John Newman's
camera case. "I remember that flash and—let's see," said
O'Dell as he examined the contents, "yeah, looks like it."

"What, if anything, did Mr. Anthoney say to you regarding
that camera?"

"He wanted to know what I thought it was worth, and if I wanted to buy it. I had two cameras, I was running low on funds, and I didn't want it. I asked him if it was hot, and he said no."

O'Dell told the jury Anthoney owed him money for marijuana. "I asked him if he had any money and first he said no. And then he said, well, hold on. And he went into Dan's room and was in there for a little bit and he came out with a roll of quarters and a roll of dimes. I said, where did you get these, at the car wash? Because I figured he might have got them at the car wash. And he said no."

John Salemi's cross-examination avoided the camera and focused on the witness's credibility.

"After you read a newspaper article about the Anthoney case, or the Newman case, you called your attorney, didn't you? And you say, 'I've got some more information, and now it's about another case, and I'd like to sell that to the police,' isn't that true?"

"Yeah," responded O'Dell. "I was hoping that I might be able to, because I might be going away for a year or so, or six months. I didn't say I want to sell it to them."

"Are you a pretty honest man, Mr. O'Dell?"

"Well, I am now. I cleaned up my act and stayed out of trouble when I got back from Oregon."

"Which would have been after you talked to the police about this case, correct?"

"Well," answered O'Dell, "I was honest with them all the way in everything I said."

"Were you honest with the grand jury when you testified in this case?" asked Salemi.

"Yes."

"Okay. Question—page three hundred eighty-nine of the grand jury in *State v. Kirby D. Anthoney*. You're talking about the coins. You mentioned that he owed you some money. 'I lent him some money when he came back from fishing.' Today

you said you got the coins because you sold him some marijuana.''

"Yeah,'' replied O'Dell. "It's just like letting [him] borrow
some money. He didn't pay me right off the bat.''

"Oh,'' said Salemi sarcastically, "so you don't think you
were misleading the grand jury at all when you said, 'I lent
him some money.' You think the grand jury would understand
from your answer that this was a repayment for a drug transac-
tion? This answer was given under oath on May fifth, 1987,
wasn't it? And it wasn't the truth, was it?''

"Well,'' responded O'Dell reasonably, "it had to do with
money, you know.''

"Do you know the penalties for perjury?''

Ingaldson immediately objected. "This is just badgering,
obviously, and clearly, he's explained his answer there.''

"The jury knows he's under oath when he testified at the
grand jury,'' said Buckalew.

Salemi went back on the offensive. "Has the prosecution
talked to you about the fact that you lied at the grand jury?''

Ingaldson again objected, claiming mischaracterization of
the evidence, and asked that Salemi not ask argumentative
questions.

"It's my understanding,'' shot back Salemi, "that Mr.
Ingaldson doesn't consider that a lie, Your Honor.''

"You don't have to badger this around,'' replied Buckalew,
"I don't care what you call it. I'll leave it to the jury to determine
what that evidence means or does not mean.''

After nit-picking O'Dell's recollections and believability,
Salemi stepped aside for Ingaldson's redirect examination. The
state only had one question: Did Mr. O'Dell receive or expect
any compensation for his testimony? The answer was an honest
"No.''

On May 5, 1988, Dan Grant, Anthoney's roommate, testified
as to Anthoney's mental state and physical condition on the

morning of Saturday, March 14. "He was pretty wired. You might say hyper or restless. I would say that he was high on cocaine at the time, or had done some previously and was suffering from the aftereffects."

Grant also confirmed the prosecution's allegation that Anthoney left the residence at 8:45 A.M.—the same time as Grant, or shortly before him. As Anthoney did not arrive at Kirk Mullins's until 10:30, Grant's testimony helped confirm the "missing hours" in Anthoney's alibi. On cross-examination, Defense Attorney Howard accused Grant of having damaged his memory by excessive marijuana smoking.

"You have a routine when you get up in the morning," said Howard. "You get dressed, you drink coffee, smoke a cigarette, and you always get stoned before you go to work, don't you?"

"Yes, sir," answered Grant happily.

"And you told the police—you were real emphatic—and you said, 'I have problems with memory, I have a problem remembering things.' "

"I said that?" Grant asked teasingly. "I might say that my memory problem is due to marijuana. Although my memory is bad, it's probably good enough to remember me telling the police that I had a bad memory."

When Howard asked Grant if he abused marijuana, Grant amused the jury by answering, "Sure. From someone-that-doesn't-use's point of view, I certainly do." The jury had a much-needed laugh before questioning returned Grant to more serious aspects. Did he still consider Kirby D. Anthoney his friend? "If he didn't do this, everyone has deserted him and he needs a friend," responded Grant.

Less friendly to Anthoney, and far less humorous, was the testimony of Carol Hawkins, mother of Kimra Atkinson. She recounted Anthoney's disturbing telephone call following the homicides in which he revealed information only the killer could know.

Vicki Irvine, the young woman who encountered Anthoney

in Chilkoot Charlie's, testified regarding Anthoney's peculiar comments the night he passed around poetry in the noisy bar. Ms. Irvine quoted Anthoney as saying, "The worst thing was that the mother had to watch." Ingaldson queried if perhaps Anthoney had actually said, "Missy had to watch." He suggested that the bar was so loud, it was possible that she misunderstood.

Kathryn Monfreda, identification technician, testified with well-earned self-assurance that she was more than qualified to analyze crime scene fingerprints. "I received training from the FBI, both in Wisconsin and at the FBI Academy in Quantico, Virginia," elaborated Ms. Monfreda. "I'm also a member of the International Association for Identification, I'm a certified latent print examiner, which means I have taken a test that's written by the foremost authorities in the fingerprint field to determine if I'm qualified as a fingerprint examiner, and which I did pass.

"On the surface of your hands and your fingers," she explained to the jury, "and also the soles of your feet and your toes, is skin that's different from skin on other areas of your body," she said. "The skin on your hands and feet is corrugated. It consists of raised formations we call friction ridges. Those ridges don't flow in a continuous line. They stop or they separate, and they form what we call ridge characteristics. The arrangement of these characteristics is unique to each individual finger and each individual palm. On the tops of these ridges are small sweat pores, which exude a small amount of perspiration. The perspiration will adhere to the tops of the ridges. When an item is touched, the impression of those ridges will be transferred to that item. That's what's known as a latent print. The word 'latent,' itself, means hidden. And that means we have to do something to it in order to make it visible. We use various techniques, and once a latent print is developed, we can compare those to known impressions. That is recordings of the ridge details of individuals who are fingerprinted by printer's ink or some similar substance."

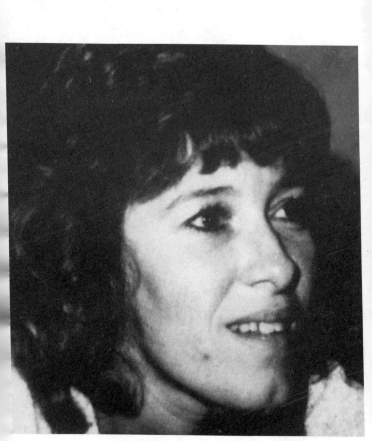

Victim Nancy Newman, 32.
(*Photo courtesy Anchorage Police Department*)

Victim Melissa Newman, 8. *(Photo courtesy Anchorage Police Department)*

Victim Angie Newman, 3. *(Photo courtesy Anchorage Police Department)*

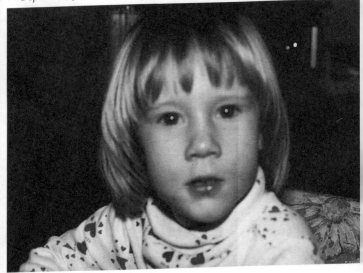

Nancy, Melissa, and Angie Newman celebrating Christmas three months before they were murdered.
(*Photo courtesy Anchorage Police Department*)

The Newmans and their two daughters left Idaho to move into the Anchorage apartment in 1985.
(*Photo courtesy Anchorage Police Department*)

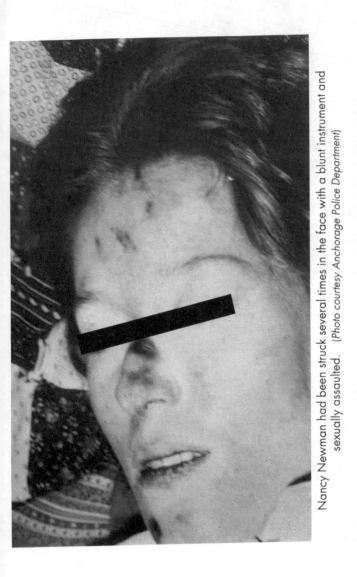

Nancy Newman had been struck several times in the face with a blunt instrument and sexually assaulted. *(Photo courtesy Anchorage Police Department)*

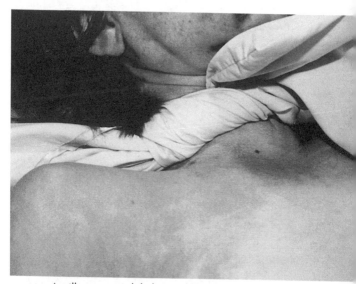

A pillowcase tightly knotted around Nancy Newman's
neck caused her death by strangulation.
(*Photo courtesy Anchorage Police Department*)

Angie Newman's hand showed defensive injuries indicating she had fought her assailant. *(Photo courtesy Anchorage Police Department)*

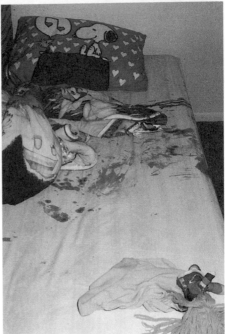

The bloodstained bed where Angie's throat was slashed. *(Photo courtesy Anchorage Police Department)*

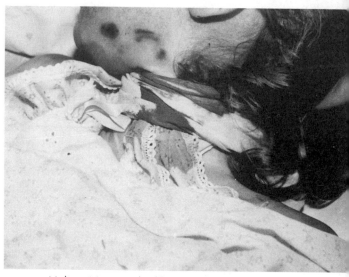

Melissa Newman had been raped and strangled like her mother. *(Photo courtesy Anchorage Police Department)*

Kirby Anthoney lived in this house, about a mile from the Newmans at the time of their murders.
(*Photo courtesy Anchorage Police Department*)

Anthoney with his uncle John Newman and cousin Melissa. She holds the camera Anthoney stole the night he killed her.
(*Photo courtesy Anchorage Police Department*)

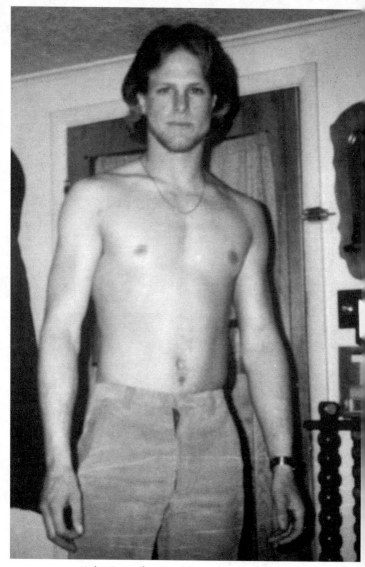

Kirby D. Anthoney, 23, prior to his arrest.
(*Photo courtesy Anchorage Police Department*)

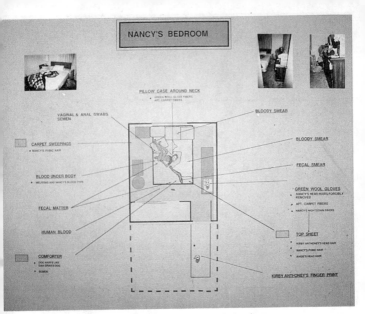

Diagram of Nancy Newman's bedroom.
(*Photo courtesy Anchorage Police Department*)

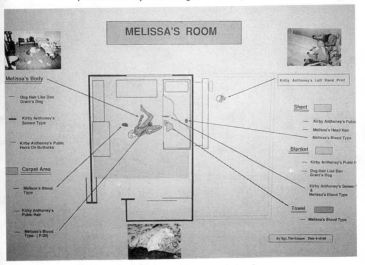

Diagram of Melissa Newman's bedroom.
(*Photo courtesy Anchorage Police Department*)

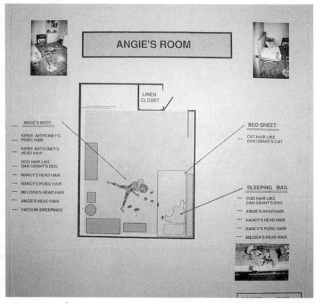

Diagram of Angie Newman's bedroom. (*Photo courtesy Anchorage Police Department*)

The cookie canister where Nancy Newman hid the tips she earned as a waitress was found open and empty on the kitchen table, indicating her killer knew about it. (*Photo courtesy Anchorage Police Department*)

Anthoney's former girlfriend Debbie Heck with FBI Special
Agent Judson Ray. (*Photo courtesy* Anchorage Daily News)

Assistant public defenders John Salemi (left) and Craig
Howard (right) confer with defendant Kirby Anthoney.
(*Photo courtesy* Anchorage Daily News)

Detective Sergeant
Mike Grimes.
(*Photo courtesy
Mike Grimes*)

Lieutenant Bill Gifford.
(*Photo courtesy
Bill Gifford*)

Anthoney wipes tears from his eyes as he is sentenced.
(*Photo courtesy* Anchorage Daily News)

NEWMAN

NANCY
FEB. 27 1955
MELISSA
SEPT. 22 1978
ANGELA
AUG. 17 1983
MAR. 14 1987

TOGETHER FOREVER

Nancy Newman and her daughters are buried together in Twin Falls, Idaho. (*Photo courtesy Carol Hawkins*)

At last, Monfreda told the jury that the fingerprints of Kirby D. Anthoney were not only in every room of the Newman apartment, but also on the inner rim of the cookie canister that once held Newman's tip change. Nineteen prints found in sixteen locations were from Kirby D. Anthoney, including the one horrid left-palm print above Melissa Newman's bed.

CHAPTER 13

The two cops who knew Kirby Anthoney best were Bill Reeder and Ken Spadafora. Neither, of course, could stand him. Thoroughly convinced that Anthoney was the cruel and inhuman predator responsible for the rapes and murders, they eagerly assisted Bill Ingaldson.

On Monday, May 16, Reeder took the stand and testified that Kirby Anthoney's alibi drifted from one position to another in response to the tug of emerging evidence. The jury heard excerpts from Anthoney's evolving alibis and altered stories about several pieces of evidence, including his whereabouts the morning of the murders. According to Reeder, Anthoney first specifically mentioned the Burger King, breakfast stop in an April 20 interview, more than a month after giving police the initial account of his Saturday-morning breakfast croissant.

"Everything was fairly consistent about time, until Spadafora and I told him his alibi was kind of weak," said Reeder, "then his statements about Saturday morning started to change. For example, when I told Anthoney that Kirk said he went right over to Beverage World, Anthoney said, 'Yeah, I told ya that, yeah, we went over there.' Well, I had the receipt right there that showed that he wasn't there until twelve-fifteen in the afternoon. His response was, 'Out of all those receipts, you have mine? Come on—throw me in jail, Bill.' ''

The drawling, personable detective also testified that Anthoney invented explanations spontaneously when confronted with possible evidence against him. ''I told Anthoney that we found recent hairs, pretty young hairs, inside those gloves—not that we exactly had his hand hairs, but I made it sound like that's what I was saying,'' Reeder explained. ''Sometimes that sort of questioning, asking such things as 'how could your hairs be in those gloves?' is going to bring out unexpected answers. If Kirby Anthoney didn't do this, and he hadn't been wearing those gloves, what's he going to say? He's going to say, 'No way, because I never wore those gloves. They couldn't be mine.' But that's not what Anthoney did at all. He invented another one of his excuses as to why his hairs would be in the gloves, another story he made up on the spot—he came up with an explanation about wiping snow off Nancy Newman's car, when there was no snow.''

Reeder also addressed the issue of the stained white shirt. He testified that he asked Anthoney, ''How can you get feces on it when you're wearing it all night?'' Jurors listened as Reeder played an actual tape recording of Anthoney's absurd and incongruent explanation—that he threw the shirt on the floor when he changed into another equally dirty shirt.

The court adjourned Monday afternoon before John Salemi could begin his cross-examination. Tuesday morning, May 17, Salemi said Investigator Bill Reeder was purposefully incorrect when he suggested that Anthoney invented the Burger King story. Salemi pointed to the transcript of Anthoney's first police interview, March 15, 1987, in which Anthoney mentioned ''going to grab a bite of breakfast.'' Reeder responded by characterizing Anthoney's March 15 reference as ''ambiguous, contained no reference to Burger King, and was offered only after [we] told him his alibi was weak.'' Salemi also challenged the prosecution's assertions that Anthoney knew details of the crimes not made public. "He was questioned extensively by police," Salemi said to Reeder. "By your very questions, anybody who had any common sense could probably figure out what you were getting at."

Reeder and Salemi fought it out Monday and Tuesday; Anthoney fought in prison on Wednesday. The Cook Inlet Pre-Trial Facility superintendent, Phillip Briggs, confirmed that Anthoney was involved in a fight with another inmate on Wednesday night, May 18, 1988. Anthoney allegedly assaulted George Roberts, who sustained numerous blows, particularly kicks around the head, which resulted in blindness in one eye, as well as bruises and contusions. Ervin Hayes, another inmate, also received a kick to the head when he attempted to restrain Anthoney during the assault.

Fellow inmates constantly taunted and mocked Anthoney, calling him "Baby Killer." The more they taunted, the angrier he became, eventually erupting into outbursts of rage. The Roberts-Anthoney-Hayes fracas was the seventh documented fight involving Kirby D. Anthoney at the Cook Inlet Facility. The dates and events were as follows:

8/29/87—fight with Dean Guy

12/13/87—fight with Sherman Smith

12/16/87—elbowed LeRoy Diggs while playing basketball, causing extensive physical damage

2/08/88—fight with Ryder Tannic, and refused to be moved to another module

2/08/88—mock fighting and loud, belligerent behavior, crisis intervention used

2/09/88—escorted out of M module following inappropriate behavior, on the same day, Anthoney threatened Sergeant Whittaker.

2/11/88—threw a cup of water on inmate Fred Barry

2/17/88—fight with William Terry

2/27/88—refused to obey a direct order

5/05/88—kicked a misdemeanant offender, Sheldon Fox, when being transported between court and the institution
5/18/88—fight with George Roberts

Based on demonstrated propensity toward violent behavior, the following restrictions were put into immediate effect: "He has to remain in leg restraints during the special recreation period. He will be placed in handcuffs PRIOR to opening the door to his room by placing his hands through the security/tray slot, and will remain in handcuffs while outside his room except when taking a shower. Ankle restraints are to be applied prior to exiting his room and shall remain in place. He is restricted from ALL program activities. When escorted from the module, he shall be placed in leg restraints and a waist chain."

To avoid problems, Anthoney's jailers kept him in administrative segregation, which is prison slang for keeping someone confined in a single cell with little or no interaction with other prisoners. "He [was] allowed out for showers and phone calls," Briggs said.

Although Anthoney was no match for a larger physical aggressor, his mouth and volume were adequate for raw expletives and offensive racial slurs. News of Anthoney's interpersonal problems with people of color in an institutional environment filtered back to the prosecution, and Cheryl Chapman confirmed to Ingaldson that Anthoney was not favorably disposed toward African Americans or other ethnic minorities, except as forced laborers or temporary sex partners.

Four weeks into the trial, Ingaldson dropped an evidentiary bombshell on Buckalew's court. According to Ingaldson, the defense had convinced Kirby D. Anthoney that cooperative ejaculation could be his best shot at complete acquittal, obtained a voluntarily released semen sample from Anthoney, and sent it off to Brian Wraxall of the Serological Research Institute in California.

Wraxall, who earned fame in 1978 when Mark Stolorow and he developed the "multisystem" method for testing three isoenzyme systems simultaneously, and new methods for typing blood-serum proteins, would perform tests on the semen sample similar to those requested by the prosecution.

Wraxall, without identifying the donor, called Dr. Schanfield and informed him that he had a semen sample for testing. The two experts subsequently met in Atlanta, where they performed numerous genetic tests. Schanfield did not know the sample was Anthoney's, and early indications were that it didn't match the crime scene sample. At the tests' completion, however, the unique characteristics of Anthoney's semen were immediately apparent.

"Schanfield immediately recognized the markers as identical to the Newman homicide sample," recalled Ingaldson. "It was that obvious. Wraxall gave the results to the defense; Schanfield gave them to me."

According to Ingaldson, the tests identified a genetic factor common to 4 percent of the population, of which 7.1 percent have the same blood type as Anthoney—B secretor. "Yeah, well, if you take all of Anchorage," Salemi replied sarcastically, "that seven-point-one percent of the population could be as many as five thousand people."

One fourth of one percent of the male population, including Anthoney, has the kind of semen found at the crime scene. Defense Attorney John Salemi argued that the prosecution could not use the test results because the state couldn't establish a chain of possession. There was no way, he asserted, for the prosecution to prove the sample actually came from Anthoney. There was also the question of whether the attorney-client privilege extended to test results. The defense also challenged Schanfield's tests as experimental and not generally accepted by the scientific community, an allegation Schanfield strongly denied.

"Had the tests eliminated Anthoney, the defense would have taken a stronger pro-test stance," said Grimes, "but as it came back favorable to the prosecution, they didn't want it admitted at all. The entire semen adventure was the hottest topic for some time. If the state could use the test results, it would be like a gift from heaven."

The prosecution, however, was concluding their presentation, and there was a potential legal fight—a long one with a possibly unfavorable outcome—over the issue of attorney-client privilege. Thankfully, Anthoney also had a rare blood type making him a B secretor, and that meant Ingaldson could tie him to the semen stains by testimony from Agent Robert Hall without having to rely on Schanfield's findings. If Anthoney had a common blood type without unusual markers, Ingaldson would have had a more complex situation. One way or another, the jury would know that Kirby Anthoney's semen had specific characteristics matching semen found at the crime scene.

Agent Hall, testifying for the prosecution, confirmed that the FBI lab results showed that Anthoney had the rare B secretor blood type, directly linking him to the semen stains found at the crime scene.

Dr. Probst, who conducted the autopsy, detailed the brutal and fatal injuries of the innocent victims. Propst and Ingaldson used large color slides of the victims to illustrate the beating and bruising they suffered before and after death. A friend of Nancy Newman's in the courtroom rushed out in tears. Anthoney, who changed his seat to avoid seeing death-scene slides earlier in the trial, didn't move, but did not look up at any of the slides.

Dr. Propst told jurors that the Newmans were killed between 7 A.M. and noon on March 14. His estimate was based on many factors, including body temperature, rigor mortis, lividity caused by the settling of blood, and the drying of mucous membranes.

Propst said he found two ounces of gray-brown material in Nancy Newman's stomach, consistent with the half cup of

coffee and cream found on the kitchen table when the bodies
were discovered. Angie had "eaten cereal mixed with fruit
pears or apples shortly before her death." Melissa, eight, whose
fingerprint was found on a spoon in a bowl of oatmeal, had a
small amount of gray matter in her stomach, "consistent with
gastric juices and perhaps some digested cereal." All three
victims had empty bladders. Propst's testimony reinforced the
prosecution's assertion that the Newmans were killed after they
got up Saturday morning.

On cross-examination, John Salemi questioned Propst's estimated time of death, citing the amount of alcohol found in
Nancy Newman's blood. Earlier witnesses testified that Nancy
Newman had about four drinks at Gwennie's on Friday night.
Under normal circumstances, all traces of that amount of alcohol should have been gone from her blood by 7 A.M. the next
morning. But Nancy Newman's postmortem blood alcohol was
.093, nearly .10—the level at which a person is considered
legally drunk in Alaska.

"Decomposing bodies produce some alcohol," Propst said,
explaining her higher than expected blood alcohol content. John
Salemi did a double take. He knew from personal experience
that Propst testified in other cases that the most amount of
alcohol produced by a decomposing body is the equivalent of
two drinks. This new view was not at all what Salemi wanted
to hear.

The defense asked Dr. Propst why he changed his professional opinion, and the witness replied that he had "reexamined
the question and now accepts the conclusions of an expert who
says decomposing bodies can generate blood alcohol levels of
up to point twenty, twice the limit considered legally drunk."

Salemi pointed to the blood alcohol levels found in the bodies
of Melissa and Angie, .015 and .016. "Why are theirs so low
and Nancy's so high if they died about the same time?" Propst
replied that children have a "different biological environment,"
and that "Nancy Newman had more gut flora, which would
produce more alcohol."

Salemi made it perfectly clear that, at least to him and hopefully to the jury, Dr. Propst's estimation of the time of death was erroneous. If Nancy Newman's alcohol level was that high, she could have died Friday, March 13, not Saturday the fourteenth.

CHAPTER 14

Ingaldson had only two witnesses left to go: Jud Ray and John Newman. Ray, Buckalew ruled, could only offer his expert opinion on the range of postoffense behavior. The phrase "postoffense behavior" means how the person acted after the crime. The defense planned to trot out Kirk Mullins and his girlfriend, Deborah Dean, to testify that Anthoney was calm and relaxed when he came over to their place—behavior one does not associate with someone who has just raped and murdered. Ingaldson wanted the jury to realize that someone who does this sort of thing is going to be worn-out and fairly satisfied after three murders and two rapes—if he was going to be agitated, that would be prior to the crimes, not after.

When Ray took the stand, Ingaldson established Ray's experience and credibility on a firm foundation. He began by asking Ray's present assignment and duties.

"I'm a supervisory special agent assigned to the National Center for the Analysis of Violent Crime, and I do crime scene analysis," he answered. "Before joining the FBI, I was with the Metropolitan Police Force in Washington, DC, in 1968, and I served with that department for thirteen months. I then relocated to Columbus, Georgia, and served in the police department for just over ten years assigned as a criminal investigator, director of patrol services and training assignments. I volunteered in the United States Army in 1966, spent a tour in Vietnam, and was in the Army for three years.''

Next came the most sensitive area of testimony, and Ingaldson knew he had to stay within Judge Buckalew's guidelines. He asked Ray to explain the investigative support unit of the FBI. The two men rehearsed both the questions and answers many times, but there was no way to accurately predict the defense's cross-examination.

''Basically what we do in the Behavioral Sciences Unit at the National Center is consult with police departments throughout the country, especially when those departments are faced with violent crimes,'' explained Ray. ''What we do is take a look at the crime scene data, which is provided via photograph. We look at all the forensic results, all of the findings of toxicology, and we sort of look at crime scenes from a nonforensic view. We're looking for things like how much emotion might have been expended in a particular crime scene, we base that on the manner that wounds are appreciated on the body. We look for evidence of familiarity with the scene and the victims, and we base that upon how much they controlled the victims and how many defense wounds might be on the victims, and that sort of thing.

''Actually,'' he elaborated, ''it's really a combination of all the disciplines that we bring to bear—anthropology, sociology, a little psychology. But most of it is just criminal experience.''

Ingaldson made it clear that Ray was neither a psychiatrist nor a psychologist. The jury was informed, however, that Ray earned a bachelor's degree from Columbus College in criminal justice administration, a master's in counseling from Georgia State University, and a master's of science in criminal justice administration.

Ray also had teaching experience at the university level

running the bachelor's and master's criminal justice program at Troy State University. "I also have teaching experience at the University of Georgia [while on] an academic leave from the police department in 1975, [I] taught at the university."

Ingaldson made a slight show of looking through his notes before continuing, giving the definite impression that Ray had so much experience that he almost didn't know what to focus on next.

"How many cases have you been involved in, both in the United States and Canada, where you consulted in the area of homicides, sexual assaults, and things like that?" Ingaldson asked.

"I would say well over two thousand."

"And have you actually done some research also, or are you familiar with a book called *Sexual Homicides* by Ann Burgess?"

"Yeah," responded Ray, "I participated in the data collection and the interviewing of sexual homicide people that have been incarcerated."

Having built a platform of experience, education, dedication, and accomplishments, Ingaldson then put Ray on an impressive pedestal by drawing attention to the high-profile cases in which he participated, including the Green River Killer investigation in Seattle, Washington, and the successful prosecution of Atlanta, Georgia, serial killer Wayne Williams.

Ingaldson then moved to the Newman case specifically, eliciting testimony from Ray that he "consulted with Agent Don McMullen along with a number of people from the Anchorage Police Department, shortly after this crime was discovered."

"I read an administrative report prepared by our office in Fairbanks," said Ray, "and I've looked at pathologist reports and I've looked at crime scene photographs and videotape."

"Can you give any absolute for-sure conclusions what someone is going to do after they commit a crime such as the crime you observed in this case?" asked Ingaldson.

"No," Ray answered. Now Ingaldson and Ray were exactly

where they wanted to be—poised on the edge of the first FBI behavior-oriented testimony in American legal history.

"Of the thousands of cases you've worked on," asked Ingaldson, "have you seen cases involving the degree of violence that you found in this present case, the Kirby Anthoney case?"

"Yes, I have seen cases like that."

"Based on your personal experience in working on these cases, and interviews with perpetrators, have you ever found any cases where persons committed a crime of the degree of violence noted in this case where after the offense the person seemed calm or subdued? Have you ever seen that?"

Before Ray could answer, Howard was on his feet. "Your Honor, I have an objection as to foundation before he renders an opinion."

"I'll offer him as an expert," said Ingaldson. "Your Honor, I would offer Agent Ray as an expert in the area of behavioral analysis of sexual homicides."

"Mr. Ray is so qualified," ruled Buckalew, and Ingaldson prefaced his question before asking it again.

"Agent Ray, I don't want to go into the profile or anything like that. All I want to talk about is, after a crime scene of the nature of this, have you ever seen cases anytime where persons act calm, maybe a little depressed or subdued, something like that?"

"Well, in looking at this crime scene," answered Ray, "and that's a basis upon which my conclusions would be drawn. Yes, it's quite common in cases like this."

"Okay. Now, from looking at the crime scene, the degree of violence and so forth from a physiological standpoint, is there any type of physiological type of explanation for this?"

"I think so—" Ray began his response, but Howard's objection cut him off.

"Again, Your Honor, I have an objection. This is outside the scope of what the state's purported offer of proof was."

The judge agreed with the defense. "I don't believe this witness's expertise is this broad."

"Let me ask a few questions—foundational questions, Judge," requested Ingaldson, "and I think I'll perhaps allay those fears."

Allowed to continue, Ingaldson took another approach leading to the same conclusion. "Based on your justice degree, and based on your continuing doctoral studies, and based on the research conducted for this book on sexual homicides—does that go into expected behaviors and so forth?"

"Yes," Ray said, "that's a phase of homicide that we looked at during research."

Ingaldson, ready to pose a variation on his original question, asked, "Are you able to give an opinion as to some of the reasons why a person might be subdued after—"

The prosecutor was cut off as Craig Howard voiced strong objection.

"I'm asking if he's able to give an opinion," argued Ingaldson.

"He's not a behavioral scientist," declared Howard. "I think it is outside the offer of proof."

Judge Buckalew understood exactly what was going on, and he was not amused. "I think we resolved that matter, and this witness's testimony is going to be limited, and," said the judge to Ingaldson, "I think you've already covered it."

"Well, okay," said Ingaldson, not giving up, "I think to allay any of the court's fears, I'm not going into profiles or talking about specific—"

Howard, aggravated, was on his feet again and addressing the judge. "Your Honor, I'd ask that any argument be made outside the jury!"

"I'm not arguing," snapped Ingaldson.

"Any further statements, any comments," continued Howard, "anything, any speeches, comments, queries—"

"All right," interrupted Judge Buckalew. He then asked Ingaldson, "What other questions did you have of the witness?

I think he's already testified to the area that I found to be permissible."

The whole purpose of Ray's testimony was to establish that in his expert opinion, the person who committed these crimes would appear calm and subdued afterward. Howard did everything he could to keep Ray from saying anything more than his educational credentials and work history.

The judge decided to excuse the jury so Ingaldson could explain the question, and the three men could hear Ray's intended response.

"Agent Ray, first of all, have I gone over with you before to limit this so you don't go into profile areas and so forth, to limit your answer . . ."

"Yes."

Ingaldson asked Ray to tell the judge why the offender would be calm after a double rape and triple homicide. "On this crime scene," he explained, "there's evidence of a tremendous amount of physical energy expended—a lot of energy. It would indicate to me that in this crime scene that the individual responsible had already begun to collect himself. And I base that on, among other things, is the attempt to cleanse oneself of—"

"I don't want to get into that area," said Ingaldson, "I just want to get into the physiological aspects based on the amount of violence that you saw. Avoid going into any other area."

Ray understood, and said, "In order to control these victims in the manner that he did, and to appreciate the wounds that were there, there was a lot of energy expended both physically and psychologically. I base that on talking to people that have killed in this manner and having a few fortunate victims who have lived through these kinds of assaults."

"I guess the point I'm getting at is, if someone's expending all this energy and this rage . . . ," said Ingaldson.

". . . he'd be relaxed, flat affect, no emotion," completed Ray.

Having presented both the question and answer, Ingaldson turned to Judge Buckalew and explained that he "didn't want to get into the areas of cleaning up afterward. I guess it would break down into two parts: The first part is the amount of energy that he saw based on the crime scene, and second, the next area I want to go into is basically expending this physical energy. It's not something that is uncommon.''

Howard, unimpressed, expressed disagreement. In his view, perhaps that much energy wasn't spent in this case. "I mean, it's not like there's been fighting all over the place, and everything is tipped over," he said. "This person is not qualified to render an opinion as to how many calories you burn to do this. I don't think there is a PhD anywhere in this country who can tell you how much psychic energy or psychological energy is spent."

Concerning Agent Ray, Howard said, ''he's a police officer, he doesn't have any background, behavioral experience . . . and we're allowing him to say—their offer of proof was to say that people who kill in sexual homicides are often mellow and spent.''

Defeated, Ingaldson gave it up, saying, ''Judge, I'll withdraw that question. I'll withdraw it and I won't go into that.''

Howard wasn't done with Ingaldson yet and requested the court ''to admonish Mr. Ingaldson to not use the word 'profile' in front of the jury. Either consciously or unconsciously. He used the word 'profile' and that was the whole reason for sending the jury out so we wouldn't hear the word 'profile,' and he used the word 'profile.'. . .''

''Don't use that word,'' Buckalew admonished Ingaldson. ''All right, now what?''

Ingaldson nimbly devised another method of getting Ray's testimony accepted—asking if Ray had seen cases where people after committing these crimes had been calm or subdued. A simple yes or no, true or false, question. Ray would answer in the affirmative.

''And then I'll say,'' explained Ingaldson, ''of course that doesn't mean that everyone that's calmed or subdued that people see after that would have committed the crime, right? Right. And that's all I'm going to ask him.''

Neither Howard nor Buckalew had any problem with Ingaldson's new approach. Before calling the jury back into the courtroom, the judge had a few questions of his own for Agent Ray. "How many days you been up here in Alaska on this case?"

"Fifteen. This is my fifteenth day."

"Okay," said Buckalew. "I want him to say a few words anyway."

Both lawyers realized that Ray's "few words" could expand during cross-examination and go into previously out-of-bounds areas. Ingaldson brought the issue to Buckalew's attention, noting that "depending on what [Howard] asks, these same answers might come up."

"Well, he's an experienced lawyer," commented the judge, "if he walks into a mine field, he's doing it knowingly. All right. Are we ready for the jury?" He then turned again to Ray, asking, "Did you do any fishing or anything?"

"I went camping, and they told bear stories, and I couldn't sleep. It's been very good being here, though."

"I just kind of lose track of these FBI people," said the judge. "They come in, they're here twenty-four hours, and they're gone."

The jury was seated, Ingaldson asked his prearranged questions, and Ray answered with one yes and two no's. After waiting fifteen days to offer his historic testimony on post-offense behavior, his statement took less than twenty seconds.

Howard approached Ray, launching a cross-examination targeted at undermining Ray's credentials, and any relevance or importance of his testimony. "Although you may have taken a couple of courses in sociology and psychology," said Howard, "your real training is as a police officer, I imagine."

"Yes, pretty much," Ray agreed.

"You don't consider yourself a behavioral scientist, do you?"

Ray paused and thought it over before answering, "Not really."

"In your younger days," asked Howard, "when you were

in Vietnam, did you ever stay up all night drinking and carousing?''

"No, not drinking and carousing. I stayed up fighting and watching people.''

"Have you ever been in a situation where you've been up all night drinking? Maybe smoked marijuana and tried to stay up the whole day?''

"If I understand your question,'' responded Ray, "I have never been up drinking and smoking marijuana all night.''

"So,'' concluded Howard, "you have no idea from your own experience how you'd react. You don't know whether that could cause you to be mellow, or would cause you to be kind of spent.''

Howard then enumerated several possible behaviors a criminal may display following a sexual homicide, asking Ray if all of these diverse behaviors were possible. "So, would it be fair to say, Mr. Ray,'' asked Howard, "that although you have seen in your two thousand cases where people commit homicides may have a flat affect, or be mellow, or tired, or spent, that there is a whole continuum?''

"Yeah,'' agreed Ray haltingly, "it's just a range of behavior that exists on that continuum that one might expect to find in cases like this.''

Fortunately for the prosecution, Ingaldson was allowed redirect examination. "What I want to focus on,'' he said, "is this particular crime—the crime scene and the analysis that you did. Would it be surprising or unusual . . . for someone to act with flat affect, more subdued, or seemingly tired or depressed? Would this be unusual?''

"Like I said, I find that response most common.''

"In this type of crime,'' prompted Ingaldson.

"Yes, in this case, based on some crime scene stuff, I would think that would be a common response,'' Ray answered.

"Okay . . . let's add one other factor in there—the possibility that this crime was committed by a relative. Would that change your answer that you just gave?''

"No."

"I didn't hear the response on that last question," spoke up Howard.

"He said no."

"Okay," said Howard, "no further questions."

"May Mr. Ray go back to Washington, DC?" Buckalew asked. "He's probably been here long enough to have perfected a homestead. You may step down, Mr. Ray. Have a safe trip."

"Thank you, Your Honor," replied Ray, but he had no intention of absenting himself from the balance of the trial.

"While Ray didn't get to say everything he would have liked to," recalled Grimes, "his testimony had to have an influence. Even if Ray's testimony was of minimal impact, the historic nature of his appearance on the stand will be acknowledged for decades to come."

Agent Ray also had a salutary effect on John Newman when the two went far away from courtroom tensions and prying reporters to the calming beauty of Alaska's pristine wilderness.

"We began talking a little bit around the edges of his family life," recalled Ray, "what it was and what his life had now become. And to watch that thousand-yard stare in his eyes, I could never forget him or what he went through. He had a need to know what happened to his family in their last moments. I couldn't relate it to him just the way it was; it would have been just too painful. But I certainly understood his need. Even with what's happened to me, I cannot fully imagine what it's like for a man to lose his wife and two daughters like that. It finally touched me that the ones who loved these people, who are left here on this earth, have to live with this thing daily."

On Monday, May 23, 1988, Bill Ingaldson called the prosecution's final witness, the one with the most intense emotional impact—John Newman. Bill Reeder, Ken Spadafora, Cheryl Chapman, and Judson Ray worked with Newman over the weekend, preparing him for the ordeal. Ray taught Newman muscle-relaxing techniques and lessons in emotional control.

"Newman got some of his crying done ahead of time, because he watched the trial for a good week before he testified," recalled Grimes. "We were, of course, concerned because this fellow had a massive amount of grief and anger, and there was the possibility that he could lose it and go after Anthoney right there in the courtroom. If the outburst was severe enough, it could cause a mistrial."

Spectators filled the third-floor courtroom, and the bereaved John Newman entered wearing a gray Western-cut suit. There had been much speculation concerning Newman's emotional state and if he would be able to make it through questioning without having a breakdown.

John Salemi requested that a flip chart easel be placed between Newman and Anthoney so the two men would not see each other. The suggestion was rejected. Instead, Ingaldson stepped out from behind the podium to ask his questions so Newman could look at him without accidentally catching a glimpse of Anthoney, who was seated only two chairs away.

Clenching and unclenching his hands, John Newman spoke in a voice taut with emotion. His labored breathing, amplified over the court's sound system, added increased tension to the already highly charged courtroom atmosphere. Jurors sat rigid; spectators cried as the bereaved John Newman answered questions about what kinds of fruit Angie preferred, and if Mrs. Newman ever used his keys.

"Would Nancy ever lend your camera to someone, without checking with you first?" asked Ingaldson. The question triggered convulsive sobs, making it impossible for Newman to continue. He pulled off his glasses and tore the microphone from his lapel before hurriedly exiting. The judge called a brief recess, after which Mr. Newman finished his testimony and answered the question. "Never," Newman replied. "She wouldn't do that."

John Newman's first face-to-face encounter with the man who slaughtered his family was far more significant in terms of emotional power than in testimonial value. His appearance on the stand was calculated for impact, and to remind jurors of the devastation to this man's life—devastation resultant from Kirby D. Anthoney. After his testimony, Newman told the press, "I did it for Nancy and the girls, and I wanted to do it the best I could."

The prosecution having rested its case, Salemi and Howard had few options. They could counter many of the theories and evidence presented by the prosecution, offer alternative theories, continue raising doubts concerning time of death and the number of assailants required to kill all three members of the Newman family.

Kirby Anthoney, declared cocounsel of his own defense team in a pretrial motion, appeared increasingly cocky and self-confident. It was as if he were on *Entertainment Tonight* instead of on trial, and he gave orders to Salemi and Howard as if they were inferior lackeys working in servitude to his superior strategic insight and legal acumen. This was exactly the type of behavior expected of Anthoney by Judson Ray because it fit the psychopathic personality.

Salemi and Howard had a few things in their favor aside from the mandatory presumption of innocence and their own legal expertise. Included among them were Salemi's theory that the crime took place at night rather than morning, the newness of the scientific approach, the absence of motive beyond crazed lust, and a cleaned-up, spruced-up defendant who was related to the victims. Certain prosecution witnesses could be called for the defense, as well—individuals upon whom the attorneys could cast doubt, insinuate impure motives for damning testimony, or challenge the accuracy of their memories. Among them were Debbie Heck and Jody Cornelius. Other defense witnesses included Deborah Dean, Kirk Mullins, Tony Marinelli, and Cynthia Crowson.

Ms. Crowson, previously unmentioned in court proceedings,

lived in an Anchorage trailer park directly across the street from the Newmans, and was a baby-sitter responsible for five children per day. Crowson testified for the defense that she baby-sat Angie Newman in March 1987, "at the beginning of the school year, until John had gone down to California, and then I had Melissa, too. Angie would vary between fifty to sixty hours a week."

Crowson said she had three girls together, including Angie, so basically they would all play together at her residence. Crowson had had two female cats and each had four kittens. The defense sought confirmation that the cats scratched Angie—Anthoney's explanation as to why there would be blood drops on his shoes. He said she liked to "clomp around the house in them."

Crowson testified that Angie's interaction with the adult felines "was kind of rough, so we tried to keep her away from them. But she liked the kittens. She would play a lot with the cats when she had the opportunity. The first time she went to pick one up, she grabbed it by the tail, and she did end up with a scratch on her arm just that one time."

On cross-examination, Ingaldson asked, "What type of scratch was this?"

"Just a little welt," answered Crowson. "It didn't break the skin."

"Did it bleed?"

"No," she replied, "no, it just kind of puffed up."

"That settled that," recalled Grimes. "If it didn't break the skin, it sure didn't bleed. Salemi, of course, had a much worse problem than the cat story—there was not one shred of evidence to back up Anthoney's alibi for that crucial time period Saturday morning."

If Anthoney were his own best alibi, he would have to take the stand—a prospect unpleasant to the defense, and an opportunity for the prosecution. If Anthoney firmly believed he could do himself more good than harm, he would waive his constitutional right against self-incrimination and put himself on the stand. "He won't be able to keep himself off," predicted Cheryl Chapman, and she was absolutely correct.

CHAPTER 15

On Wednesday, May 25, 1988, Kirby D. Anthoney, against the best advice of John Salemi, took the witness stand in his own defense. His lawyers strongly urged that he at least exercise extreme caution when answering all questions. There was the danger that he could open the door to otherwise inadmissible information, thus ruining their defense. If Anthoney claimed to be a peaceful man who would never hurt anyone, Ingaldson might be allowed to rebut such assertions with information about his Idaho felony conviction for Macing an old woman in a wheelchair, and the other assault charges in his past.

On the stand, Anthoney sobbed, cried, and insisted that he had nothing to do with the murders. This was his chance to convince the jury of his innocence, and he was going to play it for all it was worth. Jud Ray, aware of the problems Anthoney had been having with his black fellow prisoners, came up with a sly plan—get Debbie Heck to sit next to him in the courtroom. "My strategy was to get his attention," Ray explained, "and once I got his attention, I began to lean over and whisper things about the trial to her, asking her what she thought of him. And each time I did something like this, I would get closer and closer.'' Ray put his hand on the back of the bench to make it look as if he were hugging her. His goal was to increase Anthoney's on-stand discomfort. Whether this was effective or not is open to debate—for whatever reasons, Anthoney appeared a nervous wreck.

"Are you feeling a little nervous?" Salemi asked. Anthoney wiped tears from his eyes as his lawyer began a series of innocuous questions covering Heck and Anthoney's trip to Alaska in 1985, his work experience, job search, the breakup in Dutch Harbor, and why he left the *Arctic Enterprise*. "I made the decision that I wanted to leave," Anthoney explained, "but the employers had asked me to leave, but I had already made a decision to leave. It was difficult, a difficult situation," Anthoney said of the breakup, admitting that he was angry, depressed, and hurt, but not overly distraught. "It wasn't easy, but I accepted it."

On the topic of leaving the Newman residence after returning from Dutch Harbor, "it was just an uncomfortable tension I felt with myself, and that's why I initiated the move. I didn't want to be a burden on Nancy. I thought that's what I was." Salemi also had Anthoney explain why he continued showering at the Newman apartment after moving out. The answer, according to Anthoney, was that he didn't want his new roommate, Dan Grant, to get body lice. This was his way of offering a "simple explanation" for the presence of incriminating evidence on the washrag found in the Newman bathroom—a washrag containing his pubic hair and possible traces of his semen.

The prosecution team, including investigator Bill Reeder, took copious notes while Anthoney spoke. Seemingly making things up as he went along, he testified to things that had never been mentioned previously. For those familiar with Anthoney, his performance was, in a strange way, morbidly fascinating.

"It was as if he believed that he could just talk his way out of this," recalled Bill Reeder. "Of course, the cleaned-up, tearful gentleman the jury saw was not the same Kirby Anthoney I had to deal with. Then again, Debbie Heck told us that Anthoney would always lie to cover his ass. For him, lying is like an addiction.''

What Reeder perceived as a total disregard for the truth is one symptom of the sociopath, and most certainly, the psychopath—an individual whose behavior is characterized by consistently violating the rights of others, engaging in repeated assaults, and manifesting continual dishonesty.

According to Dr. Steve Rubin, ''it's a question of how accurate you want the description to be. We now call sociopath, 'antisocial,' but in the next nomenclature there will be 'psychopath.' This is a fraction—ten to twenty percent—of the criminal population, and it is different. Most were abused or neglected as children, or had role models who were psychopaths. They are egocentric, impulsive, irresponsible, emotionally shallow; lack empathy, guilt, or remorse; are manipulative; and are pathological liars.''

Although parental neglect and abuse contribute to behavioral problems, including criminal offenses, psychopaths can also come from healthy, stable, loving families, according to Dr. Robert Hare.

''It is true that some psychopaths were characterized by deprivation and physical abuse in childhood,'' explained Dr. Hare, ''but for every adult psychopath with a tragic upbringing, there is another whose family was apparently warm and nurturing, where the other children grew up as normal, conscientious people.''

''Most people who had a horrible childhood do not become psychopaths or killers,'' said Dr. Rubin, an expert on treating juvenile sex offenders. ''There are deeper and more elusive explanations for this most dangerous and disturbing condition.''

Anthoney's fellow attendees at the Mullinses' Friday night party of dice rolling and coke snorting may have also experienced unpleasant upbringings, but they didn't rape and murder anyone Saturday morning. Were dice, drugs, videos, or music the catalyst of this shocking crime, the entire city of Anchorage would have been awash in blood long ago.

Appearing clean-cut, meek, and tearful, Kirby Anthoney seemed neither dangerous nor disturbing while answering Salemi's questions, accounting for his time and deeds. Testifying under oath, Anthoney insisted that on the Thursday prior to the murders, Nancy Newman loaned him John's camera and gave him $20 in change from her coin tin. "I believe I'm the one who reached inside the tin and got it out," offered Anthoney. "A lot of people don't know that I had permission to be in that tin can."

"Was this loose change or was it rolled up?" asked Salemi, referring to the coins in Newman's tip tin. "Do you remember?" Anthoney affirmed that it was all loose change and that Nancy Newman had also allowed him to take some paper for rolling coins.

"As of March twelfth, 1987—the Thursday before the homicides—did you still have personal belongings in the Newman apartment?"

"Yes, I did," responded Anthoney, "it was just my little blue duffel bag that had some of my personal hygienes in it." Salemi then asked him if, on the Thursday before the murders, he did anything with respect to his personal belongings at the Newmans' place. "Yes, I did. I retrieved them—a blue duffel bag [containing] a hair blower, tape measure, some scissors, and some shaving cream, a couple of washrags possibly."

"Do you have any idea," asked Salemi, "what time you might have left Mrs. Newman's apartment on Thursday, March twelfth?"

"It would have been afternoon," stated Anthoney with confidence, "the afternoon sometime." This contradicted his original statements to police in which he insisted that he retrieved his bag from the Newmans' the prior weekend. Subsequently, Anthoney changed his story, insisting that he went to the Newmans' on Thursday night. Now, on the stand, he was altering his story once again. Under oath, Anthoney also said that on the same Thursday, Matt Mulherin came by his house and saw him rolling the coins he'd recently received from Nancy Newman. "I was putting coins in wrappers," acknowledged Anthoney, "the ones that I received from Nancy Newman."

On the further topic of John Newman's camera, Anthoney claimed that his next-door neighbor, Jess O'Dell, saw Newman's camera at Anthoney's home the Friday before the murders. "He came by several times to collect money," testified Anthoney. "I owed him eighty dollars for marijuana that he sold me. He came in the house and asked me if I had any money. At first I told him no. And then he was persistent about it, so I went in and I gave him portions of the coins that I had."

"Did Mr. O'Dell ever see that camera while it was at your house or in your possession?" Salemi asked. "Would it be before or after the homicides?"

"It was before—it was Friday," explained Anthoney. "When he came into the house, he asked me if I had any money for him, and I told him no. And he was persistent. So, I gave him the money that I had. Some of it, anyway. And he was by the doorway going into the hall, and he seen the camera sitting on my bed, and he asked me what it was. And he followed me into my room, and I just told him it was a camera. And he asked me if he could look at it. It was like he had some interest in it. And I let him pull it out and he inspected it, and he asked me if it was stolen. And I said, no, it's not. And he asked me how much I wanted for it, and I said, I can't sell it, it's not even my camera."

Salemi then asked his client if on the same day, prior to the homicides, he went to the bank. "Yes, Friday I went to the bank to get money because I gave Jess O'Dell what I had."

Under Salemi's guidance, Anthony recounted the Friday-night party, his Saturday-morning wake-up of Dan Grant, breakfast at Burger King, and his initial difficulty accounting for his Saturday-morning activities. Salemi methodically, almost hour by hour, had Anthoney account for his exact whereabouts and activities from the Friday-night party up to the morning wake-up visit from the Anchorage police. Anthoney acknowledged being hung over and confused when first questioned, but insisted he did everything possible to cooperate.

"I think you have to understand the pressure I was under at the time," said Anthoney. "It was a difficult situation. The police were being very hard at times. I had a lot of thoughts of my family on my mind. It was very difficult. I just couldn't remember everything that was being said even at times. It was difficult to remember days that I had done things. They started accusing me, saying I had a weak alibi."

Anthoney readily admitted lying to police during their first interview. Specifically, he explained why he was untruthful concerning drug use at the Friday-night party. "I wouldn't classify it as a party," Anthoney said. "It was just that I was coming over to visit a friend and other people showed up at the time and we visited during the night. It started out just Jeff and I. Next came Sissy Altman and then one other gentleman by the name of Mark. Jeff Mullins and I, when I first arrived, we sat around and drank a couple of beers, and I believe we watched TV, and we were sitting on the puff pillow—I was sitting on the puff pillow when Sissy arrived. When she arrived, we started to play dice. The police officers asked me about cocaine. It is illegal and I didn't want to get anybody in trouble, including myself. It was difficult for me to talk to them about it for the simple fact that I didn't trust them. The way they were approaching me on it, I felt that they may be interested in the people that I had done it with that night. Later, when I learned that the people that I was with that night conceded to the police that they had done it, I was off the hook. I didn't have to worry about getting them in trouble."

Salemi prompted Anthoney for his version of how the police gained possession of John Newman's camera. "I opened all my cupboards for them," recalled Anthoney, "and I think Mr. Spadafora asked me if I had anything that's John and Nancy's and I said, 'This is John and Nancy's,' and I reached up and handed it to Mr. Spadafora.''

Salemi then asked his client about spending Saturday with Kirk Mullins and Mullins's girlfriend, Deborah Dean—a day filled with multiple loads of laundry. Anthoney acknowledged the small stain on his shirt, the result of dog or cat manure. The stain was acquired, he insisted, when he took off his shirt and put it on the floor while he was putting on another dirty shirt before doing laundry. Anthoney then testified that he called the Newmans at least fifteen times over the course of the day. Salemi asked Anthoney to detail his actions Saturday evening, beginning with his return home from the Mullins residence.

''I received a couple phone calls,'' said Anthoney. ''Jody called me . . . Jody Cornelius. The purpose of it was so she could get out of the house. It really wasn't a conversation the first time she called. She was, like, she was talking to somebody else on the phone. She was—I couldn't make sense of it. She was talking, 'Oh, you're going to the dance,' and I'm going, 'What do you mean?' And she goes, 'Oh, I wish I could go,' and I said 'What are you trying to do, Jody, are you trying to play a game on your parents?' And she goes, 'Yeah,' and I said, 'Oh, you want to go to the dance and you're not able to get there. . . .' And I say, 'If you can get out, I'll take you wherever you want to go.' ''

Anthoney testified that he already had plans for the evening—a date with Rose Santos. He simply altered his itinerary to first pick up Jody, then Rose, and drop Jody off before proceeding to Kirk and Debbie's house. Neither Salemi nor the jury held any great interest in Anthoney's recreational plans for the evening, but Jody Cornelius lived in the same apartment complex as Nancy Newman, baby-sat for the Newmans, and claimed to have vacuumed Nancy Newman's apartment on Friday.

Anthoney testified that between 7:30 P.M. and 8 P.M., he pulled his flatbed truck into the parking lot of the Newmans' Eide Street apartment, parking in front of the Newmans' window. He went upstairs to the Cornelius apartment, stayed for about ten minutes waiting for Jody to get ready, and then accompanied her down the stairs and into the truck.

"Since you had been trying to get hold of Mrs. Newman at various times of the day," asked Salemi, "did you try to do anything with respect to continuing to get hold of her once you were at the apartment itself?"

"Well, when I first pulled in," Anthoney replied, "I realized her car wasn't there and the lights were out, the curtains were pulled shut. So, I came to the assumption that she wasn't there. And then when I was coming back down from Jody Cornelius's apartment, I figured that maybe there was a possibility Nancy had pulled in while I was upstairs and I didn't hear her car because it was a fairly quiet car. And normally what I would do is just if I was going into Nancy's apartment, was just knock on the door to announce myself and check the handle. If it was unlocked, then I would open it and go in. If it wasn't, then I would just wait for somebody to come to the door."

Anthoney further asserted that Jody Cornelius had no intention of attending a dance—her actual destination was some fellow's house in another part of town. When the two went to pick up Rose Santos, the woman pleaded exhaustion and canceled her date with Anthoney. From there, the two drove to Cornelius's friend's house on DeArmoun Road. Dropping her off, he told Jody to call him if she needed a ride.

Had Cornelius depended upon Anthoney, she would have been seriously disappointed. Canceling the preplanned get-together with Mullins, he and Dan Grant went to Chilkoot Charlie's for dancing, drinking, and socializing. When it closed at 3:30 A.M., Grant and Anthoney went home and went to bed.

Salemi then turned attention to Anthoney's alleged "flight" for the border and his relationship with the police. "Did you ever discuss with them," he asked, "your plans with respect to either staying or leaving—staying in or leaving Alaska?"

"I told them all the time that I wanted to leave," insisted Anthoney. "I told the officers fairly early in the investigation that I was wishing to leave. I was accused of not cooperating with them, but I stayed. I did everything possibly I could. And then some. When [I] finally became tired of it, I almost insisted that I was leaving. I told them that I was leaving and where I was going. Mr. Reeder was being evasive to me. And I knew that. And I knew why. I wanted my clothes and I wanted to leave. Mr. Reeder thought I did this, he wanted to arrest me. It wasn't something that I wasn't aware of because I was. But yet I contacted them and I made arrangements to go down and to talk to him about evidence that they say they had coming in, or they had come in. Evidence that we had discussed prior to this. I'd called him one morning early, and I had told him that I wanted to leave. I told him that I would be leaving. I didn't know if I would be leaving off the top of my head, when it would be, but I wanted to leave. I said I might stay around until Debbie got back off the boat. [Reeder] told me to call him, so I did. We made arrangements to meet each other at two-thirty that day. First I told him that I wasn't coming down. I was tired of it, and he talked me into coming down. I called and left a message that I would be working on a friend's truck, and I told them exactly where I would be. I said I'd be on the same side of the street I lived on, about five houses down. I'd be happy to talk with them, and I seen officers drive by a couple times, but nobody ever stopped. In my mind, it wasn't too major. If they told me they wanted to talk to me so bad, but yet they knew where I was and they drove by, but they didn't stop.''

Salemi made it clear that his client didn't take off suddenly in the middle of the night, that his flatbed truck was not in some secret place, that he didn't try to make airline reservations under a false name, or any other clandestine activity. Through questioning, Salemi brought out that Anthoney prepared for his trip by securing $300 and two gas credit cards from his mother in Idaho, and that he said good-bye to at least some of his friends before leaving, only excluding Tony Marinelli, to whom he owed money.

"I went to Kirk and Debbie's house," stated Anthoney. "I stopped by Jeff's. He didn't answer his door. He was a friend of mine. I did want to say good-bye. It's not my fault he didn't answer his door. The only person who didn't know I was leaving was Tony Marinelli, and I concede that there was no conversation with Tony about me leaving. That doesn't mean I wouldn't pay him. I visited with Kirk and Debbie for approximately an hour maybe before I actually did leave town," Anthoney elaborated, "but before I did, I stopped and I had a tire changed. I changed my left front tire, and that's because I had been out with my four-wheel drive, some of the tread came off my tire, and it wasn't able to make the trip. So, I obtained a tire and it's called a LT fifteen. A fairly large tire. And that morning I stopped and changed the tire on my truck, and I helped the man do that. And that's how some of my clothes became dirty at that point. Then I proceeded out of town. I thought it was going to be a pretty nice trip. It was when I came up, and I figured it would be going down. Well, I got to the border and it didn't turn out that it was going to be a nice trip at all. I was turned around by the Canadian police because they said I had a suspended license. I couldn't believe what they were saying!"

Following his arrest, Anthoney wrote copious letters to several people, discussing the case in detail. Salemi asked him why he sent letters such as those, and why he speculated in writing about specific aspects of the case.

"Basically because of the fact that everybody was being told that I was guilty," he answered, "that I had done it . . . even my mother . . . and I wanted them to know everything as it was for facts instead of opinions and misrepresentations . . . nor is there any indication in anything I've ever written about my guilt because I am not guilty."

At last, Salemi asked the core questions. "Did you sexually assault Nancy Newman and Melissa Newman? Did you murder your aunt Nancy or your cousins Melissa or Angie? Were you ever in the Newman apartment on either Friday, March thirteenth, 1987, or Saturday, March fourteenth, 1987?''

Kirby D. Anthoney answered no to all of the above; Salemi had no further questions.

Kirby D. Anthoney not only had a problem keeping his mouth shut in court, he was equally expressive behind bars. During his overnight stays in jail, Anthoney confessed to fellow inmate Keith Hayes that he killed Walter Napageak. One of Detective Spadafora's calculated insults served as catalyst. ''I would say things on purpose to get a rise out of him,'' said Spadafora. ''I would ask him how it felt to kill a two-year old, and other similar offensive remarks. None of those comments elicited any response—no show of anger, nothing. Then one day I got on the topic of Walter Napageak and the unsolved car wash murder—how it was obviously a sex-related homicide. Anthoney was in the backseat with Reeder, and I was driving. I looked at Anthoney in the rearview mirror and said, 'So, tell me, how was it getting a blow job from a faggot?' He knew immediately what I was talking about, and he just turned crimson with anger. With all his Mr. Macho posturing, he couldn't stand anyone thinking or knowing he'd had sex with Walter. Being called gay was worse to him than being called baby killer.''

Back in the Cook Inlet Pre-Trial Facility, Anthoney immediately told his cellmate, Keith Hayes, that the police got the car wash murder all wrong—it absolutely was *not* sex related. ''Anthoney gave Hayes, also a sexual offender, an earful of gory details about how he killed Napageak and dumped the body,'' said Spadafora, ''and he told Hayes that it was about drugs, not sex. Hayes called the police and said, 'I have some information.' We, in turn, referred him to Bill Ingaldson.''

''Once we talked to him,'' recalled Ingaldson, ''he told us

not as much information about the Newman murders, but about several conversations he had with Kirby Anthoney about the murder at the car wash.''

According to Hayes, Anthoney said he beat Napageak to death with a welding torch, cleaned up the blood using the car wash equipment, put the battered corpse in a wheelbarrow, pushed it to a nearby lot, and dumped it. The wheelbarrow left a telltale single track in the snow.

''The case against Anthoney in the Napageak murder was strong enough to take to trial,'' said Grimes. ''There was a ninety percent match to Anthoney on hair samples found and saved from Napageak's body. Of course, if he was going to be found guilty in the Newman homicides, there was no reason to go through a trial on the Napageak case. Ingaldson, however, could certainly bring it up during the sentencing phase if the jury brought back guilty verdicts.''

Anthoney also mentioned the car wash murder to his brother in Twin Falls and one of his buddies from back home. Neither, according to Grimes, was favorably impressed.

''I also strongly suspect that Anthoney murdered a weak, sickly young native girl named Donna Steve,'' Grimes said. ''Her body was found in the Echo Lake area, and it had been out there about a month before we found her. She frequented the same part of town—Fourth Avenue, the Hub Bar—as Walter Napageak. She was sexually violated and also found stripped from the waist down like Napageak and the Newmans. She was tied in almost a 'torture-tie.' She was very unhealthy to begin with. The poor girl only had one lung. We don't know for sure if she was strangled, but she was tied up with what looked like parachute cord. She actually may have died from compression suffocation—she was so frail that when he tied her up, her elbows touched each other. If Anthoney did this, which I believe is most likely, it fits in with his history of violent crimes against the weak. There were some hairs found on her body, and once we had Anthoney's samples, we had the crime lab take a look. What we got back from them essentially said that while they were markedly similar to Anthoney's, they were too decomposed to say for sure. We couldn't prove Anthoney murdered Donna Steve, but I have a very strong personal suspicion that Anthoney was involved in her death.''

CHAPTER 16

Following his May 25 testimony, court recessed. Anthoney and his lawyers adjourned to an anteroom for consultation. Emerging ten minutes later, the lawyers approached the bench. Salemi whispered to Ingaldson, "I can't keep this guy off the stand."

For Bill Ingaldson, having Kirby Anthoney on the witness stand was an answered prayer, a marvelous opportunity, and if all went well, a defining moment for the prosecution. In preparation for the cross-examination, Ingaldson consulted at length with Jud Ray and the FBI's experts at Quantico. They advised him to find something for the defendant to touch or handle—something insignificant to an innocent person, but significant if one were guilty. Ingaldson had the perfect object—John Newman's camera.

Ingaldson's plan was to start off slowly, keep his distance, and not be aggressive. "I want Anthoney's confidence to keep rising," Ingaldson told Reeder. "I want him to think he's winning." Little by little, Ingaldson intended to move in closer and closer, gradually becoming intrusive and focusing on Anthoney's inconsistencies.

Ingaldson began almost blandly, asking about how it was that Heck and he came to live with the Newmans. "This was Nancy's suggestion, that you move in with her?"

"Well, I went over to her house," Anthoney explained, "and we were just sitting and talking. I had told her that this man that I was staying with, Jeff Mullins, had a lot of people in and out of his house and was doing cocaine. And she said, 'Well, you ought to stay here.' More or less a motherly type figure. That she wanted me away from him."

Ingaldson prompted the defendant for details of his loan arrangement with Tony Marinelli, the man from whom he was buying his truck. "It was legally done," said Anthoney, "but it was fairly informal. About a week and a half before I was even supposed to make the first payment to him, I told him beforehand that I didn't think I'd be able to—[for him to] come get the truck. And he says no. He says, 'I'll work with you on this.' "

"Was part of the agreement that you could leave the state with the truck without paying for it?" asked Ingaldson.

"There was no discussion about it, no," stated Anthoney.

With no transitional remarks, Ingaldson then asked Anthoney about his love of photography. "Let's talk a little bit about your interest in cameras and interest in taking pictures. You say that after you got to Anchorage, you took hundreds of pictures and you have a real interest in taking pictures."

"Yes, we have a stack of pictures," said Anthoney, who also characterized himself as a camera "fanatic."

"Being the camera fanatic that you are, can you explain to me why you didn't want to take your camera with you on the boat?"

"Well, sir," answered Anthoney, "it was a combination between Debbie's and my decision to put them in storage. As a matter of fact, I think we had an argument about it." He explained to Ingaldson that his cameras were placed in storage prior to moving in with the Newmans, and before he and Heck went out on the boat.

"So you didn't have your camera with you to take some pictures over the Christmas holidays?"

"We talked about it and we kind of told each other it was stupid, that we should have, but we didn't," acknowledged Anthoney.

Ingaldson paused for a moment, then stepped slightly closer. "That one camera is a pretty—kind of an automatic thirty-five millimeter, automatic flash and everything, isn't it? And it's pretty compact, wouldn't you say? Now, you had never been out to the Aleutian Chain before, had you, when you went out fishing? And didn't you say that you thought that would be kind of an adventure? And it would be kind of nice to take some pictures to commemorate that event, wouldn't it?"

Anthoney, anticipating where Ingaldson was headed, cut him off at the theoretical pass by answering, "That's why we borrowed a camera while we were out there—one of those that develops the picture right in the camera—a Polaroid."

Ingaldson turned the topic back to one specific camera. He asked for Anthoney to clarify once again exactly when and why he asked Nancy Newman to loan him John's new 35mm camera.

"If I'd had my cameras," he said, "I probably wouldn't have borrowed it. But since I didn't have my camera, the interest I had would have drawn me to that camera because of the telephonic lens." He meant "telephoto lens," but Ingaldson carefully avoided correcting him. "Basically, I wanted to go four-wheeling and I wanted to go with Kirk and Jeff," Anthoney continued. "We had priorly [*sic*] discussed going to Alyeska and it never came through. But there were lots of times that we were four-wheeling with our trucks. Myself and our friends. And I wanted to take some pictures, and I would like to have sent some to Debbie," said Anthoney, adding that Nancy came over to his house on the Wednesday prior to the murders.

"I believe it was Wednesday morning when she came to the house because she was interested in what we were doing that morning, and I said I was going to Alyeska."

Ingaldson reminded Anthoney that one reason given for borrowing the camera was to take pictures down the highway to Alyeska. Why, then, did Anthoney not borrow the camera that Wednesday morning?

"Oh," Anthoney promptly explained, "that was for the weekend that we were going to go back. We had discussed it, but it didn't work out."

Anthoney insisted that Nancy Newman loaned him John's camera the very next day, Thursday, March 12. Ingaldson then produced exhibit 69, John Newman's 35mm camera, asking, "When you take pictures with this camera, what do you have to do? How do you work it?"

"You just push the button right here if it's loaded," Anthoney answered.

"And it loads the film?"

"It automatically loads it, yes."

"How about this?" Ingaldson toyed with an attachment.

"I don't know," admitted Anthoney, "I've never used it before."

Ingaldson moved in closer; Anthoney became increasingly nervous. "Does this have an aperture on it?" asked the prosecutor.

"It's basically your film right here is . . . that's basically what you want to—for your light adjustment and such. And this right here is for the atmosphere. Which is the sun, and the clouds, and basically close up."

"Do you know what an aperture is, or what it means?"

"No, not really," confessed Anthoney, who also admitted not knowing the meaning of an F stop. Ingaldson handed Anthoney the camera, asking him to demonstrate how to take pictures with it.

"Well," Anthoney stumbled, "John basically just showed me one time, and I think he showed me how to adjust this here to get really close. He was experimenting with me, showing me that he could get really close, and that's what drew my attention to this because our trucks are usually in the distance when you're four-wheeling, and you can't get a good shot. And I have some pictures of that—'' Ingaldson interrupted him, pressing him harder for a demonstration.

"Why don't you tell me, with that camera, if you had a roll of film, what you'd have to do. What settings you'd have to make and how you would use it.''

Anthoney held the camera with trembling hands and said softly, "I wouldn't know how to adjust these . . . I . . . what I would assume would—''

"What are you pointing to?'' asked Ingaldson pointedly.

"These adjustments here . . . what I would assume . . .''

"What are those?''

"I don't know . . . I would assume that John would have had these set to where it would take a picture fairly clear.''

"With any type of film?'' Ingaldson asked.

"I . . . well, uh . . . no. I would judge the film by what I was out—what kind of atmosphere that day.''

Ingaldson was now leaning right into him, pointing and playing with the camera. "Do you know what this is—these different knobs are here?''

"Uh, you just go like this and you can distance—if you get your close-up and focus, and I believe this—you close focus here, and then this—''

Ingaldson began turning a knob that made a clicking sound. "What's that clicking? There's some numbers on it—twenty-two, sixteen, eleven . . . and this thing here on the left of it, it has ASA and some different numbers. Do you know what that is?''

Anthoney didn't know, but offered that no doubt John Newman had the controls set to where "it would take a fairly decent picture.'' Ingaldson sighed, backed off, and asked another question. "Mr. Anthoney, isn't the truth of the matter, then, [is] you don't know anything at all about this camera?''

"Yes, I do," objected Anthoney, "somewhat. But not all, no."

"And you have no idea how to take a picture with that camera," asserted Ingaldson.

"If you want to put film in it right now, Mr. Ingaldson, and develop it, I'd almost guarantee you that I could take a picture with it."

"Well, maybe we'll do that next," said Ingaldson.

"I hope you do," countered Anthoney testily.

"So," summarized Ingaldson, "instead of . . . getting your own cameras, you'd borrow a camera that you know nothing about, don't know how to work it or anything. Is that what you're—"

"No," Anthoney interrupted. "I knew a limited amount about it, but I believed I could take a picture. And I still do, and if you want to put film in it, I'll show you."

"You testified, or at least implied," said Ingaldson, "that you got along fairly well with John Newman, had respect for his family and his wishes, and his desires and things like that."

"I had a lot of . . . I have a lot of respect for John," concurred Anthoney.

"And you knew John wouldn't want people to borrow that camera, is that right?"

"He was very possessive with them, yes."

"But you would kind of go behind his back and . . ."

"No," insisted Anthoney. "I didn't go behind his back. Nancy is the one who said don't tell John, he'll have a shit fit."

"Well, if Nancy did say that," countered Ingaldson, "wouldn't that make you hesitate a little bit to borrow John's camera?"

Had Ingaldson scripted Anthoney's response, it couldn't have been more damaging for the defense. "No," answered Kirby Anthoney sharply, "it's her marriage."

Ingaldson took away the camera and switched to the topics of pubic lice and Anthoney's insistence that he continued showering at the Newman residence even after moving out.

"When did you get this pubic lice, do you think?"

"I contracted them from Brian Richardson," said Anthoney. Ingaldson did not request clarification regarding the means of contraction. "That would have been in November 1986. . . ." Anthoney further stated that he didn't think he had the lice nonstop through March because he had been treating it. He did acknowledge infestation after he got off the boat.

"You heard Debbie Heck testify, didn't you? And you heard her say that she never got pubic lice, didn't you?"

"She had them, and the reason—"

"She was lying about that?" Ingaldson interrupted harshly.

"No. She wasn't aware of it—I didn't want her to be embarrassed by it and that's why I placed [Rid] in the shampoo . . . and I was successful in ridding her of it. If she doesn't have them, then I guess it was successful, wasn't it?"

Ingaldson handed Anthoney plaintiff's exhibit #142—a bottle of Rid—and asked him to read the directions.

"Shake well. Apply undiluted Rid to dry hair and scalp, or any other infested areas, and wet entirely," read Anthoney. "Do not use on eyelashes or eyebrows. Allow Rid to remain on area for 10 minutes, but no longer. Dead lice and eggs should be removed with special comb provided. Retreatment: repeat in seven to ten days. Do not exceed two consecutive applications within twenty-four hours."

Ingaldson took the bottle back from Anthoney and looked at the label. "It says apply undiluted, doesn't it?"

"Yes, it does," acknowledged Anthoney.

"I guess it just happened to work on Debbie Heck mixed in with the shampoo?"

"Well," insisted Anthoney, "there's no other explanation as to how she was free of them."

"Unless she never had them," Ingaldson countered.

"She had them," said Anthoney forcefully.

Ingaldson reminded Anthoney that Heck went to the doctor for treatment of a vaginal infection. Anthoney reminded the prosecutor that Heck "never went to the doctor to have the lice checked."

"Why wouldn't this doctor notice it?" queried Ingaldson.

"Well," answered Anthoney confidently, "I don't know if the doctor normally gets that close to look."

"Could you explain to me," asked Ingaldson, "why you'd be so concerned about Dan Grant getting pubic lice, but you wouldn't be concerned about your aunt and your two cousins getting pubic lice?"

"I was taking very extreme cautions at the house. I was cleaning myself with that stuff quite often to insure I didn't have it," Anthoney explained. He described how he always used his own towels and washcloths as an extra measure of protection for Nancy and the children, then added, " I didn't want to use Dan Grant's shower because it was filthy until I cleaned it."

"When did you clean it?"

"I think a few days after I moved in."

"And you didn't want him to get pubic lice . . . ," Ingaldson reminded Anthoney.

"Yeah, that was part of it. I wasn't sure if I was rid of them or not."

"Do you remember from the time of the murders back when the most recent time you'd taken a shower at Nancy's was?"

"I think it would have been the weekend before. March seventh or eighth, that weekend."

Ingaldson circled for the kill, asking, "When is the first time you took a shower at Dan's house?"

"After I moved in, after I cleaned the shower."

Anthoney had just testified that he moved into Grant's during the first three days of March, a full week before his supposed shower at the Newmans'.

"So this thing about the shower being dirty had nothing to do with where you take a shower, right?"

"Well, yes, it did," said Anthoney, "because if it was

cleaned, I would have gotten into it more than likely, but I didn't care to because it was really filthy."

"Up until the murders, how many times did you take showers at Dan's house?"

"After I cleaned it, probably every day."

"But you'd still go over to Nancy's and take showers now and then?" asked Ingaldson.

"No, that was after I cleaned it. I stopped going to Nancy's after I cleaned it, I believe."

"March seventh or eighth is after March first, second, or third, isn't it?"

"That's what I'm saying," sputtered an exasperated Anthoney. "I—I was clarifying that it could have been the weekend, it could have been Friday or Saturday, or the day she was off."

"I'm getting a little confused," said Ingaldson patiently. "I thought you took showers at Nancy's anyway. You kept on taking them there. And now you're saying that, well, that's not quite true?"

"No, I'm not saying that," countered the flustered Anthoney.

"So," clarified Ingaldson, contrasting Anthoney's previous assertion that the reason he showered at Nancy's was to avoid giving lice to Grant with his new explanation of Grant's shower being too dirty to use, "giving pubic lice to Dan Grant, now isn't the reason after all?"

Anthoney, thoroughly confused, attempted explaining the inconsistency between his two statements, but Ingaldson was already advancing toward his primary point of concern.

"The washcloth found in the bathroom sink—it had a pubic hair that Agent Deedrick said he matched as having the same characteristics as yours that had pubic lice on it, did he not? Do you have any reason to doubt that that's your pubic hair?"

"No, I do not," said Anthoney.

"I guess you weren't being that careful with that washcloth," offered Ingaldson, referring to Anthoney's insistence upon "very extreme cautions."

"I don't know why it would still be left in there," responded

Anthoney. Ingaldson, turning to transcripts of the defendant's police interviews, pointed out that Anthoney previously told investigators that his pubic hairs might be on that washcloth because he used those washcloths all the time. Everyone would use the same washcloths, according to Anthoney, and Nancy would leave the washcloth in the shower. He told police that he probably used it the weekend before. For some unknown reason, the washcloth with his pubic hair on it was wadded up in the sink.

"I guess you just screwed up this time and forgot to take that one and wash it," said Ingaldson dryly. "Were you pretty careful about the sheets on Melissa's bed, too? About the pubic lice?"

"I believe that the sheets that I was sleeping in was the same ones the whole period of time that I was there."

"And when you moved out, I imagine with this great concern that you took those sheets and immediately washed them so Melissa wouldn't get body lice."

"No, I did not," admitted Anthoney. "I went in there and shook them off, I believe, or I wiped them; brushed them off, I believe, is what I had done."

"You brushed them off?"

"I could have, yes."

"Well, tell me how you brushed them off."

"I don't know. I said I might have, and if I had of . . ."

"You don't remember if you did?"

"No, I don't."

"But you didn't bother washing those like you did the washcloths or towels, right?"

"No, but I was concerned about it because when I came back into the house, I seen that—I believed that they were the same sheets, and that's what I told the police officers. That I felt that they were the same sheets."

"Why did you think they were the same sheets," asked Ingaldson.

"Because of the color and the smell of them."

"Are you pretty good at telling the difference between sheets by their smell?"

Again, Anthoney's inability to make sense undermined his credibility. Ingaldson then tied Anthoney in another verbal knot concerning his knowledge of who was stabbed and who was assaulted, and his precognitive telephone statements to Carol Hawkins.

"Of course, at this point in time," Anthoney confirmed, "I wouldn't have any knowledge of that. I do know what I did tell Mrs. Hawkins. I don't believe an officer is going to ask you for your pubic hairs just to do it. Nor do I believe they're going to ask you if you own a knife just to do it. And I did tell Mrs. Hawkins that I believed that is what happened. She subsequently the next day became informed by newspapers in her hometown in Twin Falls, Idaho, that somebody indeed was sexually assaulted, and somebody was stabbed."

"All that you'd heard was that one of them had been sexually assaulted, right?" asked Ingaldson.

"I don't know," responded Anthoney tentatively. "I think I had finally been told that both of them had. At some point in time somewhere, I think I had."

"By who?"

"I don't know. There was just too many people talking about it."

"Well, were you told who was sexually assaulted?"

"Excuse me?" Anthoney had trouble comprehending the direct question.

Ingaldson simply repeated the question, and Anthoney hedged his answer of no, by adding, "But it's not hard to figure out. If Angie's the one who is stabbed, that only leaves two to be sexually assaulted."

"You mean someone can't be sexually assaulted *and* stabbed?"

"Well, that's what I'm saying, is that I drew the conclusion that it was the other two because if Angie was stabbed and somebody said that's all that happened to her, that's what I would have concluded.''

Ingaldson was moving closer now, his physical proximity matching the uncomfortable closeness of his inquiry.

''Oh, someone *told* you that's all that happened to her? And someone *told* you that the other two had been sexually assaulted?''

Anthoney quickly began backpedaling, stammering out, ''I didn't say I was told. I said I-I think I came under—in—from the information that I think I obtained from somebody else that there were two of them that was sexually assaulted, and I came to the conclusion it was Nancy and Missie because I'd already been told that Angie had her throat cut.''

''Who told you about two people being sexually assaulted?'' Ingaldson asked again.

''I think it was somebody in Twin Falls, Idaho. Or maybe even my mother. I'm not sure.''

Ingaldson's incredulity was undisguised. ''Your mother maybe told you that?''

''I don't know,'' answered Anthoney. ''It could have been any number of people that I had contact with.'' Ingaldson ignored the response and followed up his original question. ''Do you know how your mother would have known something like this?''

Amazingly, Anthoney ignored his previous response, as well, stating he heard details ''from the family, after the funerals had happened. Newspaper clippings from the people down in Twin Falls.''

''From the Twin Falls newspaper clippings?'' prompted Ingaldson.

''Could be. I don't know,'' Anthoney mumbled.

''Okay,'' said Ingaldson, ''did you know anything else?''

''I think that was just about it,'' Anthoney answered. ''The only reason why I drew conclusions that they were raped is because you guys were asking me for hairs and I drew conclusions that somebody was stabbed because you asked me about knives.''

"Okay," said Ingaldson thoughtfully. "Let me see if I can summarize what you said you knew at the time—"

"It's not that I know," interrupted Anthoney, "I assumed . . ."

"Assumed that Angie had been stabbed? When you got off the plane from Fairbanks [after being arrested], did you know how she was cut?"

"No," clarified Anthoney, "I didn't assume, I knew then. I knew she had her throat cut. My mother told me before I left Anchorage."

"And that the other two had been strangled," Ingaldson added.

He also prompted contradictory testimony from Anthoney about his leaking tire—he now claimed two such tires instead of one—and requested commentary on the lie he told at the car wash about his mother's "death." In Anthoney's version, the deception—which bothered him not in the least—took place seven days out of synch with Cumiford's testimony.

The prosecutor was about to launch another attack when his notes slipped to the floor. "When my notes fell, they kind of got mixed up in order a little bit," said Ingaldson to Judge Buckalew.

"You've got a big handful of notes," agreed the judge. "Why don't we let the jury go for Memorial Day weekend?" Buckalew then gave the jury instructions. "I want to admonish you, ladies and gentlemen, no newspapers, no TV news, no radio broadcasts, no discussions on this case with anyone. Among yourselves or anybody else. I want you all to have a good Memorial Day and a safe Memorial Day. And we'll start at eight-thirty—it will be Tuesday morning, won't it?"

As the jury filed out, Ingaldson raised another issue regarding Newman's camera, saying, "I got a roll of film from Investigator Spadafora and I was wondering, maybe, if we could have Mr. Anthoney take a couple shots with the camera and over the weekend I could have it developed."

Salemi objected, and the judge didn't understand what Ingaldson wanted. "Well, he mentioned if I got a roll of film," Ingaldson explained, "he'd be able to show me how to use that camera. Maybe I could just have him take a couple of pictures with it and have it developed over the weekend. I'm sure otherwise, you know, maybe he'll read up a little over the weekend. But—it might lose its effect, but. . . ."

"That was just some kind of thing he volunteered or you asked him about," said the judge, "and he said it before he consulted with counsel."

"I would object to what Mr. Ingaldson has requested, Your Honor," interjected Salemi. "I'm not going to talk to my client about whether he knows how to operate that camera, nor will I instruct him. I'm not sure I know how to operate it. But I don't think this would be an appropriate time to conduct that kind of experiment."

When court reconvened the following Tuesday, Kirby Anthoney returned to the witness stand. Under oath, Anthoney speculated that there wasn't time for him to do all the things he did on Saturday, March 14, 1987, plus rape and strangle Nancy and Melissa Newman and cut Angie Newman's throat.

"The murders probably took an hour and twenty-five minutes," he estimated. "There's three people. I only have two hands."

Ingaldson read aloud from letters Anthoney wrote to friends and family after his arrest. As Ingaldson read, Anthoney sobbed. In a letter to his parents, Kirby Anthoney detailed how long it would take him to commit the rapes and murders.

"Raping Nancy Newman twice and strangling her could take as long as fifteen minutes," he said. He told Ingaldson he lengthened his estimate from four minutes after learning that Nancy Newman had been raped more than once. "Cutting Angie Newman's throat would have taken one minute, while tying up Melissa, eight, and raping her would have taken about ten minutes. And whoever did it wouldn't walk in and just start killing,'' according to Anthoney. ''If I did this, I would have had to come in and talk awhile.''

Anthoney told the jury his estimates were based on ''using common sense as to what it would take'' to do everything that was done to the victims. The killer then had to clean up, find something in which to carry Nancy Newman's missing purse, plus all the loose change from her tip tin, he theorized in the letter. ''I wouldn't be caught carrying a purse out in broad daylight,'' he wrote.

According to Anthoney's account of things, less than an hour of his time that Saturday morning was unaccounted for. But there was only his word for his activities between 8:45 and 10:30. Grimes and the other police officers in the courtroom were not buying Anthoney's new version of Saturday morning's events, and neither was Ingaldson.

''What you're saying now, Mr. Anthoney, isn't really the truth, is it?'' insisted Ingaldson. ''Isn't it true that you're trying to fill up that time period, from eight-forty-five to ten-thirty?''

Anthoney insisted he was telling the truth, and then added to his Saturday memories an extensive phone conversation with Tony Marinelli, the man from whom he was buying his truck. ''I called and asked for his answering service number from his mother because I couldn't reach him,'' Anthoney testified. Marinelli, according to Anthoney, returned the call from work. Tony Marinelli, however, did not work that Saturday, and there was no record of the phone calls ever taking place.

Ingaldson then quoted from Anthoney's postarrest letters that he would break Jeff Mullins's nose. Another missive contained rants against his uncle, John Newman. If Newman believed Anthoney was guilty, he could, in Anthoney's words, ''just kiss my ass.'' Anthoney also composed unpleasant comments regarding Paul Chapman, noting that Chapman ''is going to think he's in hell when I see that fat son of a bitch.''

The letter-writing Kirby Anthoney was different from the weepy lad on the witness stand. The newly revealed demeanor more closely resembled the one known to the police. ''Ingaldson didn't let him get away with anything on the stand," recalled Spadafora. "When Anthoney claimed not to have said something to us during our interviews, or when he accused Ingaldson of misrepresenting his words, Ingaldson would play back the actual tape-recorded statements proving that Anthoney was lying one way or another."

Anthoney explained away the apparent discrepancies in his stories by saying the police insisted that he guess at things. In front of the jury, Ingaldson told Anthoney he had made slips. Once, in a letter home, he referred to the Newman door as being bolted on the day of the murder, a fact he couldn't have known if he hadn't been there. Anthoney said he learned that bit of information from Reeder and Spadafora.

"They initiated that information to me," he said. "The police are trying to insinuate that I have been saying things to people that only the killer would know. There were a lot of things that were said by the police officers that would have given a lot of people ideas—information that was leaked out through the officers that other people could have grasped, and there were people that I talked to that I'd get information from. I kept asking the police a lot of questions, but they wouldn't tell me a whole lot, but I drew a lot of conclusions from them."

Ingaldson also challenged Anthoney's newly offered explanation for several rolls of coins he was seen spending in the week after the killings. He said he went to the Newman apartment on Thursday, two days before the murders, and Nancy let him take a bunch of loose silver from her tip box. This was the same Thursday that Nancy Newman supposedly loaned him John's camera. It was during this same visit, according to Anthoney, that he was in every bedroom in the apartment, for one reason or another.

The longer Anthoney stayed in the witness-box, the less credible was his alibi. Ingladson, having dissected Anthoney's excuses and explanations, had no further questions. When Kirby D. Anthoney stepped down, the defense rested.

CHAPTER 17

"Ladies and gentlemen, I guess after the last two months maybe one piece of good news is the trial is coming to an end." With these words, the prosecutor, Bill Ingaldson, began his remarks. "Right now what I want to do first is remind you that at the very beginning when we gave opening statements, I told you one of the things that Kirby Anthoney said. He said to Investigator Reeder, 'I didn't screw up, Bill. I didn't screw up.' Also, when he was presented with a bunch of the evidence against him, [he] said, 'Okay, you've got the evidence, now show how I did it.' Well, maybe Kirby Anthoney didn't screw up, ladies and gentlemen, but he certainly left plenty of evidence behind. And certainly in his comments, his statements that he made, we can see a lot of these slipups.

"I've presented evidence to you in a lot of different forms, and I'm going to go through these. They deal with not only his mental state at the time, but the physical evidence at the scene. The entrance and exit, noise made, and the time of day that this occurred—to show that this wasn't any stranger who did this. The things that were missing: the camera, the coins . . .

evidence about the gloves, Kirk Mullins's white shirt. The explanations he gave the last several days in court. His alibis, the time of death and how they fit in with the alibis. Some of these I characterize as slipups—some of the things that he knew about that he wouldn't have known if he didn't do this. Things that he told people, some of the excuses that he gave that you all heard. The forensic evidence: cigarettes, blood and semen, hair evidence, fiber evidence, fingerprints, shoe prints.

"I'm going to talk about the flight, leaving, why he left. And finally a little bit about one of the comments he made, one of the first pieces of evidence that you saw—a portion of a letter to Debbie Heck.

"I'm going to show you evidence, ladies and gentlemen, and ask you to put all this evidence together to show not just beyond a reasonable doubt, but beyond all doubt that Kirby Anthoney is the one who committed these murders.

"When he said to Investigator Reeder, 'Show me how I did it,' not only did he show us that he did do it, he did show us how he did it. Now, that's not an element to be proved, how he did it. But sometimes it helps in understanding the evidence. What happened that night of Friday the thirteenth, and the murders of Saturday morning, the fourteenth.

"Friday night we know Kirby Anthoney was out partying. We know a little bit about his mental condition . . . he was doing cocaine, and in one of his letters to Kirk Mullins, he said he'd done as much as two grams of cocaine all by himself. What happened that next morning when he came over to Nancy Newman's house? He came over and the kids were up. Angie had eaten. I don't know where she was, maybe watching TV or something. Melissa was at the table, had just started eating. Nancy's at the table. Already smoked three, maybe [she's] on her fourth cigarette [and] was drinking coffee. He came in. We know the car was gone. We know he's come to that house before and gotten change. He was probably coming to get money again. We know he came in. And an argument ensued. Perhaps it was when he got into the kitchen, but we know that the kids were sent back into their rooms. What's a reasonable explanation? Nancy Newman, when an argument starts to ensue, is going to tell the kids, 'Go to your room,' probably because she doesn't want to have the argument in front of them.

"Well, Kirby gets Nancy Newman back into her bedroom . . . and that's when the sexual assault begins . . . he begins to choke her. We know that he got a pair of green gloves, and a pair of green gloves were used. She's strangled. She's moved on different parts of the bed. We see fecal matter on the end of the bed here. We know she's been sexually assaulted upon finding signs of semen."

Ingaldson acknowledged that none of Anthoney's pubic hairs were found on or near Nancy Newman, but pointed out that no unknown pubic hairs were found in Mrs. Newman's bedroom.

"If he's sexually assaulting her and just unzips his pants, his hairs probably aren't even exposed to her. And there weren't anyone's hairs there on her body. But we did find one of his head hairs on the top sheet . . . how did his head hairs happen to get on her top sheet? What happened to her?

"Nancy Newman is sexually assaulted; she has a bowel movement. Kirby Anthoney gets feces on him during this sexual assault. The washrag found in the bathroom has brown matter on it. And you can look at it yourself and you can smell it, if you care to. It's feces, ladies and gentlemen. It's from Nancy Newman. His pubic hair's in there. And why is that? He's sexually assaulting her, he unzips his pants . . . and look at that shirt—that white shirt he's wearing—and you all saw it. It's one of these Mexican-kind-of-style shirts that hangs out. Not the type you tuck in . . . and that's when he got the feces on him. And he went in the bedroom. He took his gloves off because he's not going to wash with the gloves on, set them on the dresser, went into the bathroom, and started washing himself off. That's how the pubic hair got on the washrag. And started washing that shirt off. Well, Melissa comes in and sees her mother. And how do we know Melissa was in that room? Because we have blood. We have blood on the foot of the bed.

We have blood going across the bed in the drops that you saw from the slides, and some of it, by the way—there's one drop on Nancy Newman's stomach, but there are other drops underneath her. That blood is consistent with Melissa Newman. Nancy Newman was not bleeding. Who does that leave? Melissa Newman. That was her blood going across that bed.

"She came in there, and what happened? I don't know if she let out a gasp or something, but Kirby Anthoney knew that she was in there, and went in and smacked her—smacked her in the nose; smacked her in the mouth. And we know he didn't have gloves on at this time, for two reasons. Number one: No one is going to be washing themselves off with gloves. And number two: There isn't any blood on the gloves. But we know that he has some blood on his hands because we see a bloody smear on this pillow.

"As Melissa Newman is crawling across that bed . . . Kirby Anthoney grabs her and grabs that pillowcase off and secures her. And you notice the pillowcase on her neck . . . there were parts where there was blood and not blood. And the reason for that is simple. Because when he first grabbed that pillowcase, he shoved it in her mouth to keep her quiet. She was probably first knocked down to the floor, and we get some of her blood on the floor. And then that pillowcase was shoved in her mouth. And she was taken to her room.

"And what happened in her room? Well, as Mr. Anthoney pointed out, it did take a little longer in Melissa's room. It probably did take five or ten minutes with Nancy. There is no sign of tearing or anything in her vaginal area. Melissa is not the same thing.

"Let's look at Melissa's room," he continued, pointing at a large diagram of Melissa's room, complete with full-color photographs. "There's a pillowcase tied around her wrist. There's blood on the edge of the bed and you can look. I don't know if you can see some—in these photographs, but you can see the blood. And you saw pictures earlier in [the] trial. It's the same diameter as the bloody smear that went across her stomach area. There's blood on the end of the bed.

"Ladies and gentlemen," he said emphatically, "Melissa Newman was choked from behind laying facedown on the bed. And you can see where the knot is. And she's strapped over this bed. And on her right wrist is where we find that other pillowcase that was used to secure her . . . he tied the wrist, wrapped it around her other hand, held her hands over her head while she's facedown. And the only spots that we see blood here—we see them on the bed here where her face would have been, and we see blood on the edge here, and we see a little bit on the towel on her bed. The towel here, which may have been from him just wiping his hand. And we see it underneath her and on the side of the bed here. And how did it get there? She's spread facedown over the bed, the right hand of Kirby Anthoney is holding her hands, and his left hand—where is it? It's leaning against the wall. And that's where we see his handprint. There is no other way for that handprint to get there. If he's laying in bed, sleeping in bed, how is this handprint—you can't do it. You cannot get your handprint at that angle. He's bracing himself against the wall there. And when he's done sexually assaulting Melissa—and it did take longer for two reasons. Number one, she's a young girl. Number two, it was the second time he ejaculated. Number three, just look at the violence to her—the fact that her vaginal area and her anal area were ripped open to be one area. That is what *he* did to her."

The jury, horrified by the recounting of details, cast a quick and unavoidable glance at the defendant.

"When he was done, she fell back off the bed," said Ingaldson, "wiping that smear down the bed and across her abdomen. The smear of blood and semen that matched Kirby Anthoney. Look where the hairs were found on her," he said, pointing to the graphic and specific illustrations. "The hairs were found on her buttocks. Right where you would expect if she's been sexually assaulted in that way. And if you look at the way her legs are, that's the only way she could have been unless he crawled underneath the bed. And she could not have been sexually assaulted from the front. She's not dragged around the room because we don't see blood all over the room. We see it underneath her and we see it on the side of her. And where does it get on the side of her? From it flipping back off the bed.

"The only place she's bleeding besides her vaginal area is in her mouth and nose. When her head hits, some blood smears out," Ingaldson again pointed directly to the corresponding photograph, "and you look, that's exactly the way it looks."

Ingaldson then turned the jury's attention to the discovery of Anthoney's pubic hairs, asking, "Is it just coincidence that these pubic hairs that match Kirby Anthoney are found on her buttocks? And you know where they were found?"

In case the jury didn't remember, Ingaldson was well prepared to remind them. "In Melissa's room . . . that's where you find nine of Kirby Anthoney's pubic hairs. Nine matches in that room. And where do you find these hairs? If you imagine a person's buttocks area, they were found up in the centerline kind of near the crack in her buttocks. Right where they would be if she was sexually assaulted . . . and where are most of the hairs? Where most of the violence was done." Ingaldson enumerated the pubic hairs found in Melissa's room, including a pubic hair with two lice-egg casings on it. "She's not carried around this room. She fell backward. What are the odds of her falling and just happening to pick up two of the nine hairs in this room . . . hairs didn't stick to anything but her—nothing else. Is this just some fluke, some weird coincidence that hairs didn't stick to the underwear on the floor, didn't stick to anything but Melissa?

"And what does he do when he's done with Melissa? Well, he goes into Angie's room. It's getting a little late now and he doesn't choke Angie. He cuts her throat. We see blood on the bed, and that's probably where her throat was cut, on the bed. And she's dragged off the bed. And if you look at the other photographs—and you'll see a book of them, you will see that going all the way through, the darkest spots are kind of near this pillow and on the edge of the bed. Which would be consistent if she was cut on that bed and then pulled off by the feet. And where is the blood? There is a lot of blood in there . . . there's spots on the wall, but most of the blood, if you look at the floor, is right around this area, this small section of the room.

"He lays her out on her back and wipes her from the vaginal area up—wipes off spot of blood clear, and probably was going to try and sexually assault her. But either he couldn't get an erection or maybe ran out of time. But we know that he was probably at least masturbating at that time because we find pubic hairs of his in the blood, and a fourth pubic hair that's immature and couldn't be matched to him. That fourth pubic hair had two [lice] egg casings on it. I'd ask you to draw an inference as to whose that could be.

"He probably cleaned up in the bathroom, at least got some of the blood off of him. We know that washrag was wet, either from rinsing out the first time washing himself off, and perhaps even wet from wiping his hands off, but we also know that in that washrag, as I said, was his pubic hair.

"Anthoney told us that the door was dead-bolted," insisted the prosecutor, then reminded the jury that traces of human blood, although small, were found on Anthoney's leather coat and his shoes. "What's his excuse?" asked Ingaldson. "Well, one of his excuses is from getting in fights. He says he got into a fight with this guy on the boat, broke up a fight or something. I pushed him, I asked him some questions about that and he backs up and says, 'Well, maybe I didn't get in a fight on the boat. I said I might have been wearing them, I'm not sure if I wore those.' He changes that because he knows that that's just not true. But probably the most unbelievable explanation he gives is this thing about the kids and the cats—he says the kids might have been scratched by cats, and they used to 'wear my shoes and walk around the house. And they might have gotten blood on them. And Angie especially liked to do that.'

Now just think about that. That's absurd! But he didn't know yet if they were going to be able to type it to one of the kids' blood. He did know that the most blood is in Angie's room. So, he said especially Angie likes to wear them around. He's trying to cover his tracks. He's trying to think of some excuse why their blood might be on there, because he didn't know what the results were going to be, and that's the best he could do!''

Ingaldson then discussed the single Camel Filter found in Nancy Newman's ashtray, ''the same type of cigarettes [Anthoney] smokes; the same saliva type as Kirby Anthoney. We know it is not Paul Chapman's cigarette, although he smoked Camels also, because it doesn't match his saliva.

''And is it a coincidence that Kirby Anthoney, in his statement to you, when he's testifying . . . about how long it would take, happen to mention something about 'I'd have to have time to talk to the persons before I could get them in their rooms'? And that's right. The time to have that cigarette. And then look what he did after that. He started walking around the house. And what are you going to do if someone does that? You're not going to go dashing out of the house. You're going to check and see where people are. See if anyone is watching you. And look at this curtain here,'' said Ingaldson, pointing to the photographic representation of the Newmans' living room. ''You'll see that this curtain in the living room is pushed back a little bit.''

Noting that the fireplace blocked an easy view out the window, Ingaldson insisted that Anthoney stepped on the fireplace to take a look outside.

''It's not a footprint that would be there if you were walking up to put a log on the fireplace. No, it's . . . even superimposed as if you step and have to twist your foot a little bit . . . no one else's footprint, but [Anthoney's] footprint, his shoe print. And we see a shoe print going out the window—his shoe print.''

Again, Ingaldson hammered away that ''this wasn't a

stranger that did it . . . it was Kirby Anthoney,'' by noting the lack of noise and forced entry.

"Now, admittedly, the Newmans lived on a kind of an end apartment. So, if there's some noise, the rest of the apartments might not hear. Because three sides of their apartment were bordered by outside. There would only be one wall that was way back in Melissa's room. So, admittedly, you're not going to hear as much noise from their apartment as perhaps other apartments. But no one heard anything. No one in that apartment heard anything. Mr. Anthoney himself says to one of his questions, if a stranger had come in there, you would expect all kinds of noise. The girls would open the door by asking first who is there. They would answer the door. So, we don't have noise. We don't have signs of forced entry. The door wasn't broken in. No sign of ransacking the house. Also look at the time of day that this happened. Would you expect some stranger to come at nine in the morning, eight-thirty, nine, nine-thirty in the morning, to come over and commit this type of crime? Some stranger? No, you wouldn't. But you would expect, based on what happened the night before, Kirby Anthoney to be over there at nine.

"Let's talk a little bit about the entrance and exits,'' continued Ingaldson. "First of all, to get in, to gain entrance here, either someone had to let the person in or the person would have had to have a key because everyone says Nancy always kept those doors locked and dead-bolted. But more importantly, let's look at the exits.

"There are three possible exits,'' he explained. "One possible one would be through the living room window because it wasn't locked. But there were no signs of dust disturbance or anything there. No signs of any disturbance in the living room window. Sergeant Gifford essentially ruled that out. Nothing disturbed. That leaves two spots to exit—Angie's bedroom, because that was the only other window that was not locked, and the front door.

"What stranger is going to go out the front door? Well, they

might go out the front door, there's no doubt. But would they
lock the door? Well, they might even lock the door . . . but
would they lock the dead bolt? Some stranger? What person,
after committing a crime like this, is going to go out in a
common area and fumble through the keys to find which key
fits the dead bolt and lock the dead bolt? The only way you
can lock that dead bolt is with the key once you're outside the
apartment. You cannot turn the knob and pull the door shut,
because the dead bolt will stick in. The door won't shut. You
have to have a key. And what stranger is going to take a key
and fumble around while someone might come and say, hey,
what are you doing? No, they're going to want to get out of
there right away. Unless the killer maybe had done this out of
habit. Unless the killer had been going in and out of the front
door and knew what key it was, and had always been locking
that so that no one knew he'd go out the front door, and could
do so in a split second. But there is only one person we know
of like that—Kirby Anthoney. He's the only person who talks
about going out that front door . . . if the person went out the
front door, the only person that would even think of locking
that would be Kirby Anthoney. Maybe because he does it out
of habit because he's always done that, always locked that dead
bolt—now he's trying to say that the police told him it was
dead-bolted, but we've had no testimony to that effect. What
did he say? He said he tried the bottom handle, and he slipped.
He said the door was bolted.''

An even more reasonable exit, according to Ingaldson, was
Angie's bedroom window. ''What did Kirby Anthoney tell you
about her bedroom window?'' asked Ingaldson. ''He said this
one you cannot see from the street as easy. You can see Melissa's easier from the street. And what did he tell you about
when he went in the window? He told you he never went out
that window; he went out the front door. Those were his own
words.''

Ingaldson focused the jury's attention on the single footprint
of Anthoney's found on Angie's dresser, a footprint which,

"because of a defect, in the shoe, was positively identified as coming from Kirby Anthoney's gray shoes that, according to him, he had only had since he got back from the boat.

"The footprint on that dresser was pointing toward the window," explained Ingaldson. Insisting that if the print were from entering the room, the toe would point "toward the room. On this dresser, the footprint was pointing out . . . the toe toward the window."

Next Ingaldson discussed the stolen items, and the manner in which they were stolen, beginning with the fact that the Newman residence "wasn't ransacked. The drawers weren't ripped open, the cupboards weren't flung open. Three things were gone from that house: Nancy Newman's purse, and the wallet in the purse; the coins from the coin tin; and John Newman's camera. There were other coin tins that look similar to the coin tin that was empty, and those weren't even disturbed.

"[Anthoney] said he'd been in that cookie tin," Ingaldson reminded the jury, "and that a lot of people have been in the cookie tin. But they don't find very many people's prints in the cookie tin. They find Nancy's and I think Melissa's on the bottom of it. And Kirby Anthoney's."

The jury's attention was directed to a photograph of the cookie tin showing its bent condition. "Look at that, and you'll see that fingerprint which matched his middle finger curved over the tin. It's right where the tin is kind of bent—it's kind of pulled out a little bit. If you have a tin full of coins and pull it out to dump those coins out, that's where his fingerprint is.

"There was a little ceramic doll that had some coins above the sink," Ingaldson continued. "Kirby Anthoney said he didn't know about that, and that wasn't disturbed. The bedrooms weren't ransacked. The things that were taken were things that Kirby Anthoney knew about, valuables that he knew about, and the coin tin. Who knew about it? Several friends knew about that coin tin that we heard. But would a stranger know about that coin tin up above the microwave?

"Is it just coincidence the condition that the tin was in,"

asked Ingaldson, ''that the bending is where his fingerprint is, is that just some weird coincidence?''

Ingaldson asserted that three witnesses saw Anthoney with large amounts of coins and rolls of coins. Anthoney's explanation—that Nancy Newman gave him coins on the Thursday before the murders—came under intense assault.

''It's kind of suspicious, isn't it, that the first time that he starts mentioning getting these coins Thursday night to any law enforcement, any police officers out of seven or so interviews—the first time he says it is in court. All of a sudden he remembers getting these coins. And he just happened to go home that same Thursday night, the Thursday night that his own roommate says that they were at the Bank Shot and went out to the bars afterward. You know the other thing about counting coins that's kind of funny? Where would you get the paper rolls for these coins? Would you just happen to have them laying around the house? It's certainly not something most people have laying around the house. We know Nancy Newman had some in the bottom of this coin tin. We didn't hear any testimony about his grabbing these paper rolls out of the bottom of the coin tin. Where would he get the rolls to start rolling the coins? Where would he get the coins? He had to come up with this thing from Nancy Newman because he knows he originally told the police he got these coins from the car wash. But once we heard . . . the number of days he'd worked at the car wash, we knew that was ridiculous. He couldn't have gotten all those coins there.''

Another point Ingaldson made regarding the coins was that Anthoney didn't have any when he went to see Kirk Mullins after the murders. ''Think about why did he go to Kirk and Debbie's. One of the main reasons is to establish an alibi, to be with someone. And, of course, he's not going to want to have coins because he knew he'd stolen coins. But anyone who was going over there to wash clothes, anyone especially going to Burger King, is going to get some coins before you go.''

The question of ''who stole John Newman's keys'' was next

on Ingaldson's agenda. The real question, noted the prosecutor, was "why would John Newman's keys be missing?"

"There would be no reason to take his keys," insisted Ingaldson. "There's no car out there. Nancy Newman's keys are right in her purse. Kirby Anthoney already had John Newman's keys, and that's how he was able to gain entrance. That's why that morning he was probably fiddling with the lock when Nancy Newman came to the door, or the kids came to the door. And she said, 'What's going on?' And that's when the argument started."

The ever-important camera belonging to John Newman again received attention from Ingaldson, who couldn't resist mocking Anthoney's self-description. "He tells you he's a camera fanatic, that he loves cameras. He's a camera fanatic. He didn't take any pictures with his own camera at Christmastime, this camera fanatic. When he went out on the boat—this new adventure, he'd never been out there before, he didn't even bother taking his cameras with him, this camera fanatic . . . when he got back to Anchorage, did he take any pictures, or even have any interest in taking pictures up until this Thursday before? No, he didn't. Why did he borrow the camera? Well, he gave a lot of reasons for that. First, it was just to doodle around. Then it was to take pictures four-wheel driving, take pictures at Portage Glacier, take pictures along the Seward Highway. And this other reason, that his camera was in storage. He borrowed John's camera. All of a sudden right before the murders he has this interest. And why would he borrow John's camera? This is the person that is supposed to have such strong feelings toward the Newmans, respect for their feelings. Someone that, according to him, thought, well, maybe I felt like I'm a burden on them, so I want to move out of the house. I don't want to bother them. So, what does he do? According to him, he's telling you, 'Yeah, I borrowed the camera from Nancy. Nancy told me first, no. I knew that John was real particular about his cameras. He never let anyone use them.' I asked him, 'Well, why would you borrow his cameras if you knew that he really wouldn't want you to?' There's no real answer to that, was there? And he says he borrowed John's camera. John was coming back the next week. He said he was going to go that weekend to take pictures. Friday he was out with Kirk and Debbie and went out Friday night partying. Saturday, according to him, he was partying during the day and drinking, smoking, watching movies. He went out Saturday night. Sunday, by the time the police came over, you know that he had no intention that day of going down to Alyeska. When is he going to take these pictures? That was just an excuse he came up with. And he had to tell you that he borrowed it the Thursday before. He had to tell the police that, because they knew that that camera hadn't been used because there was film in it from Christmastime. Twenty-three of the twenty-four shots in there had been taken of the Newman family at Christmastime . . . what person is going to lend out a camera with their Christmas pictures of their family? But the most significant thing about that whole camera is that he didn't even know how to use it, and you saw that when I was asking him questions . . . he didn't know anything about that camera. Why would he be borrowing that? Because it is all a lie.''

Ingaldson then dwelt upon what he termed ''the real chilling thing about this case''—Anthoney's attempt to sell the stolen camera to Jess O'Dell following the murders.

''We know that Jess O'Dell, even according to Kirby Anthoney, was probably telling the truth about seeing it on his bed, Kirby Anthoney's bed. I mean, he's accurate in every single thing he tells about it. [Anthoney] took it out and set it on the bed and showed it to him. The Monday after this, to try and get some money for it. He's trying to say that Jess O'Dell saw this camera on Friday and that everything he's telling is the truth except he's mixed up or lying or something and saw the camera on Friday. Well, how believable is that? First of all, the police found that camera. Don't you think that the police were pressuring him about the camera? Maybe even accusing him of stealing the camera when the murders were committed?

Don't you think that he would want to have a witness that saw him with the camera before the murders? Don't you think that if he didn't take it on Saturday, he would have said, 'Hey, Jess O'Dell saw me with it on Friday, call him up.' Of course, he would have. And he didn't. He never said that. What did he tell us? . . . A complete fabrication!''

Continuing on the recurrent theme of Anthoney's inability to speak the truth, Ingaldson discussed the green gloves.

''The gloves were obviously used during the strangulation of Nancy Newman. We find several of her forcibly removed head hairs in the gloves. We find glove fibers on her neck, the pillowcase, the ligature. We find glove fibers on the washcloth. Why would they be on the washcloth? Think about it. If your hands are sweating [in] wool gloves, you're going to pick up fibers on your hands. You go in to wash off, and some are going to transfer onto that washcloth. And we find a few of the fibers even on Melissa's nightgown. And of course the reason for that also is after going back in and grabbing Melissa, you're going to have some of those fibers on your hand. And that's when we see the chart of the fibers and where the fibers were found—the pillowcase around Nancy's neck and on her nightgown. How do we tie those gloves to Kirby Anthoney?

''His story,'' Ingaldson reminded the jury, ''was [that] 'I put the gloves on because I went to clean off Nancy's car.' If you think about it, [that] is pretty ludicrous. He couldn't say that he went out and cleaned her car off before she left because she parks in a carport. So, if it had been snowing in the morning, there wouldn't be any snow to clean off her car. So, what does he say? He says—he has to think of some way to wear those gloves—he says, 'When she came home, I went out to clean off the car.' What person, think about it, use your common sense, what person cleans snow off a car when they return? How many times have you gone in your garage when you return and cleaned the snow off your car or under the carport? Or even parked in a driveway unprotected? And you go clean the car off. No, you do it maybe before you leave, but not once you get back.

"And what about that white shirt we've been talking about," asked Ingaldson. "What do we find on the white shirt? Even according to [Anthoney's] testimony. Now he's changing it a little bit and saying, 'Well, maybe it was just a stain,' but he said in letters, he said to Kirk Mullins, he said to the police it was—looked like dog or cat shit on the shirt. And where was that? Right where it would have been if he's sexually assaulting Nancy. Right where his shirt would have been hanging down. And is that just a coincidence that Nancy has a bowel movement and feces? They're smeared on the bed. And what's his explanation for getting feces on his shirt? Think about it a little bit . . . Investigator Reeder asked him about the shirt—'How can you get feces on it when you're wearing it all night?' What does he tell him? He says, 'I took my shirt off and sat it on the floor.' "

"Who sorts clothes like that?" Ingaldson asked the jury. "Why would he take his shirt off? I mean, dump all your other clothes out and sort them and throw them back in the bag. And even if you would do something like that, why would he take the shirt off and throw it on the floor and put on a dirty shirt? That's what he says he did—he put on a dirty shirt. He says he sat it on the floor and it got some dog shit on there. And we known there wasn't any dog shit in the house. We never heard any complaints about it. Well, Anthoney thought about that and he came up with another version when he's in court. He says, 'Well, the dogs walked on it.' Well, come on. We don't see any other evidence, we haven't heard anything about footprints of dog crap along the floor. He didn't even see the dog in the house. The dog is an outside dog, and the dog is supposed to pop in there and walk across his shirt? And the only thing he noticed the dog crap on is that white shirt? Tell me why is that? Why wouldn't he notice it on anything else? Just that? It's beyond belief, this explanation that he gives about all of a sudden taking his shirt off and there's dog crap on it.

"And the other thing about that shirt that's kind of interesting," continued Ingaldson, "was that there was a hair found on the shirt which, although it couldn't be exactly matched by FBI Agent Deedrick, had similarities and differences to Nancy Newman's.

"Is it just a coincidence that his alibi starts to change during that morning?" asked Ingaldson. "Why didn't it change at other times when he's told his alibi is weak if he didn't know when the murders happened?"

Ingaldson gave the jury a guided tour of Anthoney's inconsistent statements, comparing them to the recollections of his friends and associates. "He says he went right over to Kirk's house and he got there at nine or nine-thirty, and it just so happens that Kirk says the same thing. Of course, he had talked to Kirk before the police got there. He hadn't talked to Debbie, and Debbie says much later. Debbie and Kirk get together and realize they have a discrepancy in their statements. So, all of a sudden, they come up with one time eleven o'clock, one time ten-thirty, ten. Now, when they get into court, it's ten or ten-thirty. We know what time he really got there because everyone of them says right after he got there, within a pretty short period of time, at the most a half an hour, they went to Beverage World. And we know what time he's at Beverage World— twelve-fifteen. What time did he get to Kirk and Debbie's? Certainly not before eleven-thirty in the morning. And that's giving him forty-five minutes to get to Beverage World.

"What else does he change in the morning," asked Ingaldson rhetorically. "Now he's talking about the first time washing his upper body. And why is he saying that? Because by now he's heard that Debbie Dean told the police that he looked like he had just taken a shower. He hadn't heard that before. He had to have an excuse for that. He talks about how he put air in his tire when he left the house. That's his latest. Well, he had to change that. He changed all the way along. He changed from first not going to Burger King to then maybe getting something . . . and he starts filling in later. Think about that—

doing cocaine all night. Think about all the other people that have testified in this trial that did cocaine, and said how it doesn't make them hungry. It makes them think about anything but food. And all of a sudden he's hungry. And in his statement he says, 'Yeah, I had two croissant sandwiches and it made me hungrier.' Well, he would be hungry after committing these murders and expending all this energy, this rage. He would be hungry then, but certainly he wouldn't be hungry after doing all that cocaine that morning. All of a sudden, he's going to Burger King. And first he tells you that he went in the parking lot. He doesn't say what parking lot.''

Ingaldson showed the jury a photographic display of Burger King and the surrounding neighborhood. He then asked them to look at the location of Burger King and the adjacent parking area, and reminded them that Anthoney was told that no one at Burger King saw him there.

''And what's his explanation for that,'' asked Ingaldson rhetorically. ''Well, think about it. If you're in this parking lot,'' asserted Ingaldson, pointing to the Burger King lot, ''there's more a chance of someone seeing you than if you pull around across the street. So, what does he say? He says he pulls around across to the Norge's parking lot. He changes that to cover up that area, and then he sat there for twenty to forty minutes banging his head against the window, he says at one time. Now in court he says, 'Oh, that was an exaggeration,' but he's upset. He says to the police that he was writing on a letter of his own and reading his own. Well, now he says, 'Well, no, I wasn't writing on this letter' . . . it was another one . . . one that he never mailed, and one that he says he supposedly wrote while in the parking lot across from Burger King. And he says that he showed it to the police. Well, if he really did wave it out, and show it to the police, why wouldn't he remember being at Burger King writing it? Why wouldn't he tell them that? Because it never happened!''

Ingaldson built a head of steam, rolling over Anthoney's inconsistencies with relentless vigor. This wasn't his last opportunity to address the jury, but he piled it on as heavily as possible before Salemi could give his closing arguments.

"He put air in his tires and checked his oil," declared Ingaldson sarcastically. "All of a sudden he remembers that. Why does he remember that? Because 'I was up at the border and I figured my tire would be flat.' Well, he forgot—he got that tire fixed before he left, and we see the receipt for that. And when I confronted him with that, all of a sudden he has another excuse—two bad tires.

"He wants you to believe that all these pubic lice are old," said Ingaldson, mocking Anthoney's inventive cure of mixing Rid with shampoo. "Think about it a minute. He's trying to get you to believe that Debbie Heck had pubic lice, and that he had it when he was on the boat. They had been staying together, having sexual relations on the boat, you would expect her to have pubic lice. Her testimony, clearly, is that she did not have pubic lice. Even after being examined by a doctor, [Anthoney] said, 'Well, probably because I put Rid in the shampoo.' I brought in that bottle of Rid," Ingaldson reminded the jury, "and he looked at it. The directions on the bottle said, number one—do not dilute. So, what does he do? He's telling you he diluted it and that got rid of her pubic lice and not his? Number two—it says don't put it on your eyebrows or eyelashes. Common sense would tell you there's probably a pretty good reason that maybe it shouldn't be around your eyes. So, he's saying that he put it in the shampoo that Debbie would use? And where is shampoo going to run? If you're washing your hair, you're probably going to get some on your eyebrows. And he's going to take that risk by putting it in shampoo? Even more curious than that is why would she use shampoo to wash her pubic hair? Wouldn't she use a bar of soap? He's saying that because he wants you to believe that he had these pubic lice for some time, when in fact he got them *after* he came back from Dutch Harbor.

"Every single thing," declared Ingaldson incredulously, "all the evidence he's starting to tie to this Thursday night before the murders. He's in the bathroom, he's in Melissa's room, he's in Angie's room. Gets the camera, gets the coins. All these things just happen that night in one half-hour visit. He told police he was over there Thursday *night*, but phone records show that Nancy talked to [John] twice that night, for an hour each time, and there's no indication Nancy had been talking to John when Mr. Anthoney was over there. Now, all of a sudden, he may have been earlier in the *afternoon* when he was there.

"That was a convenient excuse," insisted Ingaldson, "a convenient excuse to go into Melissa's room. Remember at that time the police were telling him things about dating hairs, dating fingerprints and stuff. Anthoney didn't know if they were telling the truth or not. He knew he was there. He had to have an excuse for these things. So, all of a sudden Thursday night, he goes into Melissa's room and gets his little bag. And maybe even changes clothes there. And he smells the sheets on the bed. He goes into Angie's room and happens to pick up toys that night. In court yesterday, he tells the police, 'Yeah, I also went into Nancy's room—I think I went in there to borrow a marijuana pipe.' He said, 'I didn't have any pipes and I wanted to borrow a marijuana pipe.' We know that's a lie, but he said he went through the nightstand looking for it. Well, he didn't know what fingerprints were found where, or whether they would be found on the nightstand because he probably was going through that nightstand when he was getting those green gloves. He's in Nancy's room. Asked about pubic hairs, he says that he might have gone in there to answer the phone, ran in without pants—carrying his pants or without his pants. That's absurd! And then, all of a sudden, later on he's remembering, 'Oh, the real reason I went over there is to borrow the camera.' And he has the camera. So, now the missing things are also in this half hour, this Thursday night.

"Remember we saw a little bit of blood behind the bathroom door," said Ingaldson, moving back toward graphic evidence, "and look at the blood spots on the bathroom light switch.

You have a blood spot just underneath one of the light switches. And there are two light switches—one for the fan that is closest to the door, and one further out that's for the light. And there is only blood under the light. Why is that? Because Kirby Anthoney knew which switch was the light, and that's the one he turned on when he went in the bathroom!''

On the topic of phone calls, Ingaldson insisted that the real reason Anthoney kept calling Nancy Newman on Saturday was to find out if the bodies had been discovered. ''He was curious and it was killing him,'' stated Ingaldson. ''Think about it, ladies and gentlemen. Why would Jody call that night?'' Ingaldson had already set up the answer to his own question—testimony from Jody Cornelius confirming that she *didn't* call Kirby Anthoney.

''He called *her!* And Jody's telling the truth. Why would Jody lie about something like that? *Jody's* telling the truth. Anthoney called her because he wanted an excuse to go to the apartment. And that's the best excuse he could have. He wanted to see if anyone found them; he wanted to feel the door himself.''

Ingaldson reminded the jury of Vicki Irvine's experience with Anthoney in the noisy bar. ''It's loud in Chilkoot's, but it stuck out in her mind about someone having to watch. And she talked about that later, and it was kind of chilling to her. And remember what her words were: 'The worst thing is that the mother had to watch.' Think about what probably really was said, and it fits what happened. The loud noises. First of all, Kirby Anthoney or anyone else is not going to say 'the mother.' If it was the mother, he'd say, 'Too bad that Nancy had to watch.' But who did see something happen? Melissa. And what did Kirby Anthoney say? 'Too bad that Melissa had to watch, or too bad that Missie had to watch.' And words like 'Missie,' which he called Melissa, and 'mother' at Chilkoot's— especially if you're thinking about something like that, that's the type of mistake you might make. But to mistake the entire sentence, no. And she talked to her friends about it. And he said that as he's sitting there writing some type of weird poetry.

"Kirby Anthoney did do it," insisted Ingaldson to the jury, "not just beyond a reasonable doubt, but, ladies and gentlemen, this is beyond any shadow of a doubt. And I'd ask you at the conclusion, after you deliberate, to return a verdict of guilty as to all counts charged. Thank you."

With Ingaldson finished, it was time for the defense to begin final arguments. During these remarks, lawyers must only address information admitted during the trial through sworn testimony or exhibits. No new information is allowed, and all conclusions must be drawn from admitted evidence.

Neither John Salemi nor Craig Howard stood to address the jury—Kirby D. Anthoney did.

CHAPTER 18

Wednesday, June 1, 1988, witnessed one of the most bizarre scenes in Anchorage legal history as Kirby D. Anthoney held sway over Judge Buckalew's courtroom for over three solid hours. None of the seventy lawyers, court employees, or police officers in court, recalled another murder case in which the defendant delivered his own closing. Judson Ray, however, was not surprised by Anthoney's action. Consistent with the FBI personality profile, grandiosity and pomposity often emerge quite dramatically in the courtroom. It is not unusual for psychopaths to criticize or fire their lawyers and take over their own defense—usually with disastrous results.

"Now I have a chance to talk without Mr. Ingaldson giving me so many confusing questions," began Anthoney affably. He casually placed his hand in his pocket, body language and gestures perfectly mimicking John Salemi. "Mr. Salemi is going to be talking with you mostly about the expert testimony," he continued, "and what I basically want to do is discuss a small portion of my life. Actually, it's the rest of my life. What I want to do now is basically talk about my relationship with the Newman family. This is a big part of my family. And it's been destroyed. And it's been taken away from me. They allowed me to stay at their house when I needed it. Nancy was kind enough to open her heart for me when I wanted it. When I needed assistance to buy a truck, they were there again.''

Showing surprising poise, he attacked Ingaldson's theories of possible motive one by one. In the process, he switched from imitating the casual presentation of Salemi to the more flamboyant and expressive style of Craig Howard.

''Mr. Ingaldson has mentioned something about drugs. He's saying that I possibly went and got more money from Nancy for more drugs. Let's look at the testimony and the evidence. I had bank records here in this courtroom that show that I had two hundred fifty-eight dollars the day before. Mr. Ingaldson wants you to believe that I spent all that on drugs. I ask you to use your common sense,'' said Anthoney. ''If somebody's after more drugs, are they going to leave cocaine laying on the mirror? Or are they not going to ask that person to give them more cocaine? There was nobody strung out on drugs. There was nobody being crazy. Dan Grant says I was a little hyper, but he says I wasn't abnormal. It wasn't unusual. Debbie and Kirk say when I showed up, I was fine; that I appeared to be tired as the day grew on.''

As for Ingaldson's theory that Kirby Anthoney snapped when Nancy pressured him to repay the outstanding loan, the defendant insisted that there was no pressure. ''There was no discussion by her asking for that money,'' said Anthoney. ''Why is somebody going to kill somebody over money? Somebody's that's loaned you money before in the past? Somebody that's allowed you into their home? Somebody that has a job?''

''Anthoney's monologue degenerated into three hours of mind-numbing blather,'' recalled Grimes. ''Although he started off sounding almost reasonable, and asserted that Salemi would handle the expert testimony, Anthoney started ranting about his fingerprints.''

"They say my fingerprints are the most in the house," declared Anthoney, "but they don't tell them fourteen of them are in the room I slept in. Neither do they tell them they are not anywhere, like I said. That's because I didn't go anywhere in that house that I shouldn't have been. That goes on and on. There's a long list of things that they would have told my friends and my family without giving any explanation to. They've destroyed my life as a relationship with my family, and they've damaged a lot of others."

"Mr. Ingaldson's taken so much of this out of context," he lamented, "I don't know if I can put it back in. He brought to your attention that I was saying something about smelling sheets. I told [police] I knew what clean sheets would smell like if it was clean and I crawled into that bed."

"Your Honor, I'll object to that and seek it to be stricken," Ingaldson recited again and again. "There's no testimony as to what he just said." When the court reminded Anthoney that "there's nothing in the record to support that statement," Anthoney simply started all over again, beginning with an unrelated topic. Soon, the objections began anew. Several times Salemi and Ingaldson would have whispered consultations at the bench with Buckalew. Anthoney had the floor, and there was no stopping him.

Anthoney turned his attention to Ingaldson's list of excuses, slipups, and lies. "I totaled three pages of it. I might have missed some," said Anthoney. "The first thing that came to my mind is 'I didn't screw up, Bill, I didn't screw up.' I didn't screw up because I didn't do anything wrong. That's exactly what I told them. Something to the effect that I stated 'You have the evidence, now prove how it was done.' That was me being sarcastic to them because I was upset, stressed out with them. Saying, 'Okay, just do whatever you feel like you have to do. You have the evidence, you say you have it, so do it.' "

Anthoney reminded the jury of Vicki Irvine's testimony and Ingaldson's interpretation of Anthoney's remarks. "He thinks it was that Missie had to watch; her testimony was that it was the mother had to watch. I wouldn't know if it was either one. I do know that Nancy would never stand by and watch something like this happen though. Never.''

Concerning Jess O'Dell, Anthoney said that his neighbor came over seeking money owed him for pot prior to the murders. ''I told him I didn't have it, but he was persistent. As I testified to, I may have gone into Dan's room and I may have gone in my room, but I'm not sure which room it was. And I won't say for sure because I don't know. All's I do know is [the coins] was in my coat pocket—a ski jacket, and that's where I placed those coins. I had change that I had borrowed from Nancy. I give Jess O'Dell fifteen dollars' worth of those coins. A roll of dimes and a roll of quarters. Jess O'Dell was only there for ten minutes approximately. But while he was there he seen the camera that was sitting on the edge of my bed. That Mr. Ingaldson so conveniently tries to accuse me with as being on my bed Thursday. And as I told him on the stand, it may have been, but I can't say as to where I had taken it off or what I had done with it. This is over a year ago. I believe Mr. O'Dell testified to the fact that when he stepped into my room, that the camera was in the closet, that it wasn't on my bed. He told the police that. He also told them it was on my bed.''

Anthoney's grasp of the language, tenuous at best, made following his line of thought difficult. Three hours of coherent, insightful arguments are difficult enough, but three hours of Anthoney's fractured prose, irregular tenses, and incomprehensible modifiers, wore heavily on everyone's nerves and patience.

''His use of the English language—his sentence structure— obviously is not from a parochial school,'' agreed John Salemi. ''He doesn't look like he had any nuns teaching him to use nouns and verbs.''

''And it wasn't simply a language problem,'' noted Grimes. ''After all, people who have accents or a narrow grasp of the English language testify all the time—some through translators.

Anthoney is a ninth-grade dropout with bad grammar and a tendency toward stilted syntax when he is trying to make an impression. But that wasn't what made it so hard to follow—it was the continual convoluted contradictions in his statements, one right after another.''

"Sometimes I would like to kick myself for using improper English," Anthoney told the jury, but the communication difficulty transcended grammar. Anthoney's contradictory comments, stacked upon each other in rapid succession, could have been part of a self-defined strategy intended to confuse the jury. According to expert Dr. Robert Hare, however, this particular communication trait is common to most criminal psychopaths—a condition that Hare termed, "mental Scrabble without an overall script."

"Lies and several contradictory statements in the same breath are very perplexing," said Dr. Hare, "and speech is the end product of very complicated mental activity. There is mounting scientific evidence that psychopaths differ from other people in the connections between words and emotions, and in the actual way their brains are organized. Psychopaths may know the dictionary definitions of words, but don't comprehend nor appreciate the significance or emotional value of words. As one person put it, 'he knows the words, but not the music.'"

"We could sit in a group of people," confirmed Debbie Heck, "and Kirby would tell lies and I would know it, but the other people wouldn't. I always just got a feeling that it just wasn't right."

This raises an important issue: If Anthoney's speech was consistently peculiar, why was he so capable of deceiving and manipulating people, and why would his friends fail to pick up the continual inconsistencies and contradictions in his casual conversation?

The answer, according to Hare, is "the speech oddities are often too subtle for the casual observer to detect, and these people put on a good show. Friends are deceived not by what is said, but by how it is said, and by the emotional buttons pushed.''

"I wish Hare could have been in the courtroom for Anthoney's three-hour performance," said Grimes. A self-proclaimed admirer of Dr. Hare's book *Without Conscience*, Grimes proudly noted that twenty copies were purchased for Anchorage Police Department detectives. "Even though Anthoney babbled away in the weird way he does," explained Grimes, "what did come through was that he was attempting to counter remarks made by Ingaldson or the police—but it was grueling. At one point, he even had the judge read the entire text of one of his tragic love letters to Debbie Heck."

This unusual event occurred following Anthoney's argument that he had no reason to kill the Newmans, and his derision of Ingaldson's theory that the anguish of his breakup with Debbie Heck drove him to murder.

"Mr. Ingaldson has given you a few ideas as to why I would want to do this," stated Anthoney. "That's absurd and I'll tell you why. First, he wants you to believe that I either did this because of the relationship that I had with Debbie Heck. Why somebody would kill somebody over somebody else's relationship, I can't figure it out. I'd like to describe to you a little bit about that relationship, give you some kind of idea actually of my state of mind. Not in the light that Mr. Ingaldson intends to show you what it was."

Anthoney then produced the letter to Debbie Heck, terming it, "the most recent compared to the other letters he showed you—this letter right here is the most recent one. He had this, but he didn't show it to you, but I am—"

Judge Buckalew interrupted him, asking, "Is this—excuse me. Is this letter in evidence?"

"Yes, it is, Your Honor," said Anthoney.

"All right," Buckalew responded, "I'd like to go through it with you, if I may. It says, 'Debbie, Hi. . . .' ''

The contrast between Buckalew's erudition and Anthoney's peculiar style provided a unique auditory experience, especially when the judge intoned, "'My life has been a lot of ups and downs. My ups with you mostly—mostly with you. And some of my downs also. But the ones without you were—weren't as good down—good as—weren't as good ups and were worse downs.' "

When Buckalew completed his recitation, Anthoney spoke to the jury, saying, "This letter was wrote before this happened . . . this was my true state of mind. And this wasn't just prior to this happening. She was on my mind. And she still is. There's parts in this letter that I want to draw your attention to. One of them is at the very end when I ask Debbie if she'll send me a picture. I tell h r I will, as well. That's what I told the police officers that I wanted that camera for. So I could send pictures. She was included in those pictures being sent to people. As well as my truck. And I do have those pictures to this day. They were not taken with that camera."

Anthoney further mystified listeners by saying of Ingaldson, "He dwells on my mental state of mind quite a bit through some excerpts that you've seen through. I'd like to go into a couple of those, but I'll reserve it for the time being.

"Mr. Ingaldson also said something about me planning ahead," he continued. "He's giving me credits in some points of having intelligence and then he's cut me down in others. He gave me credit of planning ahead about not having coins to go over to Debbie and Kirk's house to do laundry—he said, 'Of course he doesn't want them to know he had coins.' So he's giving me credit for doing that at least. And yet he's cutting me down for being stupid enough to do it in front of somebody else . . . he's trying to say that my camera—what you call it—I said it was a fanatic because I love cameras. I love taking pictures. He's trying to say that I just invented more or less to account for the camera. Well, you heard me testify that I have pictures that are at least this thick and I have photo albums with pictures in them."

Anthoney asked jurors to use their common sense and decide how many people would be able to account for every minute of their time if suddenly asked to. He repeatedly urged jurors to understand how upset and angry he became when Spadafora and Reeder elicited untrue or conflicting statements from him: "Spadafora was very hard," complained Anthoney. "You should have seen him when I was the only one with him. He was very hard. I became upset when the police officers tried to tell me that nobody remembered me being at the drive-through at Burger King," admitted Anthoney. "How in the hell is somebody supposed to remember everybody being through there? I knew it was just something else that they wanted to do to me. I gave them rough estimates as to how long it would take me to go through the drive-through. Ten to fifteen minutes. Who knows? I knew I ate my breakfast across in the parking lot. I don't know if people just shove food down their throats or not, so I assume maybe five minutes to eat. The letters did come to me at that time. When I got to Kirk and Debbie's house, I showed Miss Dean that letter. I didn't let her read it, but I showed it to her. Debbie Heck was a discussion we had that day. It wasn't very long. It was a brief discussion. Just a summary of what I was feeling and what she thought."

Anthoney further accused Ingaldson of lying about his pubic lice. "You heard Mr. Ingaldson say that I supposedly came in contact with body lice after I returned from the boat. Well, he knows that's not true," insisted an aggravated Anthoney. "I later learned that I had come in contact with body lice and that Debbie Heck had come in contact with body lice. Before I left the boat I told Miss Heck that she had body lice. This is before I left the boat. I had also told police that I had told her this. Mr. Ingaldson is trying to ridicule me on the fact that I put Rid in shampoo, and on this bottle it says 'Do not dilute, do not get on eyebrows.' Well, I guess what I'm trying to say is that by rationale the fact that it wasn't supposed to be diluted and used for over a twenty-four hour period, that if it was diluted, it wouldn't hurt to have it used over a twenty-four hour period, and that it would still have effect. And it did have an effect because Debbie Heck did not ever learn that she had body lice.

Mr. Ingaldson wants you to believe that I had just come in contact with it . . . because I'm the one who did this, and that's not true!''

Anthoney attempted clearing up his statements concerning the green gloves and the white shirt, insisting that Ingaldson and the police were twisting his statements and taking them out of context. ''They asked me if I had any gloves, if I owned any gloves. My first answer was no. That was my only answer. They then asked me if I wore any gloves. My first response was yes, yes, I had wore some gloves over at Nancy's because I wiped her car off. [Ingaldson] is trying to say to you that I did this because hairs may have been found. Because they suggested to me that there was hairs found in these gloves that were matching the back of my hands. Later on, they tried to confuse me by saying that there was hairs of my hands in there. And I caught them in that lie. And I told them that if they have hairs on the back of my hand, and they said they're comparisons. Mr. Spadafora testified to saying that they had lied to me, and I told them, I don't believe you. That was the last statement I ever gave them.''

Anthoney then produced a transcript of the actual police interview and read a portion of it to the jury:

''Ever worn gloves?''
''I scraped Nancy's window off one time.''
''What's that got to do with gloves?''
''I had to wear gloves because it was cold out and there was snow.''

''That brings us to the issue about me saying that it had been snowing,'' said Anthoney, referring back to Ingaldson's argument that there was no snowfall. ''He's trying to insinuate that I was trying to make it up about wearing these gloves because I had to place my hand in these gloves at some time. And I didn't have to, because there was no indication to me that there was any hairs in there when I first told them if I had done this. It was later . . . they tried to say that I said I wore these gloves. I never said I wore these gloves, because I don't know if they're the ones or not. And what I had told them, and what I testified to, is that I had wiped snow off Nancy's car.''

Anthoney insisted that he went to Nancy Newman's apartment on the Thursday before the murders to get his duffel bag and borrow the camera, and that while there he entered every room and picked up toys for the kids. It was then, according to him, that Nancy Newman gave him change from the cookie tin.

As for the white shirt, ''the police officers asked me what I was wearing that night and I told them. I said I borrowed a shirt from Kirk Mullins. I just casually threw in that I had a spot on that shirt. There was no mention of, do you have blood on your shirt? Is there anything on that shirt that might be incriminating to you, or anything like that nature. It was a casual conversation that I told the police officers that I had put a spot on that shirt before any questioning of it whatever.''

Attorneys usually use the final argument to weave a cohesive story from fragments of evidence and testimony. Not Anthoney. His long-winded diatribe was only ended with a personal plea to the jury: ''I just turn to you and ask you, please realize I didn't do it.''

Court was over for the day; the jury was dismissed; and the two sides gathered up their notes and went home. Anthoney returned to jail. The next morning, Salemi did his best to salvage the defense.

CHAPTER 19

"On Friday the thirteenth, Paul Chapman and his wife had what would be characterized as a small celebration and get-together which eventually included Nancy Newman," began John Salemi conversationally in his final summation for the jury. "That celebration occurred at Gwennie's Restaurant and Gwennie's bar portion of the restaurant. It lasted for, I think, the better part of two hours. It is not clear from the testimony how much was consumed. Nobody was counting. There was no need to count. But I think the evidence and reasonable inferences, using your common sense, lead to the conclusion that Mrs. Newman, Nancy Newman, had more than a couple of drinks that night. More than a couple of Bailey's. And why should you reasonably assume that? Besides the fact that people weren't counting, look at the time period. There was a two-and-a-half-hour time period where they were sitting at the bar. It's already been established that Mrs. Newman hadn't been eating at Gwennie's. In fact, she didn't have dinner at all that night . . . they then went after that two-and-a half-hour period to Paul and Cheryl's house for a further extended period of time. Mrs. Newman still didn't have anything to eat. No food was served . . . we know that when they left, Mrs. Newman didn't take her car with her.''

So far, Salemi hadn't told the jury anything they didn't know. If they wondered where he was going by telling this story, they didn't have to wonder for long. He immediately turned his attention to the car abandoned by Nancy Newman.

"Now, the explanation for that is a curious one. At least I would suggest to you it is,'' continued Salemi. "The reason that the car was left in an open, insecure lot on Spenard overnight, at a place of business which would have been closed until the next morning, at a place of business which is across from the Trade Winds Bar, a Hell's Angels hangout, was because Mrs. Newman didn't want to be alone. Apparently, she didn't want to be alone for the five or ten minutes they said it would take to drive from Gwennie's to Paul and Cheryl Chapman's. It's rather curious,'' he then argued, "in light of the fact that Mrs. Newman was at that time the sole caretaker for her two young children. Living in an apartment in midtown, with her husband thousands of miles away in Oakland, California, if she were to leave her car behind in an unguarded, unsecured parking lot, she would be left with her two children with no transportation, and in the event of a medical emergency, or some other type of emergency.''

He had the jury's enraptured attention as he slowly, perfectly, built his argument. "There is, of course, another explanation for why she left her car, and it fits very reasonably with the rest of the evidence we've talked about so far. And that is that Mrs. Newman had more to drink than has been suggested in court, and that she had enough to drink where either she didn't feel comfortable, or the people with her didn't feel comfortable, [about] having her drive even a short distance from Gwennie's.''

Salemi pointed out that the level of alcohol in Newman's bloodstream at the time of death was .093, and that a person is considered a drunk driver at a level of .10. When Nancy

Newman died, she died a .07 hundredths of a percent below the legal limit for being under the influence of alcohol if she were driving.

Heads nodded in the courtroom, but brows furrowed in contemplation—What did Mrs. Newman's level of intoxication have to do with the murders? Having knowingly raised the question, Salemi gave it verbalization and explanation. "So what? She wasn't driving. She's committed no crime. People have a right to drink as much as they want. And she had a good reason to be drinking. She was with her close friends and they were celebrating. They had cause to be happy and to socialize. Well, the 'so what?' of course, is probably obvious to you. Its significance is the sense that it casts considerable doubt on the prosecution's assertion, on Dr. Propst's finding, that Mrs. Newman was killed in the early morning hours of March 14th."

Salemi was brilliantly weaving a classic presentation of reasonable doubt. First he led up to it, then he stated it, and then he backed it up. "We all know that alcohol in the blood leaves the system over a period of time. Just because you consume alcohol, you don't stay intoxicated." He then explained that alcohol leaves the body at a rate of .015 per hour. If she were killed in the early morning hours of Saturday, "she would have no alcohol in her system.

"You start subtracting the fifteen per hour—just take the hours that she slept, and she would have nothing left in her system. There are a couple explanations, of course, for why she had a point-oh-nine-three in her system," acknowledged Salemi politely. "The first one might be that she was staggeringly drunk that night, that her alcohol level was up at two hundred fifty or something like that, and just subtracting the fifteen, she would still be at a ninety-three at eight or nine in the morning. Well, there is no testimony as to that."

Salemi made it clear that the defense was not suggesting that Nancy Newman was staggeringly drunk and overwhelmingly intoxicated. "Another possibility might be that she consumed alcohol in the early morning hours or in the middle of the night, and there is no testimony that she would have done that.''

In case the obvious significance of these facts was eluding the jury, Salemi personally clarified them. ''The obvious significance,'' he asserted, was that ''Mrs. Newman was killed several hours earlier—if Mrs. Newman were killed several hours earlier, then someone besides the person who is charged with killing these people is the real killer. Because Mr. Anthoney was at that party or gathering in the evening hours of March thirteenth and the early morning hours of March fourteenth.''

Salemi knew he had a strong argument, and he hammered away at it relentlessly. ''If you look at the evidence, this scientific evidence, another piece of scientific evidence, the type of evidence that the prosecution has asked you to rely on so heavily, you will find that there is a strong suggestion that Mrs. Newman was not killed in the early morning hours of Saturday. But in the evening, only a few hours after she stopped consuming alcohol . . . and the significance of that is obvious. If she were killed some time between ten-thirty and midnight, or one in the morning, or two in the morning, or three in the morning, this man here could not have possibly been involved in those killings.''

Ingaldson objected, decrying Salemi's mathematics. ''She would have had to have been killed ten or fifteen minutes before the Chapmans ever left the house! If she had four drinks, using the alcohol alone, she would have been killed before she ever left Gwennie's!''

The argument, to Salemi's benefit, degenerated into nit-picking over intestinal fauna, rates of decomposition, and the possible effect of antibiotics on alcohol dissipation rates. The jury became noticeably disinterested anytime discussions were technical.

Resuming his remarks, Salemi built on his argument that the murders took place at night, not in the morning, using the crime scene photos as evidence. ''If you look at the pictures, there's no coffee brewed—and everybody knew that you stayed away

from Nancy Newman until she had her first cup of coffee—
that appliance is not on, the Mr. Coffee that you see on the
kitchen counter. I guess the prosecution wants you to believe
that Mrs. Newman just took the old coffee from the night
before, on her day off, when she had plenty of time, and rather
than make a new pot of coffee—and we heard that she loved
coffee, loved her coffee, she just put some in the microwave
and that's why there hadn't been any brewed that morning. I
don't know how plausible that is. All of the victims were in
their nightclothes. That's consistent with this terrible tragedy
occurring at night.''

There were other clues backing up Salemi's version of the
murders, including a pink coat and the contents of the victims'
bladders and Mrs. Newman's stomach. "No urine in the bladders,'' stated Salemi emphatically. "Use your common sense.
I would suggest to you that it's consistent with having gone to
bed in the evening. Do you relieve yourself before you go to
bed at night? Now, food in the stomach—Nancy Newman had
coffee in her stomach. Well, she didn't have dinner, but she
did drink coffee. That's consistent with a killing in the evening.
A small detail,'' he continued, "but Angie Newman apparently
was wearing a pink coat, and it was laid I think on a sofa.
When the bodies were discovered two days later, that pink coat
was in the same location.''

Salemi then turned his attention directly to Anthoney's alibi,
stating, "You know, it's a legal term, but it sounds fishy. *Alibi.*
I'll tell you that the evidence—all of the evidence suggests
that Mr. Anthoney's whereabouts between the hours of ten-
thirty and three in the morning are certain. His *whereabouts.*
Let's talk about that. Not his *alibi.* His *whereabouts* for *certain.*''

The prosecution knew they were up against an excellent
defense team and listened intently as Salemi expertly countered
their accusations against his client. "Here's the theory of the
prosecution: They're all in their own bedroom because they
were ordered to go in their own bedrooms and they obeyed.

How about this? They were in bed. Because it was nighttime. And they were killed in the evening. The drapes were closed in the Newman apartment,'' Salemi noted, recalling testimony from Paul Chapman that one of the first things that Nancy Newman usually did in the morning, besides brewing herself a cup of coffee, was to open the drapes.

One living room drape, however, was slightly open. Ingaldson earlier suggested that the drape had been pulled back by Anthoney after the murders so he could peek outside. Salemi, of course, interpreted it differently. "The drape is slightly open toward the bottom, and that's in the living room area next to an easy chair, and that easy chair is next to the window. There is a coffee cup there and there's an ashtray with some cigarettes. It's as consistent, that drape being open, with Mrs. Newman being there, sitting there perhaps at night, finishing her coffee, drinking her cigarettes . . ."—the jury laughed at Salemi's unintentional element of humor—". . . and . . . and looking out the window because she heard a noise. Maybe she heard a car pull up. You know, you can do a lot of things with this evidence and look at it different ways. The state's theory, I think, is terribly flawed."

Next, Salemi attacked the prosecution's use of fingerprints and footprints, stating, "This whole thing about fingerprints and footprints is very strange. For example, if you look at all the fingerprints that were discovered in this particular case, lots of them related to Mr. Anthoney . . . but you look at other people who were there the day before, Friday the thirteenth, none of Cheryl Chapman. Kelly Prather Nicholson, she was there on Friday. Her prints weren't found. Jody Cornelius, who supposedly helped clean, none of her prints were found. But you find John Newman's fingerprints in there, and he hadn't been there for months. The only two footprints found in the whole apartment, Kirby Anthoney's? We know that Melissa, Angie, and Nancy Newman were living there on a day-to-day basis at the time, that Paul and Cheryl were there on Friday the thirteenth. You can't rely on the presence or absence of fingerprints," insisted Salemi. "It might be helpful if they were on a gun."

The defense also reminded the jury about the psychic visions of J.S. "Talking about the occult is kind of strange," acknowledged Salemi, "but in the context of this case it certainly is as plausible as Mr. Ingaldson's theory about how all this happened. The fact of the matter is this woman, J.S., predicted these murders. She was able, with specificity, to describe the apartment, and not in a way that she's going to pick up in the newspaper or some newscast." The defense pointed out that the Newman apartment had been sealed, and no television cameras nor press reporters were allowed inside. "You would have had some officer testify that they were in the apartment taking pictures and it was broadcast on the news if that's in fact what happened. What J.S. predicted and what came true was that there will be brutal murders, they were going to have to get the blood of the youngest child for this strange cult, satanic activity, whatever it was. And she said it was related to cult activity."

Salemi knew adding an occult aspect to the case was farfetched, so he countered that potential objection head-on. "Maybe you're saying, 'Cult activity in Anchorage, Alaska? That's absurd. We don't have those kinds of things up here.' Well, these people don't advertise in the Yellow Pages. You know that much. We have Hell's Angels in Anchorage, we've got street gangs coming up from East Los Angeles in Anchorage, Alaska. You go to Coeur D'Alene and you've got rightwing Neo-Fascists. I wouldn't expect that in Coeur D'Alene. I heard it's a pretty nice town. So, don't let the state, through Mr. Ingaldson, a soft-spoken man with a nice manner, just say, 'Oh, pooh-pooh to that stuff, you know; we don't have to deal with that.' But you do. In fact, the police did."

Salemi offered his own pointed observations about what was, and what was not, reaching the jury. He explained, "The state has a lot of money, time, and energy invested in preparing for this case—there are all kinds of diagrams, charts, overheads, aerial photos. But they didn't tell you about the blood alcohol on Miss Newman, they didn't tell you about Frank Cornelius, and they didn't tell you about the cult.''

Cornelius, an early suspect discounted by Ray because he didn't know the victims, became an important factor for the defense.

''What if he was one of two?'' asked Salemi. ''What if he was one of several? What if he wasn't involved in the sexual assault, but was involved in the killing? He lives in the apartment above them, he is alone after one A.M. on the early morning of March fourteenth. He is obviously a suspect. The police were coming to his apartment looking for him and he evaporates—he moves out right after the murders, apparently down in Seattle somewhere. He called Jody Cornelius and asked her to throw some of his personal belongings out the window after the murders. But it's ludicrous, according to the state, for us to bring him up.'' Salemi noted that once police caught up with Mr. Cornelius, he was taken to Dr. Propst where they examined various wounds, cuts, or rug burns.

''They're taking his suitcase and pulling it apart because they've got bloodstains in there, and they're sending it off to the FBI,'' said Salemi. ''The newspaper article of April eleventh said that they were waiting for FBI results because they had ten suspects they were considering—that's almost a month after these murders and they were still considering ten different people.''

The Anchorage Police Department did not actually have ten suspects on April 11—they had one: Kirby D. Anthoney.

''When I read that in the paper, I about fainted,'' Grimes later commented. ''I have no idea where that came from, or why Novaky said it to the press. Actually, that screwed up a plan we'd cooked up to really push Anthoney's buttons. We were going to have the newspaper print the profile, point by point, which Ray provided to us from the FBI. The minute Anthoney read that, it would be clear that we were on to him. We figured maybe he had a secret stash somewhere of items he'd stolen from the Newmans, aside from the camera, and perhaps he would lead us to it if he decided to make a run for it. However, because the story about the fictional ten suspects made it in the paper, we had to abandon that idea. Personally, I was really steamed about that statement to the press, and it came back to haunt us at the trial.''

Accusing the prosecution of being misleadingly selective about the evidence, Salemi further characterized Ingaldson as having choreographed an elaborate yet misleading production. ''The whole impression you're supposed to get—and I hope you see through this, is that this is a matter of science solving a crime, but it's not really that way . . . none of the victims' blood have been identified as being on Mr. Anthoney or any of his clothes; none of his blood, none of the fibers from his clothes, were found on any of the victims.''

Salemi proceeded to knock technical underpinning out from under Sergeant Gifford's testimony. ''Mr. Howard asked Sergeant Gifford about the method of vacuuming,'' recalled Salemi, referring to the alleged extensive and painstaking grid work and labeling of evidence vacuumed from the Newman apartment, ''and there was no grid.'' Salemi noted that the Anchorage Police Department was now going to change their methods because they didn't ''know where a lot of these hairs came from,'' and that labeling only identified hairs as being from certain bedrooms.

''Did they come from close proximity to the body?'' asked Salemi rhetorically. ''Did they come from other places? You've got to consider that. This whole hair thing is very hit and [sic] miss. Sergeant Gifford came in and said that using some police vacuum with a moderate suction, he picked up over five hundred hairs.'' Of those 500 hairs, Salemi reminded the jury, not one pubic hair from Kirby D. Anthoney was found in Nancy Newman's room, not even on her body.

''Of the people who were sexually assaulted, she has pubic hair,'' stated Salemi, explaining that pubic combings were performed to determine if any pubic hairs from her assailant were transferred during the assault. "Nothing was found in her pubic combings."

As for blood, Salemi pointed out that there were "significant amounts of blood" at the Eide Street apartment. FBI blood expert Robert Hall told jurors he found human blood on the leather coat and sneakers Anthoney allegedly wore the day of the murders. "But none of it is even identified as the victims' blood," asserted Salemi, also reminding the jury that there was blood on the carpet, asking, "If those footprints were Mr. Anthoney's footprints related to this homicide, wouldn't there be a little bit of blood in the footprint? Wouldn't there be a little bit of blood in that tread pattern of his—that unique tread pattern?"

Salemi concentrated on the expert testimony, constantly pointing out the imprecise nature of the test and the findings. "This whole thing about semen and blood-typing does not point the finger at any individual," stated Salemi factually. "It only serves not to eliminate a person from a much larger pool. In this case, perhaps as many as five thousand people. That's limiting it to Anchorage. What if we're going to talk about the state of Alaska? Let's use the five hundred thousand population number. Maybe we should include California, because I think you can get on a plane and go down to California from here. And maybe somebody might want to do that after they commit a crime like this. I hear there's like twenty million people in California."

Salemi allowed his expanded pool concept to sink in, then continued with a discussion of lies: "There are lies, there are damn lies, and there are statistics. And you've got the third category in this case."

Salemi attacked Ingaldson's explanation of how the crime transpired, and why Anthoney's hairs appear in some rooms and not others. "The state wants to talk about all the pubic hairs that are in [Melissa's] room," Salemi said. "He wants to explain that by saying the pants must be off. Can't find any pubic hairs in Nancy Newman's room, so he'll explain that the person left their pants on. We find some which are consistent microscopically with Kirby Anthoney, so let's take his pants off once he gets in the second room. It's getting late now in this thing, according to the state and according to their theory, it's getting late and so this person now changes the method of killing from strangulation to slitting Angie's throat. Apparently, the person is worried about time and wants to get out. That's plausible. But look at the next piece of the state's theory. The person takes the time to start masturbating on Angie or over Angie Newman's body. So, here is this person who is in enough of a hurry, who is worried about time, wants to get out, and so they just cut this young girl's throat so they can hurry up the process. But now they're going to take the time to masturbate. And I imagine it's going to take time, since they've had a couple of ejaculations already, according to the state's theory. And that explains why there's pubic hair, according to the state's theory.''

The state suggested that there were two ejaculations by one male. Salemi presented an alternate theory: two men having one ejaculation each. In the defense's opinion, one person having at least two ejaculations and then masturbating a third time was ''kind of curious.''

''The first sexual assault of Nancy Newman, the person only takes their penis out of their pants,'' said Salmei, recounting the prosecution's presentation, ''and that's why there is no hair. But for some reason, when this person wants to sexually assault Melissa, he must pull down his pants.

''Also according to the state's theory, that footprint is there [on the fireplace] because it was placed there after all this was accomplished and this person, Mr. Anthoney, wanted to look out the window to see if he could make a safe exit. The state ignores the fact that there's a mirror over the fireplace.''

Salemi then suggested that Anthoney stood on the fireplace to look at himself in the mirror to comb his hair one day, rather than to see if the coast was clear after killing three people.

''With respect to Melissa,'' argued Salemi, ''she's got this pillowcase on her wrist. It was loosely tied at one end and it wasn't tied to anything on the other end. The state's theory is that was used somehow to accomplish the rape. When you look at the photographs, it looks like it's almost ornamental, I mean it was put there as an afterthought more than anything else. I think as consistent with some sort of strange, unexplainable, maybe cult activity.''

The defense barraged the jury with numerous unanswered questions: If Melissa left her room to go see her mother, how did she end up back in her room? Why were there no signs of struggle? Why are there no defensive wounds? If Kirby Anthony was the assailant, why were there no marks on him?

Salemi also addressed the supposedly damning palm print above Melissa's bed, the one Ingaldson portrayed as consistent with Melissa being sexually assaulted over her bed. The state argued that the only way you could put a handprint like that is to lean over the bed. The defense, however, reasoned that the palm print could result from someone simply sitting up in bed, and then pushing off as they revolved or twisted to get up.

Salemi, quick to discount FBI testimony, said, ''The FBI agents are all nice people, they all dress well. They all know how to testify. The FBI sits here and they politely look at you while you ask the question, and then they revolve in their seat and they answer it, and then they revolve back here and they get your next question, then they come back, and it's all very professional. But everything they do, their tests, their testimony is calculated to advance the effort of the prosecution. Is the FBI a group of scientists?'' asked Salemi. ''Is this some sort of think tank back in Washington, DC? These people only care about prosecuting a crime. My recollection is that the FBI was not set up to do science. The FBI is a prosecution arm, or law enforcement arm, of the federal government.''

The defense used the complicated nature of Dr. Schanfield's testimony to their advantage, as well. Salemi dismissed it entirely with four sentences. ''I've got a note here to talk about

Dr. Schanfield, but I wouldn't know what to say, really. Because I don't think anybody understood what he was talking about. I think his conclusion was that eighty percent of the population has the same allotypes as he found in the semen. If the state did indeed pay one thousand dollars a day for Dr. Schanfield, I'm not sure they got their money's worth.''

Salemi pointed out that the infamous white shirt supposedly worn by Anthoney during the crime had no stain on it whatsoever. He emphatically told the jury that the FBI admitted there was no way to date hairs, nor could hairs be matched to any individual with one hundred percent accuracy. The defense again promulgated their theory, backed by their interpretation of scientific testimony, that the murders took place at night, not in the morning.

''You know,'' said Salemi, ''what this case boils down to is a bunch of maybes. And what it boils down for you is that you've got to determine whether the state has presented a case to you which you're convinced beyond a reasonable doubt that that young man brutally murdered three of his relatives and raped two of them and kidnapped one of them. What you really need to ask yourself is, are there some questions in your mind, are there still some questions. Maybe how this happened, why it happened. What's the motive? Why was Angie Newman's throat cut? Is there any possible cult involvement in this? How many people were really involved? Is this really done by one person? Who is Frank Cornelius? What was his role in this, if any? What's he look like? What was the real time of death? You know, aren't these reasonable questions?

''Here you are, twelve people who probably don't know each other, didn't know Mr. Anthoney, didn't know Mr. Ingaldson or myself,'' Salemi said in his relaxed manner, ''and you're brought together, spend a lot of time in the courtroom, probably spending more time getting to know one another. And you're called upon to make one of the biggest decisions of your life.

''There is no doubt,'' asserted Salemi, ''you make decisions about what kind of career you're going to have. Or maybe you pick a spouse who you're going to marry. Maybe you're going to plunk down a quarter of a million dollars on a house, or pay off a house that costs that kind of money. Those are all big decisions. So, it's not like you're not used to making big decisions. But the difference between those decisions and the one you're going to make in this case is that those are reversible.

"If you choose the wrong spouse," Salemi explained, "it may be painful, but you can get a divorce. If you buy a house, well, I don't know about this market, but usually you can sell it and get another if you don't like it. But the decision in respect to this case is a nonreversible decision and that's why you have to be convinced. That's why you can't play around with the standard of proof and lower it because it's a terrible tragedy. You don't want to compound the tragedy by changing the law because this was a terrible case and a high-profile case.

"You don't get to call Judge Buckalew up a week from now, or two weeks from now, and say, 'God, you know, I've been having nightmares about it, I think I might have made the wrong decision, would you mind calling those eleven other jurors and we can talk about this a little bit more?' It doesn't happen, so you've got to be sure."

Salemi entreated the jury to think seriously about the concept of reasonable doubt, and to be sure in their hearts and minds that the evidence established beyond a reasonable doubt that the man charged in this case was guilty.

"If you ask the questions that I've suggested, and the many more that I don't have time to go over in this case; if you ask yourself those questions, if you talk about them, and if you take the concept of proof beyond a reasonable doubt seriously, and if you apply it properly in this case," concluded Salemi, "you will find you have doubt, the doubt is reasonable, and you'll return a verdict of not guilty." Salemi sat down, and Buckalew called a fifteen-minute recess.

When court reconvened, Buckalew cautioned the representatives of the TV and the press. "I've been advised," he said, "that some of the jurors on the front row were viewed on

television. I'm going to conduct an investigation after this trial
is over. So, if it comes to my attention any jurors' pictures
are on television, I'm going to clear the television out of the
courtroom. All right, Mr. Ingaldson.''

This was it—Ingaldson's final address to the jury, his last
chance to convince them that Kirby D. Anthoney was a cruel
and vicious rapist and child murderer, and that the evidence
proved it beyond a reasonable doubt.

As he stood, Ingaldson knew this wasn't going to be a slam-
dunk for the prosecution. Most of the evidence was forensic,
technical, and inferential. Never before had a behavioral science
specialist been allowed to testify, even in a limited way, and
the jury knew nothing at all about Anthoney's past. All they
knew is what they saw in court, and Salemi gave an excellent
closing argument. At that point, everything depended on Mr.
William Ingaldson.

CHAPTER 20

"This will be the last time you hear anyone, so the end is finally, I guess, in sight," began Ingaldson, communicating a shared sense of release. "You heard from Mr. Salemi and you heard from Mr. Anthoney talking about some things, and now it is my chance to respond to some of those.

"In this case, all the evidence points to Kirby Anthoney," he said, immediately and succinctly getting right to the point. "All of the forensic evidence, all of the physical evidence. Blood, hairs, semen, camera, coins, footprints, fingerprints, all of it points to Kirby Anthoney."

He then addressed Salemi's attempts to undermine the prosecution's medical evidence. In the process, he took strong swipes at the questionable inclusion of secondhand testimony from self-proclaimed psychic mental patients.

"This isn't a cult killing. We see no evidence of that. We haven't heard from experts on cults. We haven't heard any evidence, anything at all to show this was a cult type of killing, a satanistic [sic] type of killing. We have her premonition, she also told police that there would be two other people killed that night because they need three every moon. There weren't two other people killed that night, and there aren't three people killed every single month in Anchorage when the moon reaches a certain phase. The day that people are convicted of something based on testimony like J.S.'s, the day that type is even able to reach a jury is a pretty sad day in our legal system. When you start hearing things like the testimony of J.S.,'' asserted Ingaldson, ''when you start hearing things like, 'why didn't the prosecution bring out this stuff about the alcohol with Dr. Propst?' Then there is kind of an attempt maybe to divert from the issues. If this is something that's important or something that is relevant, do you think I'm not going to present that,'' asked Ingaldson. ''I also didn't mention about this drug that was in Nancy's body that came from some type of gas that they use when they extract teeth. But what relevance is that toward the murder?''

Salemi had attempted raising doubts about time of death, using blood alcohol levels as the criteria. In Salemi's version, Nancy Newman consumed far more alcohol than the Chapmans would acknowledge.

''Paul Chapman testified that Nancy Newman wasn't particularly drunk or intoxicated. But what's the difference? Does that show who murdered someone, or what time it is? Is Cheryl Chapman going to try and cover up something as to time of death, and why would she do that? Why would she even know anything about that? There is no reason to disbelieve the evidence. Why did Nancy Newman drive home with Cheryl that night? And it may be, as Mr. Salemi pointed out, Nancy wasn't feeling really up to driving. Because we know not only was she drinking, but if you look at the doctor's records, she was prescribed Tylenol three for her teeth. So, she may have been taking some Tylenol. She might not have felt good about driving, and that's a very reasonable explanation.''

Because Salemi mocked the fingerprint evidence, Ingaldson began by agreeing with him. ''He's right, you know these fingerprints are kind of funny. You don't even see Paul Chapman's," continued Ingaldson. "There were some of Cheryl Chapman, but the interesting thing and the most significant print of Kirby Anthoney's fingerprint is that one over the bed. And I want you to think about it for two reasons. Number one, it came up right away. In comparison with the other print on the wall up on the closet. Why would one come up and not the other if they are both old prints? But the most important thing is, think of that location of the print."

Ingaldson pulled up a chair, and gave the jury a visual demonstration. "I'll use this chair so I don't have to sit on the floor," he said, pretending to be sitting down on a bed. "If you're sitting on the bed, how would you get your hand in this position?" He attempted twisting his hand around to match the location of Anthoney's palm print, but to no avail. "It doesn't work unless a person is a contortionist," he insisted.

Countering Salemi's remarks about the testimony of the FBI agents, Ingaldson said, "There is talk about the FBI persons, you know, that they come in and are just telling what the prosecution wants. Well, we know that's not true, because they have a protocol to go by. Because they testify in many states, and they don't want to be wrong. They also testify for the defense. They don't have an interest in the results. They're not getting paid to testify. They do their own tests—think about the reason they might do their own tests. They certainly don't have an economic incentive to make new findings.

"I agree with Mr. Salemi that some of this allotyping is confusing. The blood group substances are confusing for me, and maybe there are some people on the jury [who] know more about biology and chemistry. But Dr. Schanfield's credentials are very high, obviously. You can look at some of his background, if you have more doubts about that, in the jury room. Dr. Schanfield talked about the use of these allotypes. And it's his opinion that the same donor of semen on Melissa and Nancy and [on the] washcloth were all the same person because of this very unique, very unique semen characteristic that he noticed."

Ingaldson then commented about statements made by Anthoney during the previous day's cross-examination. "I'm sure you realize that there were many things even then that he was rationalizing and changing to fit the cross-examination. And things are changing again." To back up his allegations, Ingaldson delineated what he termed "obvious lies"—among them was Anthoney's testimony that he spoke at length to Tony Marinelli on the morning of the homicide. "We know that Marinelli wasn't working that day," said Ingaldson. "The call couldn't have happened on that Saturday. But he tries to fit it in and say it did. According to Tony Marinelli, it would have been on a weekday *before* the murders—it would have been during that time that Kirby Anthoney called him. We know he didn't talk to Tony Marinelli on Saturday, but he's trying to fill in the gaps."

More egregious was Anthoney's claim that Jess O'Dell saw John Newman's camera prior to the murders. "Anthoney tried to sell the camera to O'Dell after the killings," insisted Ingaldson, "but he wasn't able to do it. Mr. Anthoney says he gave it to the police. Well, why would Investigator Reeder lie about that? Why would Investigator Spadafora lie about getting it out? Both of them testified consistently about Investigator Spadafora getting the camera out of the closet. Why would they lie about that? If they're going to lie, they'd tell a heck of a lot better lies than that. [Anthoney] talks about getting it, and talking about Jess O'Dell seeing this. And for some reason he couldn't remember when the police are pressing him about things and accusing him of at least indirectly taking the camera, he can't remember Jess O'Dell seeing it. He can't remember until seven months later! That whole story is absurd!"

Ingaldson rapidly assaulted other contradictions in Anthoney's testimony, including him washing his upper body before going to the Mullinses'. "We hear in court, all of a sudden, for the first time, that he washed his upper body. He says that somewhere in the police reports he told the police that. We didn't hear anything about that from Investigator Reeder; there is nothing about washing his upper body in any of the police reports. Why would someone take off their shirt and wash their upper body? If they are going to do that, wouldn't they just jump in the shower?

"He talks about getting his tire fixed," continued Ingaldson, "and he said, 'Yeah, I remember because my tire was leaking.' And I said, 'Well, you got your tire fixed *before* you left.' And all of a sudden he had *two* [leaking] tires. And in court yesterday he said, 'I wish I could prove it if I could. I got a new tire.' He describes that there was tread missing from his tire, so he got a new tire."

Ingaldson picked up a slip of paper, identified as a plaintiff's exhibit, and held it in front of the jury. "Look at this receipt! It doesn't say tire on there. It says tube. What you probably would get for a leak. It doesn't say tire, it says tube."

Ingaldson then quickly turned to the topic of Anthoney's phone call to Carol Hawkins in which he informed her that Nancy was raped and one of the girls stabbed. "How would he know that? Would you assume because someone asked him for a knife that one of the little girls was stabbed? Why not Nancy being stabbed? That Nancy was the one raped? He assumed that? Would he tell [Carol Hawkins] that's what happened? He presumed that Melissa and Nancy were the ones that had been sexually assaulted. Lo and behold, those are the ones!

"We know this [crime] isn't some long drawn-out planned thing when someone came over, because everything used in the commission of this thing were things found at the scene. We have gloves consistent with gloves found in Nancy's nightstand. Pillowcases that they were strangled with were taken from the beds. I don't know what knife was used for sure with Angie, but isn't it kind of a coincidence that the steak knives in the house—of the six steak knives, one is missing?"

He paused, letting the jury contemplate his litany for a moment, and said, "I'll tell you what probably happened . . . maybe he just got there and his plan was just to have sex with Nancy and she refused. But we know that she was beat about the face before she died because there are bruises there before death, and after death. We know that Melissa was in that room at some time. Now, why did he take Melissa back into her own bedroom? Maybe he just wanted to, or maybe because there is fecal matter on the end of the bed here,'' noted Ingaldson, pointing to the enlarged illustration of the Newman apartment and pictures of the victims. ''Nancy's body is swung around here. Her legs are kind of in an awkward position. Look where her hands are? These feet were grabbed and she was swung around. She was probably sexually assaulted here and swung around after. There's fecal matter here . . . maybe he was going to sexually assault Melissa here but he didn't want to have more feces on him.'' He now had the jury's complete, if uncomfortable, attention.

''Maybe the bed's too high to do Melissa in the manner that he did it. Melissa's bed worked out just perfect for him. The right amount of height. You can see the bruises on her,'' he said, pointing to another disturbing photograph, ''inside of her knees and inside of her ankles. He had her spread over the bed. And every single thing in here, everything points to Kirby Anthoney.

''The hairs on her buttocks area are Kirby Anthoney's,'' he said forcefully and emphatically. ''The bloody smear on her stomach and on the bed, the semen matches Kirby Anthoney's. All the pubic hairs in the room, all of them are Kirby Anthoney's. No one else! Even according to his testimony, or through those letters, this is the one that would have taken more time. How does he know that? Well, we all know that. He knows because he did it!''

The jury kept looking over at Anthoney, as if picturing him in the act. The repulsion and animosity were almost palpable. ''Think of where the semen is,'' demanded Ingaldson. ''The bruises on her knees are consistent with that. Think of how you are going to secure a body—that is to take that pillowcase and tie a knot around the wrist, wrap it around the other wrist, and you can hold both hands in one hand.

"What are the odds," asked Ingaldson, "that this just happens to be a coincidence that it's his semen? Well, it is very low odds. Ninety-three percent of the population would not have that semen type. Well, we know that the person was someone who knew the family. So, is it just a coincidence that we have his hairs, that we have his semen type? Is it just a coincidence that the cigarette found in there matches his saliva type? Is it just a coincidence that the murder happened during the time period Saturday morning when Kirby Anthoney's alibi changed the most? Is it just a coincidence that Kirby Anthoney had feces on his shirt, on the lower front part, and Nancy Newman in her sexual assault had a bowel movement? Is it just a coincidence that the only valuable things missing in that apartment were coins that Kirby Anthoney knew about? Why would a stranger happen to find those coins all of a sudden above the microwave?" Ingaldson was on a roll, his intensity building phrase by phrase. "And the camera—a camera that he doesn't even know how to work.

"Ladies and gentlemen, we talked about reasonable doubt. Mr. Salemi talked about reasonable doubt. I guess in jury selection we went over what reasonable doubt means. It does not mean beyond all possible doubt, but that which is reasonable. And I ask you to follow your common sense in this case. It's true the system works when innocent people are not convicted, but it also works when guilty people are convicted. In this case not only is there evidence of beyond a reasonable doubt, but there is evidence of more than that. Really, if you think about it, think of all these things as evidence beyond *all* doubt that Kirby Anthoney committed these murders. All the testimony we've heard, all the arguments we've heard, all the explanations, none of them explain about the semen, the coins, the fingerprints, the footprints, the entrance and exit, except that Kirby Anthoney did it—every piece of evidence is explained by Kirby Anthoney doing this. There are not *any* alternative explanations."

Ingaldson thanked the jury for their time, even doing so on

behalf of Salemi and Judge Buckalew, and concluded by saying, "I'd ask you to consider this case and to return a verdict of guilty on all counts. Thank you." With that, William Ingaldson sat down.

Judge Buckalew allowed a moment of reflective silence, then said, "Why don't we take a ten-minute recess and then you can talk to the bailiffs about where you want to have lunch, and then you'll come back and I'll read the instructions and you can go to lunch. But it's twelve-fifteen. We'll take a ten-minute recess. They certainly ought to be ready for lunch right at one o'clock. That would be a safe figure."

When the court reconvened, the judge made a special point of complimenting Salemi on his defense, addressing his comments directly to Kirby D. Anthoney.

"I don't know whether you'll agree with me or not, Mr. Anthoney, but you got one of the better defenses I've seen in a long time. Mr. Salemi, that was a pretty powerful argument you made. So I suggest to you, Mr. Anthoney, if you had two million dollars in cash, you couldn't have bought yourself a better defense."

During lunch, Buckalew, Howard, and Ingaldson went over the jury instructions in the judge's chambers. A number of additions were made to the court's instructions. Back in the courtroom, Buckalew asked if Salemi had any objections.

"I've deferred to Mr. Howard pretty much in terms of the defense input with respect to instructions," answered Salemi. "And, of course, I've talked with him and talked with Mr. Anthoney after we put together the initial packet, and it's my understanding that the defense is now satisfied with instructions."

Ingaldson, however, had one more item he wished to discuss before the jury returned—"this issue about Dr. Schanfield." The issue regarding Dr. Schanfield concerned the additional findings derived from his analysis of Anthoney's semen sample.

"Obviously, we've rested, and we're not putting that evidence in, and lest there be any concern that later on, depending on the result in this case, about Dr. Schanfield or his credibility, I just want it clear for the record that the reason I decided not to put that in [because] it's clear that there is a real close question as to whether or not there would be attorney-client privilege involved and in order not to open up that issue, and depending upon the verdict in this case, along that issue, I have decided not to go into that area. So I just wanted to put that on the record.''

State of Alaska v. Kirby D. Anthoney went to the jury for deliberation on Thursday, June 2.

Jurors in the Kirby Anthoney murder trial continued their deliberations through Friday, and there was speculation that they would continue through Saturday, June 4. Any verdict reached over the weekend would be sealed and remain undisclosed until Monday morning. The panel, which was not sequestered, spent Friday listening to playbacks of trial witnesses, including the testimony of Sergeant Gifford, Dr. Propst, the pathologist who performed the autopsies, and Debbie Heck. They also requested a copy of Anthoney's driving record.

"Because he tried to leave the country before the district attorney was ready to charge him with the murders, we used Anthoney's suspended driver's license as an excuse to have him arrested at the Canadian border," commented Grimes. "When Anthoney was doing his long-winded summation for the jury, he made a big deal out of that, insisting that his license wasn't suspended."

The jury foreman, a local minister, announced that the jury had reached verdicts after only two days of deliberations. The envelope would be opened Monday morning.

CHAPTER 21

On Monday, June 6, 1988, more than one hundred people crowded into Buckalew's courtroom, spilled into the side aisles and flowed out the door. "The place was packed," recalled Ingaldson. "They put us in what we call the media courtroom—it's much bigger than the others. Everyone was eager for the verdict. Well, maybe Anthoney wasn't, but we were."

"The short jury deliberation gave us increased hope about the verdict," said Grimes. "Because of that, plus the quality of the prosecution's case, I was feeling fairly certain, but you never know for sure until the jury speaks."

Cheryl Chapman, talking to reporters outside the courtroom, said, "I just know it's guilty."

"No special effort was made to prepare Anthoney for the likelihood of a guilty verdict," stated Defense Attorney Howard, "even after jurors concluded their labors so quickly."

John Newman sat in the second row. Friends and supporters held his hand and gave him reassuring pats on the shoulder.

"Cheryl Chapman sat right in the front row," said Grimes, "strong as ever. She waited for the jury to come in, and she was quite grim. The row behind the defense table is usually blocked off with tape for security reasons, but it was opened for those of us in the Anchorage Police Department and the District Attorney's Office who came for the conclusion of this long, heartbreaking, and exhaustive investigation.''

''I went to the court the day the verdict came in,'' recalled Sergeant Gifford, ''I usually don't do that. I was sure we had done all we could, but you never know what will happen.''

With television cameras rolling, a clean-shaven Kirby D. Anthoney walked in surrounded by uniformed guards wearing flak vests. Everyone was sitting in silence, waiting for the jury to walk in, when suddenly Anthoney turned to John Newman and yelled, ''You're a fool, John!''

Howard blanched, Ingaldson's jaw dropped, the crowd gasped, and John Newman's face turned crimson with anger. A few moments later, Anthoney turned around again, calling out, ''I love you with all my heart.''

''Don't you talk to me,'' shouted Newman as he lunged for Anthoney. ''Don't you even talk to me!''

''Oh, my God, Newman went right for him,'' recalled Grimes, ''and had he not been restrained, he probably would have ripped Anthoney limb from limb. Two policemen immediately placed themselves between Newman and Anthoney until Buckalew entered.''

The jury found Kirby Dale Anthoney guilty on three counts of homicide, three counts of sexual assault, and one count of kidnapping. The courtroom erupted in a cacophony of cheers. ''Quiet,'' insisted Buckalew. ''No! No more outbursts in the courtroom, or I'll clear the courtroom.''

Anthoney pressed his knuckles against his mouth, attempting to stay a flood of tears. His attempts failed. Found guilty, a sobbing Anthoney entreated the judge to sentence him immediately. ''This is a hideous crime,'' Anthoney wailed. ''If you feel that I'm guilty of this, I feel you should sentence me.''

Ingaldson objected, insisting that Anthoney was in no condition to waive his rights to the usual presentence evaluation. In addition, the state wanted to put on record all it had uncovered about Anthoney's unsavory criminal past.

Anthoney was escorted back to jail, the crowd filtered out, and Newman and Chapman hugged each other, then hugged Grimes, Spadafora, Reeder, Gifford, and all the other police officers that helped bring Kirby D. Anthoney to justice.

"When the verdict was guilty, I was relieved," Gifford recalled, "but somehow in a case like this, there is no feeling of justice having been done. What can be done to someone who has committed a crime such as this? The horrific acts and actions committed by Anthoney are beyond comprehension. Working as close with the victims at the scene and autopsy, and then working the evidence re-creating the actions of the offender and the victims, brings a person too close to the event. Knowing what they went through, there is nothing I can think of that can bring justice to the offender."

Speaking to reporters in the courthouse lobby, John Newman addressed the near violent confrontation with Anthoney. "He doesn't want me to believe he really did it. It was like throwing a knife at me. I think we can rest as far as that the murder is taken care of," he said concerning the verdict. "It still will take a little time. I will get on with my life."

"I feel that my sister is finally at peace in her grave," Cheryl Chapman told the press. She left Alaska for Twin Falls that afternoon. John Newman followed the next day.

"The relationship between John Newman and his sister, Peggy Anthoney, who also lives in Twin Falls, is going to take years to heal, if ever," commented Grimes. "Anthoney's mother protected him as much as she could from the consequences of his behavior. His mother was his one most ardent supporter, I think, all of his life. Everyone in Twin Falls, police included, acknowledge that Peggy Anthoney did her best with those kids under the circumstances when they were younger. It's not her fault that Kirby Anthoney was a psychopath."

The relationship between Anthoney and his mother, despite his antisocial and dangerous behavior, is not unusual, according to Dr. Hare. "Many psychopaths are protected from the consequences of their actions by well-meaning family members or friends. Even those who are caught and punished usually blame the system, fate—anything but themselves—for their difficulties."

Essentially, individuals such as Kirby Anthoney have no desire for change, consider insights to be excuses, have no concept of the future, resent all authority, and detest being in a position of inferiority.

"We learned a lot from this case," said Ingaldson, the prosecutor who became an instant expert on forensics during the trial. "We learned new ways to take samples—scraping instead of swabbing, for one thing. Perhaps freeze-drying them." Ingaldson, explaining to reporters why DNA analysis approved by the FBI prior to the trial was not used in the case against Kirby D. Anthoney, said, "DNA analysis could not be used in the Newman murder investigation because not enough blood or semen was recovered for the analysis process. Perhaps because the bodies were not discovered for twenty-four hours, the semen left in Nancy Newman had been largely destroyed by bacterial action. Stains removed from body surfaces or bedclothes were collected using techniques that diluted them. Those samples were used for other tests, but when the DNA test became available, not enough was left to analyze and compare with a sample of blood police took from Anthoney. The other tests were able to isolate enough genetic markers to identify semen found at the scene as particular to only seven percent of the male population, including Kirby Anthoney."

"The Anthoney case was probably the most challenging case that I've worked on in ten years in the laboratory," said FBI Agent Deedrick, who later played a key role in the O.J. Simpson trial. "The evidence is either there or it isn't there. In the Kirby Anthoney case it was all there. It bothered me a great deal initially, when the case first came in, because I've got three girls. My fear is coming home someday and finding them dead. I wanted to work my best on this to find the right person. It's a tremendously good feeling I had when I heard about the verdict.''

The challenge for DNA testing would be the same one faced by blood allotyping—it must pass what is called the Frye test. This means that prosecutors have to be able to demonstrate that the scientific community accepts the new technique as reliable.

Judge Buckalew set August 12 as the date of sentencing, but on June 20, Assistant District Attorney Bill Ingaldson has asked for a court order forcing Anthoney to submit to psychiatric tests. Ingaldson expected the test results to support the state's position that Anthoney was one of the worst murderers imaginable, and that he deserved the most severe punishment. He could get up to 456 years, but Ingaldson wanted him to get even more. Ingaldson asked the judge to find Anthoney guilty of several ''aggravators,'' which would add eight or more years to Anthoney's sentence. These ''aggravators'' were comprised of Anthoney's criminal history, including the murder of Walter Napageak and the rape of Michelle Bethel.

Ingaldson wanted Keith Hayes to testify at the presentencing hearing, but there was one tangled complication—John Salemi now represented both Keith Hayes and Kirby Anthoney. Salemi did not want Hayes testifying about Anthoney confessing to the Napageak murder, and Salemi couldn't cross-examine Hayes without violating legal ethics. John Salemi, accompanied by Ingaldson and Anthoney, petitioned for withdrawal before Superior Court Judge Mark Roland.

''I think the reason we're having this hearing in front of you instead of Judge Buckalew,'' explained Ingaldson to Roland, ''is to prevent Judge Buckalew from any possibility of taint, I guess, that he might hear this, and it was more to err on the side of caution on behalf of Mr. Salemi and myself. It might be of some assistance to the court if I give a brief synopsis.''

''The issue is,'' said Salemi to Ingaldson, ''are you going to use this man who we represent? If you say, yes, I'm not sure why a two-minute synopsis is going to be helpful to the court.''

"Yes, I am going to use him," said Ingaldson, " but I think it's important for me to do this because I think it may shed some light on whether or not, number one, whether or not there is a serious need for the defense to even want to confront him. And the only way I can explain that is by giving the court some background information.''

Ingaldson informed the judge that a year before the Newman homicides, Walter Napageak's battered body was found near the Northern Lights Car Wash where Kirby Anthoney worked. "It's important for the court to know that nothing was released to the public about this case; about the condition of the body," said Ingaldson. "The day after the body was found, the police went to the car wash. Kirby Anthoney told Hayes, 'I was really concerned because I thought they were getting samples of the water and I noticed that there was still some blood in the area, and I thought they might find some blood in the water.' In fact, the police did go there that day, they did get water, but they were drawing water to mix with the compound to make castings of footprints. Of course, the question is, why would Kirby Anthony say something like that—knowing about the water unless he was there? The injuries to the victim are consistent with a torch-handle type of pick-type beating. Part of his ear is torn off, there are puncture-type wounds, and there was in fact a torch in [the car wash], and it was also verified that the torch head was broken around this same time. The police found that there was a wheelbarrow that was used at the car wash, and they found some paint chips near the body. An analysis wasn't done on the paint chips to determine if in fact they came from the wheelbarrow, and to be honest, I'm not sure if the wheelbarrow is still even there. I know that the car wash itself is torn down.''

"Excuse me, Mr. Ingaldson," said Salemi, "I'm sorry to interrupt. Does the court think it has enough facts now to rule on this, because I have a feeling that this is more a media speech than it is some sort of argument regarding whether or not we should be permitted to withdraw.''

"I think we'll let Mr. Ingaldson finish, Mr. Salemi, thank you. Mr. Ingaldson," said the judge, "go ahead."

"There was also a single tire track that went through the snow to the body," Ingaldson elaborated. "At first, the police thought the body had been placed in a pickup truck and dumped there. And there was not a corresponding tire track. Of course, that would match with a wheelbarrow being used. There was very little blood on the body," Ingaldson said, "and very little blood around the area, even though the person had sustained serious head injuries, and you would expect to find a lot of bleeding. The body was also soaked—completely soaked. Of course, if the body was killed in the car wash, and washed off, as Mr. Anthoney told Mr. Hayes, then that would explain why the body is wet and very little blood. So, I guess in short, there is a substantial amount of corroboration of things Hayes said. I do not dispute that Mr. Hayes is represented by the public defender agency," Ingaldson stated, "and I also know they have a right, if they want, to confront him, and impeach him. We don't really dispute any of the ways they'd want to impeach him. I guess I don't really understand the conflict if they call Mr. Hayes. . . ."

"Well, it's my understanding," said the judge, "that Mr. Salemi will be called upon to cross-examine and impeach him with materials that he's gained from confidential disclosures from his client. Which means there is in fact—it seems to me, and I want you to address, if you will, an irreconcilable conflict."

"I would agree that he would not be able to represent Mr. Anthoney and cross-examine Mr. Hayes," agreed Ingaldson. "It seems to me that all the evidence that he would impeach Mr. Hayes with is public knowledge. So I don't think there is a conflict. His conviction, and the information leading to his conviction, that's all public knowledge. So, perhaps there is something else that I don't know about and don't have a right to know about, and maybe the best thing would be an in camera offer of proof by Mr. Salemi.''

In camera means that Salemi would go into the judge's chambers and reveal the information to him alone. The judge would then decide if Salemi should withdraw because of conflict.

''I'm certainly willing to do that,'' agreed Salemi. ''We've represented Mr. Hayes in a sexual assault. There was a trial. We had a long-standing-relationship with him, and I can't say anything more about that except that I would tell the court, as an officer of the court, that there is information of which was gained in the context of the attorney-client relationship, information which is confidential in nature, information which I would use during the examination of this witness, and information which if the state did not choose to call this person as a witness, I would be compelled to call him as a witness to confront him regarding it in order to zealously represent Mr. Anthoney, in order to cast doubt upon the witness in question.''

''I'd like to hear what you have to offer,'' said the judge, inviting Salemi into his chambers. ''After hearing that, I will rule on the motion as to whether or not you should be allowed to withdraw. Okay? We'll stand in recess. You understand that Mr. Anthoney can't be here, either.''

''I hadn't thought that far along, Your Honor,'' admitted Salemi.

''Because,'' the judge explained, ''if you're simply going to disclose to Mr. Anthoney, you've violated the same canons.''

Roland and Salemi privately conferred. Within a few minutes, Judge Roland announced his ruling. ''If the state intends to use the representations made by Mr. Hayes, it appears to me there is or will be an irreconcilable conflict . . . and that counsel should be allowed to withdraw.''

''Your Honor,'' commented Ingaldson, ''based on that ruling . . . it is my intention, confirmed by talking to Mr. Newman, the victim in this case, that we'd rather go ahead with the sentencing. It would probably be in the better interest of the public and the victims in this case to continue the sentencing. So we will not present that evidence.''

"Under those circumstances," said the judge, "it appears to me there's no need for you to withdraw, Mr. Salemi.''

Roland called for recess; the clerk told everyone to rise; Kirby Anthoney said, "Excuse me, Your Honor. . . ." And court was back in session.

"As far as I understand by reading the presentence report," said Anthoney, "and knowing how the court system works, Judge Buckalew is quite aware of what's already been taking place in this courtroom. Under the circumstances, and even if it wasn't to that point, I see fit that all these accusations be brought out. And in order for this to be done, any witness that says—has said anything to the prosecution needs to be pulled in. As to whether Mr. Salemi has a conflict of interest or not, I do not know. But I want every bit that's been said in this courtroom in front of Judge Buckalew. In order to do that, Mr. Hayes needs to be pulled in as a witness. And I request that.''

"You can request that of Judge Buckalew," explained Roland, "I'm here solely for the purpose of considering the two motions which needed to be heard outside Judge Buckalew's presence.''

John Salemi had one more protective order in mind. "An alleged crime separate from the one which has just been disclosed here. And I would like to request that the court hear that. I made my request in my written materials that my request for a protective order be heard by someone other than Judge Buckalew because I thought that if it were presented to him and the protective order was granted, we would have won the battle but lost the war because he would have been perhaps unfairly prejudiced just by hearing the arguments which would detail—''

"Well," interrupted the judge, "so far as I can tell, except for Mr. Hayes, you have no complaint.''

Anthoney, confused, spoke up sharply, "I do, Your Honor. It's already been in this—''

Salemi tried calming down his client while appeasing the judge, and said, "I think he's probably not following my argument, Your Honor, and I apologize. Hold on for just a minute, Mr. Anthoney."

Anthoney, refusing to hold on, barked, "No! No, Mr. Salemi. I'm sorry. Your Honor, there is no need to apologize, and I'm fully aware of what there is to be discussed. The presentence report has this accusation in it. It has already been put in front of Judge Buckalew. He's fully aware of this issue. And that is the discussion that we are judging right now as to whether he can hear this. He had already heard it, Your Honor. And my request is anybody that has said anything to the prosecution on any of these accusations be brought in."

"You can discuss that with your counsel," replied Roland, "and Mr. Salemi can take such action, and if he feels—as a result of his conversations with you—a further conflict that would require him to move to withdraw, he may, of course, do that. But at the moment, it appears to me that I see no conflict."

"If I might continue for just a moment," requested Salemi, "one of the issues which I'm asking this court to deal with is regarding the state's intention to attempt to prove other crimes, to establish that Mr. Anthoney was involved in a sexual assault in Twin Falls, Idaho. This is separate from the car wash killing," he clarified, "and it's my understanding that Mr. Ingaldson intends to make this presentation through hearsay testimony. He intends to represent what other people have told him. And it may be double, triple hearsay. He's going to have police officers from Anchorage testify as to police reports they read from Twin Falls, Idaho, or from conversations they've had with investigators in Twin Falls—"

Judge Roland stopped Salemi's monologue and asked one question: "Is this already set forth in the presentence report?"

Before Salemi could speak, Anthoney broke in. "Not only that, it's been discussed—"

"Excuse me, Mr. Anthoney," said Salemi, "I think a great

deal of detail would come out in a request for a protective order—I think the state would argue the details. And in an abundance of caution it seems to me that it would be better for a judge who is not the sentencing judge to hear that argument. Perhaps the court disagrees with me.''

The court disagreed. ''I think it is entirely appropriate,'' said Roland, ''for Judge Buckalew to hear your motion for a protective order. Certainly, the argument itself isn't going to taint Judge Buckalew, particularly since he's been put on notice that he's a suspect in the case in the presentence report. I don't see any reason [for me] to hear that. I do with regard to Mr. Hayes. I think you were entirely appropriate to bring that before me, but—''

Salemi wouldn't give up. He did not want Buckalew considering the Twin Falls case when determining Anthoney's prison sentence. ''Your Honor,'' pleaded Salemi, ''we go to great lengths to keep this kind of information from jurors in the course of a trial. And I really don't see much difference between a judge and a jury with respect to disregarding inflammatory materials or unfairly prejudicial materials. And that's why I've made this request.''

''There are some kinds of materials,'' Roland replied, ''that can be fairly said are impossible to disregard even by a judge. But I think in general, judges are better trained and more experienced with these kinds of materials and I think judges are different from jurors in that respect, Mr. Salemi. So, I disagree with you. And what I'm telling you really is that what you've asked for in your protective order is not the kind of information that I think would taint a judge if it came to his attention, and I think you can fairly argue it before him.''

Prior to appearing before Judge Buckalew, Anthoney was scheduled for a complete psychological and psychiatric evaluation. He refused. ''I did deny to cooperate with them,'' confirmed Anthoney, ''and there was a purpose of it. One of them was on my own behalf because why should I give anything to him when he is out to get me? And again I say I take it personal.

But I also did it for another purpose. And that's because I was advised not to. I was advised not to talk to the prosecution, their psychologists. I was advised not to talk to the investigating probation officer or parole officer for the presentence report. Again, it was somewhat of my own agreement because of the prejudicial values that they see in these cases. But that's not what they say in the presentence report. They say that I failed to cooperate. Again, they are not interested in the truth and the whole matter, it's simply what they want to assert. Again, it's totally expected on their part. I don't disagree with the jury. If I had sat on the jury itself and heard the prejudicial issues that were raised, and the blatant misconduct that Mr. Ingaldson did, I probably would have done the same thing. But the state knows that if he didn't do those things, the job wouldn't have been done.''

John Salemi, on behalf of Anthoney, requested Buckalew to again delay sentencing. He granted the request, setting October 5 as the new date. Buckalew told Anthoney's attorneys that they were not required to share the psychiatric findings with the court.

''On this evaluation that I requested,'' recalled Anthoney, ''there is a doctor from the Langdon Center, I believe, who was supposed to come over and give me a thorough evaluation. What I wanted to do with that is I wanted to give it to Mr. Ingaldson so he could wipe his derriere on it. Excuse the pun. Evaluations in something like this would hold no pertinent value as to the sentencing. The evaluation was never done. I had two visits from a man who was supposed to do it. The agreement was, it was a full testing evaluation. He comes down and he sees me, and chitchats with me for a couple hours maybe just to say he's seen me and collect his paycheck. He writes a letter saying that there has been no evaluation wrote up, and he doesn't know if he can be of much help in this case. That was from observations. But testing was supposed to say different, and that was the request for continuance.''

On Wednesday, October 5, 1988, Kirby D. Anthoney, shackled in chains, stood before Judge Seaborn Buckalew one last time. "Anthoney had a beard during the trial," recalled Grimes. "He shaved it off for the verdict, and grew it back again for the sentencing. He was also wearing those tinted glasses to hide his eyes." There was no hiding from Buckalew's sentencing, and Anthoney's pent-up tension and hostility were rapidly rising to the surface.

CHAPTER 22

"This is the time set down for the imposition of sentence in the matter of *State of Alaska versus Anthoney,* Criminal Number 87-3244," intoned the judge. "Are the parties ready?"

"We are, Your Honor," answered Salemi, "however, this is at least one preliminary matter that we must take up before we proceed to the actual subject matter of the sentencing. It was a matter which I had hoped would be resolved before we started the session today."

The unresolved matter wasn't the Napageak murder. Salemi wanted an additional protective order suppressing the Michelle Bethel rape case. "What the protective order is directed at, Your Honor, is keeping from the sentencing judge information which is not sufficiently verified, or is information which is of such a nature where it would be presented in a way where Mr. Anthoney would not be in a position to confront the evidence in terms of cross-examining or confronting witnesses. We're talking specifically about what I think can be termed as the Twin Falls, Idaho, sexual assault which has been referred to in the presentence report which Your Honor has read, I'm sure.

"Mr. Anthoney was a suspect in that offense," Salemi explained. "And Mr. Anthoney wishes, if the state intends to try to establish that he in fact was the perpetrator, that witnesses who have knowledge, who are material to the case, be called so that he can confront those witnesses and so that he can cross-examine them. At this time, Your Honor, I'm going to have Mr. Anthoney sign an affidavit in open court in front of Your Honor." The signed affidavit read:

> I have been informed by my attorneys that the state intends to attempt to prove at my sentencing hearing that I have committed other crimes for which I have not been charged. I have been told that the state believes and intends to try to prove that I was involved in the death of a man by the name of Walter Napageak who was supposedly killed on April 11, 1986, at a location near where I worked at the time. I have also been told that the state intends to try to prove that I was involved in a sexual assault that occurred in Twin Falls, Idaho, in 1985 that involved a woman by the name of Michelle Bethel. I expressly deny any involvement in either of these crimes.

Salemi argued that if Ingaldson was going to present Debbie Heck's statements that Anthoney hindered the investigation by giving the police clothes other than what he wore the night of the rape, "we want to be able to cross-examine her. And we'd want to cross-examine Miss Bethel, the victim of the assault, and other material witnesses. We acknowledge that Mr. Ingaldson has the right to attempt to establish that there are other verified acts," said Salemi, "whether they be bad acts or criminal conduct that may have been committed by Mr. Anthoney. But they must make their presentations in a proper way. In a way that is fair to Mr. Anthoney; in a way that permits Mr. Anthoney to dispute those allegations, in conformity with due process, by allowing Mr. Anthoney to confront the evidence which Mr. Ingaldson says establishes his involvement in this sexual assault.''

''Your Honor,'' stated Ingaldson, ''the courts have long recognized here, and it's well established, that hearsay evidence can be used at sentencing proceedings. The entire presentence report is hearsay.''

Ingaldson admitted that he intended to argue that the court consider the Michelle Bethel incident when determining Anthoney's sentence, but decried any attempt to force Michelle Bethel to testify.

''There's no reason to put the victim through this,'' he insisted. ''I'm not sure how old she is, probably sixteen years old now. She was twelve at the time. To haul her up here and put her through it when she doesn't know anything because of the extent of her injuries, and her condition. She doesn't recall anything of that night. There is no reason to put her through that. Unless there's some reason to try and maybe punish her more.''

Ingaldson explained that Salemi only recently indicated that he wanted witnesses regarding the incident. ''I do have Debbie Heck standing by telephonically,'' he said, ''so Mr. Salemi would be able to cross-examine her. Sergeant Grimes, who had a chance to review not only the police reports, but also meet with investigators in Twin Falls a year ago, would then testify. So, I don't know how the court really wants to proceed at this time.''

''But we're not talking about what Mr. Anthoney's seventh-grade teacher thought about him,'' complained Salemi, ''or his activities outside the classroom. The state has come and said they intend to prove that he's been involved in other criminal activity of a very serious nature. Assuming that this information is sufficiently verified through police reports and affidavits, or statements to the police—once you reach that threshold that's sufficiently verified, if the defendant says, 'I deny that I was involved in that crime, and I want to call those witnesses who the district attorney is only referring to in some sort of summary fashion,' the defendant has that right.''

''Mr. Ingaldson is going to stand up and say Mr. Anthoney committed a sexual assault for which he's never been charged or convicted,'' Salemi argued. ''He's just going to get up there and say that, and then say what other people have told him about it. I want the witnesses here. I want Miss Bethel here so I can ask her, 'Miss Bethel, do you remember participating in a lineup where you were asked to try to pick out the perpetrator? Do your remember that you weren't able to do that?' ''

Buckalew wanted no further delays. ''I spent a great deal of time trying this case,'' said the judge. ''He stands convicted of three counts of murder one, sexual assault, and kidnapping, and I want to get him sentenced today.''

''Then I would ask,'' Salemi responded, ''the court to rule that you grant my protective order regarding hearsay. . . .''

''I can't grant it in total,'' Buckalew said. ''Mr. Ingaldson should have the right to call the police officers. If he can get Miss Heck on the phone and she says Mr. Anthoney told me that he did these things to this alleged victim—''

''I want Miss Heck *here*,'' insisted Salemi, ''if she can be on the telephone, she can be here. The U.S. Supreme Court interpretation is that confrontation involves a person being here. So not only do we hear what she or he has to say, but also we get to observe their demeanor, and the court would be in a position to do that. I just don't want the state to put [on] a bunch of hearsay statements, speculation, and innuendo that could affect this court's decision. I just want both sides to be bound by the rules.''

Ingaldson, pegging Salemi's argument as simply delaying the inevitable, said, ''The courts don't require a person to confront witnesses at sentencing. What I suggest to the court, since this is all information in front of the court anyway, is that I am allowed to give a brief offer of proof and to see if there's any dispute other than Miss Heck's testimony as to the facts. It's my understanding that most of these [facts] are verified and admitted by Mr. Anthoney. What I'm telling you now is information that Mr. Anthoney admitted to detectives in Twin Falls, Idaho.''

''Admitted what?'' asked Buckalew.

''I object,'' interrupted Salemi, ''you know what happens— he makes this speech about what he thinks he knows or what people have told him. You hear it and then you say, 'Well, I can't consider that.' He'll have had his say and we have not been able to confront or cross-examine the witnesses, and you're left with the impression that what he says very well might be true, and we're denied the opportunity to dispute that. So I don't think this offer of proof is proper or needed. In fact, I don't know why we're going through this because, as the court says, Mr. Anthoney sits here convicted of very serious crimes, and what effect is the fact that he's a suspect and never been charged, what effect is that going to have on this case? I think the court can probably just rule that he not be allowed to go into it.''

''My problem with that Idaho thing,'' said Buckalew, ''is that if they had all this evidence, why didn't some grand jury indict him? Why didn't they try him?''

Kirby Anthoney suddenly stood up and said, ''Your Honor, if I may offer of proof myself . . .''

''No, don't interrupt me,'' snapped the judge, ''don't interrupt me. You may sit down. I just don't want to waste a lot of time. If you really want to pursue it, I think I'm faced with a possibility of having to continue the sentencing and let you get your witnesses up here and . . .''

''Well, we don't know that, Judge,'' Ingaldson said, ''because we're arguing in a black morass now. You don't even know what the offer of proof is, or what the evidence is. Maybe you'll consider it not important. Mr. Salemi, in his most recent argument, had indicated that he thinks that this is not even necessary to this sentencing. That may be. If the court feels comfortable going forward with the sentencing without knowing about this—if you feel that it is a waste of time—then I won't go forward with it, but I would certainly want to preserve my opportunity in case people upstairs disagree.''

"Mr. Anthoney is requesting to say something, Your Honor," stated Salemi. Judge Buckalew cast a tired eye at the handcuffed defendant. "Oh, all right."

"I apologize for interrupting, Your Honor," said the convicted murderer. "I'm going to try to be as contrite as possible on these issues. I agree with Mr. Salemi, and I agree with the court that this is an academic issue and it's kind of pathetic in itself. I'd just like to tell you, Your Honor, if you give me any less than the maximum sentence . . . excuse me if I take it a little bit personal. I don't have any objections to Mr. Ingaldson bringing any witnesses in on these issues at all, or any evidence, but I want the right to dispute it. He's made accusations that I'm involved in other crimes that I have not been involved in. And I have evidence to prove that I have not been involved in. But I don't have all of it. And the reason why is because I haven't received it from the District Attorney's Office here, or the police in Twin Falls, Idaho. Which in those regards has to have a continuance because I cannot present myself in a proper manner because I don't have all the information. But the information I do have says that I'm not involved in it, Your Honor. But again, as I said, I'm not arguing. In fact, I expect the maximum sentence. And if you didn't give the bastard who did it—''

Buckalew, fed up, cut him off. "I think I should be candid with you," said the judge sternly. "I agree with the jury's verdict. There is no doubt in my mind that the jury reached the right verdict."

"I don't need a speech to the media," said Anthoney, mimicking Salemi's earlier remark to Judge Roland. "I understand your feelings. I understood it from before this trial started."

The judge ignored Anthoney, turned to Ingaldson, and said, "All right. What's your offer of proof?" As Ingaldson began speaking, Anthoney broke in.

"Excuse me, Your Honor, for interrupting one more time.

Is he getting ready to make an offer of proof on these crimes that I'm alleged to have been involved in? If he is, Your Honor, what I have just said is that I would request that the witnesses be pulled in so I have a chance to rebut, and that I be allowed to have any information that was involved in this case, which I do not have. From the police officers investigating the Twin Falls crime. Or from what the police or the investigation has here in Anchorage.''

Ingaldson and Buckalew ignored Anthoney's repetitive rant; the prosecution continued his offer of proof. ''On that day in 1985, June twenty-sixth, there was a party that was held at an area in Twin Falls. There was a ravine by this area—a common area for parties. A twelve-year-old girl was there. Mr. Anthoney had been seen with that girl earlier in the night, as other people had been. The girl was found later the next day. She was severely beaten, has permanent eye and ear damage. In fact, I have photographs of her injuries if the court decides to consider this information. She has suffered permanent injuries because of that, that still exist to this day. She was left for dead down by a creek, a ways away from where there was a bonfire. Mr. Anthoney was at that party. Some thongs that belonged to Mr. Anthoney, or at least that he was wearing that night, were found near the body.''

Ingaldson related Anthoney's peculiar explanation of why his thongs were at the crime scene, and informed Buckalew that there was little or no forensic evidence from the scene, and that the girl was so damaged that she was unable to identify her assailant.

''The police did go get clothing from Mr. Anthoney,'' continued Ingaldson, ''and here's the part that the people in Twin Falls are not aware of that came to light when Miss Heck informed us that when the police came the next day to get clothing and things from people who were at the scene, that Mr. Anthoney gave him different clothes other than what he was actually wearing. In fact, she saw his clothes and saw a pair of pants he was wearing that night. Mr. Anthoney told her that he tore the pants at the party and that he was going to throw them away, that she shouldn't say anything about it. She also said she saw stains on the pants that could be mud or blood. So essentially that's our offer of proof concerning that incident. And it's my understanding that with the exception of Miss Heck, since Mr. Anthoney has essentially admitted the rest of the offer of proof, I don't think there is really a dispute except for Miss Heck's testimony."

"I've heard those facts before," Buckalew said, "and it sounds like it was an outrageous offense. I don't know why it wasn't vigorously prosecuted. And every decision I make is going to be reviewed by an appellate court. I'm just a little skeptical of letting you use it unless you get the witnesses up."

"I don't know why it wasn't prosecuted, either," admitted Ingaldson. "I do know that Mr. Anthoney came to Alaska a short time after that. Perhaps that's the reason, since he was out of state."

Ingaldson explained that he hadn't time to bring witnesses to the current hearing and that money was also an issue. "In fact, I had originally intended to bring an investigator from Twin Falls, but I guess in light of statewide concern for money being spent on things, and in light of whether it was actually needed, I don't have those witnesses now. I think it is more important," he said, "to go forward with the sentencing not only for the community of Anchorage, but also I think for the victims and friends and family of John Newman and Cheryl Chapman, who I have spoken to. I know what they went through when the case was continued last time in sentencing."

Salemi and Ingaldson cooperated on procedural issues prior to the sentencing hearing, but Ingaldson wasn't aware until that day in court that if the case were remanded by the court of appeals, the state would still have an opportunity to present the Twin Falls sexual assault information. Once he understood that he was not waiving the state's ability to do so, he acquiesced.

"I was offering that agreement before the court ruled," Salemi chided, "hoping that Mr. Ingaldson would withdraw his need to make this offer. But he went ahead and the court has essentially ruled. I don't see there being any agreement, but I also feel this doesn't matter whether we have an agreement or not. The issue is either preserved or not. He's made the offer of proof, so I don't see that as being an issue.''

"Well," observed Buckalew judiciously, "when two persons have both graduated from law school, it makes it difficult to get an understanding between the parties.''

"It's my understanding from your remarks," said Salemi, "that you're not going to consider the Twin Falls sexual assault as having any impact on the sentence. Is that correct?''

"I've already indicated I have concern about why nothing was done about it," answered the judge. "He has the presumption of innocence as far as I'm concerned.''

"And the court would consider him innocent," asked Salemi, "even though it's heard certain representations?''

"*Presumed* to be," clarified Buckalew, drawing a distinction between presumes and considers. "I said I can *presume* that he's innocent of that. Do we have any other skirmishes we have to resolve before we get started?''

"There was no skirmish about Napageak, of course," said Grimes later. "I believe we could have charged Anthoney with the Napageak murder, and the only reason we didn't was to save the state money. As Anthoney was already convicted of the Newman homicides, there was no reason to pursue it at that time.''

Ingaldson, in retrospect, disagreed. "I don't know if we could have built a strong enough case against Anthoney in the car wash murder. Possibly, but I wouldn't want to risk it. Besides, when sentencing day came, I knew Anthoney would be put away for quite a while.''

Anthoney was belligerent one minute and whining the next, repeatedly interrupted the judge, and argued with his defense attorney, John Salemi. Together, however, they made significant efforts to minimize the unpleasant aspects of Anthoney's presentence report. The more "aggravators," the higher the sentence.

"Aggravating circumstances involve a person's criminal history," explained Salemi. "Mr. Ingaldson, as the state's representative, alleges with respect to a criminal record is one conviction for robbery when Mr. Anthoney was eighteen or nineteen years old. I don't think that's sufficient to establish a repeated source of that type of aggravated conduct. I ask the court to find that one hasn't been established."

Ingaldson wanted Anthoney's domestic-violence history taken into consideration. "I would ask the court to also consider," he said, "the statements made by other girlfriends of Mr. Anthoney, that he had in fact choked them on several occasions, and their fear of him because of his physical abuse. Specifically, Kim Atkinson, and I believe, Miss Mendenhall."

"The domestic dispute was investigated by police," countered Salemi, "I think Mr. Anthoney was arrested and then that case was dismissed by authorities. I don't think that should be considered."

Buckalew, not surprisingly, agreed with Ingaldson. "I find enough on the record to support that aggravator by clear and convincing evidence."

Anthoney wanted to minimize all his juvenile criminal activity, including his 1978 first degree burglary. "He thought it would be important for the court to know the circumstances," explained Salemi. Anthoney's first crime was breaking into the school commissary and stealing candy. "I believe other young people with him walked in, and going through an open window, took and consumed some candy."

Salemi, who insisted that "it was not properly characterized" as a bomb, confronted the allegation that Anthoney bombed a building with a balloon. "It involved a balloon with some oxyacetylene in it from a welding tank, and he was only secondarily involved in it. I think he was partly the person who hatched the plot, but his intention was to set it off in an open field. He was not near the balloon when it was actually detonated. It was his friend's idea to put it near a building.''

Courtroom spectators found these clarifications and revisions most peculiar. Anthoney was about to be sentenced for three counts of murder one, three sexual assaults, and one charge of kidnapping, and he wanted to explain whose idea it was to put a balloon bomb next to a building a decade earlier. Anthoney was most upset over a comment in the report attributed to his brother, Michael, that Anthoney almost hit his mother in the head with a wooden statue during one of his temper tantrums.

''Mr. Anthoney denies that he ever engaged in that kind of conduct,'' insisted Salemi. ''He has a letter which he gave to me last night from his mother. I would like to present it to the court. The court would probably take thirty seconds in reading it. I would like to incorporate it as part of the record, Your Honor.''

The letter, handwritten by Peggy Anthoney on September 27, 1988, was both clear and emphatic. She made no mention of the rape and murder charges, but expressed concern over remarks attributed to her other son, Michael, on September 14, 1987. According to Grimes and Spadafora, Michael Anthoney told them that Kirby once tried to strike his mother in the head with a large wooden statue. Peggy Anthoney insisted that the alleged statue incident was a lie, and that she would swear under oath that Kirby Anthoney never raised a hand to her. ''The vicious things'' said by her family, brothers, and sisters, ''were lies,'' too. She told the court that Kirby was always polite and respectful to his relatives. Because of these ''lies,'' Peggy Anthoney said her family didn't have ''the guts'' to face her.

Page 10 of the presentence report featured a summary of information provided by Kim Hawkins Atkinson. Questioned extensively by police, she didn't testify at the trial. Pregnant with her third child, she ''didn't need the stress'' of a court appearance.

''Mr. Anthoney denies he ever expressly or impliedly threatened Miss Atkinson,'' Salemi said. ''In fact, in her statement which we received from the district attorney, she said she believed that Mr. Anthoney would never hurt her.''

''Kim said that so she wouldn't have to testify in Alaska,'' confirmed her mother. ''The only way to get out of it was to make conflicting statements—she was actually advised to do that as to be exempt from going up there. We were very concerned about her health during that pregnancy, and they had enough on him that my daughter wasn't vital to the prosecution.''

The report also referenced Anthoney's drug and alcohol use, noting that Youth Service Center tests revealed an alcohol problem. It also quoted him as saying he used ''marijuana and LSD to relax.''

''Mr. Anthoney denies having an alcohol problem,'' said Salemi, ''and he has never used LSD to relax. Mr. Anthoney also disputes the presentence worker's evaluation. . . .''

Probation Officer Jo McDowell, the assigned presentence worker, submitted the following evaluation of Kirby D. Anthoney. ''Mr. Anthoney exhibits behavior patterns which are similar to those of anger rapists with cyclical patterns culminating in physical and/or sexual abuse. Poetry that Mr. Anthoney wrote indicates he recognized a build up of feelings that lead [sic] to violent behavior. These offenses were, without doubt, the most heinous and vicious attacks this officer has ever encountered. The victims died agonizing deaths and must have experienced absolute terror before their demise. Mr. Anthoney has proven many times over that he is a danger to society and should never be released.''

''Mr. Anthoney,'' insisted Salemi, ''denies that there is any history of sexual assault with respect to his personal experience, and feels that this is an inappropriate evaluation. There is no evidence to show that Miss McDowell has any particular training or education with respect to what are obviously psychological issues and particular profile type of findings. We think her statements are inappropriate and ask the court not consider her sentiments that Mr. Anthoney may be what's termed an anger rapist.''

''You have your objection on the record,'' noted Buckalew. He then turned to the prosecutor. ''All right. Mr. Ingaldson, I'll hear from you.''

This was the home stretch. The state already won the case, but complete victory meant maximum sentencing. Bill Ingaldson, well prepared as always, stood and delivered.

''In preparing for sentencing, the events of what happened about a year and a half ago certainly came flooding back to me, and I'm sure to everyone in this courtroom. People will probably not ever be able to put [it] out of their minds. I think without a doubt it's among—as Miss McDowell points out in her comments—the most aggravated, the most heinous murders ever experienced in Anchorage and Alaska in modern times.

''If you look at the facts of this case alone, and consider only the facts of this case, in order to reaffirm society's norms, and in order to give a feeling of the justice system having the ability to work at all—I think this court is compelled to give the maximum sentence on each count. The facts alone cry out for that type of sentence, and really there is no sentence that will ever atone for what happened.

''Angie Newman, a two-year-old girl who was just blossoming into life, she won't be brought back. Melissa Newman, who was eight years old at the time, was just going through kind of the awkward stage as a young girl. Her life can't be brought back. Nancy Newman, the joys she would experience as a mother, that can't be brought back. And I don't think any type of punishment this court can give will adequately avenge or reflect the pain and suffering that [they] went through when this happened. Because this wasn't just a loss—a simple loss of life of three persons.''

Judge Buckalew stopped Ingaldson's presentation by saying, ''I think for the record I should caution you that I cannot consider revenge as a factor. That's not one of the things that I can consider.''

"I'm not saying revenge," Ingaldson clarified. "You can't consider that and shouldn't consider that. But I think the goals of sentencing are many. There are five recognizable goals, and two of them I would ask the court to base its decision and place greatest emphasis on, are those of community condemnation. Reaffirmation of societal norms and isolation of Kirby Anthoney. When this incident happened, there was a great deal of pain, suffering, and terror that's certainly unimaginable. Just hearing the evidence at trial, observing the photographs of what happened, I think this court is well aware of what went on. But we have even more than that in this case. We have a person who has a history that . . . maybe some psychiatrist would say [that] this type of behavior might even have been predicted. We don't have a psychological report. On behalf of the state, I did request a psychological evaluation. I think case law indicates that the court, if possible, should consider a psychological evaluation. But Mr. Anthoney does have the right to refuse that, a Fifth Amendment right to refuse that. He did refuse through motion of his attorney, and later indicated that he was going to get a psychological examination. Of course, we haven't seen that.

"If you gauge the community's reaction to this type of crime," reasoned Ingaldson, "I suppose there are probably members of the community that say even the maximum sentence isn't enough. And that seems to be the indication of John Newman in his letter, and Cheryl Chapman in her letter to the court. So, I guess I would ask the court to do as much as it can.

"I've tried a lot of cases in front of Your Honor, a lot of real serious and awful murder trials," said Ingaldson. "This court has heard many; not only that I've tried, but many people have tried. And I'm sure that the court probably cannot recall a worse murder than this case.

"Mr. Anthoney, since the time he was very young, was involved in violations with the law. He certainly didn't have the greatest childhood. His father was not particularly kind to him and his siblings. But we know of many other people with a similar situation who turn out fine. That's certainly not an excuse. Maybe it's one fact that would help predict what happened. If you look into the junior-high age,'' explained Ingaldson, ''you see someone who according to intelligence tests is a bright person. You saw him in court and certainly he's not a fool. He's not someone who lacks mental capacities. But he nonetheless failed scholastically. He was an underachiever in school, had a high number of truancies, and eventually quit school at a young age to begin what has been a consistent pattern of criminal activity. Starting with burglaries; progressing to throwing a balloon type of bomb into a building, which I believe was a school; committing an aggravated robbery where a woman was confined to a wheelchair, after stealing from her, he sprays her in the face with Mace, indicating intentional cruelty.

''His relationships with girlfriends is one of violence. According to Debbie Heck [and] Kim Atkinson, there was physical abuse. Even when he was in jail, when you think someone would be on their best behavior while this case is pending—if you look at the presentence report concerning his activities in jail, you will see it's replete with a dozen different violations involving assaultive conduct. Two of them are particularly egregious. One of them, in December of 1987, the victim had to go through several hours of surgery. The victim of that, Travis Murphy, wrote me a letter wanting this case prosecuted, and I explained to him that the way we would handle it is for the court to consider it at sentencing. I don't know if [the letter] is attached to the presentencing report. If not, I'd like to include it.''

Travis Murphy's letter to the District Attorney's Office in general, and Ingaldson in particular, was received by Buckalew on August 9, 1988, and included in court records.

On a number of occasions, explained Murphy, he tried to press charges against Anthoney. State troopers visited him twice about this, and on both occasions told him that they did not want anything interfering with the charges for which Anthoney was being prosecuted. On December 16, 1987, Anthoney struck Murphy in the right side of the head with his elbow, causing severe nerve damage and broken bones. This was, according to Murphy, an unprovoked assault. At the time he wrote the letter, Murphy already had 4½ hours of surgery because of this assault, and was scheduled for more in the near future. Well aware that Anthoney faced ''a lot of time'' from his previous charges, Murphy didn't think that should have anything to do with the charges he wanted to file.

Another issue Ingaldson addressed was the possibility, albeit remote, that Anthoney would derive income from a proposed book about the crime. ''I guess he tried to get some writer to take up his cause,'' said Grimes. ''The thought of Anthoney making a dime off homicides and sexual assault was, of course, completely repugnant, especially to John Newman and Cheryl Chapman.''

Ingaldson asked Buckalew to rule that ''all of the royalties or other compensation be forfeited and turned over to a victim's fund. I don't know if the court can specifically rule where it be turned to, but that court rule that Mr. Anthoney must turn that money over to the state to be applied to a victim's group. Thank you.''

Before Buckalew concluded the presentence hearing, Salemi made preparatory remarks, followed by his final plea. ''My first instinct, Your Honor,'' began Salemi, ''would be to argue some of the factual issues of the trial and hope that the court might agree with me that the state, in some manner, had failed in its proof. But I know the court has, first of all, commented on its belief regarding the jury's verdict. And secondly, I know by doing that I would be avoiding the cruel reality of why we are here today.

''I remember back in the middle of the trial, perhaps one of the low moments, the court looked down from the bench— while the jury was out, fortunately, and said something about Mr. Anthoney looking scary or intimidating—''

"Did I do that?" asked the judge. Salemi didn't answer. "I just wanted to say," Salemi continued, "that except for perhaps today when Mr. Anthoney has been a little bit jumpy, and understandably so, in my mind he has been polite, he's acted in conformity with how I would expect him to. He's been nonthreatening to me in his demeanor. He's a very intelligent man."

"Well," responded Buckalew, "I haven't really felt threatened by Mr. Anthoney. He hasn't been disrespectful to this court. Although he disagrees with this court's conclusion that the jury reached the proper decision. I can understand his position, but I disagree with him."

Having made his preliminary remarks, John Salemi pleaded for mercy on behalf of Kirby Anthoney. "I know that this court has two major objectives to consider," he said. "One is protection of the public, and the other is the reformation of the individual. Both are to be given serious consideration. I can't, you can't, no one here would ignore the nature of these crimes and the immensity of them. I'm aware of the number of years that you have at your disposal with respect to the sentence you will give Mr. Anthoney. I would ask only that the court consider that Mr. Anthoney is a man who is only in his twenties, who, if indeed he committed these crimes, he's profoundly disturbed, profoundly ill, and must be pitied and must be helped if we're an enlightened society. There is no way this court can anticipate what or who Mr. Anthoney would be five, ten, twenty, forty years from now. To try to speculate who Mr. Anthoney will be at forty or sixty, or sixty-five, what he will be like would be impossible for this court. To know what he'll be like and what place he should have in society after a lifetime of punishment, when you and I are probably even no longer around, is too difficult to fathom.

"I guess what I'm suggesting," continued Salemi, "is that when that time comes, shouldn't the court at least put some other person in a position so that other person has the discretion to recognize that there perhaps has been a profound change in

Mr. Anthoney? To recognize the indomitability of the human spirit, and to give Mr. Anthoney a glimmer of hope? I would ask the court to consider fashioning a sentence that also forwards the objective of the reformation of Mr. Anthoney. And without some hope on the part of Mr. Anthoney that he can lead a different life, maybe if it's only in his last years, reformation cannot be achieved and there will be no incentive for it. As human beings, we try to temper justice with mercy, and even in these grave circumstances we as human beings try to be merciful and forgiving.''

Salemi asked Buckalew to run all sentences concurrently, giving Anthoney thirty-three years until eligible for parole. ''People do not choose in any meaningful way to go out and commit these kinds of crimes, it has to do with some profound disturbance over which they have little control. Those conclude my remarks unless the court has questions.''

The presentence hearing concluded, Buckalew called a ten-minute recess. When court reconvened for final sentencing, the brash confidence Anthoney displayed during his dramatic trial had long since dissipated. Handcuffed at the wrists and chained at the ankles, Kirby D. Anthoney launched verbal tirades against the reputation and integrity of Prosecutor Bill Ingaldson and Defense Attorney John Salemi.

''I was going to ask for a continuance today,'' said Anthoney, ''and again there's been a lot of academic issues raised here and I feel it's inappropriate. I don't oppose the sentence, even if it was the maximum. I don't oppose it if it was a thousand years. And the reason why, Your Honor, is because I know I'm innocent and I know one of these days those back doors over there—I'll walk out and I'll be free. Mr. Salemi made some suggestion that I'm an intelligent person and not a fool, as well as the prosecution. There is no possibility that anybody who did this could be sane.''

''Well, Mr. Anthoney,'' commented Buckalew, ''you know the court's position. I've already made it abundantly clear to you that I agree with that verdict.''

"You did that before the trial even started," countered Anthoney. "I was aware of that, that's what prejudice is all about, Your Honor. On some of the actions that Mr. Ingaldson has accused me of through Cook Inlet Pretrial, one of them such as Mr. Murphy—Mr. Ingaldson, he's not too interested in the truth and relating to the court that I was found not guilty on that. I agree that the man was injured, but as I've said, Mr. Ingaldson is not interested in the truth. If he was, he would have investigated further and found out what the disposition is on the Cook Inlet Pretrial record. And he hasn't done anything. But there's been numerous [instances] of that, and I won't go into them. Again," repeated Anthoney, "I feel the sentence should be the maximum. And the reason why—it's not because I am guilty. It's because if you give the person—the perpetrator, who actually did this, anything but the maximum, I would haunt you to your grave, Your Honor. There's been an issue raised about a book that's being produced, and Mr. Ingaldson seems to think or hear rumors that I want to profit from this. The author and I have agreed—and it was my suggestion and my wishes that I not profit from this. And it was the furthest thing from my mind. And between the two of us, the writer and myself, there is being papers drawn up for the purpose of me signing over anything for capital gains at all. The purpose for the book is to show the public for what it is exactly involved in this case. Period. And that's all."

Buckalew would not concern himself with publishing agreements. "I don't think I'm going to address that issue in the sentencing."

Anthoney then complained bitterly to Judge Buckalew that he had not received photocopies promised by the Public Defender's Office.

"If I could comment briefly, Your Honor," requested Salemi. "Doing the copying for Mr. Anthoney has not been a real priority of mine, especially when it's materials I've already given him more than once. Now we do have notes and cross-examination questions that we didn't provide him. We'll do that. And I'll get around to it, and Mr. Anthoney will get all of that information prior to the notice of appeal being filed. It's true that Mr. Anthoney has requested this on numerous occasions. We've tried to accommodate him where we could, but . . . we weren't able to do that in the time in which he wanted it done."

Anthoney quickly added additional commentary. "He says it's not a priority of his. He says he has six boxes. He says now that it's less than six. Which I probably agree with him. He was just dramatizing to the court. He's trying to insinuate how much it is. What is his priority toward me? What are his obligations toward the client? And that's to show the client everything that's involved in this case. Why haven't I received it? How come it's not in my hands right now? How come it wasn't in my hands before the trial started? Your Honor, I tried three months politely asking—"

Buckalew cut him off. "All right—I'm going to do sentencing. Mr. Salemi, I'll require you to remain standing and Mr. Anthoney to remain standing during the sentencing. I have a few preliminary comments I want to make to Mr. Anthoney. First off, we're not trying Mr. Ingaldson here today."

"*I* will, Your Honor," Anthoney asserted, "we're not here, but I will."

"But because of your comments," continued Buckalew, "and it's not going to affect my sentencing—"

"I didn't expect it to, Your Honor," Anthoney interrupted. "I didn't mean to interrupt you. I just like to fill in the gaps."

Buckalew paused, took a breath, and continued. "I want to put this on the record," he said, "that Mr. Ingaldson has been in my court many, many times. He's made representations to this court on all kinds of matters. He's been candid, truthful, honorable, and I just wanted to get that matter out of the way."

"Well," barked Anthoney, "can I put something on the record, Your Honor? I'd like to know where he went wrong, because he lied! And I'll prove it!"

Buckalew, neither amused nor impressed, simply said, "Now

I'm going to go ahead with this sentencing. I'm required to impose just sentencing in these matters and I intend to impose what I consider to be a just sentence.''

"Mr. Ingaldson is not interested in the truth," said Anthoney. "He wants to assert anything that's negative to the courts. And I don't even know why I'm standing here trying to justify all this BS, because—"

"I don't know why you are, either," interrupted the judge. "These murders—and we have three murders, two first-degree sexual assaults, and a kidnapping, are the most egregious cases that I've ever had contact with. Two of the victims are children so young that they couldn't have committed any kind of grievance against anyone. Counsel and this court and the jury had to look at little Melissa's picture, what the body looked like, the terror you could see on her face. It's almost like killing an angel.''

"That's what it is," agreed Anthoney. Buckalew glared at the defendant, and his voice became steel on chilled steel.

"This court had to look at those pictures, and this court is never going to forget that picture. This court is of the opinion that you're the person that did it. This court had more evidence than the jury had. It's a terrible, terrible crime. Count One, Count Two, and Count Three are the homicide cases. On Count One, I sentence you to ninety-nine years. On Count Two, I sentence you to ninety-nine years. On Count Three, I sentence you to ninety-nine years. Those three counts run consecutive with each other.'' The judge then turned his attention to Count IV, the kidnapping charge. "I don't think the facts and circumstances would justify a consecutive sentence to the homicide and the facts surrounding the restraint. On Count Four, I sentence you to ninety-nine years, but Counts Three and Four are to run concurrently with each other. Count Five is the first degree sexual assault of little Melissa. I've already indicated it's the most aggravated and obscene conduct. I've found the aggravator. I believe this sexual assault deserves the maximum penalty of thirty years. I sentence you to thirty years. Count

Five is to run consecutive to the other counts. And the sexual assault on Melissa's mother and your aunt, again it's the most outrageous conduct. I sentence you to the maximum sentence of thirty years. Count Six to run consecutive to Count Five. Because of the length of the sentence, it's doubtful as to whether you'll ever take another breath as a free man. I'm going to follow Mr. Salemi's recommendation that I don't restrict parole. I'm going to leave that up to the parole authorities, if it's ever an issue, and I doubt that it will ever be an issue. But, Mr. Anthoney, our constitution, when addressing what should be considered in the criminal law, they only mention two things—rehabilitation and the protection of the public. I have no reservation at all in stating that from what I've heard in this courtroom that you're probably the most dangerous offender that's ever been in my courtroom. And the victims in this case, the children—''

"I don't need to hear this," yelled Anthoney. "I have already been sentenced, that's all I need to know. What are you going to do, put me in jail because I don't want to hear what you have to say to the media? Save it for them, Your Honor! I don't need to hear it! I'm innocent and I do not need to be ridiculed and persecuted!"

Buckalew, incensed, turned to John Salemi, saying, "Counsel, I'm not going to have him—''

"I'm through with the courts, Your Honor," interrupted Anthoney. "I don't need to be persecuted." Then to Salemi, Anthoney said, "He's already made the sentencing. I don't need to hear his speech."

Salemi tried to calm him down, encouraging him to curb his outburst. "He needs to make remarks," explained Salemi, "that's—''

"Then give it to the media," Anthoney yelled, "because I don't need to hear that—and I'm sorry if I'm upset."

"That protects you also," continued Salemi, putting his hand on Anthoney's shoulder.

"Get off me!" snapped Anthoney.

Judge Buckalew had heard more than enough. "Counsel, I'm not going to have him gagged or make more comments. This court is in recess."

Kirby D. Anthoney, shackled, unrepentant, obstinate, and angry, promised a press conference during which he would detail the lies and misrepresentations of those who conspired against him. "When he erupted in the courtroom," recalled Grimes, "it was the same selfish rage that fueled his cruelty toward the Newmans. It had not lessened, nor was there the slightest hint of shame on his part. Under Buckalew's sentencing, Kirby Anthoney wouldn't even be eligible for parole for about one hundred twenty years."

No cathartic resolution accompanied the sentencing of Kirby Anthoney, no release from the pain, terror, and haunting nightmares for those who knew and loved Nancy, Angie, and Melissa Newman.

"There is nothing that can erase what happened, no way to return Nancy to John, no miracle that would result in the Newman children, healthy and happy, leaping into their daddy's arms," lamented Grimes. "As professionals, we're proud of the job we did on this case. I hate to think how many other people would be dead by now if he hadn't been stopped. What if Kirby Anthoney had made it across the border; what if he eluded capture; what if he kept moving, kept killing, continued his sexually charged rage-filled rampages? How many raped and murdered children? How many brokenhearted parents? How many grieved family members? How many lives cut short by one selfish man's anger and lust? If Anthoney had not killed the Newmans, he would have killed someone else—it was only a matter of time. Perhaps the Chapmans; maybe Debbie Heck. If he suddenly decided that he wanted sex with Kirk Mullins's girlfriend, and she rejected him, he could have killed her and Kirk. We don't know who he would have killed, and I don't think to him it much mattered. After all, if he could rape and murder his own family members, he would not be deterred from doing anything. Besides, look at Anthoney's history—from adolescence on, he robbed, raped, and killed.''

While the typical criminal career is relatively short, Dr. Hare has noted, ''there are individuals who devote most of their adolescent and adult life to delinquent and criminal acts. Many of these career criminals become less grossly antisocial in middle age, and about half of the criminal psychopaths studied show a sharp reduction in criminality around thirty-five or forty, but mostly in respect to nonviolent crime. Their propensity for violence, however, appears to remain constant and persistent.''

Hare was quick to point out that just because these individuals may seem to mellow with age, this ''doesn't mean that they suddenly become warm, caring, loving, moral citizens. Most remain thoroughly disagreeable individuals. They may alter their antisocial behavior, but they retain the callous, manipulative, and egocentric traits of psychopathy.''

Entitled to an appeal, Anthoney harassed his new court-appointed attorney, Rex Butler. Butler did not seek out Anthoney's case, nor was he particularly delighted to have it. ''Nobody wanted the damn thing,'' confirmed Butler, who was hired by Brant McGee, head of the state Office of Public Advocacy.

''The point of an appeal is to decide if a trial was legal and fair, not to rehash the evidence or second-guess the jury,'' explained McGee. ''Just because evidence is complicated doesn't mean the law is complicated.''

After three years enduring Kirby D. Anthoney as a client, Rex Butler asked the state court of appeals to reassign the case to ''another attorney who can devote the time to it that it undoubtedly deserves, and one who won't have to endure his rudeness, threats, and irrational behavior.''

Butler said that Anthoney threatened him for not devoting enough time to his case. ''He sought to set the priorities for his case and my office,'' he elaborated, ''and to threaten our office staff by telling them to tell me that '[Butler's] gonna be sorry.' '' Anthoney, again acting as his own cocounsel, launched a separate claim for a new trial based on his assertion that Salemi and Howard did not do a good job

"Convicted felons routinely file so-called 'ineffectual assistance of counsel' claims,' " explained Grimes, "but the fact that Anthoney was his own co-counsel rather undermined that approach. Plus, I recall Judge Buckalew telling Anthoney that he couldn't have got a better defense if he had paid Salemi two million dollars."

In 1991, three years following conviction, Anthoney's appeal was still in its early stages; the basic brief explaining what was unfair about his trial was not yet filed. One problem, according to Butler's office, was the immense volume of paperwork generated by the trial—fifty-four volumes of transcripts plus hundreds of pages of police reports and expert analysis. Butler stated that Anthoney intended challenging the admissibility of so-called genetic fingerprinting evidence used against him, and would also claim that John Salemi failed to introduce evidence that Anthoney insisted could clear him of all charges.

"If such evidence actually existed," asked Grimes, "why didn't Anthoney present [it] during his trial? After all, he was co-counsel and was obviously calling the shots. And would one believe, for a moment, that Salemi would withhold evidence that would clear his client?"

Aside from the overwhelming amounts of trial testimony and evidence, Butler also faced financial problems. A complete investigation of the case, including paid defense experts testifying that the prosecution's experts were in error, could cost up to $50,000—more than any previous case in the history of Alaska's Office of Public Advocacy.

"This is the equivalent of a capital case," said Butler, explaining the enormity of the situation. "He's got a sentence that means he'll die in prison." The state court of appeals denied Butler's request for removal and offered no explanation for its decision. "[Anthoney] wants a lawyer who will spend eight to ten hours a day, five days a week, on just his case," said Butler. "If I was standing in Kirby Anthoney's shoes, realistically, I'd probably be just as upset as he is . . . I don't think it's really personal.''

Butler followed through, preparing and presenting Anthoney's appeal to the Alaska court of appeals. Requesting a new trial, Butler argued that the allotyping blood tests utilized by the prosecution were not widely accepted by the scientific community, and the testing itself was flawed. There were also questions raised about the utilization of a private laboratory hired by the prosecution that conducted testing without defense in attendance, a point acknowledged by Ingaldson at the close of the trial.

Private labs, however, fit into the caseload mix by helping to reduce state-lab backlogs. They step in, for example, to help the prosecution ensure that a defendant obtains a constitutionally mandated speedy trial. An individual must be brought to trial within a certain period of time after having been charged in an arraignment. Many state labs are unable to finish the work and produce results in time for the prosecution. The argument against allotype test results used in court was severely weakened by the vast strides in forensic science in the years between the Newman homicides and Anthoney's appeal. In 1989, one year after his conviction, only three laboratories—one at the FBI, and two private labs—were performing DNA forensic analysis. Now, nearly a dozen private labs and about fifty state and local crime labs conduct the tests. Howard Coleman, president of GeneLex Corp., a Seattle-based private biotech firm, said that the total annual caseload has grown to more than 10,000—seventy-five percent of which involve sexual assault.

Genetic Design Inc., a public firm in Greensboro, North Carolina, reported that a large portion of their business was now database work. Genetic Design was contracted by the state of Alabama to analyze about 12,000 samples for the state's first DNA database. The database is intended to be used when there are crime scene samples but no suspect, much like a fingerprint database is used. Thirty-two states passed laws to create similar databases, legislation made possible under the Federal Crime Bill of 1994.

By 1995, when Alaska's superior court ruled on Anthoney's appeal, there was no longer any question as to the acceptability of Schanfield's scientific tests. On October 27, 1995, Judge Mark Roland concluded that "the scientific theory upon which allotyping of blood and semen is based, as well as the databases, technology, practices, and procedures employed . . . in carrying out the analysis upon which their opinions are based, are accepted by the relevant scientific community."

"Basically, Judge Roland ruled that the blood-typing evidence used in the trial was good science," said Grimes, "and even if it wasn't, there was enough other evidence offered against Anthoney for a jury to find him guilty."

Anthoney, however, was not giving up. His case could still be appealed to the state supreme court. The process, again handled by Butler, began anew. On May 5, 1999, the Supreme Court of the State of Alaska issued the following order:

Before: Mathews, Chief Justice, and Eastaugh and Carpeneti, Justices [Fabe and Bryner, Justices, not participating].

> *On consideration of the Petition for Hearing filed on 4/22/98, the response filed on 8/10/98, and the reply to the response filed on 8/24/98,*
> *IT IS ORDERED:*
> *The Petition for Hearing is DENIED*

Kirby D. Anthoney, sooner or later, will die in prison. Perhaps illness will afford him early release, or an inmate may terminate Anthoney's sentence with the swift thrust of a sharp blade. Maybe he'll grow old, wear out, and pass away—a life luxury never experienced by Nancy, Melissa, or Angie Newman. Whatever his end, the odds of reformation or rehabilitation are beyond slim.

"The crux of the issue," observed Dr. Hare, "is that psychopaths don't feel they have psychological problems. They don't see any reason to change their behavior or conform to society's standards. In fact," he has elaborated, "they see themselves as being in a hostile, dog-eat-dog world. They are not fragile—what they do, comes from a personality structure that is rock solid."

"They understand the difference between right and wrong," said Stanton Samenow, a clinical psychologist from Alexandria, Virginia, "and they understand the consequences to themselves and to others. That's not their problem." According to Samenow, what defines the violent antisocial personality of someone such as Kirby D. Anthoney is "a chilling capacity to shut off fear and knowledge of the consequences for as long as it takes to do what he wants to do."

Numerous studies have found that if children continue disruptive behavior past ages five or six, if they fail to learn the give-and-take of childhood play, and if they insist on dominating others at any cost, they are highly predisposed to become violent adults. While politicians, sociologists, and talk-show commentators debate the causes of violent crime, medical researchers have increasingly argued that people who commit such senseless and horrid acts have distinct biological and behavioral characteristics. Individuals with strong antisocial personalities consistently show low levels of the brain chemical serotonin, which functions as both a neurotransmitter and a hormone.

"I don't think anyone disagrees that there are biological factors," said Professor Frederick Goodwin, who directs George Washington University's Center on Neuroscience, Medical Progress, and Society. "We have clear biological explanations for why individuals do certain things."

Both Goodwin and Samenow emphasized that inherited factors alone don't make someone violent. In fact, while most violent offenders have low serotonin levels, not everyone with a low serotonin level is violent. They also agree that even those who exhibit antisocial tendencies into adolescence can often be reached with counseling and sometimes medication. The true psychopath, however, is far more than antisocial and does not respond well to counseling.

According to Dr. Hare, "most troubled kids can certainly be helped by counseling, but not psychopaths. Most therapy programs don't do much more than give them new excuses for their behavior and new insights into human vulnerability."

Further, psychopaths tend to dominate individual- and group-therapy sessions, refuse to talk about things they don't initiate, don't like to be confronted or questioned, and utilize long-winded monologues intended to circumvent discussions about their behavior. "Oh, that's Anthoney, all right," said Grimes. "He was always furious with us for questioning him, and his three-hour monologue certainly qualifies as 'long-winded.' "

According to Hare, attempts to teach psychopaths how to really feel remorse or empathy are "doomed to failure. They are also a rich source of excuses, such as 'I never learned to get in touch with my feelings,' which explain very little but sound good to some counselors who are willing to accept such statements at face value."

A profound inability to experience empathy and the complete range of emotions, including fear, is provided by nature and perhaps by some unknown biological influences. As a result, the ability to develop all-important internal controls, conscience, and for making emotional connections with others, is gravely reduced.

"We do not know exactly why people become psychopaths," Hare has stated, "but all current evidence discounts the notion that poor parenting is the primary reason, although it certainly doesn't help matters. This does not mean the parents and the environment are completely off the hook."

"I spoke at length to Kirby's brother," recalled Detective Baker, "and he told me how horribly Kirby was treated by their father—the beatings and all. Despite Peggy Anthoney's sincere and heartfelt efforts, she could never compensate for the horrific acts perpetrated against her youngest son by her violent and abusive husband. When he was done telling me how bad it was, I said 'that's the recipe for making a monster.' He said something like, 'Bullshit. I was raised the same way and I've never killed or raped anyone, let alone members of my own family.' ''

"Childhood is no excuse," Kirby Anthoney told the court during his trial. "That's one of the pathetic things they've always tried to relate to crimes on people like this. Is they were brought up bad, you know."

"I think there is something wrong with Kirby Anthoney's brain," stated Detective Spadafora, "some sort of mental birth defect for which there is no cure. A tragic combination of defective nature and perverted nurture created a monster. Kirby Anthoney is the best argument for reinstating the death penalty in Alaska. The death penalty was invented for guys like him. I know plenty of people are opposed to the death penalty, and I can understand their objections. But if innocent lives can be saved by sending mother rapists and baby killers to their eternal lack of reward, I'm all for it."

Anthoney's living victims—John Newman, Cheryl Chapman, and their intertwined extended families–will never fully recover. Nancy was John's very first woman, the love of his life. They had two beautiful little girls, both adored and loved.

John Newman's therapist advised him to buy a punching bag. By the time the trial was over, he had broken two and was almost ready to replace the third. Every day was, for John Newman, a fight to survive. He couldn't work, nor think straight, despite his best efforts. His only hope was that perhaps, some day in the future, the horrible emptiness, repulsive loneliness, terrible rage, morbid dreams, could be replaced by a life that had even one-tenth of the joy his family brought him.

"When the numbness and shock wears off, the 'living victims' experience certain emotional, physical, and spiritual reactions—all of which are normal," said Dr. Rubin. "Feeling anger at God, questioning your belief system, searching for answers and meaning in life and death—these are the common spiritual reactions. The physical, emotional, and mental reactions can be, however, the most immediately devastating.''

Emotional reactions may include crying, hysteria, anger, sadness, guilt, loneliness, helplessness, acute suffering, withdrawal, unresponsive emptiness, hopelessness, despair, panic, depression, isolation, separation anxiety, bitterness, self-pity, resentment, and abandonment. All these reactions, to one degree or another, were experienced by John Newman, Cheryl Chapman, and their families. For John Newman, the loneliness was difficult beyond expression.

In addition to the emotional anguish, the body is also strongly impacted by grief. Among the numerous symptoms are numbness, tightness in the throat, difficulty breathing, pain or tightness in the chest, nausea, fatigue, inability to sleep, blurred vision, headaches, glandular disturbances, lack of muscular strength, a feeling of emptiness, loss of interest in sex, dizziness, and a decreased resistance to illness.

Mental reactions encompass confusion, decreased self-esteem, lack of concentration, denial, loss of control, insecurity, disorganized thinking, regrets, hostility, searching for the deceased, thinking you are going insane, thinking constantly of your loved one, thoughts of dying, and dreams of the deceased.

Plagued by unceasing nightmares, John Newman thought many times of taking his own life. He had lived with and deeply loved Nancy Newman for fourteen years, and suddenly she was gone. His beautiful little girls were also taken from him. It's impossible to describe the terrible hurt and loneliness that John Newman was compelled to endure.

For Cheryl Chapman, the pain of losing her sister and nieces was overwhelming and devastating beyond description. She gave up her job at Gwennie's. She couldn't go back, because she would always expect to see Nancy walking out of the kitchen with an armful of orders. Heartbroken and distressed, Chapman and her husband left Alaska—they could not bear to live in Anchorage or drive by Nancy's apartment. Everything was a constant reminder of going there Sunday morning, March 15.

The geographic change did not relieve the mental and emotional anguish. The impact on their marriage was irrevocable. Cheryl Chapman had a problem relating to men after the murder, and could not stand the thought of a man's touch. The Chapmans separated two weeks after moving to the lower forty-eight. Cheryl moved in with her brother Tom, in Twin Falls, Idaho, but could not find work. She then moved to Nevada, stayed with her brother Donald, and secured employment.

Six months following the murders, she would still panic and relive everything all over again. She couldn't take a shower home alone, or sleep in a room with the door closed. A year after the tragedy, she had overcome many of the symptoms, but still could not stay by herself at night.

It took John Newman four hard years to rise above the drowning undertow of grief and depression. Day by day, week by week, month by month, John Newman, with the love and support of his close-knit extended family, and compassionate professional counseling, gradually recovered his life, his future. Today, more than a decade after experiencing the most devastating tragedy imaginable, John Newman, recently remarried, is in excellent physical, mental, and emotional health.

AFTERWORD

In 1999, a series of tragic events focused America's attention on teen violence and antisocial behavior. Congress funded extensive studies of video games; airlines edited gunfights out of in-flight movies; and the season finale of television's *Buffy, the Vampire Slayer* was pulled from broadcast because it featured scenes of high-school violence.

Seeking external motivations for irrational acts, placing blame became a national pastime. Movies, music, working mothers, poor parenting, electronic video games, lack of compulsory Christian prayers in public schools, were all viable scapegoats.

The United States Congress's investigation of video games was not dissimilar to the 1950s investigation of such pop-culture publications as *Tales from the Crypt* and *MAD Magazine.* Televised reruns of old Popeye the Sailor cartoons once came under attack for his spinach-fueled fisticuffs, and the Three Stooges' slapstick antics prompted concern that America's next generation would slap themselves silly while poking out each other's eyes.

In the final analysis, blame is only important to drunks and litigates. What we really need is an early warning system—a method of identifying psychopaths and sociopaths before adolescence—and prepuberty intervention.

Psychopaths begin showing up in court at the average age of fourteen. Once they reach adolescence, reversing the condition is impossible. Childhood intervention, however, can make a significant difference.

"Most of the children who end up as adult psychopaths come to the attention of teachers and counselors at a very early age," Dr. Hare has stated. "It is essential that these professionals understand the nature of the problem they are faced with. If intervention is to have any chance of succeeding, it will have to occur early in childhood."

In the case of Kirby D. Anthoney, it doesn't take a federal study to grasp his life's sadly predictable trajectory. In 20/20 hindsight, we see psychopathy's symptoms from his earliest childhood.

"This is a personality disorder," Dr. Hare has explained, "not simply some specific behavior such as stealing or aggression. No diagnosis is free from error or misapplication by careless or incompetent clinicians. On the other hand, failing to recognize that a child has many or most of the personality traits that define psychopathy may doom the parents to unending consultations with school principals, psychiatrists, psychologists, and counselors in a vain attempt to discover what is wrong with their child and with themselves. It may also lead to a succession of inappropriate treatments and interventions—all at great financial and emotional cost."

Dr. Robert Hare's *Psychopathy Checklist*, used to identify possible psychopaths, is a complex tool for professional use only. "Do not use these symptoms," Dr. Hare has cautioned, " to diagnose yourself or others. Psychopathy is a syndrome—a cluster of related symptoms. It is important to obtain an expert opinion. Seek the advice of a qualified, registered, forensic psychologist or psychiatrist."

Key Symptoms of Psychopathy
Emotional/Interpersonal
  · glib and superficial
  · egocentric and grandiose
  · lack of remorse or guilt
  · lack of empathy
  · deceitful and manipulative
  · shallow emotions
Social Deviance
  · impulsive
  · poor behavior controls
  · need for excitement
  · lack of responsibility
  · early behavior problems
  · adult antisocial behavior

Screening preteen children for symptoms of psychopathy is more practical, effective, and difficult than restricting video games, editing movies, or canceling television programs. Accurate psychological diagnoses involve more complexity and responsibility than composing editorials against Goth fashions, professional wrestling, pinball machines, or garish rock bands.

For the first time in history, we have diagnostic tools that may help avert tragedies such as the Newman homicides, the rape of Michelle Bethel, and the brutal murder of Walter Napageak. Prevention, of course, is preferable to diagnosis. The key to prevention may involve both nature and nurture. Through medical research, the specific brain disorder or defect may be identified, treated, or corrected—perhaps even before birth. The nurturing aspect would certainly involve a violence-free family.

"It's my opinion," said State Trooper Jim Farrell, "that striking, hitting, and berating a child causes their soul to recoil, and that repeated beatings and insults completely and irrevocably pervert their character. If all children, whatever their disability or handicap, were raised in an atmosphere of love, respect, courtesy, and kindness, we would see a significant reduction in violent crime. I realize that psychopaths can come from good families, but worse families give us worse and more violent psychopaths."

"Psychopaths from unstable backgrounds commit many more *violent* offenses," agreed Dr. Hare. "This is consistent with my suggestion that social experiences influence the behavioral expression of psychopathy. A deprived and disturbed background, where violence is common—such as in the upbringing of Kirby Anthoney—finds a willing pupil in the psychopath for whom violence is no different emotionally from other forms of behavior."

As previously explained, psychopaths lack the capacity to experience emotions. It is the emotionally charged thoughts that give bite to conscience and account for its control over behavior. This "bite" of emotion generates the sense of shame, guilt, or remorse. Psychopaths simply cannot understand these emotions because they are incapable of experiencing them. "For them," Dr. Hare has stated, "conscience is nothing more than awareness of rules created by others—empty words. Dramatic, shallow, and short-lived displays of feeling are, for example, a behavior trait of psychopaths. Careful observers are left with the impression that they are playacting, and that little is going on below the surface."

"Don't look to the cops to solve the problem of criminal psychopaths," said Mike Grimes. "By the time police are involved, it's too late—the homicide has already happened. Society spends millions prosecuting, incarcerating, and supervising convicted psychopaths. More jails, more laws, more police—these are not going to cure psychopaths, nor deter them from violent behavior. Locking them up keeps them away from innocent people, protects potential victims, and saves lives. In the long run, if the public is to be truly protected, and their best interests served, an effective treatment or preventative for psychopathy must be either discovered or devised."

ACKNOWLEDGMENTS

A horrid crime followed by an historic trial, the Newman homicides generated over fifty-four volumes of testimony, depositions, police reports, legal arguments, and court rulings. Transforming this mountain of written material, audio recordings, videotapes, and contemporary interviews into a readable narrative was a daunting assignment.

No sane human being can read this story without experiencing strong emotional reactions. My first response to the Newman homicides was shock, followed by anger toward the perpetrator of such inhuman acts. The devastation suffered by John Newman, Cheryl Chapman, and their extended and intertwined families is beyond description or comprehension. Sadly, tragic memories and emotions were stirred up anew by my research into this most heinous crime. After much consultation, John Newman, Cheryl Chapman, and their respective families chose to remain detached from this project.

I extend thanks to the detectives and officers of the Anchorage Police Department, past and present, for their kind cooperation. The same thanks are extended to the officers and investigators of the Twin Falls, Idaho, Police Department. Another measure of appreciation goes to Mark Borneman of the Alaska Court System, Bill Ingaldson, John Salemi, Jim Farrell of the Sex Offender Central Registry Unit of the Alaska State Troopers, Carol Hawkins, and Dr. Robert Hare. Materials from the published works of Dr. Hare are used with his kind permission.

Houshang and Jinous Movaffagh took me into their home and hearts while I conducted research in Anchorage. I thank them for their hospitality. I also wish to acknowledge Mr. Douglas Martin, and the eight other gentlemen with whom he consults, who took time from their pressing obligations to offer me prayerful support. Gratitude is also expressed to Charlotte Dial Breeze. If not for her creative financing techniques, researching this book would have been impossible. Karen Haas, patient editor, put it all together. Of course, there is the obligatory yet heartfelt acknowledgment of Britt, Anea, and Jordan Barer, and Dag and Bjorg Johnsen, the best and most supportive in-laws a man ever had.

MORE MUST-READ TRUE CRIME
FROM PINNACLE

Slow Death   0-7860-1199-8 $6.50US/$8.99CAN
By James Fielder

Fatal Journey   0-7860-1578-0 $6.50US/$8.99CAN
By Jack Gieck

Partners in Evil   0-7860-1521-7 $6.50US/$8.99CAN
By Steve Jackson

Dead and Buried   0-7860-1517-9 $6.50US/$8.99CAN
By Corey Mitchell

Perfect Poison   0-7860-1550-0 $6.50US/$8.99CAN
By M. William Phelps

Family Blood   0-7860-1551-9 $6.50US/$8.99CAN
By Lyn Riddle

Available Wherever Books Are Sold!

Visit our website at **www.kensingtonbooks.com.**